THE *Aloha* BUTTERFLY KISS

CAN YOUR SOULMUTT CHOOSE YOUR SOULMATE?

BABBLING
BROOKE
Books

Praise for The Aloha Butterfly Kiss

I can't recommend it highly enough. Don't walk over to Amazon to pick up your copy, run!

-TOMI TABB, AUTHOR OF DANCING WITH A ROYAL

OMG, The Aloha Butterfly Kiss is one of the dreamiest, most swoon-worthy, and most moving romance ever!

-PAOLA, ITALY, BOOKBUB

Gilbert CARES. It's rare you find an author who you can tell poured their heart and soul into the pages, but that's evident from the very beginning of the book

-MYLENE, USA, GOODREADS

Guin resonated with me so much, it brought tears to my eyes. I can't wait for the next book.

-CLAIRE, UK, GOODREADS

Guin and Locke managed to make me cry like a baby at the end of the story, even though there was nothing sad about it! But the sweetness, the deep love and understanding they share, it's so overwhelming to read.

This romantic comedy is truly lovely! So sweet and heartfelt.. I am so impressed with the quality, the detail, and infinite care taken in the creation of this beautiful story.

The author's writing style is smooth and sparkling with beauty, wit, and humor, and the romance is sweet and swoony along with lots of emotional depth and heart! I love love love this book so much. I cannot recommend this book highly enough! "The Aloha Butterfly Kiss" is absolutely a must read. 5 stars!"

I eagerly await more literary wonders from Brooke Gilbert's pen. Highly recommended for anyone seeking a charming and emotionally resonant story.

THE *Aloha* BUTTERFLY KISS

CAN YOUR SOULMUTT CHOOSE YOUR SOULMATE?

Written By **BROOKE GILBERT**

Edited By **CAITLIN MILLER**

Contents

For the community of Maui and to everyone who lost someone in the devastating fires. You have shown us what Ohana truly means. The beauty and resilience of this community is incredible to see. Please see the author's note for ways you can donate to Maui Relief. A portion of the proceeds from this book will be donated as well. Prayers and love for healing.

To Cynthia Lin and the beautiful ukulele community! Your music therapy provided a light for me on days when there was none. Strumming those strings until sometimes four or five in the morning was my only reprieve from the darkness of my illness. And chatting with this encouraging and positive community made all the difference in my world. Thank you from the bottom of my heart! And to my fellow Lupus warriors: we may not enjoy the sunlight in the same way as others, but I have found this community to be an even more beautiful source of light through your love and support. You're a beautiful force, and I see you providing your own light every day. Let nothing diminish or take it away from you!

And to Claire, who graciously answered any questions I had and helped give me the courage to tell Guin's story the way I wanted. So happy books have connected us.

For my grandparents, whose story may have been touched by Alzheimer's but only became a better example of what selfless love looks like. And to all the families who have been affected by this disease.
And to my Aunt Teena whom I love dearly. I believe in miracles and the goodness of people.

And finally, to those brave, selfless souls who have become donors for those in need. You gave the ultimate gift: an opportunity for someone else to live a longer life. And to those fearless recipients who have kept on fighting and those who are still waiting, hoping their turn will come. This one's for you.

Over 100,000 people are on the national transplant list in the U.S. More than 90,000 of them are waiting for kidneys. 17 people die everyday waiting for a transplant. Only 42,000 received one in 2022. Are you an organ donor?

1

---

1. https://www.organdonor.gov/learn/organ-donation-statistics

"Let nothing dim the light that shines from within." -Maya Angelou

Content Caution

Hello Lovely Reader,

First, I would like to thank you for choosing my novel to read. I know there are so many other books for you to select from and the fact that you've chosen mine means the world to me. You are the reason I keep publishing my writing. With that in mind, I wanted to discuss the content of my novel with you.

I believe strongly in providing content warnings, so I am going to try my best to provide them here without giving away spoilers! There are mild medical episodes that include descriptions of pain associated with Lupus and migraines with fainting. There are also discussions of organ transplant, emotional abuse with gaslighting (minimal), and mental health in relation to chronic illness and disability. This novel features a water-related accident; however, I have tried to keep the episode vague. If you would like to avoid reading the details, please skip chapter thirty.

Please note the characters struggle with ableism and the "standards" of normal body image. As is sometimes the case, especially early in a journey with a disability, the urge to hide or fit into "the norm" can become debilitating. This book is about learning to love and accept all of yourself—including your disabilities. And sometimes it takes someone else's love and acceptance before you can do that for yourself. I promise there's a happy ending for these issues.

Please be kind to yourself and if now isn't a good time to read this novel, then I will definitely understand. Perhaps, there will be a better time in the future. And if you would like modifications, there are chapters you could skip and I'd be happy to discuss those options with you. Or if you still have questions and specific triggers in mind, know that my door is always open. I'm available through Instagram (@brookegilbertauthor) and email (brookegilbertauthor@gmail.com).

This novel features Own Voices Lupus, arthritic and chronic pain from Lupus, migraines, fainting, and mental health. Themes of second chance, found family, acceptance, and forgiveness are present throughout.

I also wanted to discuss the location of this book. After the devastating fires in Maui this past summer, I thought about pulling plans for publication at the end of the year. I also debated moving the location of the book to another island. After much consideration, I kept the book as originally written before the fires took place. However, I changed the location of the scenes that took place in Lahaina.

This book strives to bring awareness to the meaning of Ohana, as well as highlighting the beauty of Hawaiian culture and its people. Therefore, a portion of the proceeds will go toward the Maui Strong Relief fund. More information about this donation is in the author's note at the end of the novel :)

This is a 'sweet' novel. Descriptive kissing. No cursing.

Please note this book includes faith conversations. This has been a part of my chronic illness journey so it is a part of the characters' as well. The conversations are short and I hope you will find them respectful.

I hope you enjoy your time in Maui! I can't wait to discuss this novel with you :)

Sending you love and endless spoons,

Brooke

Sight References

SIGHTS IN THE ALOHA BUTTERFLY KISS NOVEL

KA'ANAPALI BEACH
LANAI CATHEDRALS
WAI'ĀNAPANAPA STATE PARK
WHALERS VILLAGE
MA'ALAEA HARBOR
MOLOKINI- TAKOS FLATS

SIGHTS IN THE ALOHA BUTTERFLY KISS NOVEL

TWIN FALLS
BUTTERFLY FARM
HO'OKIPA BEACH
PAIA
ROAD TO HANA
WALILEA CHAPEL
WHALE WATCHING
WESTIN RESORT

Travel Map

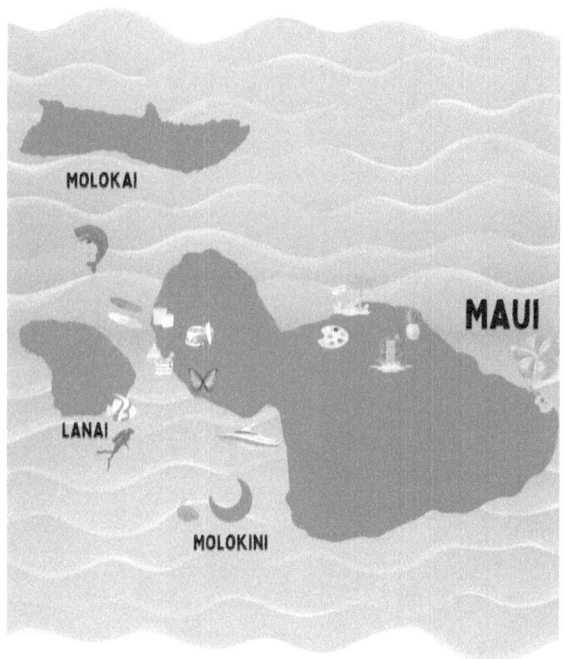

Find an interactive travel map on Squirl: https://maps.squirl.
co/book/1418

Spotify Playlist

Listen to *The Aloha Butterfly Kiss* playlist on Spotify while you read this book. It includes music mentioned in the novel and/or music I listened to as I wrote this novel. **Enjoy :)**

A sample of the playlist:
• Underdog- Alicia Keys
• Don't Start Now- Acoustic Guitar Revival
• Shivers-Ryan Updike

- Wicked Game- Cynthia Lin
- I Knew You Were Trouble- Bobby G
- Sunroof- Shelli Daniels
- I Ain't Worried- Michelle Turtle
- Island in the Sun- Weezer
- Lovely Day- The Shady Ukulele Band
- Riptide- Dev Lin
- Aquamarine- U3, Cynthia Lin
- Watermelon Sugar- INST
- Under the Sea- The Shady Ukulele Band
- Linger- The Cranberries
- Mercy- Bobby G
- The bones- Dev Lin
- Love Looks Better- Alicia Keys
- Love on Top-INST
- Sugar- Bridesmaids Quartet
- Toxic-Tiny Uke Orchestra

Spotify Link: bit.ly/thealohabutterflykissplaylist

Hawaiian & Surfer Slang

Learning more about the Hawaiian language, Hawaiian phrases, and surfer slang was one of the most fun parts of my research for this novel. Here is the list of terms and definitions used in this novel for reference.

SLANG

- *Hale-* house

- *Pale Keiki-* Midwife
- *Tutu-* grandma
- *Bennies-* a tourist, someone who isn't local
- *Hawaiian Tattoo-* sand burn
- *Bomb-* big wave
- *Doubled up on you-* multiple waves hitting you at a time
- *Washing machine- the ocean*
- *Auê!-* Oh! Too bad! Oops! Oh boy!
- *"Keiki*!- child, boy
- *Ka'u moopuna-* my grandson
- *Malihinis-* tourists
- *Ku'uipo-* sweetheart
- *Hâmau!-* silence
- *Lanai-* balcony
- *Kelani- piece of heaven*
- *Ohana-* family (one that can encompasses a whole community of people and is not just blood related)
- *Aiâ-* Oh no! Ouch!
- *Ahahana-* shame on you
- *Hûpô-* stupid
- *Lôlô-* idiot
- Quip- surfboard collection
- *Wahini-* woman
- *Anakala- uncle*
- Nalu- wave
- *Mahina- moon*
- *'O 'oe nō, aloha-* Don't worry, beautiful
- *E noho pu anei oe me au- will you sit with me?*
- Malia- star of the sea
- *Aloha-* hello, goodbye, a way of life, unconditional love, compassion, a life with purpose, a way to lift each other up, a term of endearment and great respect

• *Aloha oe ia̅ ia- love her*
• *Aloha wau ia̅ 'oe- I love you*

PROVERBS AS EXPLAINED IN THE BOOK:

• E *hele me ka pu'olo*: "leave every place and person better than you found it. Always bring something with you to make it better and leave it there for others to find. You never know when someone might need it."

• *Ka la̅ hiki ola*: "It means the dawning of a new day. We believe in the power of hope and optimism here."

• *Pono*: "It's the value of integrity and doing what's right. And knowing the feeling of contentment that comes from it. When you know in your heart you've done the right thing."

• *Ho'i Hou Ke Aloha:* "Let us fall in love all over again."

• *Ho'ohana*: "to work with purpose and intent"

Ku'ia kahele aka na'au ha'aha'a: "a humble person walks carefully so as not to hurt others."

Prologue

LOCKE

IF YOU SEE a mermaid wash up on shore you better do one of two things . . . Walk away before she steals your heart . Or . . . go to her aid being fully aware that you're not fooling anyone. She's more than capable of saving herself.

Guinevere

CHAPTER 1

"I don't understand. All my life I've been waiting for someone and when I find her, she's . . . she's a fish." -Tom Hanks, Splash

MY GRAND LANDING onto the magnificent Hawaiian shores was one of a beached whale–definitely *not* of a graceful mermaid. The gorgeous, sparkling sand beach that had originally greeted me today was now rough, abrasive, and completely uninviting against my skin. It felt like the coarsest of sandpapers as I taxied in from my rough ride under the sea and made my bumpy landing onto this beautiful Maui beach.

The last thing I recall before going under the waves was bobbing like a lost cork in the surf, enjoying the ocean for the first time in my life. I remember being surrounded by idyllic aquamarine water and thinking how bright and crystal clear it looked. And then, as if cueing *Jaw's* ominous music, huge and unexpected waves ambushed me.

I'd never seen waves like that before. They hadn't looked nearly that big from the shore, but out in the water they were seriously scary. Now I understood why this was a surfer's paradise. But for someone like me who had never been in the ocean, and was totally untrained to handle super-sized surf, it was absolutely terrifying.

As soon as I'd seen the mega waves approaching, I doggie-paddled toward the beach which lasted all of five seconds. Abruptly, the ocean swept me up mid-paddle in the wave's path and tossed me onto the shore like ripped delicates caught in the rough spin cycle of a washing machine. *Completely beached.* My black swimsuit felt mangled. Having made its way as far down my stomach as possible, like a precarious elastic band on the verge of snapping. *Well, it didn't look that good on me, anyway.* It's funny the things you think about at a time like this.

To my relief, I thought I heard the familiar yelps of my service dog, but my ringing ears were muffling everything. And I was way too embarrassed to open my eyes to check. Maybe if I closed them tight enough, my swimsuit would magically wrap itself back around me like some magic carpet. But it was too late for any wishes because I heard voices surrounding me. Humiliation made it impossible to unglue myself from the sand. No, I was only ready to burrow down deeper, except for the fact that my skin felt like it had been burned by "the fire of a thousand suns."

Suddenly, a sound cut through the noise and confusion of my mind. A deep, rough voice floated over me. Ironically caressing me, even though it sounded coarser than those nasty little granules under me. Although, I was enjoying this intrusion much more.

The voice boomed, "Ok, show's over. The current's particularly strong today. I'd like to see one of *you* battle those waves." Then a towel landed on top of me and after a few minutes, the voice washed over me again, this time with a touch of softness. "You can open your eyes now. They're gone and I've got you covered up with the towel. I'm not exactly sure about the state of your swimsuit."

Humor resonated throughout his tone, and hot embarrassment filled me. He must have witnessed my whole crash landing.

I hesitantly cracked open my eyes to see a man crouched down beside me with his elbows lazily resting on his thighs. He was right next to where my cheek kissed the sand. What a misnomer. It felt more like some wild beast mauled my face.

As he blocked the sun's rays, they created a golden aura around him. *I couldn't just be dreaming him up, could I?* I squinted my eyes harder, trying to focus my eyesight, as I looked up to see a figure with striking jet-black hair set against warm tanned skin. He had these deeply penetrative eyes. Classically handsome–if you were into that kind of thing. Think Clark Gable . . . very much giving a "you know what."

Before he could say anything else, I felt little licks all over my face. Thank goodness Sebastian had found me. Yes, I was obsessed with *The Little Mermaid* and all the creatures under the sea yet somehow I'd never been to the beach before. *I know. But look at how well it was going so far.*

I saw golden fur zooming all around me from the corner of my eyes. "Sebastian, I'm so glad you found me," I said with relief.

"What?" *Oh no, not him too. I knew it wasn't exactly normal to name a dog after a lobster, but I was in no mood to debate that particular moniker.* However, I didn't get to ask him to clarify before I felt another tongue licking me as well.

"What's going on?" I asked with confusion, not able to see anything with Sebastian leaning over me.

"Uh, I don't know," he sounded bewildered. "There seems to be two dogs. And only *one* of them is mine."

Oh, thank goodness, it was another dog licking my face. For a moment there, I was worried this stranger might have a face licking obsession, just like my dog. I loved Clark Gable, but maybe not that much.

"Well, only one is mine," I replied quickly.

"Uh, well that would explain it," he said with a laugh.

I tried looking around, but all I could see were shades of golden fur whipping around my face. This was so unfair. I couldn't see either of them clearly.

"Let's get you out of here, ok? Can you help me by grabbing the towel and pulling it around you?"

I nodded my head in reply and took some time to arrange my swimsuit under the cover of the towel. Then he began picking me up ever so carefully and cradling me in his arms. Literally cradling me, as in *Creature from the Black Lagoon*-style. Even I could admit that it didn't get much sexier than that. He certainly had the muscles. And he had a dangerously

6

attractive allure about him too. *But then again, I'd always been a little attracted to the Black Lagoon Creature. That* probably wasn't normal. While other girls were fantasizing about Ken, all I wanted was *The Creature to pick* me up from the lagoon and carry me back to his lair.

Well, this was my moment, and I was going to bask in it . . . except for the fact that my raw skin was screaming bloody murder, especially where it scraped against this stranger. I winced as he pulled me and the towel toward him protectively.

"Sorry," he said, noticing my reaction and realizing that he had probably made the wrong move. But it was oddly worth the pain to see his primal reflex. He gazed at me as he spoke, assessing the damage. Those deep pools looked at me with such intensity. I rearranged myself so the unscraped backs of my arm and body were next to his skin. The parts of me that weren't covered with sand burn. *Ahhh, much better.* "I'll take you to my *hale*–my bungalow. It's just a little way off the beach." Then he looked at me, suddenly realizing you don't just carry strange women back to your bungalow caveman-style. That *might* make someone a little uncomfortable. "Uh . . . or I have a surf shop where I could take you, but my *tutu*, grandma, is at the bungalow, and she'll be able to help you with your burns. She's a *pale keiki.*" I just looked at him, blinking with confusion. He clarified, "A midwife. She'll know what to do. We'll get your 'Hawaiian tattoo' taken care of immediately." And there was a twinkle in his eyes as he said it.

Guinevere

CHAPTER 2

"A HAWAIIAN TATTOO?" I questioned in a tiny voice.

I now had both hands locked around his neck, hanging on for dear life since the terrain had become much bumpier as we moved further up the beach. I didn't even want to look under the towel. The shock was wearing off and the pain from my sand burn was grabbing my attention. I was also increasingly aware that while my rescuer was wearing a wetsuit; it was unzipped at the top and tied around his waist, leaving his chest completely bare. Oddly, I felt like a baby kangaroo inside its mother's pouch, enjoying the comforting skin-to-skin contact. I glanced over his shoulder to see Sebastian and his dog trailing behind us. The Goldens looked quite cozy together . . . actually, pretty adorable. I saw them nuzzle one another back at the beach, and now they were rubbing up against one another every so often. I guess they were fast becoming friends.

"Yeah, you've definitely got a Hawaiian tattoo." He laughed. A boyish grin took over his features. *Why did he have to look so much like Clark Gable?* A few strands of his black hair curved down to kiss his forehead. "It's what we call a sand burn here. A lot of *bennies* get them. The waves can be pretty ferocious, especially if you don't know how to handle them. You got caught in a *bomb,* that's for sure, and then the surf must have doubled up on you. You survived the *washing machine,* so I guess that was your initiation to the island."

So many words I didn't understand, but I was just going to guess at their meaning. I wasn't gonna ask "Indie" to explain them to me. He didn't seem like the type of guy to want to translate *anything*. His attitude was way too much like Indiana Jones for that.

"Quite the initiation," I said with sarcasm.

But he just began lecturing me. "The ocean isn't something you want to mess with. It needs to be respected. There are a lot of bad things that can happen out at sea. Believe me, you were lucky." He looked down at me seriously as he said it. Really, he was just missing the fedora. His attitude was so on point. "Although it looks like you were pretty sunburned before the *washing machine* and the sand got to you."

I cast my eyes away from him, looking at the ocean, which must be the washing machine. Sunburns were a foregone conclusion for me. I had Lupus. I was basically allergic to the sun. Hence, one reason I had never been to the beach. I usually avoided the sun. I leapfrogged from one shady spot to the next when I was outside on a sunny day. And time in the sun had to be "flare worthy" because the cost was steep: joint pain, rashes, extreme fatigue, dizziness, and pounding headaches, to name a few symptoms. I wouldn't be leapfrogging anywhere after that happened.

I loved the thought of the ocean, but so far in my life, I'd only admired it from afar. It was like looking at pictures in your school locker of your celebrity crush. Or at least that had been what was in most of my friend's lockers . . . you can guess what was in mine—sunny island scenes in tropical locales. And now I had those photos scattered all over my office space. They beckoned me to suspend reality and to believe, if only for a tiny moment, that I could enjoy such a magical place.

Well, I was most certainly aware that between the sun and the sand burn; I looked like a lobster. I knew I had the "superpower" to turn red instantaneously from the heat. My faint Irish ancestry didn't help with that either. Half a day in the sun and I was ready for the Cape Cod lobster bakes. Maybe I'd at least win some good prize money.

"I guess I forgot to reapply sunscreen," I replied sheepishly, not wanting to explain my health conditions to a total stranger. I looked back at the dogs, watching them. *Well* . . . distracting myself was more like it.

"And here I thought I was catching a mermaid, but I'm pretty sure all my net caught today was a lobster. Guess that's probably for the best though, since mermaids are known to lure unsuspecting sailors to their death . . . *Auê!* I wish I'd known I was going lobster hunting today. I'm *completely* unprepared." He cracked a smile. I, however, did not.

I simply stared at him, unblinking. Then he continued on, "I guess if your dog's name is Sebastian, then you should be called Ariel? Sorry to break it to you, but you're *definitely* a Sebastian. Guess you should have chosen a different name for your dog."

"And you're *definitely* an Ursula," I bantered back.

"Wow, nerve hit . . . I got it." He laughed dryly. "Well, you should have at least dyed your hair the right color. *Cinderella* was the blonde one." His smile hadn't faded one bit. Nor had his boyish mischievousness. And I couldn't believe he'd been bold enough to comment on my highlights. He was deriving way too much pleasure from getting under my skin. Then he asked, "So I'm curious: How can you be *so* unprepared for the beach with a dog named Sebastian?"

"I am not unprepared," was my lame rebuttal.

"*Ok, sure.* I honestly don't know where to begin. Let's see . . . a second-degree sunburn, sand burns, and clothing torn apart by the sea. So yeah, I'd say unprepared," he said sarcastically.

His accuracy annoyed me.

I was amazed at how easily he seemed to carry me such a long distance, yet remained completely unwinded. *Are surfers usually this buff? He had that surfer vibe.* Well, actually, I was just going by the wetsuit. And he mentioned a surf shop. Whatever the case, I was extremely grateful he was carrying me away from that leering crowd of bystanders. But . . . he really wasn't my type . . . other than his Clark Gable looks. And I certainly wasn't ever going to be his little surfer girl. No, I was actually pretty curvy and tall.

But my thoughts turned serious as I noticed how long he had been carrying me. I thought his house was supposed to be right off of the beach. That's what he had said, *wasn't it?* But this didn't seem like a short walk to me. I hoped it was just my nerves that were making it feel longer than it truly was. I was feeling a *little* uncomfortable. I had been so grateful to be rescued, covered up, and carried somewhere, *anywhere*, that I hadn't really taken the time to think about where he was taking me. On the plus side, he had a dog. And if someone had a dog, I usually trusted them.

Okay, that might not be the best survival instinct. Maybe it couldn't even be classified as one. Ted Bundy probably had a dog. Wait, a minute! *Did he have a dog?* This was not something I should think about as I was clutching some guy's protruding neck muscles. These are the thoughts you need to have before you let a random guy whisk you away from a public place. Great, I was getting *Bundied*.

I nervously spoke up. "On second thought, I think I'm going to be just fine. I'm feeling much better now." I unlocked my arms as if I could choose to release myself back into the wild.

Deep laughter rumbled out of his chest. "What's up, Sebastian? Did you just now think that Ursula might take you back to her evil lair? I should be offended, but it's just too sad. Maybe you need to think about taking some self-defense courses."

He looked at my offended face. "Ok, seriously, my grandmother should be at my bungalow. I know it's hard to believe, but she really is a *pale keiki*. She'll be able to help with both your sunburn and your beach rash. So you're not getting boiled alive *today*. I promise to release you back into the ocean, right where I found you, as soon as possible. Well, maybe not the ocean . . . That's probably the worst place for you. Seems like you better avoid it for a while. But I *will* release you, I promise."

My eyebrows raised. He was pretty blunt. Weren't surfer guys super chill, "feel good" people? I was feeling not-so-good right now. He interrupted my thoughts. "Don't worry, you're not my type. Lobster isn't on my menu. I'm a pescatarian. Now, mermaid . . ."

My eyes flared at him. "I wasn't really worried about that. But gee, thanks." My flaming red thighs seemed to burn hotter in offended protest and aggravated pain at each one of his words. I winced as he jostled me about. The sand really didn't seem *that* uneven. Maybe he was having some fun with me.

I couldn't believe that this attractive man was having to carry my curvy butt. I looked back at our dogs. At least they seemed to enjoy our little jaunt down the beach. They look absolutely *chummy*. Sebastian was being quite the traitor; I wasn't sure how I felt about this man and, by association, his dog.

Unfortunately, "Indie" had taken notice. "What? Are the dogs doing ok? And does Sebastian realize he should follow us?"

"Sebastian is a service dog. He's extremely intelligent, thank you," I responded quickly, offended by his lack of faith in Sebastian.

"Yeah, hopefully he's more 'street smart' than his owner," he jested. "Well, as long as the dogs are still with us. I know Penny will be fine. She is extremely well-trained."

"As in Penny-wise?" I half chuckled.

"No, I did not name my dog after some killer-clown." He looked at me with amusement. "And while we're talking about Stephen King, this is not some *Misery* situation either . . . If that makes you feel any better." He laughed.

"Well, if the ridiculously oversized shoe fits." I laughed, and then I tried to guess again. "*101 Dalmatians*?"

"What?" he asked indignantly. "Is there even a dog named Penny in that movie?"

I looked at him and his clever grin. He obviously loved that I couldn't guess the meaning behind his dog's name. *He'd be so lucky to have his dog named after an adorable Disney film character.*

"So she's just a good luck penny?" I queried, underwhelmed.

"She's nothing for you to worry about," he said swiftly.

"Wow, nerve hit," I parroted, expecting a witty rebuttal, but he didn't say anything else. Instead, I felt him suddenly turn and cut up through the sand. We moved inland through a community of soft cream buildings. The furrowed expression on his face told me there was a fifty percent chance this was going to end up on a true crime podcast. And his shark's tooth necklace was looking a little sinister to me now.

The beach was becoming smaller and smaller, making me even more nervous. I swallowed hard. *Okay, more like a seventy-five percent chance now.* We headed toward a cluster of bungalows. It was the cutest community I'd ever seen. I could just imagine neighbors yelling across to one another and asking to borrow some coconut sugar. The thought warmed my soul. *How nice it would be to live in this paradise.* Well . . . paradise minus the one He-Man sized fly in the ointment. But I would not let that ruin this little fantasy for me.

There was a woman standing on the top story of a bungalow's wooden lanai, cleaning a rug. She was striking the rug ferociously with the end of a broom. It was like witnessing a scene straight out of an old black-and-white movie. I was just waiting for Jimmy Stewart to walk out the screen door and scold her in his trademark comical manner for cleaning the rug improperly.

The woman squinted in the sunlight and shielded her eyes with her hand. She looked to be in her mid-seventies with beautifully tanned skin and jet-black hair lightly peppered with gray.

"*Keiki*! What are you doing?" she said in a warm, but scolding tone. "*Ka'u moopuna*." She tsked loudly.

My rescuer just shook his head and began briskly climbing the outdoor stairs to the top lanai while the dogs bounded up behind us. This older woman must be the midwife and grandmother he had talked about. She must have been referring to him as her grandson. I looked at him and he just raised an eyebrow.

When we'd reached the top, he stood before the slight woman. I felt extremely awkward with the towel still wrapped around me as I clung onto her grandson. I cringed thinking about my burned skin underneath the towel and what it might look like.

"Oh, *Keiki*. I don't think I'm going to want to hear this . . . but what happened?" She looked at me with reddened cheeks and obvious concern.

I would have burst out laughing at her unexpected reaction except for the fact that I was too embarrassed myself. Well, I didn't need to worry about where this stranger landed on the serial killer spectrum, at least . . . not at this moment.

Locke

CHAPTER 3

I COULDN'T BELIEVE I had carried this woman home. This seriously was just my luck. I would be the one to find this type of buried treasure. But it wasn't every day that a tourist made such a grand entrance by washing up on shore like a stranded mermaid. And as much as I had learned to stay away from women my age, I just couldn't leave her washed up on the beach, surrounded by all those rubbernecking tourists. This woman's pain and humiliation wasn't something that needed to be included in their Instagram feed.

And just like that, without another thought, I had gone to her aid, warding off the beachcombers like they were snakes in an *Indiana Jones* film. Thankfully, it hadn't taken too much effort to get the *malihinis* to move along, especially since they'd already seen most of the "show" anyway.

What I should have done was just carry her up higher on the beach, set her on a towel and ask her if she was okay. Then I could have left her there to recover some of her dignity. *Alone.* I'm sure she was more than capable of taking care of herself. She didn't need some grand rescue. *Why hadn't I done that?* It would have been so simple. *I was feeling really stupid.* I could have at least let her walk after she collected herself. But a primal force overtook me. I went full Hulk and carried her back to my bungalow. Now I was ready to club that caveman over the head and barricade him in the cave farthest away from me.

Hopefully, Tutu could quickly take care of the "Little Mermaid" and she'd be on her way. One more attractive tourist I wouldn't see again. And I'd have done my good deed for the day. Maybe for my karmic reward, Tutu would stop harassing me. She'd been way too concerned about my lack of a love life or more specifically my lack of a wife. Yes . . . a wife . . . *not* just a girlfriend. She'd moved *way* past that. Actually, she was concerned that maybe I wasn't even interested in women. She'd even introduced me to a man at one social gathering. I had literally spat out my drink on the poor guy who apparently had been very interested in me. And while I was flattered, that wasn't the problem. Tutu didn't have my preferences wrong. Well, maybe she did . . . I *preferred* to be alone.

Tutu didn't seem to understand this concept. It only caused her to push harder. I guess I got my hard-headedness from her. And being her only grandson didn't help matters. I didn't especially think I should be the one to continue the family legacy, anyway.

But when I had carried this woman up the stairs, my grand-mother had beamed like I'd given her a new lease on life. She'd tried to hide it by reprimanding me, but she couldn't conceal her joy–neither her excitement. And I'm sure 'Ariel' had noticed it too. I just couldn't believe she'd gotten both sunburned and sand-burned. I'd like to say I didn't see nasty burns that often, but unfortunately, that would be a lie. You wouldn't believe what tourists would do or tour companies either, for that matter. Neither one seemed to have enough respect for the power of the ocean or the sun. Mother Nature was just a joke to them, but they quickly found out who got the last laugh.

My mind quickly snapped back to the present as Tutu started busily moving around the inside of the house, asking me lots of questions as the mermaid continued to grip me even tighter. Her bright blue eyes shined worriedly. *Really, she looked like an animated princess. And I probably looked like some villain shrouded in black.* With that vivid image in mind, I set her gently on the sofa where Tutu had thoughtfully laid down some blankets. Now that Tutu understood this was more a *Baywatch* call than a "Bachelor" situation, she looked nothing short of deflated.

But to my surprise, the mermaid clung tightly to me when I tried to release her onto the blankets. It was like I was trying to release her back into the sea and she didn't want to go.

As I gathered my thoughts, the dogs caught my attention. Ironically enough, our dogs seemed to be experiencing puppy love. Penny had already invited Sebastian into her doggie bed, and they were happily curled up together on the living room floor. I was going to have a talk with her. You didn't just open your heart up to a stray like that. But all I could do was silently laugh as I glanced at them, seeing them nuzzling each other. Because it was obviously way too late for *that talk.* I think they already imprinted on each other. *Did dogs do that? Or was that only with ducklings? Yup, it was definitely puppy love.* When I looked back, I caught the mermaid smiling at them, too.

I glanced down at the towel. For her sake, I wasn't really sure if I was ready to reveal what was underneath it. So I continued to hold her as we stayed in this awkward limbo.

I offered what I could. "I'll leave the room and let you have some privacy. Tutu can look and see if she can help. I just have to extract myself." I chuckled, trying to make her feel better about the situation.

She shook her head repeatedly. *No? Why is she saying no?* But her grip made me realize she wanted me to stay. *Why? How can I possibly make anything better or safer for her?* Wow, this mermaid really wouldn't last long at sea. She had terrible survival instincts. She'd take the first shiny lure that came her way.

"No?" I asked, and she shook her head some more.

"Don't go. Please stay. You'll be honest with me if I don't understand everything. . . *I think.* Distract me somehow in the meantime, *please.*" She said anxiously.

I nodded, still stunned, but oddly, there was nowhere I'd rather be.

Locke

CHAPTER 4

"*KEIKI*, move now. How am I going to look at the woman with your arms still around her? And you're going to have to go somewhere else so I can properly examine her."

I looked at Tutu's furrowed, sun-kissed brow and then back at the mermaid. "Right, and that would be–" I began.

"Locke, please remove your arms *now*."

I did as I was told, untangling us like a fish removing itself from masses of seaweed. I tried to maneuver around her as gently as possible, but 'Ariel' still winced.

"Stand by her head, facing away from her, and I'll have a look. I'll make a tent with a towel for privacy too. Hopefully, some cream and bandages will do the trick." I looked dumbfounded at Tutu.

"*Distract her, Keiki.* You can do that. Tsk tsk." She busied herself with her examination.

"So . . . " I began, trying to come up with something better to say this time as she winced again.

Tutu apologized. "Sorry, dear, but at least it's not as bad as I expected. Your swimsuit is actually in pretty good shape–it didn't tear. I'll be able to remove the towel in a minute. I'm sure your sunburn is making the sand rash much more painful. Although I have to say your skin is more inflamed than I'm used to seeing. You're also swelling quite a bit, and your body seems to have reacted more than I usually see with something like this. You're getting a rash, too. My guess is you already had some sun poisoning–"

"It's my Lupus," Mermaid said matter-of-factly, not once looking at me, only gazing ahead. I had no idea what that meant, except it sounded very similar to the Hawaiian word for wolf. And she sure didn't look like a wolf to me. No, she still looked very much like an enchanting siren of the sea.

"Ahh, *ku'uipo.* I see, I see. The sun's not good–"

"I know," she said hesitantly, stopping Tutu again. "I usually never go to the beach. Staying out in the sun makes me feel pretty miserable, so I try to avoid being outside in the direct sunlight anymore. But I wanted to have a beach experience at least once, especially while I was here. I've dreamed about taking a beach vacation for such a long time. Maybe if I had my Lupus under better control . . . But I was tired of waiting for the "right time" for my dream vacation. Plus, there was also a huge ukulele convention here that I didn't want to miss. I just underestimated the strength of the sun and apparently the waves, too."

Tutu responded thoughtfully. "I understand, *ku'uipo*. We need to make sure we watch your burns carefully, though. And you're going to need to be much more cautious in the sun. It is much stronger here than most people realize. The ozone layer keeps getting thinner. I'm going to get my medicine bag and make a healing cream."

The mermaid thanked her, and Tutu hurried off, rapidly talking to herself.

I don't know why I was scared to look at the mermaid now, but I was. "So," I offered for a *third* time, sounding like the idiot surfer dude cliché I hated so much. I was a man of few words, but that made the situation worse today. My usually blunt conversational skills weren't exactly what you wanted in this type of situation. But I was trying my best to be comforting and put her at ease.

I made yet *another* attempt at conversation. "So, where are you staying while you're here? I'd be happy to drive you there once Tutu finishes treating you. I don't think you need any more surf or sun for today. Seems like some rest would be best for you this afternoon."

She didn't respond; rather, she gazed at our dogs instead. I wondered why this Lupus thing required her to have a service dog. I noticed that the patch on her golden's blue vest was like the one on Penny's bright red one. Penny was wearing red, even though she had clearly cast her vote for a neon pink vest in the pet store by excitedly sniffing it. But I just couldn't bring myself to put that color on her yet. Of course, I had eventually been *persuaded to* buy her both the pink and the red vests, even though she had yet to wear her pink one. But her soulful chocolate eyes were wearing me down *every* day. Penny always seemed to get *anything and everything* she wanted. She already got way too much table food, and the vet was constantly lecturing me about it. But Penny meant the world to me, so I couldn't deny her anything. Not even a pink vest. Even if she was color blind.

Although, right now I was a tad bit annoyed with Penny, since she was quickly becoming his "little spoon." *And what kind of name was Sebastian for a dog, anyway?* I looked at "Ariel," willing her to break eye contact with our dogs. The encouraging looks she was giving them would only make it harder when it was time for them to leave. I sure hoped to heaven Sebastian was neutered. The last thing I needed was baby lobsters running around–that would be trouble for sure. And if 'Ariel' was their grandmother . . . Well, I could already tell that co-grand parenting with her would spell trouble . . .

"Uh, well, that's an interesting question," she remarked slowly.

My head snapped back to her. "Interesting how?" My eyes narrowed. "You're not planning to sleep on the beach *White Lotus*-style, are you? You know, there are rules against that here."

"No, I was just waiting until my lodging became available later today. So we've only been living out of my rental car this morning, *thank you*." Then she looked at me skeptically. "Well, I was going to stay at a hotel, but I've never traveled with Sebastian before, and I hear there can be a lot of confusion with service dogs. Usually, they only allow small dogs in hotels, and they're not always receptive to service dogs. You know, *Bruiser*-sized. Not . . ." She looked at Sebastian. "Not full-sized *Beethovens*."

I shook my head, clearing it. "Bruisers?"

"*Legally Blonde*," she said, quickly, as if that should clue me in.

"Yeah, ok. Then that's what you should have named your dog, Mermaid."

She shot me a perturbed glance. The word "mermaid" apparently ruined it for her. I laughed silently as she spoke, "My name is *Guinevere*, not 'Mermaid,' thank you. Guin for short, and no, *you* can't use that."

My eyebrows snapped up at her 'don't mess with me' rebuttal. I paused before venturing, "You never know if resorts are going to accommodate special requests even for service dogs, but they are required by law to do so."

"Yes, I know. I *did* my research," she said with the same annoyed look. "But I didn't want to take the chance of a resort refusing him, so I decided on a different option."

"Ok, *Mermaid*. And this option would be? . . ." She shot daggers at me, which I rather enjoyed if I'm being honest with myself. "So, where did you decide to stay?" I tried again, but she said nothing; instead, she raised one eyebrow at me. I laughed heartily.

She reluctantly spoke. "I feel like you're going to judge me. I don't know *exactly* where the place is. But, when I received my convention ticket, they included an online bulletin with the names of locals who offered to host people who would attend the ukulele convention. I guess it's like VRBO *Aloha-style*."

I couldn't stop laughing as she stared even harder at me. "And you were worried about *me*? You're planning on staying in a complete stranger's home for the rest of the week and *I'm* the stranger danger?" Her laser beam eyes were burning a hole through me now and I was thoroughly enjoying it.

She glared. "I knew you would judge me for this, so that's why I didn't tell you earlier. There was a nice online message board where you could talk with the hosts and get to know them, so it's *not* completely random. The paper with my host's address is in the pocket of Sebastian's vest, but I'm having second thoughts about it now. Maybe I should just stay at a hotel, although I imagine they're probably all booked by now with the convention. Perhaps you can look at the address and see if you know where it is. I was hoping I was close so I could go 'check-in' this afternoon. But with my sense of direction, I'll probably end up on the wrong island."

She called Sebastian over and I rummaged through his vest pocket to find the paper. She continued, "You see, I'm not crazy. It's just that this family has an emotional support dog, so I knew they would be more understanding about my service dog. And I also thought it would be a better option with my special dietary needs–that I would have more control over my food choices." She glanced down at her arm quickly. "And I really enjoyed the online chats I had with the adorable older lady who posted the listing. We had a lot in common. She used to play the ukulele, that's why she wanted to help support the convention. And she said she had the sweetest grandson that took care of her . . ." Her voice dropped off with a dawning realization.

She looked at me, horrified, as I stared at the address on the piece of paper.

"*Why* is my address listed on this piece of paper?" I asked in shock as I stared at Guin. "*Tutu!*?"

"*Sweet* grandson?!?" the mermaid said in utter disgust, her eyebrows arched in disbelief. Out of the corner of my eye, I could see a slow shadow making its way into the room.

"Yes, *Keiki?*" Tutu's sweet, demure voice cut through the electrified air. Her "elderly" voice sounded so frail now that I'm sure even the mermaid could clearly tell she was laying it on thick. It was her get out of jail free card. She stood in the living room doorway surrounded by our home's beach bungalow decor, a perfect fit for this woman. Her long floral dress matched the light blue walls perfectly. Like a chameleon blending in with her surroundings to avoid getting caught.

"Do *you* want to explain *this* to me?" I handed her the piece of paper..

"Oh, I've been meaning to talk to you about that," she said innocently.

"Talk to me about it? When exactly? Check-in time says three o'clock," I said sternly. "It's now *almost* two thirty."

"Well, we have thirty minutes to talk about it," she replied nonchalantly.

"Tutu!"

"Oh, Locke, where is your aloha hospitality? Of course, no resort is really going to want to take a dog that size, even if it is a service dog. You know that. This is Maui. They don't expect people to bring large dogs to this island. Especially ones that aren't celebrity teacup-size. And it's only natural that she wants a place to stay where her larger dog would feel welcome." She looked disapprovingly at me. "When she contacted me, I had to say yes. Just look at those two sweet dogs together." Tutu glanced over at them now, mirroring their pitiful eyes.

She turned to the mermaid, "I'm so sorry, dear. I didn't recognize you from your picture. You look so different in your ... beach attire." I guess that was a nice way of describing what the mermaid looked like after getting pummeled and dragged under the water, somersaulted over the sand, and spit out onto the shore.

I stared at Tutu. And then I looked back over at the mermaid's face, whose mouth obviously would not close anytime soon. This was *just* perfect.

The mermaid responded to Tutu, "I didn't recognize you either. Your photo was so pixelated on the site. I actually couldn't see you very well."

I looked at both of them, trying to think fast. "I have some friends," I jumped in quickly. "I'll see if they can find a place for you to stay."

Tutu huffed. "*Keiki*, we have a perfectly good place for her to stay. All the arrangements have already been made," she hissed. Her disappointed look fell on me.

I looked at her and felt like I was in kindergarten again. This was as bad as when I'd used crayons to draw a family mural on Tutu's kitchen wall. In my defense, there were a lot of murals in Hawaii, so I thought it was justified.

"Yeah? And what room were you planning to 'check' her into?" I asked sarcastically.

"*Keiki*!" She looked embarrassed and quite upset with me.. "We will figure it out. We have more than one bedroom. It's alright. We will make sure *she* is taken care of," she said, eyeing me.

Yeah, your room or mine, I thought. But her determined look fiercely settled on me. "Of course," I interjected swiftly, "I'm sure we could set up a spot at the surf shack for the mermaid to stay overnight until she's able to find a hotel. And she can have the whole place to herself until I open the shop in the morning."

Tutu tsked even louder this time. "*Keiki*, the surf shack, *really*? That's the best you can do?" Her eyes penetrated through me. I thought I had made the mermaid a pretty nice offer because there was *no way* she was staying here. The surf shack had once been a house, so it had a full bathroom, and my office could easily be made into a place for her and *Sebastian* to sleep overnight. I still couldn't help but say Sebastian's name sarcastically in my mind.

Tutu's voice broke through my thoughts as she repri-manded me. "Guin can stay *here* with us–*as planned*, Locke."

"Really? . . . Because I think 'planned' is a pretty loose term here," I shot back.

Even though the bungalow was technically my house, Tutu ran things like it was hers and I was usually more than happy to let her do so. She knew how to do most things better than I could, anyway. After my grandfather passed, I moved Tutu here with me since I hated the idea of her going to assisted living. I was happy to drive her whenever she needed to go and to provide whatever help she required. But I really wanted to be there for her mentally whenever or however I could. And usually her mind was much sharper than mine–when it wasn't working against her.

I looked at this sweet, yet very tough woman who had nursed me back to health when I'd needed it the most. I could never say no to her. But I was really surprised that she'd be totally fine with a complete stranger staying with us. I mean, how much could she even know about this woman, if anything?

I tried again to reason with Tutu. "I'm sure I can find her a perfectly fine place to stay. Much nicer than here. I'm sure she doesn't want to–"

"*Keiki!*" was all she abruptly said, as if I was embarrassing her. This was a rare request; she hardly ever made any.

"Ok." I nodded quickly. The mermaid had been looking between us with hesitancy. I turned to her. "Would you like to stay here?" I asked, extending a reluctant invitation. I made eye contact with her for only a moment.

"Oh, um . . . what did you say about some of your

friends?–" She asked as Tutu came over to stand beside her. Tutu continued stirring the healing cream she had concocted in one of her iconic coconut bowls. Her mortar and pestle were stirring vigorously now. Scents from the coconut oil, vitamin E, aloe vera, lavender, chamomile, and other essential oils awoke my childhood memories. Watching my grandmother work had always calmed me. A sense of home. It had always been a special treat when I could watch her healing hands do their work. But these days she wasn't able to do much of that anymore. Seeing her like this again was really comforting. It hurt me so much to see her lose parts of herself. It especially hurt knowing there was nothing I could do to give those missing pieces back to her. But at that moment, one of those pieces had reunited with her and it was beautiful to see.

After a few minutes, Tutu put her hand on the Mermaid's towel and asked if she could remove it since everything was covered. The mermaid nodded. I watched as Tutu applied the cream gently to the burns around her swimsuit. Then I winced thinking about how tender her skin must be. The burn looked so painful. And Tutu was right, it was really inflamed. Even *I* could see that.

I was determined to make Tutu happy, so I extended another invitation to the mermaid. "Really, we both want you to have somewhere comfortable to stay, a place where Sebastian will be welcomed." I said the dog's name with the best smile I could manage. Although I think it probably looked more like the Joker's grin. Nothing against the dog. He was absolutely adorable. Well, other than him moving way too fast with Penny. I guess I was one of those protective dog dads.

"Oh, well, if the surf shack won't be too much trouble, that would be wonderful. Plus, I can go shopping when I have insomnia." Her laugh was a melodious Disney princess laugh. I felt like I'd been transported under the sea. I imagined her singing, "I've got gadgets and gizmos a-plenty . . . " as she breezed down the surf shack's aisles enjoying a midnight shopping spree. My eyes winced at the overzealous image burned into my brain. And I shuddered at the fact that I actually enjoyed it.

"Well, I don't know what you'll think about surfing gizmos–" I began as my eyes traveled to where Tutu's hands worked on her left arm. It was covered by something that looked a lot like a wetsuit sleeve wrapped around her elbow. I hadn't seen anything like that before. We certainly didn't carry anything like that in the store. Tutu started to remove it, but the mermaid pulled away reflexively. Her face took on a protective shield.

Tutu looked at her with a gentle firmness and "Ariel" relented. I watched Tutu unfurl the sleeve with a grace and gentleness that had been honed in our family for generations. My grandmother came from a long line of midwives. As her only grandchild, she had been determined to give me the tools to become one. She would not let gender roles stop her. It's just that I didn't have a very nurturing personality. At least not with strangers. I had always been pretty shy, especially growing up. And it was probably my lack of a bedside manner that really put the nail in that coffin.

My eyes locked onto the mermaid's arm. Tubing poked out at the top of the elbow sleeve as more of her arm was revealed. It was peering out at me like an anticipatory answer to a question that I knew would greatly change the course of things. Tutu's dark chocolate eyes snapped up and connected to the mermaid's sorrowful blue ones as if the answer was just revealed.

"Locke, the surf shack will not be good enough," Tutu said sternly.

"I've got a really comfy blow-up bed–"

"Locke! *Hâmau!*" She was asking for silence while also demanding that I stop my suggestions. Tutu's eyes looked over at the service dogs and then back to "Ariel." "It's unnecessary to separate them." She spoke with a hoarseness in her voice now. Then she spoke to the mermaid, "But, it's up to you. What would you like to do, *ku'uipo*?"

"Guin," she replied softly.

"Guin, I don't think Locke ever properly introduced us. You'll just have to excuse him. He thinks brutes are in style. He certainly has been taught better manners than he's showing today. You can call me Tutu if you like, but my name is Kelani. What would you like to do? I can take better care of you here though. And either way, the mermaid laughed at my expense, which I knew I deserved, and considering the day she'd had I definitely wouldn't begrudge her the relief. But as we waited for her response, I didn't seem to be able to stop glancing at her tubing. I knew it was rude, but I wanted to understand, and it seemed I was the only one in the room who was lost. She kept proving to be more and more of an enigma to me. And with each clue I got, the more she intrigued me.

Finally, glancing away from her arm, I looked at *Guinevere.* I guess I should get used to her real name, even if I wouldn't give her the satisfaction of using it, especially if I was going to be the only one not allowed to use her nickname. I spoke with what I hoped was an encouraging tone, "Yes, Mermaid, I think it would be cruel to split up the dogs. You really are welcome to stay here. The situation just took me by surprise," I said, as I looked at the happily snoozing dogs. *Who am I to impede puppy love?* At least someone in this house had found some.

Locke

CHAPTER 5

I COULDN'T BELIEVE I was actually holding my breath as I waited for her response. The mermaid was taking her sweet time too. I thought we had offered her a pretty sweet deal. And our accommodations were obviously pet-friendly. Plus, our bungalow came with a "holistic healer." It didn't seem to get much better than Aloha VRBO.

I knew nothing about Lupus, but I was remembering a few things about medical tubing. I'd seen Tutu check ports before, but that was usually for cancer, and I only remember seeing them in someone's neck or chest. At that thought, my mind whirled with questions. Now I really wanted the mermaid to say yes. I was afraid of what might happen to her if she was left to her own devices.

After a substantial amount of time, Guinevere said, "Yes, thank you. But only if you are *absolutely* sure."

"Ok?!" I said, maybe with a little *too* much excitement in my voice. She seemed surprised by that. I think I startled myself too. It was like my subconscious had taken over.

"If you're sure . . ." she said, this time with *much* more pause. As if my unexpected excitement was making her reconsider. She looked up at me with those big doe eyes of hers. Ones I had tried to avoid looking into as I'd carried her here.

There was this self-conscious look in her eyes as she continued, "It would really be nice to stay somewhere that understands about dogs like Sebe and my unique restrictions," she whispered. And that punched me in the gut–the feeling of not wanting to always have to explain yourself and be the "different" one hit me hard. To want to be somewhere people understood you.

But Tutu replied before I could say anything else. "Yes, we're sure. Don't worry about anything. We want you to have a wonderful stay here and hope you'll enjoy your time at the ukulele convention." Tutu was absolutely beaming. Then her expression took on a more serious tone. "We need to make arrangements for this, if you haven't already," she said softly as she assessed Guinevere's arm and the mermaid nodded in response. Tutu smiled back and turned to me. "Locke, would you please make us some hibiscus tea while we discuss some things?"

I stood there a little shocked that Tutu was already kicking me out. It didn't appear they were going to explain anything to me, certainly not anything about the tubing in her arm. Tutu was keeping me busy preparing the tea. I had certainly had more than my fair share of experiences as Tutu's sidekick, but this time I wanted to stay in the room. But I knew Tutu's ploys all too well. She used to run me for tea when she didn't want me to see or hear something.

"Ok," I replied, with nowhere near the enthusiasm I had expressed earlier. I turned and then pivoted back and jokingly asked, "Do mermaids drink hibiscus tea?"

This time there was a genuine smile from her. "Well, if there's not a seaweed one available, they do," she volleyed back at me.

"Oh, I could find–" I began.

"*Locke*," Tutu said impatiently, and I hurried toward the kitchen that was feeling not so much like my own anymore.

As soon as the light cream-colored, swinging shutter doors closed behind me in the tiny kitchen, I went to put the kettle on to boil, trying to distract myself from my annoying curiosity. But my mind latched onto the muffled sounds of their voices. I heaved a sigh of exasperation as I left the kettle and leaned against the wall beside the swinging doors, trying to hear their conversation. I knew it was wrong, but since I hadn't made the best first impression on her, I knew I would not be welcomed into her trust circle anytime soon. I seriously looked like one of *The Three Stooges* with my ear pressed against the doorway. This was why I needed to stay away from women. My capacity for showing interest had been reduced to this. And I was sure to get smacked on the nose by the door in the process and I rightly deserved it too. But hopefully, I would hear some of their conversation before that happened.

I looked over at the kettle, hoping it would boil so it wouldn't be *too* obvious what I was doing. I brought my attention back to my spot by the door, just in time to catch the tail end of their conversation.

"Will you be able to drive?" Tutu asked the mermaid. "I sure wish I still could. Locke has to drive me everywhere these days. He really is a good man. Life just hasn't been very kind to him," Tutu continued. I sighed at the remark. The mermaid didn't need to know anything more about me . . . I hoped Tutu hadn't already said too much while I was busy putting on the teakettle.

"Oh yes. I have a rental car and I can drive. Really, please don't worry about me. Usually I'm better at taking care of myself. I just didn't do a good job of it today since it was my first day at the beach. And well . . . I guess I didn't do too well with the reservation either." She let out a tiny laugh. "But I've been easily distracted lately . . ."

"Of course, of course, *mao ku'uipo.*"

I wondered if Mermaid had any idea Tutu had been calling her "sweetheart" this whole time. I laughed. Tutu hardly ever called anyone by that name anymore. It was one name she'd called her patients when she'd practiced midwifery. However, it seemed to have a different connotation for the mermaid than it had for her patients. It was jarring to hear Tutu call her by that name. But, it was also a relief. Another piece restored. Another reminder of how much had been taken away from Tutu recently. *How was this woman bringing so much back to her in one casual interaction?*

Tutu continued, "I completely understand. I used to be better at taking care of myself too. And I used to take care of other people who lived around here as well." Even from this distance I could hear the sadness in her voice. And it gutted me. I felt like the unlucky fish who wasn't getting thrown back into the sea.

The kettle started whistling, and then I heard it go silent in the other room. Apparently neither one of them wanted me to hear their conversation. Fair enough after my unwelcoming manner earlier today. I finished preparing the tea and hurried back out to Tutu and Guinevere. I'd placed monk fruit and pineapple rock candy on the tray as sweeteners. I kept the rock candy stocked at the surf shack for motion sickness and I kept it handy during boat excursions. We'd started using the excess in our tea. It was pretty addictive if you asked me.

"So, is it all settled?" I asked casually, pretending like I wasn't interested in the details.

Tutu grinned, apparently seeing right through me. "Yes, *Keiki*. It's all settled. If Guin needs some help to drive, I told her you would be more than happy to help, even though she has insisted she will be fine. But you never know. We all need help, every now and again."

I swallowed, looking at Guinevere, wondering where I'd be driving. I knew it must have something to do with her tubing and condition. I wondered if either of them was going to tell me about it now. No, I'm sure after how I'd acted, I was going to have to earn that trust. People didn't just confer all their secrets to me like they did with Tutu. Whatever was going on, it was serious. And talking about it obviously hurt, so exposing that pain would only be for a select few. I could relate. However, I rarely got the luxury of choosing. That's why I tried so hard to disguise mine. Kind of hard to do on a tropical island, but I managed, or at least well enough if people didn't know where to look.

I glanced back at Guinevere. There was so much vulnerability in her expression that even her *Little Mermaid* mask couldn't hide it.

I tried to reply more gently, "Yeah, of course I can drive

you. That's the best part of being a surf shop owner. You're expected to be unreliable and keep sporadic hours. If you aren't a 'free spirit,' people feel cheated, like you're not the real deal. I'll just pop over to the shop and put the closed sign on the door, or I'll get someone to cover for me," I remarked, hoping to hear another melodious, sea siren laugh . . . which I got. I couldn't believe how much I liked her laughter. How much I *wanted* it. I kept feeling drawn to her. Maybe it was because she seemed like she needed a friend, and just like me, she was too stubborn to ask for one–to open herself up to one. And that thought melted some of the protective glacier around my heart, which was kinda ironic since I lived in a tropical place and had warm Hawaiian blood running through my veins and all that . . . But there were reasons my heart had turned arctic, and I needed to remember that.

I stood up quickly, eliciting a startled look from my grandmother. "Where are you going, *Keiki*?"

"Uh, I just remembered I need to close up the shop for Dean. He'll wonder what happened to me." I quickly gave my excuse.

"Dean will be fine. You said you took the rest of the day off," Tutu said, remembering my words clearly. She would only occasionally forget small things, for which I was very grateful. But now would have been a really convenient time for a memory slip. I just needed some time to clear my head and surfing was my way of doing that.

I'd just swing by the shop first to check on my new staff member, Dean. I knew he'd be fine, but he still looked really nervous when I left him in charge of the business. Probably because Dean hadn't been able to find a job that came with health insurance which was something his family desperately needed. And it seemed that an arrest at a drug bust, followed by a misdemeanor charge had something to do with it. As a result, Dean had been desperate for a job to support his family and pay their overdue medical bills, but the charge seemed to follow him wherever he went. After hiring Dean, I learned that cannabis was used to help ease his wife's pain from cancer treatments. It also allowed her to eat, gave her some quality of life, and allowed her to spend time with their children. We usually all have pretty good reasons we do desperate things, and Dean seemed like the type of man to have had *a good reason*. The type of man I was more than willing to give a second chance. And so far, I was more than glad I had.

Calling my bluff, Tutu went over and picked up our old rotary dial phone. The spiral cord wrapped around her worn finger like an old friend. Yes, we actually had one of those phone relics. I guess you could call us nostalgic. The phone had been one of Tutu's many finds at our local area flea market. Within minutes of talking to Dean, she had her answer and was telling me to sit back down. That was my grandmother for you.

"Dean said he is more than capable to watch the surf shack and for you to go enjoy your night, Locke," she said pointedly, calling my bluff. "Although if you'd like to take Guin to get her things first, that would be okay too." *Oh, so that would be fine, would it?* Tutu continued, "We probably need to bring her car back here. I doubt it's a good idea to leave it in the public beach access parking lot all night." She glanced over at the mermaid and then back to me, realizing that Guinevere wasn't in any state to get her car right now. Then she spoke again quietly, "Better just get her things, *Keiki*."

Guinevere protested, but I finally got the car keys from her. This woman seemed even more stubborn than I was. But I'm assuming since she was relenting, the fatigue and pain from the burns had worn down her resistance. Under normal circumstances, I'm sure this endeavor would have been like getting Penny's favorite chew toy away from her: impossible.

"At least let me pour some tea for you and help you get situated so you can rest while I'm gone," I said as I stared into her wild, stubborn eyes. Eyes that looked fiercer than the stormiest seas—and we'd weathered some beasts.

"Ok, thank you." She swallowed. She seemed wary of this new gentleness from me. I would be too. Barracudas were usually harmless until they saw something shiny. Maybe the mermaid thought she was the new shiny thing.

As I poured her tea, I explained about the different sweeteners on the tray, trying to figure out what she might like. Then I went to get some pillows and a few more blankets for her. When I returned, I noticed that Tutu and the mermaid seemed quite content as they peacefully sipped their tea together. It stirred something inside of me. Tutu definitely seemed to have things under control and would make sure the mermaid got some sleep. So I gently laid the blankets and pillows down beside them and took that as my cue to leave. I didn't know what would be said while I was gone, but maybe that was the whole point. Tutu was clever that way.

Locke

CHAPTER 6

WHEN I RETURNED to the bungalow, I found a sleeping mermaid on our tropical palm leaf-patterned sofa. She actually looked docile. A laugh escaped me, and I hoped it wouldn't wake her. Somehow I had a feeling she'd be even more fiery after being awakened. A sadistic part of me wanted to find out. Instead, I carefully set her bags by the door. I'd left the dog carrier and food in my car for now. I lightly tiptoed around her, sliding past the sofa and stepping out onto the lanai where I was always sure to find Tutu. She was sitting on the wicker glider as the late afternoon sun dulled, finally offering some relief from the heat. It was the first cool break in humidity for the day.

My grandmother looked so relaxed sitting in her rocker under the grass tiki umbrella. It was a sight I always loved to see. Tutu enjoying life was infectious. You wouldn't think she would enjoy touristy-type things like kitschy grass umbrellas and bodacious tiki huts, but those sorts of things made her smile. And it was wonderful to see.

I came up behind her and put a hand slowly on her shoulder. She jumped at my gentle attempt to let her know I was there. It was pretty much our tradition.

"*Keiki,* stop doing that. How can you walk so quietly? Especially for someone *so* tall." She held her hand over her heart like I'd just stopped it.

"Just graceful, I guess." And she laughed at my facetious remark. I grabbed a chair and pulled it over to sit beside her. There was a tranquility in being together like this, looking out at our little community. Faintly in the distance, over the buildings, we could see the water. It was our little piece of heaven–*kelani.* The same as my grandmother's name. But I believe the serenity came from Tutu.

She glanced over at me. The tanned skin between her eyebrows furrowing in rows of concern as she asked, "Are you going to tell me what happened today? Or would you like my imagination to fill in the blanks? You know, I'm *very* creative." She smiled mischievously, and I knew I *wouldn't* prefer that option. She continued, "I never expected such a grand entrance for our check-in service. Of *all* the women on the beach, Locke." She laughed at me.

"Right, I guess I just somehow sensed you were up to no good . . .I mean, she was on the shore near our beach access walkway. So glad her sense of direction kicked in today." And Tutu just shook her head at me. "So, are you gonna tell me what happened when I left now?" I volleyed right back, hoping she might take the bait. But she just looked at me, like she could see straight through me and was offended that I thought she could be fooled so easily. I knew better, but it wasn't like I had a lot of other options for finding out more about our "houseguest." It was worth a shot.

"Locke, you better ask her yourself. I will not betray the *pale keiki's* bond of trust. Just like I wouldn't tell her certain things about *you*." She looked at me with her worldly gaze, the "trump card" that always one-upped me. There was no denying it. She always beat me at the game of Rook, too. Her look served as a reminder of how much more life experience she had than me.

I lifted my brows and then looked out onto the community surrounding us. Sometimes I forgot how much we tucked ourselves away. "How about you tell her a bit about me, and I get to know a little more about her right now?" I playfully asked.

"No, *Keiki*, I don't think that's how this works. But I'm glad to see you're willing to negotiate. Only *interested* men barter." Her smile was radiant. I wasn't sure if I wanted to make her *quite* that happy. Tutu continued, "You'll have to be careful with this one, *Keiki*. In *all* ways. And however she reacts–if you decide to tell her about your situation–you need to remember to put her needs first, above your own."

I grimaced. That hardly seemed fair. The Hunchback got to hide away in his cathedral, the Creature in his cave, and the Phantom in his dungeon . . . surely I could do the same. It's funny, lately I'd been watching and reading things with a different perspective. I was now that person who felt deeply for flawed characters and their situations.

I responded to Tutu's remark, "And are you going to tell me why I need to be careful?" She just stared back at me, her solid features unmoving. *Right.* I sighed. "That's what I thought." At least it was worth a try.

She softened as her curiosity took over. "So, tell me what happened today."

"Oh, so you want to know about earlier today, but I get nothing in return? Is that how this works?" I bantered lightly with her.

"*Keiki*, of course, that's how this works. I'm your tutu, and if you really love me . . . " Her voice trailed off.

"Alright, alright, save your energy. I wouldn't want you spending it on my behalf. You knew this was always going to be the outcome." She smiled widely at me. "Well, I took Penny to play fetch, and I was checking out the surf to see if it was going to be worth getting my board, when the mermaid washed up on shore, right in front of me."

"The mermaid?" she interrupted, eyebrow cocked.

"Yeah, *the mermaid*," I said matter-of-factly. "I felt a little like Major Nelson. But instead of finding a magical Jeannie, I found a distressed mermaid. And just think how much trouble she caused him."

"You can't call her that, Locke," she said firmly. "And I know you love that show. You can't hide it from me. I'm not the only one who's enjoying TV Land with the mischievous blonde in a bottle."

I rolled my eyes playfully. I'd never give her the satisfaction of admitting it. "Well, Ariel is the other name option since

Guinevere has made it clear we are on a formal name *only* basis."

Tutu snickered at my words. "That really irritates you, doesn't it?" she replied through her laughter. I scratched at my skin, which suddenly seemed aggravated. "I don't think it will be long until Guin warms up to you and lets you have a few more privileges. You just have—"

"To earn them?" I parried. More laughter escaped from her. Apparently she found my annoyance comical. "Doesn't protecting her from a crowd of rabid tourists and carrying her back to my home count for something?" I looked out, fixing my eyes on the ocean and not on Tutu.

"No, Locke, it doesn't. Not with this one. *Not even close.*" I rolled my eyes at her, and she continued, "Do you know how you must seem to someone like her? You're like a brooding *Rocky*. That's intimidating."

"Well, then she should know I'm not going anywhere. I'm—"

"I wasn't done," Tutu interrupted me. "You're not exactly warm and fuzzy, *Keiki*. And with this one, you're going to have to learn to give a little something more in order to get to know her better. And I believe you're going to have to be tender. Think of those funny movies with 'The Rock' trying to be gentle. You can do it too. I believe in you. Look how sweet you are with me. How friendly and compassionate you are with the people that are *Ohana* to you."

"That's different. It's you." I scoffed. "And that's 'family.'"

"Well, at least we know you can be sweet. But most of all, I'm glad to see you *are* interested."

"I'm *not* interested," I replied a little too quickly.

Tutu chuckled. "Ok. Well, since you're *so* uninterested, it shouldn't be a problem to be gentle and patient." She looked at me, assessing how I handled her comment. I folded my arms as she continued. "*Keiki*, there's a lot for you to learn. Why don't you just talk to her and ask her what you want to know? How about I make a nice dinner, and then the two of you can take the dogs for a walk on the beach . . . *together*. A nice sunset walk. The dogs seem to get along very well, so maybe they will provide you with some inspiration."

She tittered. As much as I wanted, I couldn't get the corners of my lips to fold downward. It was impossible with this woman. So I said, "Penny sure dived right in."

"Yeah, I think you could learn something from Penny, Locke."

"Penny doesn't even know if he has fleas. And I'm the one who's going to be left patching her broken heart when they leave." My voice rose slightly.

Tutu's eyebrows raised. "Are you *sure* we're talking about Penny?" I just stared at her, aggravated that she'd called me out on it. "I don't think she's the one you need to be worried about." She eyed me back. "Plus, Penny has you . . . and *you* have me. But there is a terrified and lonely woman on your sofa, even if she doesn't show it. One that could use a friend. And I think you could use someone who understands you too. I'm not getting any younger."

"You're plenty young." At my words, a sad smile spread across her lips.

"Maybe . . . but parts of me are not." And those words fractured me. She started to get up. "I'm going to make some Mahi Mahi and plantains. How does that sound?"

I stopped her, placing my hand softly on her shoulder. "It sounds like that's going to be very nice for me to make while you rest." Now she rolled her eyes at me.

Tutu replied, "Really, *Keiki*, I have lived my *whole* life taking care of myself. I know how to do it. I won't break."

"Maybe so, but I think you've earned the right to let someone else do it for you." She put her hand over mine at my words. And I could feel the thinning of her skin and the increasing weakness in her hold. Slight changes I had noticed in the last couple of years. I had always seen her as indefatigable and unbreakable. Noticing these changes chipped away at me. And they were all I could think about as I softly slipped back into the house as quietly as I had come.

Locke

CHAPTER 7

I WAS TRYING to be as quiet as possible as I rummaged for pans in the kitchen. Guinevere was still sound asleep on the sofa, and I wanted to let her rest for as long as possible. The sun and the events of the day seemed to have really taken it out of her. I'm sure whatever else she faced in her life was exhausting her too.

I was pretty excited about my stealthiness when a pan suddenly clattered out of my hand. "*Aiâ!*" The word came out of my mouth loudly. I quickly rose, peering over the counter and out through the archway to see if I'd disturbed the mermaid, but I didn't see any signs of movement from her.

Satisfied, I went back to my business. I wasn't a stranger to this kitchen. Tutu and I did this dance most nights. When she first moved in with me, she had insisted on doing all the cooking, but after much discussion, she had finally relented and allowed me to take over the cooking. At first, it would have been better if she hadn't given in since I was a truly terrible cook. As a single guy, I had only cooked fast convenience foods. My menu comprised all the iconic and long-lived chefs– Boyardee, Campbell, and Ragu. So when Tutu taught me how to cook, it had been a culinary crash course. And crash and burn, I did. I charred almost everything I cooked and not in a good, flavorful way. That seemed to be my hidden talent in the kitchen. But Tutu had been patient and helped me along. Now I was very grateful that I could make something other than grilled cheese that didn't come in a can.

Tutu had taught me to make many Hawaiian delicacies, and that had connected me to our heritage in a way I hadn't expected. So I was finally making peace with cooking, especially since I had found audiobooks to keep me company while I worked in the kitchen. I loved underwater mysteries or classics involving the sea. Sometimes I'd put on YouTube videos of surfing techniques or even sea life documentaries on the Discovery Channel. Yes, I couldn't seem to get enough of the ocean. But I had a bit of a guilty pleasure . . . dog books . . . sappy ones about lovable puppies. Extra points for a book about a service dog. Although finding books with one wasn't easy. And you could forget about finding a book with an owner like me. But my somewhat surprising audiobook preferences was just one way that I was a misfit.

Thinking about dogs, I glanced back out to check on

Penny. I wanted to make sure that Sebastian was still being a "gentlemutt." I turned to sneak another peak into the living room when I saw Guinevere standing on the other side of the bar counter in the open archway startled me.

I reflexively put my hand to my forehead from the surprise. "Uh, I was just trying to check on the dogs," I explained.

"Oh, really," she asked suspiciously. It was like she'd read my mind. Then she suddenly burst out, "*The Big Bang Theory*!"

"What?" I looked at her like she was crazy.

"Penny's name . . ." she explained.

"Oh, no," I replied with satisfaction. She reached for her back pocket to get her phone, and I grabbed it from her hands. She began protesting, but I responded, "No, that's cheating. Use your brain and wit, or it doesn't count." I went to hand the phone back to her, but not without a few fake-outs first because they were just too tempting. She looked too cute trying to grab her phone from me. But the moment I had that thought, I quickly put her phone easily within her reach. *Dangerous.* This woman was trouble. We'd entered code Locke-you're-an-idiot territory.

"So," she asked, distracting me as I tried to get another look at our sleeping dogs. From here, Penny seemed ridiculously happy and quite content to still be Sebastian's "little spoon." *He* should be the little spoon. I didn't like this. She was a strong, independent–

The mermaid interrupted my thoughts, "So you *can* actually cook? I never would have pegged you as an apron-in-the-kitchen type of guy." She eyed Tutu's vibrant, flamingo-patterned apron that was wrapped around me. Frills and all. Another alarming surprise about me. She better get used to them.

"Yeah, Mermaid, I can cook. Or at least you can see for yourself and let me know in about five minutes. I'm hoping this is something you can eat. Tutu suggested the fish and plantains, since they would be healthy."

"Yes, thank you. I just have to watch my potassium." But she seemed rather distracted as she said it. A knavish grin overtook her expression. "So cooking is a regular event for you, and yet . . ." Her eyes continued to roam over me and my absurd apron. Tutu had found it in one of her friend's souvenir shops. She enjoyed "shopping local" and supporting her friends, plus she absolutely loved the tourist stuff. She'd always been good humored like that. "*This* is the apron of choice?" she said, grinning widely and waving a hand over the ridiculous apron.

"Yeah, Mermaid, *this* is the apron of choice." I lifted my arms out from my sides to show it off, and she pinched her lips together to keep from laughing. I turned my back to her and called over my shoulder, "You should see Tutu's."

The mermaid was already in the kitchen to check out my apron. Her scent surrounded me, a heady cloud of Tutu's "lotion potion" and a faint trace of sunscreen. I inwardly growled. I was prey to mermaid scent . . . "Siren enchantress" pheromones meant to lure weak seafaring men like me. *Darn it, I shouldn't be this susceptible.* Surely, I was certainly stronger than this.

I abruptly moved away from her, and she looked at me with a surprised lift of her brow. Her quizzical expression seemed to ask what she'd done. That tugged something loose inside of me. *Gentle and patient, Locke.* That's what Tutu had suggested.

"Um, Tutu's apron is in the pantry." I nodded toward the closet and her eyes lit up at my suggestion. "You don't need to help me with dinner, but if you'd like, I can show you how to cook the plantains. Unless you'd be more comfortable sitting at the bar countertop and resting–" But I didn't even get to finish my sentence before she started shaking her head enthusiastically at my invitation. Brief bursts of laughter escaped me as she made her way to the pantry. And then I heard her laughter–the "under-the-sea music" was alive and well again. She'd obviously found Tutu's apron designed to look like a tiki girl with 3D coconuts on the top and a neon grass skirt on the bottom.

"You're not going to switch with me, are you?" she asked as she came out of the pantry.

"No, Mermaid. That was half the appeal to you helping in the kitchen," I said with the straightest face I could manage while she held the apron as far away from herself as possible.

"Well, for five minutes I don't think I need an apron," she replied.

"Oh no, I think you're a flight risk for any activity. An apron is mandatory." She scowled at me. I responded, "Only thinking of you." Then I nodded at her in the *most* gentlemanly manner I possessed. This elicited one of the best facial expressions I'd ever received. "Well, you could have a seat at the bar. Probably better for you considering the day you've had."

The apron went on within a second flat. Having someone around who was as stubborn as myself was definitely going to come with some perks. It was going to be fun. I knew how to swipe all the elevator buttons with one stroke.

"No way," she said, eyeing me. "You promised me life changing plantains. *That's* what I want to see, Mr. Muscle."

"Mr. Muscle? Is that all you've got?" I asked with a teasing jab and raised an eyebrow.

"I'm working on it. I'm badly burned in more ways than one–"

I held up a hand. "No way am I giving you a pass,

Mermaid. But *please* take your time. Maybe you can figure out the significance of Penny's name in the meantime too."

Her eyes narrowed at me, but beyond her look I saw appreciation. I could tell how much it meant to her that I didn't think she *needed* a pass. And underneath it all was a fire and determination in her that was kick-starting mine. One that said she wanted to prove me right.

"Ariel" took her time and softly approached me like I was a dangerous sea creature. As if she was trying to get a closer look but being careful not to scare off the sea-life. I reflexively reached out to bring her closer to the stove, but then remembered her skin was too tender to be touched. That was a *good* thing to remember. I *shouldn't* touch her. My heart was way too tender for that. It was best not to form *any* attachments. Her touch had already had too much of an effect on me earlier today.

There were mixed emotions on her face as she watched my hand make its slow retreat, but she came over to me, anyway. Her scent grew stronger with each step she took. I closed my eyes briefly, trying to fight it, but it was no use. Her baby blues looked up expectantly at me. Waiting for her lesson.

I stumbled out with, "Uh . . . So . . . Well, you want to cook the plantains last because you need to watch them closely." I looked down at her, not really registering a word I'd just spoken. "And uh. . . They burn really easily." My words were trailing off as I became increasingly distracted by her closeness.

I kept staring at her eyes. There was something in them that threatened to pull me under. And her blonde hair fell seamlessly around her heart-shaped face. Because, *of course*, it was heart-shaped.

"Locke?" she questioned when I just stood there, gazing at her. "They burn?" she said, trying to remind me.

"Yeah." I cleared my throat. I looked down at the plantains so I could finish my explanation. No more getting sucked into those blue vacuums. Little riptides of doom. "I like to sprinkle a little coconut sugar on them. If you only have bananas at home, you don't need the sugar. They will caramelize just fine on their own. Just use some coconut oil so they're extra-smooth . . ." I prattled on, and then darn if I didn't sneak a look at her. The riptides immediately pulled me away from shore. And oddly she seemed to look a little lost herself. But maybe I was too far gone to see clearly now, lost at sea, mystic mirages confusing me.

I felt something rub against my leg, and then the mermaid toppled over onto me. The spatula dropped from my hand with a thud as I instinctively reached out to catch her as she landed softly in my arms. Now I'd really made things awkward. My eyes locked onto hers in this way-too-romantic embrace. I could hear her gulp as she stared back at me. Finally, I pulled my eyes from hers and looked down at the culprit. I found Sebastian rubbing up against her leg and licking her hand. He must have startled her when he was trying to get her attention and she lost her balance, because I sure didn't think women were just spontaneously falling into my arms.

Guinevere seemed to have reached the same conclusion as her eyes spotted Sebastian too. She began explaining, "Sorry, he's alerting me. I woke up feeling off today with a bad migraine. But my medicine's been keeping it mostly at bay until this evening. I guess it makes sense that I might have a migraine with everything that has happened today. But I can't always predict them like he can. I've got to get somewhere safe . . . in case I faint. Sebastian's usually never wrong. Sometimes I can avoid it though. Sorry for once *again* forcing myself into your arms." She laughed lightly, but I could tell she was uncomfortable about it. She really thought I *didn't* want her there.

"No, I'm the one who should be sorry. Your skin must be painful to the touch," I whispered, because what she had just said couldn't be further from the truth. I very much wanted her here. And that was the problem. It just *wasn't* a good idea, romantically. "Ok, let's get you to the sofa."

"It's ok, my skin doesn't hurt *too* badly. My front took the brunt of it, so my arms aren't too painful." She smiled at me and I felt my heart melting a little more. "But, um, sometimes I only get a couple of minutes as a warning before I faint, so sitting down on the floor here is best." She looked up at me from underneath hooded eyes. And it was the first time I felt like I could see a little unguarded piece of her.

My lips parted to speak again, but I was not ready to let her go yet. I had this primal instinct taking over me where she was concerned, wanting nothing more than to protect her and not knowing how best to do it. But Sebastian came back and licked her hand again, pacing beside us.

"Right, ok," I said, quickly cutting off all the stove eyes. I kept her in my arms as I lowered us to the floor, and she gave me a little shocked look. I guess I was supposed to let go, but I just couldn't do it. Everything in my body wanted to hold on to her as I had earlier today. I continued holding her in my arms as I asked, "So what's best? What's safer? Holding you like this or placing your head on my leg . . . ?" I looked at her with nervousness.

There was this stunned look on her face like she couldn't speak, but when Sebastian licked her hand again, it jolted her back to reality. She said, "Um, can I put my head on your leg?" And I nodded with what I hoped was reassurance and lowered her down to my left thigh. All the while, Sebastian kept pacing back and forth. She looked at him, then back to me. "It's amazing to me he can smell so well, even when he's in the other room. Somehow he always knows when I'm about to have an episode."

I was shocked, too. It really was incredible what Sebastian could do. I saw him lay on her legs next. Comforting her and trying to help with her blood pressure, I suppose. Then I asked, "Is there something else I need to do for you? Elevate your legs? Get you water?" I asked this with more nervousness now. I was way out of my league here. Occasionally, I helped tourists who became distressed from the heat, but they had usually *already* fainted and I just helped to bring them around.

"Uh, can you . . ." Her words were becoming more fuzzy, like everything was heavier. I could tell she was becoming more disoriented, sleeper. And Sebastian was now licking her hand madly and nibbling on it too. "Those things sometimes help, but . . . Just let me come around if I . . ." And then, as if she had just drifted off to sleep, she was out. And so I just waited, doing what I thought she had asked of me. Not attempting to wake her even as Sebastian started nudging her.

And when her eyes fluttered open after what felt like an eternity to me, I wondered if waking up to me would cause her alarm. I'm sure she wasn't even going to know where she was. Maybe I should have left her in peace. But she bobbled her head around, looking for and finding Sebastian. I guess he was always ready, waiting for her to find him. But then she looked up, as she realized that her head was resting on someone's thigh. My voice got trapped in my throat. Her hazy, exposed eyes stared up at me and then back away as they went shy. Then she looked back up to me a little more daring.

"Hey, Mermaid," my voice managed in a smooth tone, for which I was thankful. "You should have told me you were really *Sleeping Beauty*." And then she smiled. "How are you feeling?" I realized my hands were still on her head and shoulder, and I wondered if that was okay.

"Yeah, just a little embarrassed is all. I just need a couple of minutes. I'll feel strange for a while after passing out. So we'll have to sit here awkwardly for just a little while longer. I really hope I didn't ruin dinner."

I couldn't believe she was worried about dinner or the awkwardness of this. Most of all, I hated she was embarrassed. "Guin, please don't be embarrassed–you shouldn't be at all– and dinner will be fine. What can I do to even the playing field? Because I know that saying 'don't be embarrassed' does nothing." I knew this all too well from my own experiences.

"What?" she asked, nothing but shock on her face.

"Ok, so when I was five I had this Ariel piggy bank," I began.

"Locke, what?"

"Just let me even the field, Mermaid." She looked at me with disbelief. "And I carried it *everywhere*. I even slept with it. I was obsessed. The kids at school even teased me and called it 'my girlfriend.' Now that's your embarrassing Locke story for the day. Although, this,"–I waved to her–"is not embarrassing. So we're not really even, but if it helps you feel that way . . ."

I trailed off as she reached up for my hand on her shoulder and grabbed it as a way of thanks. Her little sea siren smile rested beautifully on her face. I was so done for. I was the Thanksgiving turkey that smoked up the entire house because everyone forgot it was in the oven. And now she knew *exactly* how much I had loved *The Little Mermaid*. And not just any character of the characters, but Ariel herself.

"So you do go looking for mermaids," she couldn't help but reply.

"That's not what I said. I was only five." But she was grinning so widely I couldn't help but enjoy it. "Fine, I will not complain about catching one. How's that?"

"It's good. Really, good." Her impish expression only heightened. But then she seemed to realize where we were again. "Uh, I think I'm ok now."

"Are you sure? Let's just sit you up slowly," I suggested, but I could tell she wanted to get up and out of here as quickly as possible. My mermaid story wasn't anywhere on par with the vulnerability of what she had just exposed to me and with no choice either.

After a little while, she said, "I should take Sebastian out. He probably could use a potty break." But really, I think she needed the break. She kept looking down at my hand on her arm. The one I seemed unable to remove from her. I hadn't been able to break our point of contact.

"No, I can do that," I said, also looking down at our connection. "Let me take the dogs out. You can stay here."

"No, that's ok. I'm sure you need to tend to the food and finish the plantains. I don't think I got *all* the instructions on how to do that." She laughed, and my face twisted in embarrassment. "Plus, if you think you're bad at burning things, then you obviously haven't seen me in action. Never leave me in charge of the kitchen."

Then, like a cold splash of water, she was up and out of my arms, and I was watching her collect the dogs to go outside.

Guinevere

CHAPTER 8

AFTER LOCKE DIRECTED me to an outdoor area for the dogs and I finally convinced him I was feeling well enough to go with them, I took my exit. I *needed* some fresh air, especially after what had just happened. Some time to think and space to process what Locke had just witnessed. I didn't want to stick around any longer than necessary to see how he would react or how he might change in his interactions with me after one of my episodes. And I especially didn't want to see how he would look at me now.

And as the fresh air and its botanical fragrance greeted me, the more I realized I needed a break from Locke's intoxicating bungalow and its cheeky, frilly aprons. *And him.* Most of all him. But not for the reasons I would have imagined. Everything had been all too perfect in there.

I hadn't lied; I was a disaster in the kitchen. I'm not sure even Tutu could have salvaged me in the cooking department, although she seemed to be a miracle worker. Her salve was already helping heal my skin. And that shocked me. Not that I had ever doubted her abilities, but usually, when my body reacted to something, it was slow to respond to treatment. It usually got a lot worse before it got better.

I think part of her healing power was her personality. Tutu had been so kind to me when Locke left to collect my things. She sat and listened with a comforting expression while I shared some of my medical journey with her. She never looked shocked or showed pity towards me. And she assured me she wouldn't tell Locke what I shared with her, and I believed her. Tutu seemed to be a woman of integrity.

And the few things she'd shared with me about Locke made me want to believe that he had integrity too. But I wasn't sure what to believe yet. I couldn't decipher what he thought about me, so I sure wasn't ready to wade through my thoughts about *him*. Especially when I kept falling into his *very* well-defined arms, honed from his love of the sea and the time he spent there. And as much as I hated to admit it, that made him even more attractive to me. And this only confused me even more because I usually wasn't attracted to muscular men. If you told me there was a bodybuilding event, I'd be the first one looking for the door. But Locke seemed to have developed his muscles naturally as a byproduct of his surfing lifestyle and his work at the surf shop. Tutu had told me a little about his work before I'd drifted off to sleep. Then she'd tenderly tucked the blankets around me, just like my mom had done when I was a little girl. I didn't realize just how much I'd missed that. Care and concern had cocooned around me with Tutu's simple gesture.

Well, no matter what was his "secret" to working out, even I could admit it *definitely* worked to his advantage. But I was the *last* person who wanted to go there. His obvious annoyance with me, and the way he got under my skin so easily, offset all of that "handsome" for me. I was usually the type of person who had to get to know someone before becoming attracted to them. But I guess being swept off the beach by someone–and actually *wanting* someone to do that for you–kind of blew everything else out of the water. Thankfully, I had enough to do to keep my mind busy, so I'd have *no problem* staying away from him or any thoughts about his attractiveness. I just had to stay out of his arms. And definitely no more cooking lessons. No more lessons of *any* kind. He'd gone sweet on me, and "Tender Locke" was trouble. A Bermuda Triangle of gentle, masculine oxytocin. And my traitorous body responded to it *all*.

My mind continued to whirl with thoughts of my "dilemma" while I patiently waited for the dogs to finish their business. Penny and Sebastian were completely adorable together, and their attraction to one another seemed to really irk Locke, which made it that much more enjoyable for me. Once the dogs finished sniffing the ground and each other, I brought them back inside. I gave them each a treat from a jar covered with paw prints and sand. And I gave them the treats on their doggie bed so they would curl up together again. I *really* loved firing Locke up especially about their obvious attraction for one another. And sure enough, he rolled his eyes at the sight of them snuggled up together.

But to his credit, he said nothing about it. "The food's ready if you feel up to eating." He looked over to me briefly and then started plating the food. Not exactly the reaction I had expected after what he had just witnessed. I hesitantly came into the kitchen to help, waiting for fifty questions or for him to tell me what I should be doing with my body, such as resting. But he didn't.

He must have been somewhat distracted by today's events because he was still in his wetsuit–or maybe he just lived in it. As I got closer to him, I saw that same indent on the lower leg of his wetsuit. The one I thought I'd noticed when he was distracting me from Tutu's care. The shape of the right calf seemed different where the indent began, too. Locke turned to me. I'd obviously been looking at him far too long.

"What?" he asked.

"Nothing, I was just waiting to help." I looked at his skeptical eyes. Maybe there was a reason his response had been so different toward me today. Maybe he *could* understand.

He nodded, handed me a plate, and called for the dogs to follow us out onto the porch. Locke was more than happy to break up their love fest. He really didn't seem to have a romantic bone in his body.

I wasn't sure how dinner would go, but we actually had a lovely time. And I had to admit that Locke was an incredible cook. Tutu had done *very well* with him. Even Sebastian agreed. I kept sneaking him pieces of fish, which I thought Locke would be very disapproving about, but to my surprise, he kept doing the same with Penny. There was *no way* you could not share a few table scraps with these adorable four-legged friends. The looks they gave could melt even the most hardened of hearts. Sebastian had the "pound puppy" look down. He could look so hopeless you would have thought he'd *never* seen a meal in his life. In reality, the vet wanted him to lose five pounds. But if he was happy, I was happy. I was trying to do better about the table scraps, but one look from him and my resolve broke. He was *my everything*. He had saved me in more ways than I could count. Just like my music had. And that's why we were here. There wasn't anywhere I went without him. He truly was my "soulmutt."

I looked over as Locke fed Penny a piece of food. Her tongue happily lapped up the table scraps with the special eagerness of a golden. My wayward eyes drifted to Locke's annoyingly handsome face. And it was covered by the softest expression, which only weakened my reserves. I wondered if Penny was his soulmutt too. And that thought made nagging questions pop into my head again. I focused on Penny's little red vest and discreetly looked at Locke. *Why does he need a service dog?* I'd tried asking Tutu for more information, but she wouldn't tell me anything. She said to trust her on the fact that Locke had a good heart.

His eyes caught mine, and I looked away quickly because there was an actual possibility that my nosiness was going to be interpreted as a "come to momma" invitation. My radar was busted, anyway. I couldn't even protect myself. My "invisible" illness didn't feel so invisible anymore. I always ended up having to talk about it more than I wanted. It always made itself present somehow, like today. It could be seen on my skin, in the pain on my face, and in the sadness in my eyes. My AV Fistula had just become a walking "take advantage of me" sign. And I had officially closed that neon sucker down. I didn't let new people in lightly. This was special. But the sign lit up immediately for Tutu.

And that's why I agreed to Tutu's suggestion that we take a walk at sunset after we finished dinner. Locke and I hesitantly looked at each other. Our gazes reluctantly met at the same time. Like two lobsters caught in a trap, sizing up the other unlucky soul accompanying them on their misadventure. I sure hoped we would fare better.

"*Keiki*, this is Guin's first sunset here. You should make sure she enjoys it." She pursed her lips. "It's Sebastian's too."

He shot her an unreadable expression and, without turning to me, said, "I didn't think about this being your first night here."

"Yes, it is. I flew out Saturday evening and got here really early Sunday morning. But I'm really tired, so I can wait to see it another night. It will still be 'my first Hawaiian sunset' some other evening." I said, quickly.

"No," he interjected. "If you think you're up for it, let's go. The sunset is really beautiful from the beach. I'll walk the dogs so it's easier on you. I have a feeling they'll want to walk side by side anyway," he said with mild irritation. "Let me just feed them first. I can get Sebastian's food out of my car, or he's welcome to share some of Penny's. I cooked chicken, rice, and green beans for her this week. I'm afraid he might get jealous."

I just looked at the man, blinking. *He did what?* This man with his cool but please-back-away-slowly exterior cooked meals for his dog? And he was offering Sebastian gourmet meals, too?

I hesitated. "Uh, are you sure? He'll be fine. I feel bad for you to–"

"Don't. I'll feel bad watching him eat dry food. Plus, I

don't think Penny would ever forgive me," he said with a hint of humor.

I nodded, thanking him the best I could through my disbelief. Tutu was silently taking in our exchange like an old fortune teller reading the tea leaves. "*Keiki*, let me feed the dogs. You go on. I don't want you to miss the sunset."

"But the dogs will enjoy it–" he started.

"I think it'll be easier for Guin this way. You just take her. As long as she's comfortable going without Sebastian. You can take the dogs some other night. When she's more settled. And the dogs seem tired from the events of today. I'm sure they'll enjoy resting on the porch with me."

I looked over at them, and they seemed pretty content lying on the porch together. Sebastian even had his paw resting sweetly on Penny. I was really worried I wouldn't be able to convince him to come back home with me. And now I had to compete with gourmet food too.

I swallowed dryly and eyed Locke from the corner of my eye, and I noticed he seemed to do the same to me. Not having our dogs as a distraction didn't seem ideal, but at this point it didn't seem up for discussion.

So we both nodded graciously to Tutu and thanked her for watching the dogs. Locke reminded her that he had his cell phone if she needed anything. And then to my complete surprise, Locke escorted me out the door to the beach in a truly old-fashioned, gentlemanly way. And it was then that I worried a little about what I had agreed to do. Because I was feeling drawn to this man and there wasn't even a hint of a sunset in sight.

Guinevere

GENTLE GIANT. Those were the words that kept racing through my mind. *Maybe* I'd misjudged Locke. *Maybe* Tutu was telling me the truth . . . and her portrayal of him was the *true* Locke. *Perhaps* I was seeing the real, unvarnished version of him, and everything else I'd seen earlier today had been a mask.

Each little thing he did was making me at least consider the possibility that I may have misjudged him. . . . especially considering the literal and figurative doors he was opening for me. He'd already shown such care and concern for my well-being. Both in big and small ways. All the little things he was doing were really getting to me. Things like making sure I had a jacket and shoes to stay warm and avoid sand burrs. Keeping his hand on my back as he guided me toward the beach so he avoided touching the burns on my body. Opening his home to Sebastian and me. Staying with me when I fainted and was in such a vulnerable state. And most of all, his wonderful relation-ship with Tutu. It was all adding up to a genuinely nice guy, making me want to give him a fresh start. Wipe away those initial negative impressions from my mind. Perhaps we'd had a rough start in more ways than one–including the embarrassing and painful way I'd met him–which may have influenced the way I saw him *more* than I realized.

Maybe he could be a friend. God, I needed one. I was drowning in a sea of strangers, and all I wanted was for a friend to grab my hand and offer refuge. I wanted to prove more than anything I still had something left to offer. That I could still contribute to a friendship. Maybe more than anything, I'd been hoping to make some new friends at the ukulele convention through our shared love of music.

Locke guided me down a shell-covered path, through the coastal community, and toward the beach. To my surprise, I recognized very little. My perspective of the beautiful coastline differed completely from earlier today since I was now viewing it on two feet. And the walk seemed much shorter since my nerves weren't worried about what serial killer propensities Locke might have. After a short walk, the water slowly came into view. The photos of the Maui coastline that I had memo-rized from my home office daydreams were suddenly coming to life right before my eyes. The sun was dropping lower and lower in the sky, crushing the blues into magical warm hues of reds, golds, and vibrant oranges.

I looked over to see Locke's jet-black hair dancing in the sea breeze. He seemed just as captivated by the sunset as me. I honestly don't think you could have guessed which one of us was the tourist. And in the waning sunlight, I felt like this was the moment to try for a fresh start. To see if he might be a person willing to take a risk on me. And if I could let myself take a risk on him. Because maybe, *just maybe*, he needed that too.

The ocean's waves lapped in the distance, a serene sound that enveloped me in its soothing embrace. The sparkling aquamarine water still glimmered, making the most of what was left of the day, its hues slowly turning into a deep sapphire. The ocean was making every last moment count. As we drew closer to the water's edge, only the expanse of soft sand separated us from the sea's soothing crashes onto the shore.

Locke looked down at me, and I felt it was time. "Guin," I said to him softly. "You can call me Guin."

A large boyish grin spread across his face. And his tone immediately changed. It was light and happy. "Well, *Guin*, do you want to walk a little or should we just choose a spot to stop and watch the sunset?"

I really didn't want to admit I was already tired from the walk down here after my very "eventful" day. Plus, I hadn't been able to sleep on the flight like I'd hoped I could. And I was always exhausted after my treatments. I hadn't scheduled enough time between the treatment in the morning and the flight in the late afternoon. I knew if I had my treatment on the day I left it would buy me an extra day before needing another round. And I wanted all the time I could get, yet I'd probably been too greedy.

I was just about to speak when he said, "Let's just sit for now. That way you can really soak in the view. After all, you only get one first Hawaiian sunset. I know I'm probably not your *first* choice for sunset companionship, so I'll try to make up for it any way I can."

I laughed at his sarcastic joke as he found a pleasant spot on the crest of the shore, one that the waves had carved out at high tide. Locke spread out a vinyl-backed blanket on the peak and lent me a hand to help me down to the sand. *Gentle giant indeed.* As I looked at him sitting beside me, he reminded me of the lion with a thorn caught in its paw. Penny was a reminder of that thorn. I wondered if there was ever going to be a way to ease that pain. I was pretty sure I'd never be able to remove it, but there was a naïve part of me that wanted to see if I could help in some way.

We hadn't said much to each other on the walk. I think we were both afraid of saying the wrong thing. Too worried about stepping into tender territory. But with the sea breeze hitting my painfully burned skin and the sun cascading into a burst of coral colors in the sky, I felt that same feeling tugging at me as from moments ago.

I looked at Locke, who seemed to share the same wonderment I felt at the sunset's kaleidoscopic display. A boyish grin spread across his face as he gazed out across the ocean. He slowly turned his handsomely tanned face toward me, apparently noticing my glances. I was not exactly good at being subtle. I guess that was my social awkwardness. "Guin . . ."

"Yes?" My breath hitched. Something about hearing my name from his lips made my heart beat rapidly.

"Um . . . I don't know what Lupus is," he said vulnerably

and then turned to look back out at the sunset. I smiled at his words. Maybe he wanted a friend after all. Maybe I was *still* risk-worthy . . . at least to someone. "And I don't have the first clue about what it was I saw today." He nodded, looking down at my left arm gently. "Uh . . . and I would like to know what treatments you were talking about earlier today if you feel comfortable telling me." There was a detachment to his words as if he wasn't getting his hopes up.

My mouth fell open slightly after hearing his words. Then he pivoted his head back again toward the sunset. It obviously had taken a lot of courage for him to ask me those things.

I softly said, "Yes, I would like to tell you."

He looked back at me, an eyebrow raised in disbelief. *Yes, it surprised me just as much.* It wasn't like I normally shared my diagnosis or anything this personal with someone so quickly, but there was something about this island and apparently *this man* that made me want to do things differently this time. Perhaps push myself out of my tiny comfort zone.

With a small upward quirk of his lips, my stomach bottomed out. Why did my new "friend" have to be so good-looking?

But his smile was what I needed to push those boundaries and begin my explanation, "Well, Lupus is an autoimmune condition that attacks different parts of the body. It was named that because it causes the skin of the face to look like a wolf bite—or at least that's what the thirteenth century physician who named it thought. I prefer butterfly rash. And my condition is attacking my kidneys. That's one of the most common organs that Lupus attacks. Mine just is aggressive," I said, giving him my very rehearsed "technical" answer. It helped to have a medical explanation memorized. I could detach myself from the situation that way. I could just purely state the facts and not allow myself to get emotional. This was my coping mechanism. After my explanation, I looked at Locke's eyes and it surprised me to see there was actual interest there.

I was going to stop there, but his intense gaze encouraged me to continue. "So I have kidney dialysis three times a week. I had my last treatment the day I left to come here, so I won't need another one until Tuesday. That bought me some extra time until the next treatment . . . but my kidneys are failing. That's why I'm on dialysis. I'm on the national transplant list. I didn't think I'd have to go on the list . . . but things haven't worked out the way I hope they would." That tightening in my throat and prickling in my eyes started again. It happened every time I thought about that last part.

I took a few breaths. "The transplant list is really long so I don't know when, or if, I'll receive a kidney. And I've always dreamed of coming to the beach ever since I was a little girl, so I thought, why not go now? It felt like the right time, especially with the ukulele convention being here this year. The ukulele has gotten me through many of my darkest hours and I learned to play online from one of the convention's featured artists. She's also one of my favorite musicians. It's incredible what she's done–she's created such a supportive online music community. When I couldn't leave my house, I found comfort through music and the ukulele platform. Music saved me when I was too lost to see I needed help. And when I heard so many people with dialysis continue to travel and live their lives as normally as possible, it encouraged me to do the same. I've never traveled before, but I really wanted to try . . . So that's why there is tubing in my arm," I finished as nonchalantly as possible, as if I hadn't just dumped a lot of serious medical information in his lap.

He stared at me as if trying to figure out how much more

there was and how much more he could ask. There was a deep sadness in those intense, volcanic eyes, and then they melted into something much softer. "I'll ask Dean to cover Tuesday so I can take you to your next treatment," he replied without a second thought.

"No, that's not why I said—"

"I'd like to take you . . . If that's ok." His face slightly colored when he realized how straightforward he had been with me. So many emotions were bubbling up inside of me, along with sparks of electricity. I nodded and thanked him. He didn't know what his offer meant to me. I couldn't remember the last time someone had really wanted to go with me to dialysis.

He cleared his throat. "Uh, so is no one a match . . . I'm sorry, I shouldn't ask," he quickly corrected himself.

"No, it's fine. I would wonder the same thing. But no, not yet." He nodded, and his brow furrowed at my words. He kept nodding silently, almost to himself. Like he was trying to figure something out.

"And Sebastian?"

I could tell he was getting more comfortable with his line of questioning. I answered, "He's with me for so many reasons: anxiety, emotional support, alerts, flare care, bringing me things that can help when I'm too sick or dizzy to get them myself, and even medication reminders. He can even bring me a blanket, my medication, or even a bottle of water if I need it during a flare. If I were to become distressed, he would try to draw attention to me or he would use one of the alarm buttons in the house. He's my golden shadow . . . The *best* part of me."

"Distress, *right*," he teased. "I don't think needing a kidney is just distress."

"Has anyone ever told you that your bedside manner could use some work?" I joked.

"Yeah, that's why I'm not in midwifery and why I'm a surfer instead." He laughed back. "I'm sure I would make Hugh Laurie's character on *House* look like *Mary friggin' Poppins.*"

"You're not that bad off," I teased. Then I really looked at him as the colors in the sky deepened their hues. I chilled, goosebumps pebbling my skin. I was chilling from my burn and from my body attacking itself. *Something it loved to do.* I wrapped my arms tightly around myself, trying to ward off the shivers that would likely come next. I managed, "What about Penny?"

"Oh, uh–" he spoke as he handed me a blanket, having taken notice of my shivering. The blanket was actually a tropical quilt that looked as if it was handmade. I imagined Tutu must have quilted it. I spotted another one beside him. Two quilts, that was good. This evening was already way too romantic. No need to share one quilt. The romance factor needed to ease up a bit on me. My dating survival instincts were signaling system overload already.

Once I was under my quilt, he said, "Uh . . . Penny is for emotional support, mostly anxiety." I looked at him blankly when he didn't continue with his explanation, and he sighed. "Mermaid, I don't like to get into it." I looked at him in disbelief. When he looked back at me, our connection seemed to him to continue.

He lingered. "My friend was in a water accident a few years ago before I opened up the surf shop. There are so many water accidents that happen at the beach or out on the ocean. People don't take the ocean seriously enough, and many of the tour companies around tropical locales don't even take the proper precautions. They're just out for a quick buck. That's why I wanted to make sure I opened a shop that taught safety first and made sure our visitors had fun but stayed safe. And that they learned to respect the power of the ocean. I wanted to make sure I taught *e hele me ka pu'olo*. It means to leave every place and person better than you found it. Always bring something with you to make it better and leave it there for others to find. You never know when someone might need it."

I couldn't believe that was it–that he wasn't going to tell me any more. I stared at him, hoping he'd open up to me.

He sighed, relenting. "My friend is ok now. Well, as ok as he can be. But it was a really horrible accident, and I was there with him when it happened. Then I watched him get airlifted and taken to the hospital. They didn't allow me to ride in the helicopter with him. I had to meet him and the first responders at the hospital." He closed his eyes and looked as if he was getting weak, or maybe a little light-headed, just remembering it. His hands clenched. "Anyway, Penny helps. It was Tutu's suggestion."

"I'm so–" But I stopped myself. Locke seemed like the type of person who wouldn't want to hear 'I'm sorry.' He would say it's not your fault. But when people said it to me, I found comfort in it. Well, I guess it all depended on *who* was saying it and *how* they said it.

But right now, there were no other words left at my disposal. "I'm sorry. I'm so sorry you had to go through that. Both of you." There was an aching depth in my voice that I didn't expect. I obviously felt more for this man than I realized.

His lips turned quickly upward, and he nodded. "Well, at least our service dogs found each other. Seems like they're a perfect fit." He laughed, and I did too, even though I was shivering harder now.

That was the price I paid for being in the glorious sun, my body reacted like it was poison. Locke reached out his arm and invited me into him for extra warmth. I hesitated, not knowing what to do. But I moved to him slowly as he continued to look outward, as if he didn't want to see what decision I made. Or maybe he just wanted to give me the space to make it.

He let me situate myself against him so I could find the least painful position for my burns as I eased into his body warmth. Ironically, he was like the sun. He was nothing but warmth. And when his arm enveloped me, I relaxed against the first true new friend I'd made in a long time.

Locke

THE SUN WAS SETTING on the gorgeous shores of Maui–shores that never faded in their beauty to me. They were my constant. My true north. Besides Tutu and Penny, they were the things that I could always anchor myself to. But tonight a new sensation met me as I sat on these familiar shores. One I had forgotten existed, and it was overpowering me.

Guin's warmth enveloped me, amplifying the effect of this novel sensation. And it was then that I couldn't help but feel an overwhelming sense of guilt. She'd shared so much with me and I had shared so very little with her. *What was wrong with me that I couldn't even wager a minor part of myself with someone like Guin?* Her intimacy and honesty nestled against me and it only made me more rotten. I always thought when I met someone like Guin, someone who was brave enough to be so completely vulnerable, I'd be able to overcome my fears. But all I felt was an overwhelming need to protect myself even more.

As I held Guin in my arms and watched the sun set on the magical shores of Maui, it was *all* hitting me hard. How badly I wanted *to have this* with someone. The sun edged nearer to the horizon, and I could almost feel myself holding my breath as the sun dropped lower. *Why?* I had survived the day–even the sunset with this woman. Did I really think I couldn't survive a few night stars and sea air?

My hold instinctively tightened at the thought, and she turned to look at me with those larger-than-life eyes. *Bambi eyes. Great,* I had just made my way back from the last riptide. Now *here I go again.*

I sailed off on a sea of siren scent with the intoxicating melody of her voice as she talked about the sunset. I instinctively leaned forward, a little closer to her, as I spoke, "Maybe we'll get to see the green light. Legend has it that if you see the green flash when the sun drops below the horizon, then you will never go wrong in matters of the heart. It doesn't happen often though. And it's really hard to see. But maybe we'll get lucky."

"Have you ever seen the green flash?" She turned to me, surrounded by my arms and the beauty of the night.

"No, Mermaid, I never have. But maybe I never looked well

enough." I spoke at a clipped rate because there was more pain there than I wanted to admit or for her to see.

I dared to glance at her through the corner of my ever-growing heavy lids. She was lulling me into a peaceful state. "Are you warm enough? Do you want the other blanket?" She nodded, and I laughed. "Yes, to which one?"

"Another blanket." She laughed in response, and I grabbed the blanket and spread it over her. At that moment she looked so serene and vulnerable as she sat staring at the sunset. But her calm serenity was in complete juxtaposition to the deep sadness in her eyes. And I don't think she was just overcome by the sunset's beauty.

And it made me wonder why I hadn't told her the complete story about why I had adopted Penny. It actually seemed like she had a shot at understanding me. I could already tell we were alike in a lot of ways. And yet, I'd only told her part of my story. But at least that was a start, and it was further than I'd ever gotten before with anyone.

And just like that, the green light flashed before our eyes. She turned to me with a wild smile on her face. "Was that it?" she asked me with pure excitement. She looked like a kid who had just arrived at Disneyland for the first time.

"Yes, Mermaid. I believe it was." I chuckled incredulously. A beached mermaid and a green flash. What was next, buried treasure? Come to think of it, maybe it was buried right beneath her feet. She seemed to have a certain magic about her.

I returned her expression with raised eyebrows and a smile of wonderment. *Could it really be this simple? Could a mermaid really wash up at my feet?* Maybe the sea was sending me an apology. I was just sorry it had hurt her in the process. Our eyes locked so intently that I knew the sea had indeed laid her at my feet for a reason. But I just wasn't ready to acknowledge it yet. I wasn't ready to take the risk, but apparently the sea thought I'd waited long enough. Tutu thought so too. And those baby blues were beckoning me, and I was wading deeper and *deeper* with every passing moment. *Okay.*

Her light hand breezed up to my face and tried tucking back some of my hair that kept obscuring my vision. Her blue eyes searched back and forth over mine. They were like the gentle lapping of the waves ebbing and flowing, in and out. And now I knew I was completely gone. I'd waded in so far that all I could see was blue.

Her light touch traveled to my neck, and her hand stayed there. *God, it felt good.* A touch that seemed attracted to me for all the right reasons. And then she came nearer, and my body didn't hesitate to respond to every little movement she made. As if it was being moved by the sea, left to the mercy of its push and pull. Mindlessly, blissfully . . . carelessly. Those soft lips were nearing me. And I wanted them so badly. Yes, I wanted them–

"Bad idea, Mermaid," I said so abruptly that I didn't realize the words had come from me. I was still in an underwater sea haze. It was like an automatic protective shield had deployed without my permission.

Guin let out a little strangled sound and moved back as far away from me as she could in my arms. A wounded sound of rejection escaped her. There was a sharp pain on her face. And I hated I caused it, but it was bad enough that our dogs were already attached to one another. We didn't need to follow their lead.

"I'm sorry–" I started, but she didn't let me finish.

"Don't worry about it. I could really use a friend. I never should have confused the two," she said firmly as her cheeks flamed. I could tell how embarrassed she was. No, not embarrassed. *Humiliated*. She thought I didn't want her. I was so torn. Telling her the entire story was dangerous, but not letting her know wasn't fair to her either.

"I could use a friend too. Sorry if I misled you. I wish confusing the two things wasn't a bad idea." Hopefully, I'd said just enough, so she knew it wasn't her.

I let the words linger and then broke our connection to lay back on the blanket and give her some space. She could choose how far away she wanted to be from me now. But the stars were peeking out brighter, and I didn't want her to miss this part either. Not because of me.

Slowly, she came to join me, but I noticed she stayed much further away from me this time. I turned my head so I could take her in, if only for a few moments. I wanted to see her as she experienced the Hawaiian night sky for the first time. Her hair spilled all around her face and the dusk kissed her features in a way that made me smile.

"So, are you going to the ukulele convention tomorrow or would you like to do something else?" I asked hesitantly. My fingers drummed on my leg to distract me. "I'm sure I can ask Dean to watch the shop for me. I hired him so I would have more time to work on business logistics and also so I could lead more water excursions. So as long as Dean's comfortable being by himself all day at the shop, I'd be happy to show you around the island."

"I think there's a welcome luau tomorrow night for the ukulele convention, but other than that, I should be free," she said with nonchalant vagueness.

"And does the mermaid want to explore dry land or . . . ?" I waited. I didn't know if she was going to do *anything* with me after the rejection that had just taken place. But I was pretty sure she was going to make me ask.

"Maybe . . ." she replied vaguely.

I laughed. "Mermaid, I'm trying to spend some time with you." I tried to keep my tone steady without letting any vulnerability seep in. This *was* me asking. She looked at me, unimpressed. Obviously that wasn't going to cut it. "Princess Ariel, I would like to spend time with you . . . Would you spend the day with me?" I couldn't believe I'd just asked that question.

She rolled her eyes upward and kept them there in a pondering motion that signaled she was considering my invitation. I blew out an exasperated breath. She laughed, and it warmed me.

"Yes, I would really like that," she replied.

"Ok," I said, trying to hide the excitement I felt when she agreed. "Well, there's so much for you to do while you're here. For starters, I feel you need a surf lesson." She laughed at my words, which only made me more determined to put it on the list. "Also, there's some pretty great snorkeling if you're up for it. You can see a lot of the sea turtles around the crescent-shaped island of Molokini. And we can take the surf shop's tour boat out if you'd like. A private tour." Her face brightened. "There's also the Road to Hana. It has a lot of waterfalls along the way. A popular one is Twin Falls because it's only a short hike from the road and has a pool at the base of the falls where you can swim. There are also a lot of waterfalls in the tropical rainforests of the West Maui mountains and around Mount Haleakala. You've definitely got to see Mount Haleakala, if you're up for some walking one day. And, of course, there's always the beach."

"That all sounds amazing."

"Even the surf lesson?" I asked in surprised.

She laughed even harder. The melody of her laughter was so infectious that I wanted it to take up residence inside of me.

I was hoping it would stay. She answered my question. "Yes, even the surfing. I want to have a good beach experience. And I obviously need instruction . . . and I've read about the dolphin sunset cruises. One of them even included onboard dancing."

"That would be one of my competitors," I said with annoyance. "Dolphins, I can do. Maybe even a sunset sail . . . but not dancing. You'll have to book a different cruise company for that one."

"Ok, fair enough. Well, I got two out of three. That's not bad. Now, I know the best way to ask you for things." She laughed coyly.

I looked at her sternly in response. Really wondering if that was the plan all along. But somehow, with her obvious love of music, I highly doubted it.

I noticed her shivering again and invited her back over to sit beside me with a wave. She came closer, and it gave me relief that things were okay between us again. But what was supposed to be a practical way to stay warm felt much more like snuggling. This was not helping me; somehow, I'd already missed her. She'd felt too far away.

We lay together as the stars shifted in the sky, while I tried teaching her some constellations that Tutu had taught me. She argued with me about most of them, telling me none of them looked like their names. She doubted me on most of them. And I absolutely loved every second. And it was just like that–with her in my arms–that I woke up hours later to find us wrapped tightly together. She had burrowed closely inside my rebellious arms that knew exactly what they wanted and wouldn't take "no" for an answer from me.

It was then that I realized, under the glistening night sky, that we weren't any better off than our dogs.

Guinevere

CHAPTER 11

I AWOKE TOTALLY unaware of where I was. I'd felt someone rustling beside me and realized I was indeed in the arms of a man. Not a usual situation for me. And it was then that I realized I was lying under the shining stars of Hawaii. I can't believe I'd forgotten that minor fact. And I really couldn't believe I'd fallen asleep like this. With *this* man.

Locke was partly looking at me and partly looking up at the

stars somewhat awkwardly. And he looked just as confused as I felt. He'd obviously woken up before me and was trying to figure out if he should wake me. Maybe he thought it was all a bad dream–some poor, sleep-deprived, lapse in judgment.

He cleared his throat. "Uh, I was just debating if I should wake you, but you looked so peaceful. We must have drifted off to sleep while we were talking. Guess I didn't realize I was that boring."

I let out a little laugh. "No, that's not it. But I can't believe you don't want to sleep on the beach. I would definitely have thought that would be your thing."

"Well, as many times as I've done it, I can tell you it's actually not that much fun. I keep trying it because it sounds so ideal, but when the morning dew rolls around, followed by the humidity . . . It's not exactly as much fun as it sounds. Everything always looks better under the stars and then the morning rolls in with a rude awakening."

"Sounds like my health journey. Every new treatment is the night sky. Hopeful and romanticized. And then when things don't work out, reality sets in and the optimism fades."

He looked at me empathetically. "I really hope you still go looking for stars, Mermaid. Never stop stargazing. *Ka lā hiki ola*. . . It means the dawning of a new day. We believe in the power of hope and optimism here." And then he turned his head toward me. And what I saw on his face was plain *want.* His expression shot a bolt of electricity through me.

It completely confused me. His expression *must* be toying with me. Almost kissing him had been such a lapse in judgment. It was just that I had this weird, *irrational* attraction to him. And I was sure the stars, and the moonlight weren't helping. That magical Hawaiian night sky had carried me away. I would make sure it didn't happen again. Especially because he'd been so clear on *not* wanting to kiss me . . . But only his words that were clear and everything else he did was sending a different message.

He spoke, and his voice was so unexpected that it startled me. "We should get back now. Save you from the morning. Trust me, this is the best part."

And it felt like he was talking about himself too. What kind of *harsh morning* did he feel like he was hiding?

"Ok, that sounds good," I answered, but his eyes stayed fixated on mine. A stormy look of deep contemplation furrowed his brows.

Locke slowly removed himself from me, and I helped him gather up our items from the sand. I took one more moment to look at the bewitching night sky. I was a little worried he might never bring me back here. It felt like something got unearthed here that he really wanted to stay buried.

"Come on, I'll bring you back again soon. I promise," he said as if he could read my mind. But somehow, I doubted he would.

WE ARRIVED BACK at the bungalow in a serene silence. The sound of the waves had helped to guide us back, their lulling rhythm moving our feet along. The light blue house was lit by a few porch lights, and it looked like a romantic beach bungalow from a fairy tale. One of those special places off the beaten path you wanted to succeed, but you also secretly hoped would remain quiet and unspoiled by too many visitors.

As soon as we came through the door, the light of the TV

and the sight of Tutu on the sofa with both dogs beside her greeted us. She was snoring softly while they intently watched the TV screen. Their large, soulful eyes were mesmerized by the television as their paws hung off the sofa, their heads fixed with keen concentration. The *101 Dalmatians* scene was melting my heart.

We slipped in as quietly as we could so as not to disturb Tutu. I felt bad for leaving her so long to take care of the dogs. But I didn't have time to feel bad for too long before I noticed Locke quietly pacing around the room, wrestling with some kind of predicament in his head. Tutu had awoken during Locke's "silent" brainstorming and was now pretending to watch *I Love Lucy* on TV Land. However, I could tell she was really in complete amusement of her grandson. It was hard to be more entertaining than Lucy, but somehow Locke was managing it.

Eventually, he came over to me, arms over his chest as if he'd finally solved his problem. And in the flickering light of the TV screen, I could see concern on those ruggedly hand-some, boyish features. "Uh, Mermaid, we don't have a guest room. I don't think Tutu thought about that when she extended her invitation. Tutu sleeps in the guest room." He paused. "Um, how about you take my room and I'll sleep on the sofa. I'd sleep at the surf shop, but I need to be here with Tutu."

"Good thinking, Locke. You better give her your bed," Tutu interjected as Locke jumped back in surprise. I let out a giggle. It was too funny seeing this tough guy startled.

"Tutu!" Locke put his hand to his chest.

"Yes? . . . Did you have a pleasant walk?" There was almost a wink in her voice.

"Yeah, I'm really sorry it's so late. I think we were both just exhausted, so we fell asleep while I was showing Guin the constellations. Apparently I'm not as entertaining as you were when you taught them to me. I think I bored us both to sleep."

"That's not true," I interjected.

"Ahhh, *Keiki. Constellations* . . . So that's what they're calling it," she said incredulously with a little bob of her head. Tutu didn't seem to buy his explanation for a minute.

"Tutu, I promise. *Constellations.*" Locke drew out the word.

"*Constellations.*" She nodded gravely. "Well, the dogs have eaten and they've been out again for their bedtime walk, so I'm just going to go to my room. That way you and *Guin* can sort out whatever arrangements you would like."

Now, I actually felt like I saw a wink. She must think her grandson needed a lot of help if she was trying this hard to be his wing woman.

"Tutu . . ." He gave her a look, but so much amusement filled her that he just said goodnight and helped her up from the sofa.

"Take the night off, Locke, I'll be fine," she said as she waved him away and started walking slowly to her room, bracing herself against the tropical patterned wallpaper in the hallway for support. It seemed the evening hour affected her balance more.

Locke moved my suitcases after seeing Tutu was okay to make it to her room. And immediately, I tried to stop him. "Please, let me take the sofa. I'll be more than comfortable here. The dogs can even stay with me," I pleaded.

"Doesn't work like that. Mermaids don't sleep on couches."

"Ok, I'll take the bathtub then."

"You've seen *Splash* one too many times," he said dryly, moving my suitcases. I had little strength these days, so I didn't even try to stop him.

Instead, I ran to the hallway and stood in front of the opening. "Locke, no."

"I'm coming through. So it would be best if you moved, Ariel. And I promise to make Ursula's lair as inviting as possible. I just have to straighten up a few things."

I felt terrible about taking his room, especially since he hadn't been aware of Tutu's *Aloha VRBO* plan. He wasn't kidding about the moving part though. All that muscle was coming toward me. You didn't play chicken with a freight train. So I figured it was best to get out of the way and try to convince him some other way.

He made it to his room with me right behind him. I could hear the TV playing softly in the background. Locke had left it on since the dogs were enjoying it so much. He obviously had the biggest soft spot for his family. With no other options, I stepped through the threshold, but I wasn't prepared for what I saw. I thought Locke's room would be *super* masculine. I'd expected bold, deep colors and lots of surfer decor or accessories. Heck, I wouldn't have even been shocked by MMA or professional boxing posters. But this . . . *Never this.*

I would have thought I had the wrong room, except that Locke was busy straightening things up. That part seemed to track, but that wasn't what surprised me. Since the room was almost completely clean, he was just picking a few things up off the dresser and nightstand. And then he got in a *hope chest* to look for new sheets. As he pilfered around in the packed chest, I took time to look around his room in stunned awe. I seriously would have thought this was his grandma's room. It looked like the quintessential classic Hawaiian bedroom. First, there was the hope chest and the bamboo furniture pieces with their woven accents. Then, there was the hand-sewn quilt on the bed. No doubt another one made by Tutu. And the walls were a soft, happy sage color with tropical foliage accents and yellow print patterns scattered throughout the room. *Completely unexpected.*

And then there was the hope chest that served as a window seat, complete with a long cushion and a folded quilt placed on top of it. This would make for a wonderful reading nook. I could see his grandma sneaking in here with a cup of tea to snuggle up under the throw, read a book, and look out the window to observe the surrounding community. It was the perfect spot to "people watch."

Locke turned to me as he threw some things out of the hope chest so he could get to the extra sheets. Or at least that's what I thought he was looking for. There were clunking sounds as things thumped together, and I was curious what things he stored in that chest. *Maybe the mixed martial arts gear was in there after all.*

Locke stopped when he saw my face. My mouth was hanging open in disbelief. "What?" he asked suspiciously.

But I couldn't get my mouth to work as it hung open. "This is *your* room?"

"Yes, Mermaid. Something wrong with *my room?*" I shook my head rapidly, trying to distract myself from the giggles that were forming. He asked pointedly, "Ok . . . what *were* you expecting? What *exactly* is wrong with it?"

The Creature's cave, that's what I was expecting. "Oh, nothing. I just thought it was Tutu's room." I put my hand up slightly over my mouth. I needed to physically shut myself up. It was only going to get worse. He looked at me like I was crazy.

"I mean, it just looks so calming . . . so nurturing." I *couldn't* shut up.

His eyes went wide. Then he laughed and said, "Maybe that's why all my *few* dates have left so quickly."

"No, I don't think that's it." I pinched my lips together harder. He looked beyond shocked now and we just stood there, staring at each other, each in check at this game of chess.

"Maybe mermaids *are* more comfy on couches," he said pointedly. But now I'd changed my mind and actually wanted to sleep in this Hawaiian grandmother's haven.

"No," I demurred. "It's perfect here. I just didn't think this would be your vibe–" I was going to stop myself this time before the mass exodus of embarrassment continued out of my mouth.

"Well, as long as you're sure." He chuckled and laid some sheets on top of the hope chest. My eyes were scanning over the bed, and it was like he knew I was looking for something. "Is there something you need? If there's anything else you can think of, please ask me," he added, as he assessed me and then moved toward the bed to strip it.

"Oh, no, this is great." But he looked as if he didn't believe me. "I can definitely change the sheets though. Let me at least do that." I went to stop him.

"I know mermaids are used to the sea but I'm sure these sheets are even too salty for you. I'd feel better doing this myself. I feel like sand and salt are always stuck to me somehow. We'll probably find the remains of a sandcastle hiding underneath here. I'd rather you not be around for that." He laughed and looked at me as he continued, trying to shoo me away. I wouldn't relent though. He continued "So what are you *not* asking for? I bet I have it or I can get it. I promise I won't judge you. I mean, I should. I feel like it would only be fair after letting you into my 'old folks' hideaway," he said playfully. The jab couldn't be missed.

"Uh, no, that's ok." I tried to grab the fresh sheet from him and finally succeeded.

"Come on, Ari–. . . I'm sure I have it."

I grinned cheekily. "You think I'm Ariel. You've said it twice now."

"No, it's just difficult because you already took the obvious choice for your dog's name," he argued, as he pulled harder on the sheet. My Lupus hands couldn't seem to grip well at all tonight, especially when they were so swollen from my time in the sun. I hated to think what they would feel like in the morning. And as if to prove my point, the sheet boomeranged out of my grasp and hit Locke squarely in the face.

"Whoops," I said with a hesitant half grin. "I'm sorry." He nodded faintly, as if he didn't believe that for a second. "It's my gimpy hands, that's all, *I promise*." He nodded again. This time, a little more believable.

"So, what are you not asking for?" he said, eying me.

"Uh, I was just looking at the pillows."

"Do you build a pillow fort or something?" I could tell he would not forgive the smack in the face any time soon.

My face flamed because he wasn't too far off. "No," I drawled. He laughed heartily at the way I exaggerated the word. "Fine, if you must know, my friend suggested I get a pregnancy pillow for my joint and muscle stiffness and for my GI pain. She got one when she was pregnant and thought of me. I was too embarrassed to get one, so she gave me hers. And . . ." I rolled my eyes. "Now I can't sleep without him."

"*Him?*" Locke laughed louder. "So, does your pillow have a name?" He waited, but I didn't satisfy him with a reply. "Well, I wouldn't want to separate you two. The least I can do is find you a temporary replacement. *Please*, let me find you some pillows. Prince Eric 2.0 coming up." He went into the closet and quickly pulled out several pillows and started arranging them on the bed. I was mortified. And then to top it all off he went back into the closet and came back out with a wig to place on the top pillow. Now I wasn't sure I could even sleep in that bed.

"I don't think you need any more guests," I said with annoyance.

"I don't know, you might change your tune after your stay in 'Grandma's haven' with Eric 2.0. And don't worry, the wig was part of last year's Halloween costume. It's my favorite holiday. I might even be persuaded to let you have the wig if you get too attached." His deep chuckles were getting more pronounced as he said, "There's a bathroom down the hall and then another one off the living room. Let me know if you need anything else. No matter *what* or *who* it is." The way he said that last part had me glaring. He collected some of his things as he continued laughing. And then he said goodnight and left me with my ridiculous pillow-man.

Guinevere

CHAPTER 12

I WOKE up with both dogs curled up beside me on the bed and Eric 2.0. (Minus the wig, thank you. I had put that back in the closet as soon as Locke left). I wondered if this was a special treat for Penny or if she got to be on the bed most nights. Something told me that Locke had such a soft spot for her that she got to be on the bed any night she wanted.

And I *may* have done a little snooping while I was in the

closet putting the wig away last night. I was itching to explore his world. I wanted to be part of it. Oddly, seeing the extensive wetsuit collection and surfer paraphernalia had put me at ease. I even saw a telescope tucked away, probably inspired by his time learning constellations with Tutu. I was actually enjoying learning more about him. Slowly, I moved toward a shelf filled with treasures he'd collected from the sea. I wondered if he'd started collecting when he was a boy. The thought made me smile as I looked at the small bowls filled with shells, sharks' teeth, corals, and lava fossils. The ocean memorabilia must serve as small reminders of special days spent at the beach or out on the ocean. Each a little vessel to hold a memory. And the shelf helped further my understanding of his love of this place and the home he called the sea.

My thoughts returned to Sebastian and Penny, who looked so cozy together. I didn't want to disturb them, but I knew it would take me a little time to get my joints warmed up for the day, so I decided I better get moving. Mornings were especially painful for me. And this morning I was paying for the time I spent in the sun yesterday. All my joints were inflamed and swollen by the sun's UV rays. The arthritis symptoms and the headache caused by the sun were really slowing me down.

I WENT over to my luggage to change and noticed my face reflected in the driftwood mirror over Locke's chest. The red butterfly wings were prominently displayed on my face today. I could see a rash vividly forming across my nose and cheeks. At least people would just think it was part of my sunburn.

I finished getting dressed and pocketed my medications to take before I let the dogs out. At least my joints were feeling a little more oiled.

The dogs were now excitedly waiting by the door. Sebastian was scratching the door as he so often did in the mornings. This was my signal that he was ready. A sign that I was going too slow. *When wasn't I?*

As silently as possible, I crept out of my room with the dogs close behind me, only to find Locke still passed out cold on the sofa. His tall limbs clearly didn't fit. They were all askew as he lay on his stomach, hanging off the sofa like a bendy Barbie. I chuckled at the image.

Without a moment to lose, Sebastian raced over to him to do what I could only imagine must be a "safety check" as he started feverishly licking his face, followed by Penny with equal concern. Her tongue started licking the other side of Locke's face for good measure. I went over to wave them away from Locke, not wanting to be the reason he woke up. But the harder I tried to move the dogs away from Locke, the more insistent they became. And, of course, when he stirred, they backed away, instantly satisfied, which left me hovering over him.

His head shook in alarm, and then his eyes went wide at seeing me. He closed them tightly as if clearing his head. "So that's how a mermaid kisses," he said groggily, squinting up into my eyes. He reached out his hand aimlessly and finally found one of the dogs. Having gotten his bearings, he sat up and the blanket started to fall off of him, revealing his shirtless chest.

"Hey." I put out a hand and turned my head away. "Put a shirt on, 'Thor.' No one called *The Avengers* today."

He chuckled and swatted my hand away. I'd heard rustling,

so I was assuming the shirt was on, but only turned back when he said, "Ok, I was *only* shirtless. But thanks for comparing me to Hemsworth."

"No–" I began protesting.

Locke volleyed back, "You *specifically* said Thor. You had your pick of the *entire* team. Really, you could have just left it at *The Avengers*. I think he's the fan favorite, anyway." He practically winked as he spoke.

"No," I protested some more. "I get confused. The green one," I fired off rapidly.

"Yeah, Mermaid, you can't really mix up the Hulk with Thor, but thanks for trying. Although that one is probably more fitting." A sigh escaped me. He continued talking as he sat on the edge of the sofa facing me, "Sorry, Penny usually gets me up really early. I didn't think anyone would see me. Or at least that was the plan."

I saw a hint of red on the side of his leg where the blanket had fallen away. "Wait, what's on your pajama bottoms?" I questioned with amusement.

"What?"

"You heard me."

"I just meant I would have slept with my shirt on if I thought anyone was going to be up this early," he said, pulling his blanket higher.

What he really meant was he would have worn different pajamas. "Nope. I want to see the PJs." I sat down in the sunny yellow recliner by the sofa, unmoving. The dogs were looking at us as they waited by the door. And I knew with no doubt there was no way he'd make them wait to go out and play. Mornings were Sebastian's favorite time since they were cooler, so I was betting Penny was the same way. Either he'd have to show me his pajamas, or he'd have to get up and take out the dogs. And I doubted he was going to do that with a blanket wrapped around him.

Locke looked at them. Then at me. A disgruntled expression took over his features. Finally he stood up, although making a big production of it as he used the armrest of the sofa to stand; then lowered the blanket to his knees and quickly pulled it back up. He was like a shy schoolgirl who was too embarrassed to show off her new bikini.

"I'm sorry, what was that?" I asked playfully, and he lowered the blanket back down slightly. I stood up, satisfied. "Thank you. I'll let the dogs out as I think about that satisfying mental image." He groaned louder while I practically skipped out the door, the image of his bright red pajama pants with Golden Retriever puppies on them keeping me company the entire way.

WHEN I RETURNED, the dogs were bounding around playfully, full of energy. Locke was now in the kitchen, dressed for the day. Ironically, dressed for him was a wetsuit unzipped at the top, the arms hanging down from his waist, and a T-shirt, which I'm guessing was for my benefit. He already had some supplies out to make pancakes.

How long had I been gone? *Man, I really move slowly.*

I went up to the kitchen island, grabbing a bamboo bar stool covered with a banana leaf pattern similar to the sofa.

"Don't you get hot in those wetsuits? I mean this is a tropical island?" I asked.

"Thanks, I wasn't aware, Ariel." He rolled his eyes, and I

smirked at him. He hadn't caught himself again with the nick-name. So I *was* Ariel to him. Good to note.

He continued to answer my question, trying to breeze past his name slip. "I guess I'm just cold-blooded."

I had so many jokes, but I proudly contained myself.

His raised eyebrow seemed to suggest he realized as much. But he just moved on. "Trust me, it's nice wearing a wetsuit in the water. We'll pick one up for you at the shop. You especially need one now to protect your burn."

I groaned. "I don't really think 'ocean toddler chic' is my thing. That's how it's going to look on me–like a baby's over-sized onesie. Besides, my body temperature runs hot."

"Good to know," he replied with a joking nod. An unap-pealing expression took over my face as I thought of the heat induced headaches and rash that was sure to ensue. "Wow, you really need to market my merchandise," he said in total amuse-ment. "And besides, I think that's how everyone looks, but it will protect you. Just try one and see. There are some thinner suits you may like better. And if not, then I have some rash guards that block the UV rays. They have much better protec-tion than a long-sleeved T-shirt. One of the rash guards even looks like a cute long-sleeved dress. Maybe that will be more Disney princess-appropriate."

Daggers, that's what I shot at him. And he just laughed, turning back to the ingredients on the kitchen counter. "Your concern is very kind. I appreciate it," I replied. He laughed harder, knowing it had been difficult for me to say those words, especially considering all of his jokes. I looked back at the counter, changing the subject. "So what are you making? And are you going to let me help? Or are you too afraid I'm a lost cause in the kitchen?"

"No, not at all. I bet you can learn to make Tutu's famous

pancakes. What? Too many carbs?" he asked as my lips turned downward.

"No, they cause too much inflammation. Gluten, sugar, salt . . . And now I have to be even more careful with my diet because of the dialysis."

"Well, it's coconut flour and coconut sugar. And I use a little sugar. I let the pineapple and plantains sweeten the batter. It's sort of like a Piña Colada pancake. And I don't have to use much salt. But . . ."

I hurried over. My feet excitedly led me to the prep counter. His contagious, baritone laughter warmed me as he watched my reaction. I was supposed to limit potassium, but some coconut and plantains would be alright. This was one reason I'd been so excited to find a host. I knew food accommodations were going to be tricky for me and access to a kitchen would be invaluable.

I glanced over to the dogs who were sitting in front of the doors, watching us intently. Sebastian didn't have any trouble following Penny through the swinging doors. They were now waiting for morsels. Locke started instructing me on which ingredients to blend in the bowl. He handed me a whisk to mix the wet ingredients together in one bowl and then another one for the dry. But my swollen hand had a difficult time grasping the utensil. And within the first few seconds of blending the dry ingredients, the whisk slipped out of my hand and sprayed flour over the side of the bowl closest to Locke, covering him in a fine mist of white powder. The flour aerosolized in a spectacular spray pattern. I cautiously looked at him out of the corner of my eye, trying to assess the damage as my weak hand tried again to regain its grip on the whisk.

He looked down slowly at his tight black tee and black wetsuit that the flour had covered so perfectly. The colors and textures of the materials were a perfect canvas for my "flour shower."

Locke's eyes stayed fixed in a downward look as he said through a disbelieving smile, "I really wanted to look like a drug lord when I went into the shop today. Now, they really will think my shop is a drug front."

I tried placing my hand over my mouth to muffle my laughter, but it didn't help. I think this was going to be my default pose with this man. Before I knew it, he had reached into the bag of flour and placed a handful of the white stuff on the top of my head. It cascaded down over me like an artificial snowfall in a Hallmark Christmas movie.

"Mine was an accident," I exclaimed as I looked at him.

"Mine was *not*," he replied. "Welcome to dry land, Mermaid. Just explaining gravity." He teased.

I reached for the flour bag, but he placed his hand on top of mine, shaking his head in a serious warning. I grinned wider. His eyebrow raised in a challenging reply, and that was all the encouragement I needed. I was just about to go for it when I heard the shuttered doors swing open.

"*Keiki*! What are you doing? Are you five?" Tutu surveyed the mess all over me and looked us over. "*Ahahana*," she said, shaking her head. She seemed to say shame on you. I shyly looked at her and then at the dogs with their cocked heads, attempting to figure out what they were witnessing.

"Uh, I was just showing Guin how to make your special pancakes," he replied.

"Well, I certainly don't do it like *that*." She tsked. Tutu moved toward the pantry to get her apron, assuming it was time for the 'grown-up' in the house to take charge of the situation. "Why don't you wash up and I'll finish showing Guin how to make my pancakes."

"No, I've got it. I'll bring you some tea out on the lanai in a minute." Tutu looked at him with concern, apparently not expecting this response. I think she thought the best thing would be to bench him.

Her face raised in surprise. "*Okay, well* . . . I'll be right out on the lanai if you need me to step in to help–"

"Really, it's fine. I'm going to help Guin clean up, and then I'll be out."

Her radiant smile was actually contagious. "Well please, *be thorough*," she said as she sashayed away with a little extra pep to her step.

Locke

CHAPTER 13

COOL BLUE ICE. I was lost in it. Seriously, it was all I could see as I started patting a damp rag over her face and hair in an attempt to clean off the flour. *Aía.* This was not okay. I was supposed to be cool and aloof–the closed-off one–and yet her crystal blue eyes looked like ice. Big beautiful glaciers. Yet somehow, between the two of us, she seemed to be the warmer one. *How ironic.* The pools of blue were causing me to get lost in my daydreams. I brought my attention back to the present as I wiped more of my handiwork from her face. I was having trouble keeping myself in check. I reminded myself: *I am uninterested. Completely uninterested.* I needed to show it. But it just wasn't working today. It apparently had stopped working last night, and I was feeling *hūpō*–stupid, just stupid.

My hand with the cloth stopped beside her cheek, and I gazed deeper into those blue eddies, feeling a rush of adrenaline kick up inside me. It felt like a whirlwind of sand had been disturbed on the ocean floor. And I knew it would not be settling soon. Then suddenly, a soft creak sound severed the small, precious space between our faces.

My eyes shifted toward the doorway to see Tutu just standing there. She'd probably been standing there for a while now. I guess her curiosity had gotten the better of her. I stood frozen with my hand in place. Then as if realizing she'd been caught, I saw Tutu quietly tiptoe backwards out of the kitchen. I lowered my hand with the cloth and handed it to Guin.

"I'll have the tea out to you in a minute," I called over my shoulder to Tutu, but I knew that wasn't the answer to the question Tutu had wanted to ask.

As soon as we'd finished cleaning up, the three of us enjoyed a nice breakfast on the lanai. Afterward Guin and I left Tutu there to enjoy the rest of the morning. She loved just sitting and observing our community, and was completely uninterested in joining us on our surfing expedition. Most likely because the *little matchmaker* wanted me to have more time alone with Guin. So I took Tutu her sewing basket and supplies, before we left for the shop. This had become our morning ritual most days. I think Tutu was quite happy to have both of the dogs to keep her company today. Sometimes I would take Penny to the shop, but lately I had been leaving her more often with Tutu for companionship.

But her happiness today seemed to stem mostly from the

fact that I was taking Guin to do something. This proved accurate when Tutu came racing out the front door to catch us before we left, waving a waterproof camera in the air and insisting we take photos. Where she found the old thing, I don't know. It looked like something from the early 2000s. She obviously had high hopes for this outing. But I just came back up the stairs, nodded, and agreed I would use it. She smiled proudly at this accomplishment.

I kissed her cheek, joking with her, "Behave while I'm gone. Don't sew anything too crazy. No naked tribal patterns. . . or weird romantic voodoo ones that you plan to place over me while I'm sleeping." But she knew I really meant that she shouldn't meddle into anything where Guin was concerned.

Tutu responded, "I will, if you won't. *Try* to have some fun. Give happiness a chance." She smiled at her request to which I could only raise my eyes and surrender. I guess I set myself up for that one.

A FEW MOMENTS LATER, I was surprised to see Guin already standing beside my Jeep in the parking lot, waiting on me.

"How did you know which one was mine?" I asked with surprise.

"Lucky guess." She smirked. And it irritated me in the best way that she was right.

"Alright, hop in before I change my mind." I could see her eyeing the dinosaur of a camera in my hands. "Yes, Mermaid, pictures will be taken of your surfing attempt today, so better give it your best effort. No one says 'no' to Tutu."

"How about we lose it in the sea?" She laughed suggestively. "Or the surf shop," she added quickly.

"No, I actually love the idea of documenting this adventure." Her unamused face made me smile. But it wasn't long before she warmed up and joined me.

And she kept that joyous expression as we made our way to the shop. She seemed to love riding through the tree tunnels with the Jeep's canvas top removed. It was too bad her body was so allergic to our tropical paradise because she seemed to love it. I think the whole tropical atmosphere was good for her soul, and she seemed to enjoy drinking in every moment. Every flickering sunbeam of light through the palm trees seemed to unwind her, relaxation seeping into her core.

It was nice to witness, to see the transformation taking place. I'd taken a lot of visitors around the island, but none of them seemed to have been as affected by the island's charms as her. Maybe because her soul held so much sadness, she really needed the light to penetrate it.

I pulled up to the surf shack with its bright yellow exterior painted with hibiscuses, large waves, and surfboards. The local art students at the high school had painted the mural, and it was my favorite part of the surf shack. It made me happy to come to work here every day.

Mermaid's nodding grin at the mural seemed to agree completely with me. "*This* is yours?"

I wished she would stop saying that phrase to me. It was making me feel like I needed a personality makeover. Maybe I should take the not-so-subtle hint to loosen up a little around her. Maybe if I could imagine her as a guy friend, then I could do that better. But as soon as I looked at her, I knew that would never work. I'd never had a friend this attractive. *Sorry, Reef.* I just nodded in response, giving her a pass because I'd definitely brought it on myself, and then I welcomed her into the shop.

Hawaiian music recorded by local artists was softly playing as we entered the shop, along with the sounds of tinkling wind chimes. Stained glass displays by local artists lined the front of the shop, featuring water fountains and more elaborate art pieces. I enjoyed carrying some of Tutu's friends' art and felt fortunate to have it in the store. Plus, their art made the window displays way more attractive. But my favorite area of the shop was the cozy corner I'd dedicated to Tutu's quilts and hand-sewn items. They weren't exactly what you expected to find in a surf shop, but then again, I wasn't exactly who you'd expect to find in one either, so I guess it all worked out.

I saw Guin pinching her lips together in that way she did when she was trying to hold something back. *What now?* She probably was finding amusement at my expense for the "grandma vibe" in my store.

"Mermaid? . . ." A deep rasp came out of me.

She pinched her lips harder in response. "Um, hmm?"

But I didn't have time to question her any further when I heard Dean's voice at the counter. His warm, relaxed tone of voice always gave me a sense of calm and happiness. "Locke, hey! What are you doin' here? You're supposed to have the day off."

"Well, I was bringing Guin to get a wetsuit," I said as she glanced at me questioningly. "Or *possibly* a rash guard," I said relenting. "I'm going to try teaching her how to surf today. Although, I've been told it's not possible."

Dean came out from behind the faux tiki hut counter as we made our way towards him, winding through the round racks of aquatic gear. "If there's anyone that can teach you, it's this guy," Dean said to Guin with his jovial voice, sticking out his hand and then introducing himself. She took his hand but seemed skeptical about his words. "Really," Dean continued, "he's not as scary as he looks. He's actually a pretty excellent teacher. He just needs a reminder that we aren't all the Hulk. Plus, he's a softie too. You'll see."

"Alright, alright," I said to Dean, who was just as big of a softie as me. His two girls had already gotten to take full advantage of his employee discount on more than one occasion. I looked toward Dean. "Do you want to help Guin find something to wear in the water? I'll just wait at the front. I'm sure she'd prefer you to help her. Just put her merchandise on my 'mermaid rescue tab.'"

Dean looked at me with the biggest smile. "Out catching mermaids again, huh, Locke? I told you that was too dangerous for you." His contagious laugh filled the space. "I don't believe I know our inventory well enough to fit mermaids properly." He glanced at Guin, then back to me. "Yup, you better take this one. I believe mermaids prefer seafaring men anyway, and we both know how badly I navigate out on the ocean." And with that said, he firmly sat back down at the counter.

Well, at least that last part may have been true, but we were working on it. And at least his family got to enjoy spending time on the water with us while we trained together. And they laughed a lot at his expense, which he took like a champ. But I knew he was wrong about Guin's preference. No way would she prefer me to help her over someone so innately warm and friendly as Dean.

But Dean just sat there unbudging. And the man could be strong-willed when he wanted to be. Most of the time, he usually went with the flow, but it would be just my luck that he would choose now to be one of those times when he went against it.

I glanced toward Guin with an apology already on my face. But oddly, she had this little upward turn to her rosy lips, and that twisted my insides.

I put my hand on the center of her lower back in a spot that I thought would be a safe distance away from her burned skin. "Ok. This way. Let's see if there's something that fits your tail."

She tried to look back at me with one of her playful glares, but ended up only smiling more. I stopped in front of a rack of the most feminine wetsuits I carried. They actually had a really flattering shape, or at least that's what the female surfers had told me, and I figured, if I had any chance at all of getting her in one of these things, that this was the way to go.

"These aren't so bad, Locke. They're actually kinda cute." I saw her fingering the material as she eyed the floral and geometric patterns that ran down the sides of the suits. "Ok."

"Ok?" I said in disbelief.

"*Yes*," she said, relenting. "How does sizing work?" she asked, and I started pulling one out for her to try. "*Oh no*, I'm curvy. You can't just pull one size. My thighs throw everything off. So whatever you think you know, just discount it."

She laughed. But I could tell this was a sore subject. However, I really knew what I was doing, and I didn't want to admit to her that I had checked her out *way* too many times to be wrong. And I was extremely familiar with her shapely legs– the ones that drove me a little mad. *I rolled my eyes at myself . . . just avoid the blue pools, Locke. You lōlō–such an idiot.* But there I went again, staring into the blue abyss, unable to stop myself from going under.

Trying to have some confidence, I didn't pull anything else.

"Why don't you try this one and see if it fits. Is this the color you like best?"

She eyed me skeptically. "Yes . . ." I laughed at her disbelief. It had been pretty obvious. Plus, I noticed her way more than she thought I did. "But it'll just be easier if you let me have several—"

"It'll just be easier if you have some trust in me today, please," I replied.

Her eyebrows raised quickly, and her pupils dilated. Then, without another word, she went back to the changing room. And after she vanished, I selected two more sizes because I just had a feeling I was going to need them. I was usually right about the wetsuit sizing—call it a surfer's gift—but today; I had the unmistakable feeling that I was going to be *very* wrong. And next I went in search of a rash guard because I had an even stronger feeling that I was going to need it.

Locke

CHAPTER 14

DEAN'S CHUCKLES emanated from the counter after I returned from my little adventure hunt.

"Oh, shut up," I said jokingly.

"You're in *so deep*," he said as I came over to the counter. He was laughing even harder now. "Your 'mermaid rescue tab?'" I was sure she could hear us, but I liked this man's laugh too much to stop him. "You've trained me well, but I wouldn't know how to ring that one up."

"Well, you're going to have to get creative in a few minutes," I replied.

He chuckled. "I don't know. I don't think she's walking out of here with anything."

"Yeah, *not even me*," I added.

"I didn't say that," he started. "You've just met your match. I think it's more of a 'rescued lobsters tab.' When they find each other, they mate for life, ya know–"

I stopped him; I had seen that *Friends* episode. I was just about to lob some comment back to him when Guin stepped out of the dressing room at the back of the shop, looking around for a mirror. But then I remembered there was one in the changing room. *Was she looking for me?* That had to be it. The most beautiful woman I'd ever seen was looking for *me*. And she looked stunning. That wetsuit was doing things to me. As in sexy Catwoman-level. It was seriously making me come a little unhinged.

My mouth must have fallen open as my eyebrows raised because Dean said "lobstered," not so quietly and emphatically. I eyed him and shook my head, but he only continued chuckling somewhat quietly. "Get your little claws in motion, Locke. She's waiting."

I looked at him more sternly and then proceeded toward *her*. Guin stood silently, having spotted me as soon as Dean's laugh rippled through the air. I jerkily made my way back to her, slightly stumbling. It felt like I was back to my dorky school days. My entire mouth went dry. Even my usual protective shields of humor and coolness were failing me now. Nothing seemed at my disposal and I felt laid bare.

Guin blushed as I looked at her, maybe a little too inappropriately. Google reviews did not need to hear about this shopping experience. I'd be sure to get five stars on the "ogler" emoji scale and zero chili peppers.

She looked down slightly, tucking her hair, and said bashfully, "Uh, it fits. Sorry for doubting your abilities."

But I really couldn't care less about being right or having her trust my abilities. There was this tightness in my chest that needed to ease up and leave me the heck alone. And it's all I could focus on, well, besides the gorgeous woman in front of me that was causing it. When I said nothing, Guin just looked at me, waiting for a response. All I could think was that I needed to find her the ugliest rash guard possible, stat. I would not survive the day with her looking like this. I would never look at *Catwoman* the same anymore . . . or a wetsuit.

I inhaled thickly. "So, it fits?" She nodded shyly. Funny how she only got shy around me. *Okay, words, Locke. Find some. Stop ogling her like a perve. She doesn't want you looking at her in this way. Be professional and look at the fit. No, that doesn't mean the curves of her butt.* If she wanted a freak show, she could have gone–well, actually she probably came to the right place.

"Uh . . . I've got a rash guard too," I said abruptly, staccato movements guiding my hand out toward her with it. "I think you were right. Better try it on. That's the best way to go." I hoped she would change into anything else besides this Locke bait trap.

Guin responded, "No, I really like the wetsuit. It actually feels *so* good. The material is much cooler than I thought it would be, and it's kinda silky. I love the way it feels against my skin. It's soothing. I'm surprised," she remarked slowly.

Great, this was just turning me on even more. Why? I don't know, but it felt like her remark applied to me. Like maybe she was finding me to be surprising and maybe a good fit for her too.

I countered, "Well, if you're sure. Why don't you try this one on for size, just in case you prefer it for snorkeling or something. We need to keep you protected, and I've got some great zinc sunscreen that doesn't hurt the reefs. And UV hats and umbrellas too, if you need that."

The smile that bloomed across her face made my heart pound. She responded with less shyness, "That's ok. I brought a hat and sunscreen. But I will try the rash guard." I was shocked she didn't fight me on it this time and she actually smiled as she looked at the one I had picked out.

I went back to the counter area, picking out other things I thought she could use based on what little she'd told me and what I'd overheard. I set them on the counter and got a bag for them while Dean jotted down the inventory.

We were still working on the list of inventory when I noticed Guin coming out of the dressing room in her normal clothes, disappointment washing over me. Since Guin didn't come out with the guard on, I took that as a sign that apparently I stared too much. *Great.* She made her way to the counter, setting her purse on top with the guard and suit, ready to pay for them. I just shook my head at her, to which she lobbied back a head shake of her own. A silent war ensued between us, and Dean continued laughing.

"I can't accept your 'under the sea' currency. Your Mermaid money's no good here," I told her, which only incited her further.

"Don't worry, it goes toward saving the lobsters," Dean managed through a chuckle, and I glared at him. But she did oddly seem to accept his explanation, so I just let it go as he continued with amusement, "You kids have a good time. I want to hear how well he does today, Guin."

"Oh, I will definitely give you unbiased feedback," she said joyfully. And I knew plenty of feedback would be given. I just doubted that it would be unbiased.

I grabbed the other bags sitting on the counter, which made Guin's eyes open wide. She was just about to protest, but I said quickly, "it's for the reefs. Those sunscreens are really terrible for them."

"And don't forget about the lobsters," Dean chimed out with a pretend sad face that even he couldn't quite manage.

Guin protested. "There's no way that's *all* sunscreen, Locke. No, let me pay for this. It's way too much. You've already done enough for me. At least let me support your shop."

But I just shook my head. If it was this hard just to get her the gear, I couldn't imagine what teaching her to surf was going to be like.

Amongst all the sea maiden charm, I'd almost forgotten the most important thing for today's excursion, *the surfboard*. This woman was seriously unraveling me. "Come on, you can check out my 'quip' and if you end up liking to surf, then we'll get you your own board."

She looked at me curiously, and Dean interjected. "Don't worry, that's slang for his surfboard collection, Guin. He thinks we all know the lingo. Don't feel bad, I'm still learning too. But you must be special if you get to take one of his boards out." I gave Dean the eye which I knew was only going to egg him on further.

"Oh, this I have to see," she said eagerly.

HER AMUSED TONE CONCERNED ME, but I led her back through my office and to the garage beside the old house where I kept my personal gear. The reinvented garage was also my private workshop where I worked on surfboards and customized them to meet each individualized surfer's needs. I customized them not only for functionality but also for personal style with custom designs. Maybe I'd gotten some of my creativity from Tutu. I could only hope to be so lucky. But since I really didn't want that added to my old lady tally, I figured I would just show Guin my personal boards. I tried to guide her away from the covered workspace. I liked to keep it that way, so no one could see what I was working on and nothing could damage the unfinished pieces.

But like a moth to a flame, or more aptly, like a mermaid to a shiny lure, she went right over there. Of course. I should have known. Zero interest in the *quip*.

"What's all this?" she asked, curiosity taking over every note of her voice.

"Nothing, just some basic shop repairs."

She laughed. "Nothing is basic about you, Locke."

I curled up one side of my mouth. She was way too good at calling me out on *everything*. It was just a matter of time until she figured out things I really didn't want her to know yet. I knew I wouldn't be able to hold her off for much longer.

"Ok," I replied hesitantly, slowly uncovering the work area, and her eyes widened. She went over and started absorbing the colors and textures. Her fingertips reached out, itching to explore the board on the workbench, and then stopped, remembering herself. But I nodded and chuckled. Her fingertips brushed over the board with an ease and grace. I felt my body tingle in response. The board was like an extension of my soul. And she was exploring every uncharted inch.

"These are gorgeous," she said as she turned around, looking at me differently now, clouds shifting in those blues. I cleared my throat, not used to being looked at this way. Not tenderly. Not with pieces of me unearthed. She asked, "Did you work on all of them?"

I moved toward her, the sunshine streaming in through the garage bay windows, reflecting off her golden streaks. There was an electricity that seemed to surge between us, like electrons raging in the air before a big storm. Anticipation stirred inside of me. Our bodies moved closer together as I approached the board that I had just lacquered this weekend. After a coat of wax, it would be done. This one was special though. It was for a diabetic who had lost his foot recently. He'd surfed his whole life and wasn't ready to give it up. One of my specialities was customizing boards to fit physical needs. It took a lot of trial and error and patience, but I loved it. And seeing the look on someone's face when a board finally fit them was the biggest reward.

I looked at the board and explained to Guin how this one was unique. "Ever since Reef's accident, I guess I've just had an interest in customizing boards. If you don't have a 'normal' body type, it throws off your center of gravity and the way the board works. We have to go through a lot of trial and error in order to get the board just right. But it's so worth it. When we finally got Reef's board right, it was one of the best days of both of our lives. Being able to restore someone's love of surfing and give them back that lost piece of themselves is the most rewarding thing I've ever done in my life. I have people come in here thinking there's no way they'll ever be able to learn to surf–or if they're former surfers, they think they'll never be able to surf again–and we figure out a way to do it together."

Most of them have heard Reef's story. I think it's what gives them the courage to come in. It makes the process less intimidating and maybe less embarrassing. Although there's *nothing* to be embarrassed about. But in our cookie-cutter world, it seems being anything other than a gingerbread man makes you defective–an outsider. But all it takes is one new mold to start a whole new chain reaction of thinking."

With every word I spoke, her body kept gravitating closer to mine. She was bathed in the tendrils of sunlight shimmering through the weathered glass. Her beauty wasn't lost on me. "Reef is very lucky to have you," she said, with an appreciation in her tone. "And so is this community. This is amazing, Locke."

"It's the other way around, believe me." I looked at her, as if I was really seeing her for the first time. There was such sincerity on her face. And her eyes seemed to linger on mine as if she was seeing me in a new light as well. It was such a raw moment. At least it was for me. I brushed my hand gently against her arm, as if I just needed to touch her again. "Come on, let's go see if we can find you a good enough fit for now. I still have some of my beginner boards from when I was a boy."

Locke

CHAPTER 15

UNBELIEVABLY, Guin had chosen my favorite board from when I was a teenager. It was my first serious board, and it had so much wear on it. I'd wiped out on it so often as a teen trying to learn harder, more elaborate tricks. But I think that's what attracted her to it. I was learning that Guin was attracted to weathered and messy. She wanted character. And because of this preference, her choice of boards had sent little electrical currents rippling throughout me. As soon as she had run her hands over it—chosen it—and turned back to face me with a grin, I was gone. There was this unfamiliar desire in me.

So, in true 'Locke' style, I'd tried to push my feelings aside and went outside to load the surf van. All in order to stay busy, instead of taking her by the waist and kissing her up against that surfboard, as I so desperately wanted to do. I spent the whole time trying my best not to look at her, so I gave nothing away. And before I knew it, we were staring out at the ocean from Kapalua beach, boards in hand. I noticed as we did so, she looked terrified. And in the short time I'd known her, fear wasn't something I was used to seeing on her face.

I planted my board in the sand and went over to her. I figured it was going to take some time to get her comfortable in the water before we could go out very far into the ocean, but I wasn't expecting her to look quite like this while standing on the beach. I gently placed my hand on her shoulder, and her glowing crystals stared back at me. Wisps of her hair had escaped from her bun and were lightly blowing around her face.

I tried to reassure her. "Hey, I'll do everything possible to make sure you're ok. I'm sure you've heard that a lot in your life, but it is accurate right now. I've taught a lot of tourists how to surf. And they've *all* survived. I promise."

She laughed at my words and looked at me carefully as if drawing strength from my gaze. She bravely went out into the water.

I found a relatively calm, shallow area beyond the wave breaks for her to try practicing getting on the board. But she continued to stare at the board like it was one of those gremlins. Her eyes kept watching for it to morph into something else. Well, I guess we were about to break the rules of sunlight and water if that was the case.

"It's ok," I said, trying to ease her worry. "Just try getting on the board and I'll be right here to help. I will not let you get hurt."

But she continued to stare hesitantly at me. As her cheeks increasingly turned pinker, she explained to me, "Locke, I'm not in very good shape. I mean, even stairs exhaust me. Some days I sit down halfway through them. I probably don't have the muscles to–" she started.

"Mermaid, I will place you on the board if you need it, but I don't think you will. This is Hawaii. The island gives you this secret energy. I like to say the island has its own heartbeat, its own magic. Just listen to the heartbeats of the island and let them calm you. Just try it."

Her pink lips twisted upward at my words. And then, somehow, magically, she was on the board. "I did it! I–"

The board started wobbling as she lay on it, clutching it tighter. I instantly reached out to grab her, wanting more than anything to make good on my promise. I looked at her face the whole time, letting it guide me. I really wanted her to have a good time. More than anything, I wanted this island to be a wonderful experience for her and for her to never feel embarrassed here.

Relief washed over me when the board steadied. I was so happy that I'd righted her, I almost didn't hear her when she said, "Locke, did the island give you 'secret energy' to grab my rear? I'm pretty sure the heartbeats weren't telling you to do that." Her head twisted toward me in amusement and looked at my face with raised eyebrows. I was too embarrassed to look down at my hands, but my eyes reluctantly trailed down to her body which lay flat against her board. And there they were, the offending objects, both of my hands were splayed as widely as possible across her butt.

I quickly released her like she was a hot potato, sending the board back in motion and it rocked more vigorously now. "Locke!" she said laughing, but I could see her white-knuckle grip on the board.

"Sorry," I said as I reflexively grabbed her again.

"Locke!" She laughed out again. I looked down to find the same placement of my cursed hands. I quickly slid them up to her back. Surely that was a safe place for my hands. I closed my eyes even though she was looking right at me. "Do you always have this problem with your lessons? I can see why your shop does *such* amazing business." She continued laughing.

I answered quickly, "No, not at all. It's just you." I pinched my eyes tighter. Those words were actually painful to hear leaving my mouth. I didn't need to be saying that to her. "I mean, I promise I'm not a perve." *Wonderful, Locke. Only perves use the word 'perve.'*

"I never said you were, but let's keep the hands on the back, please." Her smile greeted me when I finally met her eyes. I couldn't believe she was actually giving me the benefit of the doubt. When did that change?

"Yeah, I *should* be able to do that," I said, making fun of myself. She laughed even more at my words.

I finally got her situated and comfortable on her board. And she learned to ride out into the ocean so the waves could pass us by. We paddled out farther, past the breakpoints of the waves, so we could enjoy the calmer water and float with ease on our boards. The beach looked so small from this distance, like a miniature world, and this was easily my favorite sight–my favorite spot. But it was quickly being surpassed by who sat beside me. The gentle waves were rocking her in such a beautiful way. Just when I thought she couldn't get any more attractive, this island proved me wrong. The tightening in my heart was surely in agreement.

As my eyes lingered on her, I could tell she was nervous about trying to do anything more with her board. She seemed pretty fearless to me, but yesterday had been brutal, and this morning she was vulnerable. And as much as she tried to put on a brave front, I was pretty sure I could see through it. I wondered if this meant she'd be able to see just as easily through mine.

I looked her over, glad I had finally convinced her to wear the wetsuit. The last thing her tender skin needed was more sun. But her baby blues caught mine as I did. Little waves of endorphins rushed through me with her reciprocated gaze.

"Are you feeling alright? Is your skin and the tubing ok in the wetsuit?" I looked at her appraisingly, as if I could take an inventory of her pain. I had a pretty good feeling that she was an expert at hiding it–at saying she was fine. But I didn't want the Disney version. Not now. Actually, never with her. I wanted the documentary. The real. That French new wave stuff no one ever sat through. Ok, there were a few that Tutu had shown me that I enjoyed–especially *Cléo from 5 to 7*–but I wouldn't tell Tutu I enjoyed them, for fear of what else she might make me sit through. But I could imagine wanting to sit through everything with Guin and I wondered if she could ever imagine that with someone like me.

Guin stared down at her arm, the one I noticed she always devised to stay as obscured as possible. It was hidden now with the wetsuit on, just the way she seemed to prefer it, and that tore at me. Because I could already tell how much she felt she needed to hide it.

She slowly glanced back at me. So I said, "Any time you

want to go in, let me know. You can always rest back home until it's time for the luau. I don't want you to miss that."

But she just continued to look at me. "I'm ok. My skin actually feels a lot better today, thanks to Tutu's healing salve. I can't believe how much better it feels. The sleep helped too. Sleep is one of the few things autoimmune conditions really like. But there's just not enough sleep in this world. I need to pull a Han Solo and sleep in a frozen state for a year," she joked.

She paused, and I could see exhaustion sketched on her face. Honestly, it looked like she hadn't slept at all. So I suggested, "Maybe we should head in. Today was a good start. We can do more another time. I can set up a place for us to rest on the beach. I've got that UV protection umbrella in the van." I was glad I'd brought one of the VW vans I'd fixed up for the shop. I kept all sorts of gear stocked in the vans for our tourist excursions. You never knew what you would need. I always liked to be prepared. Dean enjoyed teasing me about whether I was leading an excursion or setting up a tiki bar. We could probably convert one van to some type of food truck.

Guin gazed at me and said, "No, it's peaceful out here. Unfortunately, I just don't have the same energy I used to have anymore, especially since I started dialysis. Maybe one day that will change." Her eyes filled with a sadness that seemed to stretch out as endlessly as the horizon on the sea.

I nodded at her, glancing over at her swaying on the board beside me, letting the disbelief of this moment sink in for a second–this moment I thought I'd never have. The sea gently rocked me with its lulling rhythm as I enjoyed sitting beside such a gorgeous woman. And not just any beautiful woman. One who might understand me. And now my hopes were bubbling to the surface again.

"Yeah, this is where I like to come to escape. Even from

myself. I can turn my thoughts off here. Or at least the negative ones. I can just leave everything on shore and give the rest to the sea. It's a freeing place to be."

"Your 'best-version' place," she replied.

"Yeah, I guess so. I feel like my best version here. Do you have a place like that?" I asked, a genuine curiosity taking over me.

"I guess wherever I am with Sebastian or my uke. It's hard to be a bad version of yourself while petting your dog or making music. So I guess I don't really have a specific place . . ." Her words trailed off as she looked toward the shoreline. There was something haunting about them–a sense of homelessness. As if she didn't have a place to call her own. I couldn't imagine, my identity was tied so closely to this place.

She looked down hesitantly at her arm. "I don't really feel like the best version of myself anymore. I feel kind of incomplete these days. I wake up every day with my body unable to do what it's supposed to do. Already battling itself before I even start the day. Hard to feel like your best version when you wake up that way. Like you're already at a deficit, you know?" And then she shook her head, like of course I wouldn't know.

I reached out slowly and pulled her board closer to me, needing to be nearer to her. "I may know more than you think, Guin. I mean, my personality is *such* a huge deficit." She laughed at my attempted sarcasm. "No, I'm pretty sure you don't have trouble being the best version of yourself."

The look I was met with just made me grip her board tighter in response. A silent electricity brewing, a storm of emotions moving between us. I looked deeper into her eyes, the ones I was beginning to crave as much as I knew I shouldn't. *I should just stop kidding myself.*

A small voice came out of her, one I wasn't used to. "I

think about it a lot. Am I living as my best version? If my name gets called off the list, do I deserve it? I mean, why should it be *me* over someone else."

Now it was her eyes that searched mine. *Really, me?* But this woman made me want to dig deep. *Really deep.* I wanted more than anything to provide her with what she needed. She was opening up to me now, and I realized how fragile this opportunity was. I didn't want to blow my chance if I could help it. So I dredged up something I never did for anyone: that day with Reef. It was as close as I was going to get to relating to her situation and connecting to her emotionally. Those suppressed feelings slammed into my chest so hard I could almost feel the wind getting knocked out of me.

"After the water accident, Reef and I were determined to live every day as our 'best selves.' But it's so hard to do, especially after you have the crystal clear realization of all the ways you were doing it wrong from having a near death experience. But all you can do is try. I learned that's the important part, because it's impossible not to get it wrong most of the time." I pulled her board even closer, the distance dwindling between us. "But Guin, when you said you didn't think you'd have to be on the transplant list. What did you mean?"

"It's complicated," she said, looking away from me. I pulled at her board gently and the motion snapped her head back to me, our eyes locking. She sighed hesitantly. "I was really lucky I got on the transplant list, some people aren't even eligible for various reasons. But most people on the transplant list wait five years for a kidney because it's the organ that has the longest list. So when my family and friends heard I needed a transplant, most of them got tested right away. I felt awful about it—that I needed this from someone. But . . . ." She just gazed away.

"Hey–" I began, not knowing what I was going to say, but trying to bring her back.

Her eyes filled with sadness when she turned to me. "It's surprising who in your life wants to be tested for a kidney transplant. Some people you expect, but some you don't. My boyfriend didn't even get tested. He seemed to lose interest when I had to drop out of graduate school and work from home. I never knew where my 'value' came from until I got sick. Was it because I was pretty? Because those people vanished when some of my hair fell out, rashes took over, and steroids blew up my face. Was it because I was going to have an important job? Because those people disappeared when I had to withdraw from school. Or was it simply because I wasn't worthy of unconditional love? Because my baggage was suddenly too much for them? Not just my condition, but all the emotional and mental health that went along with it? The good times were replaced with the hard ones, and that's when I needed someone the most."

I guided myself further along her board, gravitating toward her. I was like the ocean current and she, the moon. "Please tell me you don't believe that superficial view of your worth. Please tell me you know that integrity of the heart is the most valuable human possession. The only worth of any significance. Not profession, notoriety, money, or social standing. That the care we give and the way we treat people are the most important attributes we possess. And from what I can see, you are *so* worthy. Please tell me you know that . . . And if they call your name from the transplant list, please tell me you'll say 'yes.'" I looked at her, my eyes wandering over hers with intentionality. "We have a saying here–it's called *pono*. It's the value of integrity and doing what's right. And knowing the feeling of contentment that comes from it. When you know in your heart you've done the right thing. *Pono* is what matters here. That should be the value of a heart."

She seemed to nod at me, but I didn't know if she was just doing it because that's what the moment called for or because I was getting through to her, so I continued, "There's something Tutu has always said to me and I never really understood it. Not until recently. Um, I don't know if your journey has included faith or not, so I don't know what version of this you would prefer," I asked, trying to be respectful.

I looked at her for guidance. I had a guess of her preference by things she had said, but I never wanted to assume. She swallowed and looked back at me. "It's complicated, Locke. Which is the authentic version? Give me that one."

"The one with faith," I said slowly, and she nodded. "Ok .. . Tutu said we shouldn't use the word 'deserve' because we're never going to live up to the impossible standards of 'deserving.' Rather, we should see it as our 'Esther timing.' Perhaps this is our moment for which we were created. Perhaps it is *our time*. It's a gift of grace. Another moment, at some other time, will be someone else's. And we should be happy for them when it is because we will have our time too. So we have to take our moment and do with it the best we can. We can't waste it by comparing ourselves to others or living in the 'what-ifs.' And we certainly can't waste it in question. Because it's a gift. Even if it's a moment of struggle–a Goliath trial–it's still our moment to choose what we want to do with it. And not one moment of this life should be wasted because how we use our life not only affects us, but everyone around us."

My eyes roamed over her, assessing if I had messed up the explanation with my interpretation of it. I wasn't always the best at expressing myself. I said quickly, "Tutu should be here. Her viewpoint on it is so much better. She's the one you should talk with . . ." My words trailed off with waning self-assurance.

"No." She swallowed with difficulty. "No, I think you're doing a pretty incredible job all on your own." And she just stared at me. Her bewildered blue eyes shifted from disbelief to something much more beautiful to see: a faint hint of peace–maybe even acceptance.

Guinevere

CHAPTER 16

WE BOTH STARED at each other as I floated mindlessly on Locke's childhood surfboard, like a tiny leaf on the ocean's vast surface. I felt so light in this moment, but also infinitesimally small. Just like the stray leaves I loved to watch swirling around on the rippling currents of the lakes back home. My childhood water elements certainly looked very different from Locke's. I'd grown up loving the water ever since I could remember, spending fun afternoons on the lake near my grandparents' house. I recall being fascinated with the way the currents moved. That same childlike fascination and feeling of weightlessness came back to me as I rocked gently with this man and the sea.

But I had not expected such a profound life lesson today. I guess I should have. After all, Locke was the brooding, silent type–prone to introspection. Well, maybe not so silent when it came to me, I was learning. And I may not have learned how to surf, but I certainly took so much more away from my time spent out on the sea today.

Locke's words continued to distract me as he tried his best to teach me a few surfing techniques. Finally, he decided we should call it a day, so we rested on the beach before washing off the sand at the Kapalua showers and driving back home in his Jeep. I was happy for the drive so I could contemplate his words as we drove under the flickering sunlight, glinting through the leaves of the palm trees.

But as wonderful as my time with Locke had been today, I was excited to be reunited with Sebastian. There was always an instant calm that washed over me when I saw him. Sebastian worked hard to take care of me, so it was a luxury that he could stay home and relax with his new canine friend since someone else could look out for me today. And then it hit me . . . how much I trusted Locke to do that. *Look out for me.*

Locke might not be able to detect an upcoming Lupus flare like Sebastian could, but he could help if I needed medical attention–he'd already proven that. However, it would be hard to replace Sebastian because he wore a lot of doggie hats. But I had a feeling Locke could be great at helping me, too. Oddly, Locke had even helped with my anxiety. He'd been able to calm me on more than one occasion, which was one of Sebastian's best skills. Doggie therapist was one of his top–and most earned–titles. One of the best ways he relieved anxiety was by providing me a sense of peace since he could alert me to impending flares. He had given me back my independence.

Sebastian had a special way of letting me know when a flare was coming. His special cue was to nudge my hand. The harder the nudge, the worse the flare was going to be. And if I got a hand lick, as Locke had witnessed, that meant I was in danger of fainting. Many service dogs were scent-trained with cotton balls, but Sebastian had just naturally started alerting me on his own. And when I figured out his alerts, I could enjoy more freedom and quality of life. I started going places again and with much more confidence than before. I had such a better idea of what I'd be capable of doing that day. Sebastian gave so much to me–he showed me the definition of selfless love and the meaning of a true friend. I could have never asked for a better companion or partner.

So I was happy that Sebastian was getting to enjoy some time being a "regular" dog. I wanted him to have as much of that type of time as possible, especially since I never had to worry about him taking care of me. I knew if I needed help or a warning, he would stop whatever he was doing. He would even disobey commands–intelligently disobey–in order to alert me.

But I was still amazed that I'd let Locke take on Sebastian's role today. It was an enormous step for me. I wondered if Locke had any clue just how big a deal this was for me. I figured he must have some idea, because as soon as our dogs greeted us at the bungalow door, I couldn't miss the look on his face. And it was then that I realized I must have taken the place of Penny today too. We both lowered to the floor auto-matically in greeting to our dogs. And as we received our dogs' exuberant kisses, I was reminded that there was nothing quite like being welcomed home by a dog. Their unconditional love overwhelmed me every time.

Our faces slowly turned toward one another as if realizing how similarly we felt about our canine companions. And it ignited such longing inside me, sparking in my stomach and spiraling its tentacles outward. And the feeling seemed to be echoed in Locke's eyes this time. Both of our gazes began drifting ever so slowly downward toward the other one's lips, a heat rising between us.

I couldn't be imagining this–projecting this–could I? But his intense molten eyes had such a deep hunger in them I didn't think I was misreading him. Desire was melting like lava over me, kindling my skin. I swayed in his direction as if I was being mindlessly pulled toward him once again. But then I remembered the beach and pulled back. His words echoed in my mind, making me second-guess everything I was feeling.

His lips parted to say something, just getting ready to speak when Tutu entered the living room.

"Oh, Locke," Tutu said with her hand on her heart. "You surprised me. I didn't know you were back."

Penny gave him a giant lick on his face to solidify his welcome home, and then Sebastian did the same to me. I grinned at Locke and laughed, glad something had eased the mounting tension between us. Tutu laughed as well.

"I see you're still out capturing mermaids. Perhaps you're getting better at it." He looked at Tutu with a cautionary warning, but she didn't let that stop her. "Why are you back so soon? It's a beautiful day! Too much sun and heat for Guin?"

I responded to her question, "I actually did better in the sun today. Locke was kind enough to help me find something to wear. I think the wetsuit he chose really helped protect my skin from the sun. But we came back early because I'm going to the ukulele convention's luau tonight. I thought I'd rest a little before I started getting ready for the evening."

Tutu smiled. "I'm so glad Locke took good care of you today, *mao ku'uipo*. And tonight's luau should be fun. As you know from our chats, I used to play ukulele back in the day. There's a beautiful community of people here. I really miss playing. But I have enjoyed connecting with the instrument again by being part of the online community and listening to the music." There was a faint sadness and longing in her voice.

"You miss it? Why don't you play anymore?" I asked, looking into her faraway, chocolate-colored eyes for answers.

"Yes, I miss it, but that was years ago. I had a little ukulele band where I met–" She stopped. "Oh, you don't have time to hear this. You need to go rest and then have time to get ready, Guin. This is a big night. You're going to meet so many wonderful people. Music unites us in such a beautiful way. It's one of the few things in life that welcomes people from all walks of life with open arms. No one's a stranger and everyone is family. Music is home. Music is love."

I looked over at Locke. There was a mixed expression on his face. So much love but also deep sadness. I wondered about Tutu's story and what was being left unsaid. And I really hoped I wasn't about to overstep . . . but I felt compelled to invite her.

I asked Tutu, "Why don't you come with me tonight? I'm sure everyone would love to meet someone who has experience playing in ukulele bands. It's a meet-and-greet this evening. And I'm allowed to bring a guest with me."

Tutu looked at me hesitantly. "Oh, that's very kind of you, dear, but this is *your* night. Maybe another time," she said with a far-off look.

I persisted. "I'd really love for you to go with me, if you'd like to go." I looked at her with deep understanding. She needed music just as much as I did. And from my experience, I felt I could spot someone who desperately needed it. "Please," I added.

Her small, hesitant smile spread into a much larger one, full of joy. She enthusiastically replied, "I still have one of my ukuleles I played at concerts. Let me see if I can find it so I can show you later after you've rested. I'm going to look for something festive to wear too. Thank you, *Ku'iupo.*" She glanced at me with such love, that it warmed me. Then she dashed off toward her room.

Locke slowly got up from his kneeling position, his eyes bringing me up with him. "Guin, can I talk to you out on the lanai?" he asked slowly. I nodded quickly. *Great.* What had I done? *This was bad, wasn't it? I'd way overstepped, hadn't I?*

We left the dogs pressed against the sliding glass door. Their pitiful faces told us they didn't want to be separated from us anymore today. "Guin-"

"I'm sorry," I interrupted, not able to hold off. "I didn't mean to overstep. It's just that she looked so sad when I mentioned the convention. And I just wanted to-"

Now he cut me off. "Guin, that's not what I was going to say. I *really* appreciate you inviting my grandmother to join you at the luau tonight. Life's not always been kind to her, especially the last couple of years. It's just . . . There are some things you probably should know. But I also wanted to suggest you still take Sebastian with you . . ." He trailed off. I could tell this was extremely painful territory for him.

Locke moved toward the railing and placed his hands on it, leaning forward. I could see his back muscles tighten and pull together. I made my way slowly over toward him. I wanted to place a hand on his back, but it didn't seem like a gesture he would want right now. As soon as my hand moved in that direction, I pulled it back. I had no idea how to comfort this man. I wasn't even going to pretend to try. Instead, I just stood beside him.

"Locke—we can all stay in. I don't have to—"

He looked at me, shocked that I would consider doing that after all I'd gone through to get here. "No, Guin. I want you both to enjoy yourselves. It's just . . . I rarely talk about this. There are some things I've learned about Tutu since I started living with her. And she has asked me to keep some things private, even from the rest of my family." The look he gave me seemed to search my face for trust.

"You can trust me. I know all about wanting to keep parts of your world private. About not wanting to share certain aspects that are too painful."

His eyes met mine and then went back to the horizon. Locke inhaled sharply before continuing, "I feel bad telling you this without her knowing I'm sharing this with you. But I think it's important for you to know." He sighed as if deciding how much to share with me. "Tutu first started having memory and coordination problems—tripping and falling more often. After one of her more serious falls, I moved her here to recover with me and that's when I saw she really needed my help. That she actually needed a lot more help than I realized. And we worked so well together that I asked her if she wanted to stay here and she did. She has helped me so much throughout my life, especially when I needed it the most. I felt it was the least I could do for her and I found that I really love having her here."

I nodded, but he didn't really seem to see me. His eyes stayed fixed out to sea as if trying to catch the distant glimmers of sunlight on the ocean between the buildings of the community. Then he turned his face back to me.

"Guin, her memory is fickle. Same with her coordination and simple daily functions that our brains are suppose to remember how to do. So she had to give up midwifery. On good days it doesn't seem like there's any reason she shouldn't be able to continue helping people. It's hard to watch her sit around here instead, sewing or keeping herself busy. Something to keep her mind off of things—keep her mind off of all the things she misses, such as caring for her patients. Anything to keep her mind busy. Ironic, isn't it? I try to keep her company the best I can when I'm not at the surf shop, but I am no replacement for her patients. Far from it. So your being here is a huge blessing. You have no idea."

"I didn't know—" I began.

But he seemed to need to continue while he could. "I just wanted to make sure you knew. Just in case something should happen tonight. . . I mean, I know she seems perfectly fine, but that can suddenly change. She won't exactly be here with us. She won't really be herself. And she may need help. And I know you have a lot to think about already. I don't want to—"

"I'll be fine. Really. We'll be fine." But my mind started whirling. If my flare got bad enough or I passed out, I wouldn't be of any help to Tutu. I'd be the one that needed help. I felt incredibly useless.

Locke looked at me. "I can go with you, just in case. I just didn't want to . . . invite myself, not without explaining the reason." He looked so incredibly uncomfortable.

I sighed heavily, and that stopped Locke. He looked at me self-consciously. There was empathy on his face, as if he knew how awful it was to have our freedom taken away. I knew he must hate offering, as if implying we needed someone with us.

Well, I had my own medical equipment; it was Sebastian. But I guess I couldn't be Tutu's, not like Locke could be. I had really wanted to give this to her.

"Where is the convention?" he asked, and I could see his wheels turning, trying to problem-solve.

"It's going to be held on a restaurant patio on the beach. It's at the Whalers Village shopping center." I pulled it up on my phone and showed it to him. Locke knew the restaurant and even mentioned that his friend, Reef, worked there as a bartender.

Locke said, "That's perfect. How about we head that way in a little while? We can take a walk down the beach if you like. Tutu loves walking the beach in the evenings. And you can see some shops if you're up for it. And I'll sit on the beach while you and Tutu enjoy the luau. I can wait somewhere nearby. I'll let Reef know about Tutu. He'll be able to help if she needs anything. Tutu sometimes gets confused when she's not somewhere familiar. It will be great to have both you and Reef there to help her. That way, it will be like I'm not even there."

Locke spoke with gratitude, "Guin, this is so wonderful, what you're doing for Tutu. *Thank you.*" His eyes looked deeply into mine. And I really hoped he was right. I hoped I could still do something helpful for someone. I wanted that more than anything.

Guinevere

CHAPTER 17

THE SLIDING door closed behind us as we came back inside to the cool, air-conditioned home. Thankfully, Tutu was still in her room getting ready. I wouldn't want her to know that we had been talking about her on the lanai. I knew all too well what it was like to be the topic of *those* discussions. Even with people that had your best interest at heart, you couldn't help but feel uncomfortable. So, the last thing I wanted was for

Tutu to feel that way too. And that's why I suddenly saw Locke in a new light.

I really appreciated all the care he was taking to give Tutu a nice evening out that she could safely enjoy and still feel like the evening belonged to her. It was incredibly sweet and thoughtful of him. And Locke had also taken my feelings into consideration too. Never once bringing up my limitations, only trying to make the evening work best for us and make sure both Tutu and I would be comfortable. He'd wanted to be fair to me. It was *me* who strained against my limitations and saw them so vividly.

With this dawning realization, I left Locke so I could get ready for the evening. He graciously offered to take care of the dogs and feed them dinner. He really was very considerate. Not at all what I had expected. He was going to make some woman very happy one day. Because the world he'd created here seemed pretty close to the perfect paradise. A supportive family harmony with important values. And a man who was so considerate.

Absent-mindedly, I started going through the things in my suitcase. My hands dug slowly through my clothing as brain fog hung over me. I'd definitely been out in the heat too long today. My spoons were running out. They were all going to be in the dishwasher pretty soon—aka; I needed to be resting in bed. I sat on the mattress for a moment to gather myself.

This was not the time for low energy. I needed all the spoonfuls of energy I could get today. I wanted to borrow some, but I knew it didn't work that way, and these days I started off with even fewer than before. Sadly, I could tell it was already time for my treatment tomorrow. I sucked in a big breath of air, looking at my suitcase like it was a gigantic to-do list. How I wished I could enjoy the simple task of getting dressed for what should be a fun evening. But my eyes continued to stare at my suitcase as if it could somehow magically levitate and come dress me *Beauty and the Beast* armoire style.

I heard a tapping noise, then Locke's voice called through the door. "Do you mind letting me know when I can get some of my clothes so I can change for the evening? And I'm just about to take the dogs outside to play for a few minutes, if that's ok with you."

I went to the door and opened it. Locke was standing sideways since he'd been leaning up against it. He straightened and coolly adjusted himself upright at the sight of me. I guess he hadn't expected me to open the door, but I was going to need his help. I'd barely unzipped my wetsuit in the back. I was exhausted and my hands were so swollen that I was having a difficult time pulling down my wetsuit zipper.

"Hey–" I began.

"Hey," he said with a soft edge to his voice that I wasn't used to hearing.

"Do you mind unzipping me?" I asked, with exhaustion filling my voice.

His eyes widened, and a tiny smile crossed those handsome features. "Sure, I'm still on mermaid rescue duty," he said, cracking a bigger smile.

I turned and pulled my hair up out of the way. His hands found my zipper and pulled it down ever so slowly, making my pulse soar. I couldn't believe something this simple was having such an effect on me. I was holding my breath, trying to remain unfazed by his movements. When his hands reached the bottom of the zipper, they just stayed there. I heard a sharp intake of breath as my full back was on display. I turned my head to look at him. He had this lost look in his eyes.

"Uh, yeah. You're all good now. Let me know if you need anything else." He shook his head slightly, snapping out of his dazed state. "If you want to rest for a little while–"

As if on cue, the dogs came bounding in through the door. Obviously, it was Sebastian's way of saying he'd had enough of this separation thing, and Penny was ready to be back in her room again too. Both dogs bounced up on the bed together and hung their heads off the edge, their now iconic pose. I looked at them longingly. A nap sounded amazing. It was like Locke could sense it too.

"I guess the tribe has spoken," he said as he gazed at the dogs, chuckling.

"Ahh, I think so. Thank goodness. I'm just going to take a shower–a real one this time–and then I'm coming back to do the same thing," I said with a yawn.

He glanced at the bed. "No need to wash off before napping. My bed's seen way worse in the sand and salt department."

"Really?" I said with relief, not really knowing how I could summon up enough energy to take a shower at the moment. "But sunscreen really sticks to fabrics, you know."

"Yeah, I'm really not that type of guy. I don't care at all."

"If you're sure." I moved toward the bed to lie down on top of the covers as he nodded, dragging an oversized cover-up over my bikini as I slid off the rest of my wetsuit. My legs honestly didn't feel like they could support me any longer, and my body definitely didn't want to remain in an upright position.

"I can leave the room first if you need to get your things to change."

"No, that's ok. I'll get them later." Locke headed for the door. Penny bolted upright and Sebastian cocked his head toward her in concern. I had taken Locke's bed and now his dog. I felt terrible about it.

"You can stay . . . " My words trailed off, unsure of myself.

"Oh, uh . . . That's ok." He looked at Penny as he said it, but then his eyes glanced over to me and to the other empty side of the bed. I must have looked disheartened. There was plenty of room on the left side, especially with the dogs in the middle. Then he continued, "I mean, I can stay if you want the company." I nodded, not understanding why I was so incredibly shy around him. The dogs immediately relaxed when he sat down beside them on the opposite side of the bed from me. And I did too. It was the weirdest feeling of an adrenaline rush mixed with the calming sense of home. This was going to make for one interesting nap. At least the dogs were between us this time. And it didn't take long until his husky baritone and the dogs cuddling beside me lulled me into a peaceful sleep.

BUT THAT'S DEFINITELY *NOT* how I woke up. No, I woke with the dogs at *our* feet. Because I was very much in Locke's muscular arms, and he was cradling me, *again*. Was this our default position? Seriously, it was like we were magnetized. I blame the dogs: they started it first. And apparently we were just as good a fit together as they were. It was like I was the key to his "Locke." Every one of my curves blended into him seamlessly as my head lay on his chest and he hugged me to him.

Okay, *now* my heart rate was spiking. I wasn't supposed to fall for anyone. That was the last thing I wanted to do. But somehow, when I was in his arms, it felt like he'd already caught me.

I was now working on damage control. Trying to figure out a way to wriggle out of his hold without waking him, so I could go shower and we could pretend like this never happened. We'd obviously both gravitated toward each other. We were *both* in the middle of the bed. *Magnets.* Like the gravitational pull of the sea's currents today.

Carefully, I picked up his arm to begin my escape when he pulled me even closer, tighter. No, no, no this was not good. I could feel his heart beating against my chest and it was melting me.

I hadn't thought of this man as warm or cuddly, not in the slightest. But I sure was beginning to. Of course, when I was trying to save myself from embarrassment, he would pick this time to let his softer side shine. I started moving ever so slowly to inch my way off the bed when my foot accidentally tapped Sebastian, who spun around in surprise and bounded up to check on me.

"Oh, my God," Locke said in alarm. "Guin, I'm so sorry." The words came out as he was looking at his arms engulfing me. I was in the sea of Locke. Can't say I minded being in the masculine cocoon again, but I didn't really want him to know how much I was enjoying myself.

"Uhhhh," I grimaced. "Locke, you didn't do anything. I was just trying to take a shower without waking you, and you made that a little difficult by pulling me closer. You were probably dreaming about a surfboard or something," I teased. Then I continued to explain, "It takes me a long time to get ready, and I didn't want to make us late." His expression seemed to relax as he sighed in relief.

"As long as I didn't go full caveman on you," he said, laughing a little anxiously.

"Well, maybe just a little," I teasingly laughed, as I tried to contain my smile at just how much I had enjoyed it.

IT DIDN'T TAKE LONG for Sebastian to follow me down the hallway. He now lay on the cool bathroom floor as I started getting ready. He accompanied me everywhere, even here. I knew it seemed strange to most people, but bathrooms weren't a good place to pass out alone. Hard tile floors didn't make for a soft or safe landing. And if I didn't let Sebastian come into the bathroom, he would scratch the door to get in anyway, so it was best to just let him in. He always wanted to stay with me, getting anxious if he couldn't see me, especially if he wasn't able to smell my scent well enough for an alert. Showers made that part harder. I had an alert button at home that he could hit in case of a worst-case scenario, especially if I couldn't call for help myself. Sebastian had given me the freedom to stay by myself. I just hoped Locke hadn't noticed Sebastian accompanying me, or if he did, I hoped he would understand.

Within a couple of minutes, I heard this timid knock on the door. "Uh, Guin, you forgot this on the bed. Kind of think you'll need it for tonight."

Please don't be my bra. I looked at my pile of clothes, but the bra was right on top. *Phew.* I cracked the door, poked my head out and of course, Sebastian did too. Locke just looked down at him. Then a little smile crept across his features. I guess he found it cute which eased something in me.

He began explaining himself. "Uh, as much as I'd enjoy not giving this to you, I figured I'd do the gentlemanly thing. It was sort of laying on the bed."

Underwear . . . no. "Just take it back, Locke," I said with complete embarrassment.

"Ok, well, I'm here, and it is a gorgeous dress. But if you want to go full Lady Gaga. . . I like it." He laughed at his joke.

Oh. I looked down at the pile. I guess there *was* underwear in the pile. But how could I *miss* that there wasn't a *dress*? The brain fog had gotten really bad.

I sighed and stuck my hand out the door as I retracted my head to retreat, waiting for the dress to land in my hand. But nothing came through the door except for his voice. "So . . . I guess Sebastian needs to stay with you instead of going outside? Or Penny and I can wait on him."

"Yes he does, but how about the dress? Or are you planning on wearing it?" I asked.

"I wasn't the one that left it behind," he teased.

"*Brain fog*, Locke. Not a sexy scavenger trail hunt." Embarrassment covered my tone.

"Ok, ok. Don't get your panties in a twist. I hope you have those." He chuckled as he placed the dress in my hand. My *bright, deep red* one that I thought I'd be bold and wear. I didn't even know if I'd get up the courage, but now that he'd seen the dress, it would kind of be hard to back out.

"Yes, thank you," I replied.

"Ok, so what about Sebastian? Is everything alright?" he asked.

"Oh. Huh? . . ." It took me a minute to remember what we were even talking about. "Um, just take Penny out. I'll probably be too slow for Sebastian to join you. Thanks for thinking of him though."

"Oh, ok." Then after a pause he said, "Oh, Guin, Do you need me to move the shower chair somewhere for you? I mean, you're welcome to use it . . . wouldn't want to deny you any part of the Grandmother's haven experience. "

"Oh." I hadn't even thought about the things Tutu might need. "Oh, um, that's fine," I said as I checked behind the curtain to see the hand railing as well.

At the rustle of the curtain he laughed and said, "if you're sure. Just let me know if I can provide anything so it's the *ultimate* haven experience." And with that I heard him close the door the rest of the way for me.

I realized he may have used the dress as an excuse to check on me. But I didn't want to provide answers to the questions that I knew were coming. So without giving him a chance to ask any, I thanked him and closed the door.

After my nap and my shower, I had recovered some of my energy and was relaxed from the warm water. I wrapped a towel around myself so I could do my hair and makeup first. This was something I'd given up doing a while ago. However, tonight I was determined to find the spoons. I'd steal them from tomorrow if I had to.

But I just continued to stand there wrapped in my towel, looking at myself in the mirror, not able to find the energy to take the next steps. My fistula was staring back at me. At least I had found a sleeve that matched my dress to cover it. I'd packed several sleeves specifically for this reason. But *I* would still know the fistula was there.

And the sad fact was that I couldn't remember the last time I felt genuinely pretty. I certainly didn't feel it now, even after I'd finished my hair and makeup. I reached for the red dress I'd packed with the hints of floral embroidery around the bodice and hem. It was a gorgeous bluish-red hue and it would be beautiful on someone, but I just didn't think that person was going to be me. Then I remembered the intense looks Locke had been giving me. Maybe I was still desirable. *Maybe*. It gave me the courage to at least hold the dress up in front of me. And then I saw his expressions dance across my mind, felt his warmth, and it gave me a little more strength to believe in myself. To feel I was still beautiful. To dig deep and find that part of myself that still wanted to believe I could be.

So I slowly put the lovely dress on, looking at my reflection and felt so many mixed emotions. Next I put the sleeve on in an attempt to disguise the messy, undesirable parts of me. But it didn't make a difference. I actually felt wrong putting the sleeve on. It didn't make me feel prettier. And a piece of me wondered what Locke would do if I didn't wear it. But I wasn't that brave. I was just glad that I found the courage to feel pretty enough to wear this dress.

I took a breath and exited the bathroom, allowing the beauty of the fabric to surround me with confidence and be my guide for the evening. I tucked my items away in my suitcase and headed out to the living room, where Tutu greeted me. She sat up swiftly, looking like she'd dropped twenty years. She looked absolutely gorgeous in her floor-length Hawaiian dress with a plumeria flower clip that pulled her hair back on one side. The deep, royal blue color of her dress brought her beautiful complexion to life.

"Guin," she said, coming over to me and taking my hands in hers, "you are absolutely stunning," she beamed.

I felt warmth rush through me. "Thank you, Tutu, but you are the beautiful one. Wow." Her face flushed a soft pink, and she had a warm glow about her. I asked, "Are you ready to leave? I think Locke said there are some shops in the village we could check out before the luau starts."

"Oh yes, the village shopping is really nice. You're going to love it, Guin."

"Great, I'll go get Sebastian and we can leave now. I don't think we need to bother Locke. We can have a girl's night out." I was feeling more anxious now, and I didn't especially want Locke to see me like this. Surely, I could take care of Tutu and myself for *one* evening.

But as if he could read my mind, or most likely he heard my comments, here came the man. Although, he'd lost his hardened explorer vibe. "Indie" cleaned up nice. *Real nice.* He walked in from the porch dressed in a casual black button-down and black pants. Usually I'd make some Johnny Cash joke about the "man in black," but he looked so sexy I couldn't get one humorous bone in my body to work. No, I think they'd all melted.

"Leaving without me?" he asked jokingly. "I promise I won't crash your party. I have a date with two adorable dogs on the beach." Except he looked *way* too nice for the beach. No, he looked like he was going to a photoshoot for People's "Sexist Man Alive." And they probably did those in Maui too. *No, nuh-huh.* I wasn't going to see this man set all aglow by the Hawaiian sunset looking like *that. Dang,* he should come with a warning label: lonely women may become unhinged–salivary glands likely to be activated. I mean, come on.

Really, Guin, you sure know how to pick a house host. Good going.

There was a little devious grin forming on Tutu's lips. I guess the Donald Duck heart eyes popping out of my head were a dead giveaway, but then I realized she wasn't really looking at me. No, she was looking at Locke. And *he* was looking at me.

And oh my, was it a look. *A good one. It sizzled.* There was a tortured look in his eyes as they scanned over my dress and slowly traveled back up to meet mine. My eyes, which had suddenly gone timid on me. *He did not intimidate me. He didn't. I wasn't interested. I didn't have any feelings for him. I didn't–*

A low groan hummed in my brain, recognizing defeat. I *was* attracted to this caveman. Obviously. My body was telling me so. And obviously my body was the last thing I should be listening to, considering it thought attacking itself daily was such a *brilliant* idea. Okay, so this was *not* a good idea . . . If he would just stop looking at me like *that* . . .

"Guin, you look–" But our eyes locked in a stalemate at his words. He shook his head slightly and closed his eyes momentarily. *What was that?* "You look very nice," he said, quickly.

Tutu interrupted, "*Keiki*, really? *Nice?* Your grandmother looks 'nice.' Guin looks *beautiful, stunning, gorgeous* . . . We'd even take hot or sexy over *nice.*" She rolled her eyes.

"Nice is *nice*," he said, confused, holding up his hand in a gesture that echoed that sentiment.

But Tutu just shook her head exasperatedly. She ignored his remark, obviously not knowing what to do with him as she said, "I'll show Guin my ukes some other time so we can go on to the luau now. Let me just grab a shawl." She hurried off and left us standing there awkwardly.

"You do look–" he tried again but stopped, unsure of what to say. "The dress is really beautiful." But he didn't seem to be admiring the dress. His eyes fixed firmly on *me*.

"You look really *nice,* too," I said with a playful smile.

"Thanks," he said uncomfortably, still letting his gaze stay transfixed on me. "I better get the dogs ready."

But he just continued to stand there, making me feel a little weak in my knees and thankfully not from a health issue. No, this lightheadedness was a blissful feeling. It was quite confusing and new to my body. And best of all, he never once looked at my sleeve. No, he was looking at *me*. *Seeing me.* The man in black was bringing out a light in me I thought had dimmed long ago.

Locke

CHAPTER 18

NICE. *Nice, Locke? Really.* But I couldn't let my true thoughts come out. I was afraid once they started coming out, I wouldn't be able to stop them. So I redirected with something . . . safe. At least the dogs were an excuse to extricate myself from the situation because I couldn't seem to stop staring at her in that beautiful dress. And I'm sure that's the last thing she wanted, especially from me. I was debating if it really would be better if I just stayed home. I'm sure Tutu would be fine, especially with Reef there. Maybe that was the better call. I felt really weird about all of this. I didn't enjoy invading their special time. This felt like an impossible situation where I was surely going to get it wrong.

Just stay home with the dogs. Decision made. She'd offered to take Tutu out for a special evening. And Guin didn't need someone intruding. I really didn't want to be that guy, anyway.

I went back over to Guin and softly said, "I think the dogs will be happy to stay here with me. The dogs and I can take a walk when it cools off later. Unless you want to take Sebastian with you," I added quickly.

She looked at me hesitantly, "Oh, well, I'm sure Tutu and I will be ok, but . . . we'd *like* you to come with us." There was a demure tone to her voice. "You probably don't really want to go shopping, but–"

"No, we'd–I mean the dogs and I–would like to go with you. Although Penny not every place welcomes Penny like Sebastian. She doesn't have the same legal rights since she's an emotional support dog. But we can walk around with you."

"Really? That doesn't seem right," she said, offended on Penny's behalf, which I found adorable.

"Yeah, it's up to the shop owner. Some are cool about it, but others aren't."

"Oh, well, we can still enjoy walking around together." Her blue eyes looked up at me as she extended the invitation. And I'd never been so happy to be included.

THE DOGS HAD JOYOUSLY PARADED down the beach together. Funny, when they were together, they looked like a couple of puppies again. They seemed so carefree. I guess love did that for you. And I was definitely warming to the sight of Sebastian with Penny. I was even willing to admit how cute they were together. But only to myself, never out loud. And definitely *not* to the mermaid.

When we reached Whalers Village, Tutu and Guin happily made a beeline to the shops. I could tell Tutu loved having a shopping friend–and one that saw her purely in that light too. Nothing more than a fun companion. She wasn't a label–old, frail, or unpredictable–because of her diagnosis.

The twinkling light bulbs that criss-crossed over the square were already glowing as the sun's first rays began dwindling. I didn't realize how romantic this square was until I came here with *her*. Now, I was acutely aware. Her red dress was clouding everything, making it all rosy. Blanketing it in a *La Vie en Rose* hue. Couldn't she have worn *any* other color? It must be a special shade used by sea sirens. Maybe that's why so many fishing lures were that color too. Just like that I was ensnared. *Already*.

I led her over to a special place in the square that I wanted her to see, hoping for a distraction. This had always been my favorite part of the square ever since I was a little boy, and I still loved it here. And to my delight, there was a huge sand sculpture magnificently displayed in the remaining sunlight.

We stood in front of the sand art and Guin looked up at me with happy curiosity, waiting for me to explain. "There's a local sand artist that changes this scene weekly throughout the year. It's one of my favorite spots."

Although I really couldn't believe what I was seeing, I should have known better. The entire island was already in love with Guin. Its heartbeats matched hers. She was meant to be here, obviously. The enchanted mermaid that was highlighted in the sand sculpture seemed to wink and grin at me in triumph. The display had a complete under-the-sea theme with the sea enchantress as its centerpiece.

"Really, your *favorite* spot? Is it always this way?" she asked coyly. I could see her eyeing the mermaid with amusement and Tutu grinning widely. Her playful tone continued. "Did you call ahead and order this, Locke? You really shouldn't have."

"Ok, Mermaid. This isn't my *obsession*," I blurted.

"Really, so what *is*?" She laughed wickedly.

That's *not* what I meant. It had come out all wrong. She unraveled me. And that dress was unnerving me too. I needed to back away. Red was a danger sign in nature, so I should have known better. *Wouldn't any caveman know that?* Nope, I had all the annoying qualities minus the helpful ones.

"My grandmother is *right* beside you, Guin," I said with total embarrassment.

"Yeah, and she wants to know too," Tutu said with mirth. "I've tried setting you up so many times. So what is your obsession? Please tell me where I went wrong."

I responded, "Well, starting with women instead of men would be good."

"What?" Guin burst out laughing. "No way. Really, Tutu? What else did you try?"

Tutu opened her mouth, but I stopped her. "Ok, that's enough. You ladies have dived into Locke's warped psyche long enough for one day."

"Don't listen to him." Tutu laughed. "Mermaid is *his fetish. Clearly.*"

"Tutu, *please* don't make me regret coming along on this girl's night out," I begged.

"Oh, but it wouldn't be a girl's night if you didn't regret it a little." She laughed.

"Ok, let's find you both a shop with lots of 'bobbles and thingamabobs' to distract you both, *stat*." I sighed helplessly, not understanding how this had gone belly up on me so quickly.

"It's really beautiful, Locke," Guin said seriously, looking at me again and then returning her attention back to the sand art. "I love all the artistry in the curved details of the sand. You can tell he shaped it with passion. I can't imagine the time it took."

Just like her. That's exactly what I saw when I looked at her. The love and passion that shaped her life. Her fiery outlook. And, of course, the beauty of her curves.

I swallowed hard and responded, "Yes, this man has been creating sand sculptures for decades. I can't imagine working so hard on something that's going to be wiped away so soon after its creation. But giving something–perhaps all–of yourself for the pure enjoyment of others asking nothing in return is genuine sacrifice, true love. Something that will leave a lasting mark even when it can no longer be physically seen. The joy it brings will remain in people's hearts and be passed on to others."

Tutu smiled at me. "That's my grandson," she said, nudging Guin with pride.

Guin smiled back at her. "Yes, I see where he gets it. You raised a good one." She glanced appreciatively at me, melting my heart even more.

"Alright," I said, clearing my throat. "I think I promised you some shopping."

I hung back behind them as they took the lead. I actually enjoyed window shopping with them. They were quite the pair. A little of Laverne and Shirley mixed with Lucy and Ethel. Guin definitely brought out my grandmother's humor. Even if some of it was at my expense–well, okay, most of it. I hadn't seen it in full force for a long time. Leave it to the mermaid to restore that piece of my grandmother too. Maybe she was an enchanting mythical creature after all.

I stayed with the dogs outside the storefronts while they went inside. Very few shop owners allowed Penny inside. But Sebastian was being a real "stand-up" canine and didn't leave Penny's side. I couldn't believe they were so attached to each other already. *How could you fall for someone that fast?* I guess that was puppy love.

Out of all the shops, Tutu and Guin's favorite was the one featuring local artists specializing in glass-blown art and plumeria jewelry. Their art pieces were uniquely beautiful with a taste of local flavor. And surprisingly, the shop owner even let me accompany Tutu and Guin with both of our dogs, which was quite the fun experience. However, maybe they *should* have barred me entry. I wasn't prepared for the combination of these two in full shopping mode. I was worried I was going to come out with a plumeria necklace wrapped around *my* neck. They were *that* persuasive.

I was waiting under the romantic twinkle lights when Guin and Tutu came up beside me. They had a few purchases in tow. I still couldn't believe how fast they were bonding. I looked at them and realized that yes; they were wearing matching plumeria necklaces. *Well, as long as I didn't have one too.* They really were such kindred spirits, and it made my heart sing. I was glad they'd had so much fun and got to be so carefree. My grandmother never had the chance to have many friends of her own. And she'd always had to blend into the background, careful not to be the center of attention. She'd become invisible. And she certainly never got to be carefree like tonight. I was glad she was finally living her moments, too. I was so glad she could now.

"So, is it luau time?" I asked as they nodded at me. "I'm just going to say hi to my friend, Reef, and then I'll take the dogs down to the beach. They deserve some play time in the sand after all that shopping." I took the lead this time, not out of some primal male thing, but a survival thing. The enchanting call of the mermaid's movements had scrambled every brain cell in my mind.

When we reached the outdoor patio of the restaurant, I went to find Reef while the ladies checked in with the host. Since the guy in charge of the list knew me, he was fine to let me stop by the outdoor bar with the dogs before I headed to the beach. The welcome party was arranged for the patrons of each ukulele musician's online community, and each musician had chosen the place for their group to meet. Since the convention was so large, this allowed for a more intimate setting and patrons who met online could finally meet each other in person. Guin's musician had selected Lelani's patio on the boardwalk of Whalers Village.

There were festive banquet tables set up on the patio and lighted tiki torches glowed against the beautiful backdrop of an orange sky. Needing a break from my inebriated reactions to enchanting mermaid calls, I quickly found Reef behind the bar. I was relieved to see his good-natured smile. How easily he got along with people always impressed me. I'm sure his tips were incredible. I'd give anything to have a little of his congenial qualities, such as being more open and easy-going with people.

"Hey Reef," I called across the bar to his friendly face that melted hearts.

"Hey, Locke. It's been awhile. The last time you were in

here–" He trailed off. We didn't need to remember the last time he tried to wingman me. Let's just say Icarus flew too close to the sun that day.

I decided it was best to just move on. "Hey, uh, this is kinda uncomfortable. I don't really know how to ask . . . but could you just watch out for Tutu tonight? She's here with our house guest who's attending the ukulele convention. You know, usually–"

He cut me off without a second thought. "Of course I'll keep an eye on Tutu. I totally get it. Not that long ago I went through the same thing with my grandmother. Tutu's mind seemed great last time I saw her, but I know how each day can be."

My shoulders relaxed at his words. Reef was a fantastic, stand-up guy. Of course, he would understand. So many people had suffered through this same process. That we were helplessly watching our loved ones fight this battle was heartbreaking. It was bad enough watching them practically disappear, but also knowing that millions of others lost the same fight before there was any hope of a cure was devastating.

"Yeah, we're lucky. Tutu has always been sharp. They say playing a musical instrument has helped. The music patterns have helped to keep her brain sharp. I just wish she hadn't stopped playing. Maybe this will bring her back to it." I glanced over my shoulder at Guin, my heart spasming. It was feeling more and more like she'd been sent to us for a reason.

"Well, whatever I can do. Really, Locke. I want to help." There was this long acknowledgement between us, then a spark lit in his eye like a match in a dim room. "So, that's the *wahini*, huh?" A loveable grin was taking over his handsome face as he looked at Guin. I said nothing, and he smiled bigger, laughing deeply. "Oh, man. Locke's in trouble. Well, I won't wingman you on this one, Icarus." Yes, the nickname had stuck. Unfortunately.

"Shut up. There aren't enough feathers in the world to get me off the ground."

"Dude, you say that, but she's eyed you *three* times since you've been over here. And I think it's about time you could use a little fire to melt that icy heart of yours and maybe thaw the ice from your feathers so you can try flying again, too."

I rolled my eyes as he raised his eyebrows and looked pointedly at Guin's red flame dress.

"Well, why don't you and Dean hold a convention about it and then get back to me. I hear those are popular these days," I said, looking around.

"Oh, I know Dean's got my back. Don't you worry, he'll fill me in. I need some new surf equipment, anyway. We'll hold a 'Free Frozen Icarus' meeting tomorrow."

"Whatever, thanks again, Reef." I turned to go, and he grabbed my forearm, looking seriously at me.

"Locke, not all women are like that, ok?" He nodded to the fateful bar stool. "You can't let what happened with a few dates ruin a chance at happiness for you."

"Who could blame them?" I replied and with a sad look, he let me go.

Locke

CHAPTER 19

I MADE my way through the crowd on the patio with the dogs in tow. This was one restaurant that was cool with Penny being with me on the patio. I was about to pass Guin and Tutu on my way down to the beach when the person they were talking with caught my eye. And within a second, she'd spotted me as well.

The sweet Hawaiian girl I'd known since childhood was calling my name and motioning me over to their huddle. She looked so grownup in her flowing floral skirt with her long jet-black hair elegantly tied back and a purple orchid lei around her neck. I hadn't seen her in ages. I guess following her dreams had kept her pretty busy.

"Locke," Tutu exclaimed. "Look who is Guin's ukulele teacher. It's Luna. Isn't that wonderful? I was just telling Guin that I used to play occasionally music with Luna's uncle. He was in a ukulele band, too. How is your uncle, dear?" she asked Luna.

"Oh, uh, he's doing ok. I think he just has had little to look forward to recently. He's been . . . Well, he's just not been himself. I wish there was something to help cheer him up. It used to be music, or at least I thought so," Luna spoke quietly. She turned to Tutu. "He was always so envious of your band, Cass. I think he secretly wanted to be a part of it."

"Cass?" Guin spoke up.

"Oh yes, that was my stage nickname. We were called 'La Vie en Stars.' I was Cassiopeia, but everyone called me Cass."

"She's being modest," I spoke up. "She was part of the most popular ukulele band on the island."

"Yes, please don't tell my uncle, but I wanted to be you when I grew up," Luna remarked. "I mean, he was a huge inspiration to me. He taught me so much and has always been like a grandfather to me, but *you* . . . well, I always wanted to be like you."

"Well, I think you far outdid yourself on that," Tutu said kindly. "You've brought people from all over the world–from all different walks of life–together. That's the beauty of music in its purest form. It focuses on what matters most: a person's heart and soul."

Luna beamed, and Guin spoke up, "I agree, Luna. Your music has been such a light–like a rescue flare for me. And I can't even express what the gift of making music has meant to me–it's helped me through some of my darkest times. I didn't know just how much I needed music therapy. What you have done through your music–connecting us all and giving us a medium of hope and positivity–can't ever be repaid. And then offering a few of us tickets to the convention . . . that was beyond generous. Thank you so much for giving me a ticket."

I could see the emotion radiating off of Guin. But it took a while before recognition seemed to register with Luna. "Oh, yes, of course. I'm so happy you could join us. And you'll get to meet the other two ticket winners tonight. Everyone who entered the raffle had incredible stories about their musical journeys. I wish everyone could have won. Excuse me, I'm sorry to rush off, but I need to do the mic check before we get started. I have too many embarrassing stories from not doing that properly. But Locke, stay. There's plenty of room. No one that comes with Cass will ever be turned away," she said, smiling at Tutu and then hurried off toward the stage.

Everything was going smoothly, so I was just about to take that as my cue to leave when an aged, gravelly voice called out from behind us.

"Cass? Is that you? It's been ages."

My feet swiveled around to see a man a little younger than my grandmother. He wore a vintage fedora hat and suspenders, looking like something right out of a 1940s jazz club scene. Maybe his clothes were actually vintage from that era. They looked pretty authentic.

As his deep voice breezed past us to my grandmother, I saw her face pool with emotion. This was someone she was going to have no problem remembering–even on a bad day. That I could tell. He was the good kind of past. The type you actually wanted to catch up to you.

"Louis?" Her voice barely came out. But the look in her

eyes said it wasn't a question. And his eyes met hers with intensity. *How did I not know this man?* It was feeling like my grandmother had this whole secret life that I knew nothing about. Although this guy didn't look like just a fan. No, there was something more here than just the love of music burning deep in his weathered eyes.

"Yes," he breathed. And we all just stood there as they stared at each other. There was a long, intense pause. Then finally, he continued. "How have you been, Cass?" There was an aching tone to his voice. Not such a simple question, apparently.

I looked at Guin to see if her face had any clue what we were witnessing. She seemed much more intuitive than me. But she just stood frozen, not daring to move.

"I didn't know you'd be here tonight, I–" Tutu trailed off.

"Well, I just moved back recently from the States. I came back here to be with my family and my niece. She's like a granddaughter to me. She's quite the music legend herself now. Just like you. I think you were talking to her . . . Luna," he stated. It seemed like he didn't think my grandmother would know of his connection to Luna. I guess he didn't think she'd kept up with him.

"Luna . . . yes, I know . . . you're back?" Fragments left her. "When?" Then she shook her head. "Well, it's only natural that she would be a legend. You were definitely one yourself. California never knew what was coming."

Ok, now I *was* lost. I wanted to interrupt to get clued in, but there was no way I was disturbing whatever was going on here.

He chuckled. "Well, it wouldn't have if you had come along with me."

My mouth fell open, and I saw a light pink streak of color cross my grandmother's face. *Whoa, what had we stepped into?*

I attempted to rescue my grandmother, who still seemed a little shell-shocked. "Hi, I'm Locke. Kelani's grandson. Or Cass I guess I should say? And this is Guin, who's staying with us during the convention," I explained as I shook his hand. "How do you know my grandmother?" I queried.

Louis seemed taken off balance at the disruption to their private world of reflections and stares, but he regained his composure and replied, "Oh, well, I knew your grandmother a long time ago. We were both trying to find our way as musicians around the same time. Playing any gig we could to keep doing what we loved. Although, your grandmother had a few more years' experience and a lot more talent than me. I kept trying to sway her to the 'dark side of the moon' and to come play with my band, but she never did. I even named our band 'Stars Fell on Me' and I thought she would have fit perfectly."

Something told me that the stars that fell on him were Cassiopeia. And that the band was named specifically for *her*. *Well, this was a fine mess we'd walked into.*

Tutu spoke up, "Louis is being extremely modest. Luna definitely got her musical genes from him. He left the island when he got a jazz contract over in L.A. It was a big deal, especially back in the day. Ukulele wasn't as popular as it is now, especially outside of Hawaii. And he played other instruments too. His saxophone playing still haunts me to this day."

"Your music still haunts me too," Louis replied quickly.

Why did this conversation feel oddly intimate? Maybe this was how musicians flirted. Whatever it was, I felt that Guin and I needed to let them have a little privacy to work through whatever musical dance they were doing. It seemed like this waltz might turn into a steamy Argentine tango.

Tutu demurred, "You always had a soft spot for my music, that's all. You were the actual star."

"Thanks, Cass. But we know it was my muse that made me special." There was a burning intensity in his eyes.

Okay, I was getting out of here. My grandmother was on her own. As she obviously needed to be. I was getting out of the musical foreplay zone. But I felt her grab my arm. *Okay, maybe I wasn't getting out of here.* I recognized that look in her eyes. And it sliced through me.

So I stayed and spoke up, "She's certainly good at that. She's been an inspiration to all of us." Then, hoping to diffuse the situation, I pointed to an area of tables and said, "I think Luna said Tutu and Guin would sit over there. I'm going to help them find their seats before things get too busy."

"Oh yes, of course. It was nice to meet you." And then Louis turned to gaze at Tutu again. "And Cass it was . . . Well, it was *so good* to see you again."

She nodded in return and I felt her grip tighten on my arm. Then I led Guin and Tutu over to the random area where I had pointed, not knowing if that was indeed their spot at the banquet table. I leaned down to Tutu and asked, "Are you going to tell me what that was all about?"

"Not now, Locke. Later," she breathed.

Guinevere

CHAPTER 20

THERE WAS NO ASSIGNED SEATING, but if Locke somehow had missed that tiny fact, I certainly wouldn't share it with him. Because I wasn't sure what I had just witnessed either, and Locke seemed to want to get Tutu out of there. I wouldn't impede his fake excuse of an exit as we made our way over to our "spot" at the outdoor table.

"So I can leave Sebastian with you, or I can take both dogs

down to the beach," Locke said quietly to me. "If you need anything, Reef is at the bar. He's been a good friend of mine since childhood. I promise you can trust him."

I looked down at the dogs. "Thank you. I think I'll be fine if you want to take Sebastian to play with Penny. We'll be sitting most of the time, anyway. I can keep him here with me, if it's easier, though." Then I looked at Locke's compassionate eyes. "You could stay with us, though . . . if you want."

His intense look rippled down my skin in response. "No, that's ok. You two enjoy it. I've got a date with the dogs. I'm going to find something to eat, and then we'll be down at the beach if either of you need anything." He smiled at me. I think he wanted to be sure Sebastian enjoyed his time here as much as me. My heart twinged at the thought.

And then, I watched him walk away . . . the man in black, followed by two of the most adorable golden fluffs of fur trailing loyally behind him. They seemed like such a contrast. Locke looked like someone who would have an aggressive guard dog, not sweetly adoring goldens. But I was wondering if Locke was really a golden inside–maybe he was the hidden sunshine or unexpected rainbow after a storm. Maybe there really was a light burning brightly behind that dark, closed-off exterior. And perhaps underneath my shiny exterior, I was the skeptical one. That would be ironic.

Tutu's sweet voice broke through my thoughts. "Reef is such a nice guy. He and Locke have been friends since child-hood. They became even closer after their accident. There are so many other wonderful people here tonight too, that I hope you'll get a chance to meet. I really hope you'll enjoy your time here, Guin."

"I already am Tutu, or should I call you Cass now?" I teased. Her face beamed at me shyly. There was a glow about her now, brought out not only by the music and the person she used to be but also by her mystery man. "There's no way I'm letting you off the hook about playing for me now."

And she just laughed. "Ok, ok. I will *mao ku'iupo*. I will."

"So who–" I was just about to ask more about the enigmatic man when a loud, sharp mic adjustment interrupted me. Then Luna's voice crooned over the speakers.

"Hello, and welcome everyone. I wanted to take this opportunity to welcome you with a few songs. I'm not exactly good with words, unless they're lyrics, so I thought it might be best to express myself through music tonight." The crowd erupted in applause. Everyone here was definitely a fan. "But first, I'd like to introduce two very special musical legends that have significantly influenced me. The legendary Cassiopeia and my uncle Louis. I wouldn't be the player I am today without either of them, and I was wondering . . . " She eyed Tutu and then scanned the room until she found her uncle. "Well, I was wondering if they would like to join me. Would you two please stand up so we can give you a round of applause?"

The crowd went wild as they stood. Apparently most people recognized them, or at least could gather what a big deal they were in our musical community as Luna continued speaking about them. As she introduced them, I only heard half of what she was saying. I was too focused on Tutu and how she must be feeling. Locke hadn't given me too much information about her condition, but I was nervous about how it might affect her playing. And he had said she hadn't played in years. I was pretty sure Luna wasn't privy to this information or she wouldn't dare put her on the spot like this.

My palms were seriously sweating. I was supposed to be looking out for her, but I wasn't sure what to do in this situation. My insides were twisting uncomfortably. But Tutu was standing, looking calm. *Calm?* Her eyes had found Louis' from across the patio. And suddenly, I felt like we had been transported back to another time. Tutu and Louis were moving in lockstep toward the stage, and I wondered if all the noise was just muffled in the background for them as well.

Luna had both a baritone and tenor uke brought up on the stage. She asked, "Would you like to play with the band or play solo? You can make the song choice. Tonight, we'll combine, 'La Vie en Stars' and 'Stars Fell on Her.'" She laughed.

Louis replied, "Could it just be Lani and I . . . if that's ok? I think we can manage on our own for a song or two," Louis said, looking at Tutu. His eyes stayed on hers. "And we'd like to be called 'Somewhere Under Our Rainbow.' At least for *one* night."

Luna's smile was huge. "Of course, Uncle."

She brought over two stools that Louis arranged together, practically touching one other. He gently went over to Tutu and reached for her hand. His eyes scanned hers as if worrying she would not accompany him–*once again,* apparently. He whispered something we couldn't hear, and she nodded. It seemed to be something like, "Do you remember?"

And just like that, they were on their stools, knees touching and swaying together to an unheard rhythm. He leaned over and whispered into her ear. Her face bloomed to life, and she nodded. A smile of familiarity and love played on her lips. And then they strummed together seamlessly as if they had never been parted. And Tutu *was* amazing. Apparently her musical memory hadn't left her at all. Or maybe it was these particular songs. *Or him.*

They started with a rendition of "You Can't Take That Away from Me." It was a much slower, sensual version that leaned into all the jazzy aches. Giving way to those hard minor seventh and ninth jazz chords as their hands traveled all the way down the neck of their instruments like I never dared to do. And I had a feeling this song had such a personal meaning for them. Because at that moment, we weren't in Hawaii anymore. We were in the golden age of underground jazz clubs, and their love had escaped prohibition.

And then they sang "Somewhere Under Our Rainbow." They had made subtle changes, but they made a big impact–definitely making it their own. Louis started, and then Tutu echoed her reply. This was their love song. A duet dream of a faraway place where they had always existed together, and apparently always would. Protected under the rainbow of their bond–of their love.

A tear fell down my cheek when a deep voice startled me from behind. "*Why is my grandmother*–?" Shock penetrated each of his words.

Locke obviously hadn't left yet. He sat down beside me as if in slow motion, his eyes glued to the stage. "What's going on?" he asked in a trance.

"I think your grandmother is falling in love . . . *Again*," I said through my emotional haze.

"But she hasn't played . . . She hasn't wanted to play . . ." He sat there shocked. But as stunned as we felt, none of us were prepared for what happened next.

No sooner were the last words of the final chorus out of her mouth and the final chord strummed than Louis dropped the ukulele to his side. He leaned the very short distance toward her, bridging the gap of whatever years and space had been created between them in a matter of moments. And then his lips were on hers. In front of everyone. Both of his hands caressed her face so tenderly, yet with such desperation, as she sat motionless with the ukulele in her lap. He had let his emotions pour out through his music and it continued in the way he kissed her. A deep, tender desire rolled off of him and languidly flowed onto her.

But as he pulled back from her, she sat frozen as he continued to look deeply into her eyes. I was so moved that I felt disappointed that I couldn't see her expression. But she seemed suspended in time as he continued to hold her in his hands as if she were his lifeline.

I turned toward Locke, who looked equally stunned. I don't think he'd processed *anything* yet.

"Locke?" I questioned. Trying to get a read on him. But it wasn't working.

Luna came up to the stage and moved the mic up to her height so she could address the crowd. After the raucous round of applause for the couple, she merely carried on as if Tutu and Louis weren't sitting there frozen in the background. I'm sure she'd had to work around other weird situations before. And finally, Tutu and Louis escaped from their trance, and Tutu moved off the stage without looking back. Luna took that opportunity to say, "Let's have another round for the amazing Cass and my uncle."

With catlike reflexes, she grabbed her uncle before he could leave the stage. "But before you go, *'Anakala,* I think you've got one more song in you. Can we play one together like we used to do when I was a young girl?"

He just looked at her dazedly, but nodded. I guess Luna wanted to allow Tutu some time to collect herself. It was extremely kind of her. Especially considering how shell-shocked Tutu looked as she slid into the seat Locke had pulled out for her.

He grabbed the empty chair beside Tutu and pulled it behind ours so he could check on her. "Tutu, are you ok?"

I could see his dark eyes pooling with concern as he leaned forward into her field of vision, trying to catch her attention and snap her out of her rainbow trance.

Finally, she said, "I'm fine, Locke. Just a little stage acting. I'm not used to it anymore at my age. It used to be just another Friday night routine." She laughed dryly.

The corners of Locke's eyes drifted to me in concern, not buying any of it and looking to me for help. "If you're sure," he said skeptically, getting up to leave. But she grasped his arm, clarifying that he was to stay here with us for the rest of the evening. I guess if one of us flanked her on either side, then she felt secure. But it seemed Louis would probably stay away after being left on that stage. Although, I wasn't sure. He had just pulled off one of the boldest moves I'd ever seen. Leave it to a man in his seventies to 'show up' every guy I'd ever met.

Or at least I thought he was in his early seventies. There seemed to be an age gap between them. Maybe he'd pined for her when they were younger. Like an "older woman" crush. And perhaps it had all been stage acting for her but not for him, and maybe he'd confused the two. But what I'd witnessed when they were singing had felt so real. So palpable that the audience was quiet enough for you to hear your own breathing.

Tutu finally spoke as Luna's gorgeous ukulele music floated over us. "I think I could use something to drink before the luau starts." And by Locke's surprised expression, I could tell this wasn't a normal request, but he wasn't going to say anything.

"Of course, I'll go get you something," Locke said quickly.

"I can get it," I offered. "Why don't you stay here with Tutu."

Locke hesitated, but finally relented, and I made my way

over to the bar. Behind the bar top, I saw a very tall and slender yet muscular man. He must be Locke's friend that Tutu had mentioned earlier in the evening. The man came toward me immediately, grinning. "Cover for me, Nalu," he called as he came over to me. "You must be the mystery woman. Hi, I'm Reef."

"Guinevere–Guin," I said, introducing myself. I couldn't believe he knew about me. I guess Locke had already told him that someone was staying with them. "I don't know that I'm the 'mystery' woman though. Tutu tells me you're friends with Locke. She said you all have been through a lot together."

"Oh, you're the mystery woman alright. I couldn't get anything out of Locke. He's *locked* up tighter than Davy Jones' locker." He laughed boyishly at his pun. "And yes, I'm *that* friend. We've survived a lot together, even the worst day of our lives. But we were lucky. We survived, and I guess we're even closer now . . . So what kind of spell have you cast on my friend?"

I fumbled but finally said, "Locke didn't tell me much about the accident, but I'm so sorry for what you must have gone through. I can't imagine. He doesn't talk much, but I *think* he's warming up to me now . . . But is he always like that?"

"No, but he doesn't talk too much." He laughed. "Consider yourself special. Locke is . . . complicated. But that's not who he is with everyone. He's a really great guy. Locke would do anything for his friends, family, or the community. He's warm and generous."

Are we talking about the same man? I eyed Reef questioningly.

"I know, I know." He held up his hands. "Just trust me. He's still all tough, but he's the best guy. You get him around women, and he's all rough decoy. But that's because they've not always been too kind to him. Believe me, it's a little justified. The protect his heart thing, I mean."

"But I don't understand. He seems like he has a lot going for him if he would just, you know . . ."

"Yeah." He chuckled. "But after people mistreat you, especially for things that you can't control, then you start to close down. Optimism and the benefit of the doubt go out the window. Or at least that's my official bartender analysis. Kinda comes with the mixology territory."

"But what could make these women treat him—"

Suddenly Locke's voice boomed behind me. My eyes went as wide as Reef's. I didn't even turn around to look. "Tutu decided she's going to go back home for the evening to rest. She's going to call it a night. She had a great time, though, Guin. Thank you. That's the most excited I've seen her in a *very* long time . . . Uh, I'll come back later to walk you home if you'd like. I can leave Sebastian with you." There was a detached coolness to his voice.

"Oh." Embarrassment laced my tone, like a kid caught misbehaving. I wanted to crawl under the bar. "Of course. I'm so glad she had a good night. Hopefully, she can come back with me another time for one of the convention's sessions. If it's easier for you to take the dogs back now, that's fine with me. I'll be ok." I finally turned around to face him, although somewhat reluctantly. My voice was quiet. "I'll go back to the table with you. I guess Tutu doesn't need that drink after all."

Locke's eyes searched over me, and then he looked at Reef, sending some type of silent message I couldn't begin to decipher.

Guinevere

CHAPTER 21

LOCKE RETURNED to the luau faster than I had expected. The ukulele music had given way to hula dancers and local music performers for the evening. The tiki torches set the dark night sky ablaze, and the air was balmy with the scent of the sea.

Quietly, Locke slid into the chair beside me. I turned toward him and softly asked, "Is Tutu ok?"

"I think so. Still not really sure what happened. She wouldn't say much." He glanced toward the stage. "Are you enjoying the Polynesian music and dancing? These performers are very talented. I grew up here and I still don't understand how they're capable of half of what they do."

I turned my eyes back toward the stage. The women were moving fluidly in their grass skirts and keeping time flawlessly with the music. And I don't think I'd ever seen a group of men who looked more physically fit. Their tattoos glistened in the moonlight as they effortlessly tossed poles in the air and energetically beat their drums. "Yes, they've blown my mind. They're fantastic."

I looked at the man sitting beside me, now directing his attention my way. I wondered what he might look like up on that stage. He'd probably hold his own extremely easily. *What was it with the men on this island?* My eyes roamed over him, gazing at the black shirt stretched taut across his arms and chest. And knowing exactly how it felt to be held against his muscular body.

"Just wait until the flames and knives come out at the end." He laughed. And then, as if on cue, the men came back on stage carrying both things. And Locke's laugh only deepened. I definitely wasn't prepared for this part of the show since all I could imagine now was Locke on stage with them the whole time. And something told me that "Indie" would manage just fine.

When the men finished their finale, Luna came back on stage and encouraged the performers to take a final bow. She cozied up to the mic and said, "Ok, we're going to move on to our last activity of the evening . . . something that will help us get to know one another a little better. We're going to play a little game of 'pass the coconut.' But no worries, they're just baby coconuts." She laughed. "Everyone please stand up," she instructed as she began dividing everyone into teams.

"Have fun," Locke said to me.

"What? You're not going to play the game with us?" I asked, in mock disbelief. No, I'd seen *Charade*. I saw how well that had gone with an orange, and I was pretty sure this was going to be equally embarrassing.

"Yeah, Mermaid, I'm just watching. I'm not part of the convention. *Have fun*," he repeated with mirth and raised his eyebrows.

I started moving toward the designated area, noticing Locke was the only one still seated. He might just be more hard-headed than me.

Suddenly, I heard Luna's voice boom out from the mic. "That means you *too*, Locke." He shook his head at her. "Yes, you stayed. Just be glad it's not 'coconut smoochie.' But if you keep it up, I can change my mind. Maybe you would *prefer* to play that game."

He got up right away, apparently afraid she might make good on her threat. I felt him follow behind me. However, when we started lining up, he moved to make sure there was at least one person between us.

Luna's voice gave further instructions. "Please stand beside who you sat next to at your table."

Locke rolled his eyes and glared at her but moved over next to me, doing as he was told.

"Thank you," she said triumphantly. I could tell she was taking great pleasure from this game already. Tutu had told me that Luna and Locke had grown up together, so I'm sure they loved to tease one another.

It was then I noticed Locke was looking at me like I was a

stick of dynamite. "You can't catch Lupus, Locke," I informed him.

"Thanks, Mermaid, but I'm aware," he said stiffly.

Well, it seemed like he was afraid of catching something. What, I didn't know.

Before I could say anything else, Luna began giving instructions. "The object of this game is to be the first team to pass the coconut to the end of the line without touching it with your hands. Also, you can't let the coconut touch the ground. If it does, then your team has to start all over again. We'll place the coconut in the crook of the neck of the first person in each team's line. When we say 'go' you may begin passing the coconut to the next player in the line. We hope you'll enjoy this little get-to-know-you game. Afterward, please stay as long as you like and get to know one another better. We'll have T-shirts for the winning team members."

"Heck of an icebreaker." Locke scoffed. "Only Luna. She would pick the most socially awkward game possible."

I saw his eyes watch in amusement as the coconut made its way down the line with awkward and painstaking slowness toward us. It sounded so much easier than it looked in practice. I was already regretting not sitting this one out. Surely, I would be the one to drop the coconut. I actually had a bit of a team activity phobia. I remember being called "stupid" repeatedly by a little boy for costing my team time in a competition when I was really young. Ever since, I preferred watching instead of participating.

When the coconut arrived at the woman standing next to me, I fumbled pretty badly trying to retrieve it from her. I kept apologizing as the coconut slipped below her neck, and I went fishing lower and *lower*. But she just laughed in good humor.

Finally, around her belly button, I secured it. I would have been laughing, too, except it was *my* turn to pass the coconut next.

Locke's eyes caught mine, and he stood there frozen, looking at the coconut in the crock of my neck. Our eyes fenced off against one another, neither ready to make the first move and tangle with the other. After what felt like way too long a pause, I called out, "Locke! Not contagious, remember?" I tried to snap him out of whatever he was going through.

"Fine, Mermaid!" He grunted, attempting to grab the coconut with his chin but being completely unsuccessful at securing it. And it was at that moment that I became acutely aware our faces were colliding. The smoothness of his face caught me by surprise, and his chiseled features didn't seem so intimidating up close. He actually seemed pretty docile in this vulnerable position.

But I didn't think that for long as the coconut started moving upward and he tried to get a grip on it. He started blazing a trail up my neck with it. "Locke, what are you doing?" I mumbled through my smashed face. "*No one* has gone in this direction. How do you expect to grab it like this?"

"I'm well aware, *thank you*. It started moving, and it was either up or down. I thought I would invade your personal space less if I went in this direction, but I'm thoroughly regretting that decision now," he mumbled with the coconut in a precarious position, squished between our cheeks.

"Locke, I'm serious, we are not dropping this coconut." But I wasn't sure what he could understand through my squished lips.

"Working on it, *Mermaid*," he hissed out.

"Ok, well, let me help you," I suggested as he stayed frozen on my cheek, completely at a loss what to do.

"I wish you would," he said sarcastically. And our eyes darted toward one another, almost making us drop the bloody thing.

"I don't feel so inclined now," I mused.

He stared at me. "Don't make me say please. There is an entire team to consider. Just do it for them, not me." But I continued to wait on him. "*Please.*" He was really floundering.

"I'll take it with you to the next person," I relented.

"Great, we'll drop it for sure. No way are we working that well as a team," he said skeptically. I just looked at him like *really, do you have a better option?* Then finally, he said, "Fine, ok. I'll position us so we are facing each other and try to hold us together. Then we can move together and give it to the next person."

I nodded slightly and then realized my mistake as the coconut shifted. He grumbled and called out my name in warning. Then, determining that I was staying still for him, he began repositioning. There was no way our team was winning at this rate, but I also really had no frame of reference. I felt suspended in time, as if the world had stopped, just for us.

Locke moved the coconut, and before I had time to realize what he was doing, it lodged between our lips as he faced me. My eyes went wide.

A laughing voice over the mic said, "I told you we weren't playing coconut smoochie, Locke. Guess you wanted to play that game anyway," Luna's teasing voice called out to us.

There was a red bloom on Locke's face that seemed to spread onto mine. We were certainly close enough for it to be catching. I was so embarrassed that I was about to pull away to speak, not caring what happened to the coconut, when Locke grabbed me. He gripped me tightly, placing his hands on each side of my face, and tilting my face toward him, effectively locking our heads in place. Solidifying this weird romantic embrace. His eyebrows raised in a way that told me he would not let us drop it. And this actually relaxed me. I guess I trusted him more than I realized.

He navigated us toward the next person in line. Their eyes went wide. I couldn't believe how easily I moved with Locke. But it wasn't every day you kept ending up in the arms of such a strong and attractive man.

The unspoken message between our eyes said this would not be easy, but Locke definitely wasn't giving up at this point. He was invested. With my head in his very capable hands, he guided us to deposit the coconut. This was officially the weirdest "kiss" I'd ever been given. But oddly, one of my favorites. As we laid our heads on the man's chest so that he could take the coconut with his chin, I couldn't stop searching Locke's eyes. It was slightly required for the activity, but there was also something else that had entangled me in their depths. And the people gathered around us didn't even faze me.

But the weirdest part was how we just stood there gazing at each other, with his warm hands still enveloping me as we straightened. Everything was still positioned the same, *minus* the coconut. Like we felt the need to keep hanging on to each other.

Finally, Locke cleared his throat, and ever so gently, he moved his hands as if he might break me. "Sorry about that, Mermaid. Hope I didn't embarrass you too badly."

But I noticed neither of us stepped back or moved away. I finally said, "No, not *too* badly. It was fun. Thanks for figuring out a way to make it work. Usually, I'm the one to let my team down. I just didn't want to be that person here. I guess the island has a secret energy after all. "

Yeah, I thought that the secret wasn't a key but a Locke.

I added, "I hope I didn't embarrass you too much."

"No . . . Not *too* badly. I had fun," he teased back with a smile, opening his mouth to say something else when I heard a loud eruption. Somehow, our team won. Although I really do not know how. Other teams must have dropped their coconut *a lot*.

Locke laughed and raised that wicked eyebrow of his. I could see his wheels turning. The thought of us in matching T-shirts was utterly ridiculous. "We will have a strict no-matching policy." He pointed to me as he spoke.

And I just grinned at him. "Some rules were made to be broken, Locke."

Locke

CHAPTER 22

THIS WAS the type of experience I was hoping to avoid at all costs. And keeping my distance from her had been impossible. I wasn't scared of catching some ailment. I was afraid of catching were feelings. Of being caught by a mermaid specifically. I was too afraid that she would react the same way as other women had recently. But that darn coconut had set off a reaction in me. And now I was staring helplessly into her eyes, believing that she might be different. That maybe, just maybe,

Tutu was right in telling me I should at least take the opportunity to find out.

I finally released her, feeling a little like Louis up on that stage. And what a position that would be. I didn't want to be that out of control or hopeless for someone–feeling like I was at their mercy. At least Louis was lucky: Tutu would be careful with his heart. But I was wondering if maybe Guin was that type of person too. I sure hoped I hadn't made her feel uncomfortable–overstepped too much. But she continued standing in front of me, not backing away.

"Uh, I'll leave you to mingle. Just let me know when you're ready to go back," I said, trying to salvage things. And without waiting for a response, I walked back to the table to wait for her.

I was a little surprised at how quickly she returned to the table. Or maybe I had just been so deeply lost in my thoughts that time had gotten away from me. Lost in thoughts about coconuts and under-the-sea creatures, and a dog named after a lobster. I'd been surprised that Guin hadn't wanted Sebastian to stay with her tonight. It seemed like a big step for her to take, and it spoke to how much she trusted us already. She seemed comfortable with Tutu, the ukulele community, and even with Reef at the bar. The Hawaiians were good people. They would definitely take care of her. Because that was *Ohana*. And these people would take her in as one of their own. I knew Tutu already had.

My thoughts turned to Reef specifically. He was a good guy, and I knew he was single. I actually thought maybe Guin and Reef would be a fantastic match. Maybe I should have done a better job of introducing them. We'd both been through a lot, and he deserved a good, kind woman. And that's why I didn't understand why I had gotten so territorial and prickly when that thought crossed my mind. I should have been happy to see them talking at the bar together. But when I'd overheard their conversation and the direction that it was headed, I had gone into full cactus mode. I guess it mattered little. Reef seemed to think I was interested in Guin and I knew that meant he wouldn't go anywhere near her. So it was a moot point. I wouldn't try to push them together again, especially if it meant they might finish the "special" conversation they'd started. And a part of me, that obnoxious caveman part, sighed in utter relief.

I saw a flash of color before my eyes. Bright, neon aqua. I traced it back to the mermaid's hand, past the curves of that dangerously beautiful red dress, and up to her smile as she held out the brightly colored fabric to me.

"I thought I would choose the color I knew you'd like best. I just knew you'd hate the black one." She grinned wickedly. "And as luck would have it, my size was the aqua color too."

A little sea serpent grin spread across her rosy lips. A color that echoed her dress perfectly. She was naturally beautiful. And that just about killed me. Or at least killed my plans of not noticing her.

I pushed through the noise of my mind and responded to her teasing. "Of course. Because it's not like I'm already wearing all black," I mocked. "Really? Neon aqua?"

"Now, Tutu and I will always be able to find you easily," she replied.

"Yeah, because I don't stick out enough already as it is. I'm only 6'4", Mermaid." And for many reasons, I already felt like a neon glow stick in a pitch dark room.

She asked, "Seriously, is it the right size for you? I can exchange it if it doesn't fit. I wasn't sure how 'He-Man' sizes worked."

"Oh, so you'll exchange it for a different size, huh?" She laughed at my words. "I already stand out pretty well, but in this you'd have to be blind to miss me." Her face fell. Oh no, why did I feel like I'd made some really inappropriate joke? "Hey, I'm sorry. I love it. The size is right too. No one ever gets that right. You should be proud, Mermaid."

I began putting the neon glow-in-the-dark shirt on. I can't believe in under five minutes, she had me in this absurd thing. *What the heck?* This woman seriously had super powers.

"It's not that. It's . . . It's fine. You don't need to put the shirt on." But it sure didn't *seem* fine to me.

"I'm never taking the shirt off." And she laughed at me. But something made me reach for her arm as I stood up. I sensed there was something still bothering her. "Is there something you want to talk about? We've got a little time while we're walking home if you want to tell me and my neon safety shirt about it."

"Ok," she agreed slowly, and her response made me wrap my arm around her shoulders in an attempt to fend off the sadness that was overcoming her. We began our descent to the beach, down to the shoreline, and Guin's eyes had already found their way home to the moon. I stopped to join her, my eyes landing on the luminous *mahina* with hers.

"So what was it I said?" I asked, neither of us taking our eyes off the glow.

"*Blind.* And it wasn't you. I'm struggling with some things in my life right now." She sighed as if to catch her breath. "One of my online friends is going to lose her sight because of her Lupus medication. They didn't catch it soon enough. If they'd done a certain eye screening at her annual eye exam, they would have caught it early enough to prevent her vision loss," she said with pained detachment. I could see how much she felt for her friend and also how scared she was for herself too.

"Wow, is there anything this Lupus thing can't do?" I asked. And she laughed. At least my comment was easing her tension. "Seems like it's a supervillain of disorders. Now that's a real Ursula." When she stopped laughing, I asked, "I'm really sorry, Guin. Is there anything that can be done to help? And can you . . . are there things to help prevent it from happening to you?"

"There's nothing to be done for my friend. But she's staying positive. I don't know what I would do in her situation. My whole life revolves around reading and creating images since I'm a children's book illustrator. I'm so visual. I can't imagine losing my sight. Well, I could have the books read to me, but there's no way I could do any of my illustrations. I think about the what-ifs sometimes. But that's dangerous. And I go to my eye appointments religiously. I'm so scared, I plan to never miss one now, that's for sure. Unfortunately, my friend's one of the unlucky ones. There are warning labels on the medication, but it seems so unreal that they would actually happen . . . until you put a face to them. I still can't believe it's happening to her . . . So it's really important not to miss any of your eye exams."

I swallowed hard as my toes dug deeper into the sand with each step we took, and my arm pulled her closer, nestling her tighter into me. All I wanted to do was protect her. This primal part of me seemed to come out in full force with her. And it had from the first moment I saw her. She probably wished I would knock it off. But I couldn't help it. As much as I tried to switch it off, she just kept bringing that instinct out in me. She probably thought, with my rough exterior, that I was always like this. I most certainly was not—just with her. She had some pheromone that triggered the hard-wired caveman in me. And man, she smelled good. The swirling sea breeze's tangy air mixed with her sweet floral jasmine scent made me feel intoxicated. I was pretty sure I just smelled like "salty pirate." *Lovely.* Hopefully, the breeze wasn't blowing my scent back to her. But she seemed content just to gaze at the moon with me. And that unsettled me. I wasn't used to this.

When we arrived back home, I quickly said goodnight to her. I could tell she was exhausted and needed some rest. I had asked her about the details of tomorrow's morning appointment on the walk back, just before we'd reached the bungalow. And she'd given them to me–albeit reluctantly. I could tell she was still unsure about the whole thing. But I was glad I had asked my questions so she could go right to bed when we got home. She looked completely drained. Not a drop of energy was left in her face. It was chalk white.

I asked if she needed anything, but she said she was alright. I doubt she would have said yes even if she did. That stubbornness we both shared was coming out in full force now. It made me wonder what happened when two forces of nature collided. Probably best not to find out.

At least she'd had a good time tonight at the convention and that made me happy. I'd even gotten her to wear our team's winning T-shirt for the walk back home, and that seemed to be a pleasant distraction for her. I think she saw our team win as a victory for her.

Thoughts of the ukulele convention shifted my attention back to Tutu, reminding me that I wanted to see if she was alright. So, after saying goodnight to Guin, I went in search of her. I found Tutu on the lanai enjoying the night sky, tendrils of her hair blowing softly around her. Not wanting to disturb her tranquility, I quietly slid open the glass door.

I slowly made my way to her side and leaned against the railing. Penny had followed me outside and her large chocolate eyes looked up at me with concern. She must have sensed something was amiss, especially if she hadn't wanted to stay with the mermaid and Sebastian. I rubbed her head as I leaned against the railing, trying to get Tutu's attention. But her eyes stay transfixed on something in the distance, so I spoke gently, "I just got back home with Guin. She seemed to have a good night." When she didn't respond, I tried looking at her more directly. Still, I got nothing in return. Finally, I asked, "Are you going to tell me what happened at the music convention tonight?"

"What do you mean?" she replied evasively, her eyes never leaving the horizon.

"Well, Louis, for starters. Like, what's his story? I've never even heard about him before tonight. And please don't tell me what I witnessed was a stage kiss. I'm not completely hopeless. At least I know genuine romance when I see it."

Her face sunk into a tired mask. "He's just an old friend, that's all."

"Really? You look at old friends like they're the Romeo to your Juliet?" I teased.

Her brown eyes widened. Then she smirked. "No, I prefer the Lancelot to my Guinevere." And then she winked at her cleverness, as she masterfully deflected my question.

She turned her head to look through the sliding doors to locate our medieval princess. But Guin wasn't anywhere in sight. She was probably already tucked away, exhausted from the strain of the day. It had been a lot. And I'm sure she wasn't looking forward to tomorrow's appointment.

I countered, "Well, the 'L' is the only coincidence you've got there. My name is actually closer to that of the Loch Ness monster he'd be fighting. That's way more accurate and you know it. Now stop deflecting, it's not working. And you're far too sweet for it, anyway."

She sighed. "Well, at least you didn't fight the medieval princess part." I rolled my eyes playfully, and she laughed. "Speaking of, I heard how you helped Guin when she fainted last night. You may have more *pale keiki* in you than we thought. And you're always taking care of those tourists on your excursions. Maybe I didn't fail our long line of midwives after all." She laughed sweetly.

"Ok, Grandma. Well, since I didn't fail you, I think I should get a reward . . . like *the true* story." I eyed her.

Then she replied with seriousness, "It's really nothing, Locke. Louis just got carried away tonight reminiscing about the good old days. We both got overwhelmed at being reunited with the ukulele and once again being able to do what we've always loved doing. It's an experience we never thought we'd get to have again."

Yeah, reunited in more ways than one. And apparently with the person you love too.

She seemed to look at me suspiciously, not liking where my thoughts might lead me. "Louis was younger than your grandfather and me. He was an amazing musician, but our band was full. And so, he formed his own. Occasionally, we would play together for group concerts and benefits. When that happened, Louis and I would play together a lot."

I looked at her, my eyebrow raised. "Ok, so what's the non-musical story? The one where he fell in love with you?"

"Locke," she said exasperatedly.

"Or did you end all of your concerts with hot, steamy kisses? I guess it *was* the 60s and 70s. The era of free love and all that. But somehow I don't see Grandfather allowing any shenanigans. He was extremely–"

She cut me off before I could say more. "Locke, it's complicated." She sighed, looking at me. Then she finally relented, knowing I wouldn't easily give up on getting the story. "I'll tell you because you're my favorite grandchild–"

"I'm your *only* biological grandchild," I interrupted.

"*But,*"–she rolled her eyes–"we're never talking about it again. And what I share with you doesn't leave this lanai."

She looked at me, assessing my response, and I held my hands up in defeat and agreement.

"Romeo to my Juliet." She tsked. "Seriously, where do you come up with this stuff? Okay . . . It was the summer of '69. Woodstock year."

I nodded, ready for her to get to the good stuff, but she just eyed me as if to say, 'Don't rush me.'

"I met Louis at the free concerts I performed at the Waiʻānapanapa State Park. I didn't know who he was for a long time. I just knew his face kept showing up at all my concerts. But slowly, he began approaching me at the concerts. First, sweet compliments, then more in-depth conversations about my music. And soon, Louis began music studies with me on the ukulele. But never intending to play in front of an audience. It was just for himself, a type of music therapy for the soul. He was about six years younger than me, which was a lot at that stage of your life. I thought I was just a mentor of sorts." She laughed. "He gradually started becoming more confident. Before I knew it, he started asking if he could stay and play with me after my concerts so he could start honing his craft. To learn from me. Our moments together in the little grotto and on the park beaches' black sandy shores were some of the most intimate times for me.

"Louis knew that your grandfather and I were dating and that we had formed a band together. And I really enjoyed just playing for myself and not for money, but your grandfather really wanted us to have our own band and he was most persuasive. I just wanted to spread my love of music and my love for the people of the island through my free concerts. I didn't want to take the joy out of one of the few things I ever had for myself. But your grandfather was as insistent as ever.

"Louis never pushed anything. He would just compliment me. Nothing more. And always from a safe, respectable distance. We kept our teacher-student relationship professional, and that's all I thought he ever wanted. Louis didn't even ask to join our band at first. I don't think he thought he was good enough. But he worked really hard, and I tried to teach him everything I knew. There's so much you're able to share with someone who is ready to soak up as much knowledge as possible. Someone whose heart and soul are so open. One who is ready to give something back to the world. And then it wasn't him who was asking to play with me any longer, but the other way around. It was me. *I'd* fallen for him. So easily in fact, that I didn't even know it had happened. But I saw everything much clearer once I realized that. And then one night under the stars, with the last chords of our ukuleles still ringing out, he told me he loved me. And I knew then that he'd loved me from the start. "

I was shocked, but more than anything, I didn't understand. "You'd fallen for Louis too? Why didn't you break it off with Grandfather? It makes little sense."

"By that point, I was too scared to leave your grandfather. And there were pressures from my family too. Pressures I couldn't outrun. The age difference between Louis and I, as well as his background, were frowned upon. And that he wanted music to be his career was unacceptable in the eyes of my family. As for your grandfather, our ukulele band was a way for him to sew some of his wild oats and rebel just a little. Then he could go back to his regular life where he could safely return to his family's money and begin a respectable career. And I thought it would all work itself out. But that's not what happened. By the time I realized I felt something more for Louis, I was already in too deep with your grandfather."

She continued, "For Louis, ukulele was *the* destination–the only place his soul could land. Music was his life. When he received an offer from an interested music producer to come to California, he wanted to take me with him. But I wasn't strong enough to go. I would have had to disappoint and disentangle myself not only from your grandfather but also from both of our families. And you don't easily get away from powerful people. You *don't* disappoint them."

"Grandma, I wish I had known . . . I just didn't know–" I began. I'd had a complicated relationship with my grandfather to say the least and I knew there were things Tutu kept from me. I'm sure she still did, even as she told me this.

"It's ok, Locke. I've learned there are many types of love. There's a mutual understanding that's built on friendship and a life together. And it's beautiful in its own way. That's what I had with your grandfather. And then there's the all-consuming love that swallows you whole and tethers your soul to another person so closely that it scares you. That's what I had with Louis. And when I look at the ukulele, I don't see your grandfather . . . I see Louis. That's why I've put it away for so long, especially recently. I can't lose them both–Louis and the ukulele."

Tutu shifted in the breeze. And I looked at her sternly. "It's not too late. It's never too late for love."

"But it is. *It is for me. Now,* I'll start forgetting more and more, and then I won't remember at all. I was too scared to go with Louis, and now it's not fair to let him have what's left of me. I made my own choices. So, Locke, you better choose wisely because when someone comes along who consumes your heart, it shouldn't be treated lightly. True weakness is throwing love away."

"Tutu," I interrupted, the tears in her eyes really breaking me now. Snapping me like a hurricane effortlessly destroying trees in its path. "It's more complicated than that and you know."

"No, standing up for love isn't complicated at all. Living with yourself every day after you don't is the really hard part." She stared at me, her glassy eyes looked like eerily calm waters before the storm. "When you're young, you think it'll be easy to find a love that fits you that well again, but you're wrong. There will be other loves, but never like that one. Stand up, Locke. Stand up for love when it's your turn."

I couldn't bear this. I had some idea of what my grandfather was like, but I always knew it only scratched the surface and that she would never tell me the complete truth. Tutu wanted to provide enough sunshine to hide the darkness, but it was impossible to completely cover someone as dark as he had been. To everyone else he was the life of the party. He was the "good time" guy–as long as he was getting *his way*. The one everyone wanted to be friends with because he held *all* the power. And I knew one thing was for sure: you never truly knew what went on in a relationship. And you never truly knew who someone was behind closed doors.

"It's ok, Locke. Don't look like that. You get used to not being seen at my age." She tried to laugh. "You get used to being invisible. No one looks at you anymore. And that's probably a good thing for me. But no one has ever looked at me the way *Louis* did. I wasn't prepared to be seen in that way ever again. I got used to being invisible with your grandfather. But not invisible enough to disappear–not in the way I wanted to, anyway . . . and I'm not sure I can even let myself be seen anymore. But you, Locke–you have a chance to be seen. *Take it.*"

I looked at her sternly, wanting more than anything to make this right. "Only if you make a deal with me." She turned to face me, the moonlight caressing her hardened features. "I know you've seen *An Affair to Remember*. And I've seen the end where Cary Grant accepts her exactly as she is. So I'm going to put this in terms you may accept. Louis *is* Cary Grant. Stop being stubborn. Finally, let him have his chance. That's all a man really wants. You may think that chance has an expiration date on it or requirements for when it can happen, but it doesn't. But it matters if you never give him a chance. Are you really going to do that to him? Because I'm pretty sure from what I saw tonight that the last person you're going to remember will be *him*. And when that fails, the music will still be playing. Because he'll be there to play it for you."

"Locke, I can't–" Her glassy eyes watered over.

"Are you telling me you couldn't years ago and you're going to *choose* not to now? What if now is *your* time to stand up?"

"I had a good life with your grandfather. That was my story–"

"You had a controlled life with my grandfather, and now you get to write your own story. None of us knows how much time we have, so we all better use it wisely."

"It was a different time, Locke. Your grandfather was of

another generation–" Tutu began helplessly, making excuses for him as she always did.

"No, we are in the twenty-first century. We've not been in a different time period for a while now. There are no excuses. Nor should there ever have been." I saw the way he belittled her midwifery, the way he controlled the finances, the household, her friends, and the way she was expected to be perfect in *every way*. No wonder she didn't think Louis would want her "the way she was now." No wonder I thought no one would want me "this way" either.

My voice softened. "There's a reason I knew you would understand what I had been experiencing with dating, and there's a reason we're so bonded together. But I've also seen you break free recently. You're able to stand up for yourself now. Society is different. Your situation is different. And *you* are different. This is *your* time. And Louis is waiting."

"Locke–" The word trembled bravely.

"He doesn't want *perfect*. He wants something much better: *you*. So stop trying to be perfect. Let someone finally appreciate *you*. Let them actually love *you*."

She nodded silently, barely able to speak. "And we have a deal. You'll go with Guin tomorrow?" Her words were barely above a whisper.

"What?" I asked in disbelief. "Tutu, I don't understand how that has anything to do–"

"Just do it for me, *please*."

"Yes, I will go with her tomorrow. I already had plans to go with her, anyway." And she smiled endlessly.

Guinevere

CHAPTER 23

THE MORNING SEEMED to come sooner than possible. I wasn't ready to go to a new dialysis center. I had finally found comfort in the familiarity of the one back home and with the nurses who staffed it. Anxiety always overtook me when I had to go to a new medical place, and this would not be an exception. You just never really knew what to expect or how you would be treated.

Maybe that's why I'd moved through my morning routine like molasses, trying to draw everything out. But my movements definitely sped up when I saw movement out on the lanai. As nice as Locke's offer was last night, I really thought it would be best If I went alone this time. So I kicked my movements into double time when I heard the porch door opening–which, granted, was not fast with my morning pain.

"Hey," he said, coming in from the porch, coffee in hand. "I was just about to check and see if you were ready to go."

"Oh, everything's fine. I've got my Lyft app open and there seems to be a ton of them in the area that are rip, roarin', and ready to go."

Rip, roarin', and ready to go? Really, Guin. That *Chattanooga Choo Choo* southern charm was really coming out in full force now.

"Oh, uh, ok." But he looked oddly disappointed. I thought he'd be relieved. "Well, I promised Tutu I would take you." He paused. "And I *wanted* to take you."

Want. That little pesky word shot right through my heart. When was the last time someone *wanted* to go to dialysis with me? To be fair, my grandparents would surely have wanted to go with me, but they had their own health problems, and I didn't want them to be burdened with mine. But now, here was someone who *wanted* to go–what I'd been longing for this whole time. Surely, I wouldn't push that away, would I?

"If you're sure you *want* to go," I replied. "It's not exactly pretty, especially if you're squeamish. But it's not like you need to go inside, though."

"Mermaid, do I strike you as someone who does stuff they don't *want* to do?"

No, he certainly did not. His unfaltering gaze, coupled with the one eyebrow raise, was enough to set me in motion. I finished collecting my things and went to retrieve Sebastian out of habit. They allowed him in most medical facilities, but then I stopped as I looked at Locke. I realized I actually trusted him enough to leave Sebastian here again. Locke's care with Tutu told me I could trust him. And so I took one of the biggest steps of all and laid Sebe's harness back down. And I was met with this big smile from Locke that slowly crept over me, taking hold gently and then all at once. He even offered me a to-go coffee and eggs since, apparently, he'd made extra. I stared at him, feeling a little mystified. Any man offering to-go coffee was more than an Achilles heel for me.

It wasn't long before we arrived at the dialysis center on this cool, dewy morning. We had arrived early, so we both just sat and stared at the dialysis center's stark entrance from Locke's Jeep, neither of us making a move to get out. Time seemed to stretch like an elastic band before us, and it would only be a matter of time until it snapped back.

Locke swallowed and looked at me, but I continued to stare straight ahead. I realized then that I wasn't ready for him to see me like this. Maybe I should ask him to come back and pick me up in a couple of hours. But I felt he was most certainly going to want to come inside with me.

"Are you . . . Are you ready?" he asked hoarsely. I could tell he did not know what to expect or what to say.

"I guess. Um . . . dialysis usually takes about three to four hours. Can I just call you when I'm done? I really appreciate you driving me here," I said as I dared to look at him. All his features fell, like a collapsing house of cards.

"Oh . . . uh, yeah . . ." He stared at me. Concern filled his perfectly tanned features. He ran a hand through his inky black hair. It became mussed in a sexy way, of course. "Uh, I'd like to . . . I mean . . . Do you want me to–" Then he just stopped, looking defeated.

"It's fine, Locke. Really, no one wants to sit in a dialysis center. Believe me. I'm fine. Thank you." *Why had I thought he would be any different?* Of course he didn't really want to go in. No one did. It was one thing to drive here, but to face it, to look at someone's frailty and mortality was different. Disturbing. Unpleasant. I should have known. This was really more of Tutu's doing.

I reached for the door handle, but he stopped me. "*I* do. I was just waiting to be invited," he spoke slowly.

"You make it sound like a party," I remarked with detachment.

"Guin," he said sternly. "It's private. I never want to intrude on your privacy. Of course I want to sit with you."

"I'm sure you have work to do. It's not that big of a deal, really–" I began the song and dance I usually did to protect myself.

"Guin, stop being more stubborn than I am. I promise you, it's going to be exhausting."

"No one has ever really wanted to stay with me before." I paused, thinking about his sincerity. *He really meant it, didn't he?* "Locke, will you stay?" I asked nervously. And my stomach's butterflies were kicking up a storm inside of me. A kaleidoscope of emotions rushed through me.

I had friends say they would like to come with me, but they never actually followed through on the idea. I got it–I wouldn't want to sit at a place like this either. *Why did he?* Whatever the reason, I would take it. Just to have someone there would be so nice–no, it would be amazing.

"You can do paperwork or something," I added quickly.

And his lopsided grin melted my heart. "Nope, I'm definitely not doing that. I just want to be with you."

And with that, he got out of the car before I could even respond. His words bypassed everything and went straight to my heart, making it pump harder and faster. Making me feel so alive–so special. And maybe, just maybe, *wanted.*

And from there, it was all a blur. All I could think about were his words as I checked in for my appointment. I'm pretty sure I answered most of the intake questions incorrectly, even giving my date of birth for my name. I remember doing that at another appointment and the nurse had laughed at me. But that time, I had been incredibly nervous. It was my first time. This time, though, I had a *good* reason for my distraction. It's amazing how different life can look with the right person. The way we care for one another is truly the way we leave a mark on the world. How we make a difference. Even if it feels as small as a flap of a butterfly's wing. Because that can be the most powerful of all. And I was pretty sure Locke was that butterfly's wing flap for me.

A young blonde nurse led me back to a recliner with all the intimidating machinery standing beside it. I turned to take in Locke's reaction, my eyes scanning his face. Terrified of what I might find there. But he didn't seem grossed out, freaked, or weirded out. He just stood still beside me, unmoving. A Stonehenge kind of man. Completely unexpected and unexplainable, but always there. Someone you could depend on.

I noticed a tinge of sadness in his features now. And he put his hand on my arm soothingly as the sweet nurse motioned me over. Even when she connected my fistula up to the machine he just sat there, *looking at me.* This was the part where I'd expected he would need to take a walk or suddenly remember he had somewhere to be. But not Locke. He was completely unphased. He just continued taking me in. And me, I realized, was now this machinery too. And somehow, someway, he seemed completely okay with that. Like it wasn't ugly because it was connected to me. I never realized how painful it had been for me to see people walk away, needing to not see that part of me, not until Locke stayed. Until he had no problem looking at me–*every* part of me.

I reclined all the way back in the chair. Medical recliners were never comfortable. Not like the ones you had at home. I don't know why that was. And the sight of my blood running through the tubing always made me queasy. I wasn't someone who got queasy easily, but when I saw my blood or that of a loved one, it was different. And I hadn't gotten immune to the sight of mine, as they told me I would.

I must have been turning a little green as I squirmed in the chair because Locke reached for my left hand with no warning. Of course he had sat on my left side with all the tubing in it. He certainly wasn't the slightest bit squeamish. It felt like a moment from *A Walk to Remember.* And as much as I loved that movie, I really didn't want to live it. But now, it was one of the few I related to. It wasn't like there were many romances starring main characters like me. And I doubt they were told by people like me. And they certainly didn't get the classic "happily ever after."

But doesn't everyone deserve a love story and more importantly, an HEA?

Locke's grip tightened hard on me, and I was pretty sure that part wasn't in the movie. He wasn't especially gentle right now. No, I think he was a little scared. This all just got very real for him too, and I could feel the exact moment it did. There was this wild look in his eyes like my worth made the stakes too high. So he just kept gripping me tighter. I was going to say something, but his look stopped me. And then I only wanted to feel his hold tighten. I was so glad I was finally feeling something good in this chair. I'd either been in pain or numb in it for much too long now, detaching myself from everything and everyone. Wearing a shield of pleasantness which was really my way of surviving. But I was drowning right under the surface of the facade.

"So do you usually get to bring Sebastian? Am I in his spot?" Locke teased, obviously trying to distract me.

"If I say yes, are you going to let me pet you?" I laughed, and he grimaced playfully. But at this point he'd probably let me do anything, judging by the look on his face. *Great. I am that pathetic.*

"I guess you can't bring your uke here either, huh?" he asked, obviously thinking of my "best version" places.

"No, they would probably frown upon that seeing as I can't play it that well yet and I can't sing."

"Yeah, there's no way I believe that," he replied.

"Oh no, believe it. It's therapy, but *only* for me. Maybe my playing is okay, but not the singing. Ironic, since that's kind of a big part of playing the uke. But there's something so soothing about the instrument. Playing takes my mind off of everything. Well, singing does too, but only when no one can hear me. Guitar had always been on my bucket list and I had just started learning to play it when I got sick. I guess that's why you shouldn't put anything off in life. We never know what trouble the next day will bring—what version of ourselves we may find. When I got sick, my swollen joints wouldn't allow my fingers to press down the strings hard enough to play the guitar. I even tried using the lightest strings possible. So with the skeptical hope of finding an instrument that I could play, I was led to buy my first uke. Its lighter frame and strings allowed me to play it. Sometimes we just need to be guided to what has been waiting for us all along."

"I believe that too. Something similar brought me back to surfing." He smiled at me. "So did you just stumble upon these online classes too?"

"Yup, my immune system was too compromised to attend in-person classes, so the online uke community became a home for me. I joined this group because the teacher instructed all the songs on YouTube that I wanted to learn. I'm obsessed with jazz standards. And it became the best type of support group for me. Instead of joining a local Lupus support group, I joined a music community, and it became part of my therapy too. While I'm sure we all joined for different reasons, I believe we all had a reason we needed music. No musician plays without a reason. There's a part of their soul that needs healing that only the notes can reach."

I squirmed some more under the heated blanket they had brought me and glanced at the machine. Probably at least three more hours left, and the blood was still making me just as uncomfortable.

Locke glanced quickly at the machinery humming quietly beside me and looked back to my face. Then an enormous grin took over his face like a tidal wave rolling over everything in its path.

Oh no. What is he planning?

He used his other hand to pull out his phone and started scrolling. *Oh. He's one of those guys.* He probably had a sports channel on his phone or something else even more entertaining. Well, that's okay. I was used to distracting myself at these appointments. At least I had his physical company.

I was getting ready to pull out my phone to look at Buzz-Feed or Bored Panda–something that would allow me to go down a mindless rabbit hole. I certainly wasn't about to do my usual thing, which was adult coloring while listening to ukulele music or rom-com audiobooks. I was just about to unlock my phone when he turned his phone screen around to me.

"Ok, take your pick."

My mouth fell open. Book thumbnails covered his screen–and not just ordinary thumbnails–no, these were sweep-you-off-your-feet high romance covers in a *very* specific niche.

"What?" he questioned. "You don't like romance novels? You strike me as a romance reader. Am I making too much of an assumption here?" A look of worry crossed his features.

I stared at him harder. "Yeah, but not spicy-surfer-dude romance novels."

His husky laughter rumbled over me. I looked intently at the shirtless surfers who looked like they might collapse underneath the weight of their muscle. Ok, now I was just picturing Locke on these covers. Now I got the appeal of the Fabio cover. Then my eyes found the enchanting mermaids and Locke's finger hovered over them in suggestion. No way was I reading this in front of him.

Locke began, "Sorry, it's not like I have much practice with this. I don't really know what I'm doing here. There was a tropical filter in the romance section, and that made me curious, so I searched for surfer romance."

"Yeah, well, maybe never do that again," I teased, as he laughed at my words. But I appreciated his thoughtfulness, and I did like the idea of a surfer romance for *way too* obvious reasons. "Um, I'm just going to apply some filters if that's alright," I said as I took the phone from him.

"Ok," he said with an infectious smile as I returned the phone to him. "Wait, the mermaids are gone. What did you do?" He interrogated me suspiciously. "You're not playing fair. They probably got filtered out too." I laughed until he said, "If I'm going to read to you, then I can at least have a mermaid."

I looked at him in wonder. I just thought he was getting a book for me to read. That gesture was sweet enough in itself.

"Wait, what?" I asked a little shakily.

"Don't make me say it again, Mermaid. I'm planning on reading to you so we can both 'enjoy' it. Why do you think I picked mermaids and surfers? I need it to hold my attention somehow." He laughed anxiously.

My heart tightened and this time when I pinched my lips together it wasn't to keep from laughing. "They're *all* perfect. Whichever one you want." I could barely get the words out. My eyes were burning.

"Well, I'm scrolling until I see a mermaid then," he said jokingly as he clicked on one to buy.

A tear dropped from my eye and I brushed it away quickly, hoping he wouldn't see.

"It won't be that bad, I promise. I surely can't be that awful at reading. You can't cry *yet*."

I let out a shaky little laugh as he peered up at me and then back down at the book. He began flipping through the pages on his screen, giving me a few moments of privacy to collect myself. Suddenly, this deep, seductive voice came out of him. He sounded like a terrible radio ad for online dating. A honey trap for lonely women. I burst out laughing as he began the first chapter from the male's perspective who had set out traveling on the high seas.

His eyes snapped up to me, larger than I'd ever seen them before. "What? Nothing is funny yet," he deadpanned.

"Locke, your regular voice is fine," I burst out.

"What do you mean? *This* is my regular voice. I'll do character voices later when I get to them." His words only made me laugh harder. And the people in the chairs beside us had already started looking at us even before my laughter. At least they looked thoroughly amused. Oh, I hoped this was family friendly. Somehow, I didn't think he'd skip *anything*.

Locke just gave me a weird look and then returned to the book, full sexy, baritone voice on display. It was like I'd entered an underground jazz club with a sensual-voiced disc jockey. My cheeks were flaming. But then came the character voices. I don't even have the words to explain them. For someone so rough-edged and serious, he sure didn't mind making a fool of himself. You would have thought he was reading in a children's ward, although the material would have been a *little* inappropriate for them. Now some nurses had stopped by to "check" on the patients for much longer than usual, loitering in amusement. But at least everyone had big smiles on their faces. They were looking at us like we were adorable. And Locke had no clue. He was way too engrossed in his narration.

When the nurse finally–yet reluctantly–came over to check on me, Locke stopped and looked up at me with a smile.

"You're almost done," she said. "Just about thirty more minutes. You have quite the man. You two are so cute together. We might need to hire you as staff."

"We're not–" we began at the same time but then stopped when we saw her huge grin.

"I'm really lucky to know him," I said, looking at him and something seemed to come untethered in him when I did. His gaze was so magnetic, I felt like I might melt away under its intensity.

"Well, don't stop now," the kind nurse said. "We want to see if the guy gets the mermaid."

"Yeah, me too," Locke said quietly.

And my blood suddenly felt super-charged throughout my body. What was this machine doing to me? Then he abruptly looked back down at the book and read to me for the rest of our time.

Locke

CHAPTER 24

I COULDN'T BELIEVE I was reading this book out loud. I had never read a romance book in my life. Not even when Tutu had been in the hospital. We had always talked or worked on her quilting. And I was really feeling like the punchline here. I couldn't be further from the men on these pages because, of course, there was not one, but two "Fabios" fighting for this mermaid. But Guin seemed to enjoy it, and that's all that mattered. And she seemed to enjoy it because I was reading it to her, not necessarily because of the perfect male characters. But maybe I was wrong. *Were* these the type of men she liked? Perfect to a fault? Chiseled and physically flawless, always knowing what to say to a woman to woo her in every way?

Okay, Locke. You don't need to be worried about what Ariel likes. That is not your business. Just entertain her. But as time went on, dang, if I wasn't intrigued not only by the story but also by *her* responses. I kept sneaking peeks at Guin to see how she was reacting to the storyline. And I had to admit this eReader thing was pretty addictive because I was ready to buy the whole trilogy.

The nurse came back over just when the two Fabio pirates were duking it out. Of course, soaking wet from the raging storm in an epic battle on the plank of the ship. Guin was actually giggling helplessly at the absurdity of it all–or perhaps it was my character voices.

"Unfortunately, I think you're done for the day." The nurse actually looked dismayed. "But we're not too busy if you'd like to stay and finish the book. Seems like you're pretty close to the end and you're sure keeping everyone entertained."

"Oh," Guin said with an embarrassed tone. "As entertaining as Locke is, I think I'd actually fall asleep. Thank you, though."

The nurse nodded with understanding. "Dialysis really takes it out of you, doesn't it? Go home and get some rest, sweetie," she said, disconnecting her from the machine.

Guin thanked her and looked at me silently. I could sense her unease at the intimate treatment I had just sat through with her. So I tried to break the tension. "Are you sure you don't want to hear the ending? I feel like we're close to finishing. And I'm totally team Fabio–with golden locks–I think he's going to win. Although all that hair may slow him down or get tangled in his sword."

She laughed at my attempt at romance humor. "No, that's ok. Really. We can finish another time. I have to come back again . . ." She let her words trail off. *Was that an invitation?* "I won't subject you to any more outlandish romance right now."

"Does that mean–" I looked at her, actually hopeful she'd extend another invitation.

"Will you . . ." But she didn't seem to be able to finish. She kept weaving her fingers in and out of themselves. I could almost see a basket-weave pattern forming.

"Well, I'd like to come back so I can find out what happens." My heart hammered out the words.

"Really? The book's not too boring?" she asked. I knew we were *not* talking about the book. Although those men were intimidating. No one could live up to those standards, most certainly not me.

"No, absolutely not." She sighed at my words. "Although, is this what it really takes to get a mer–a woman?" I asked half-jokingly, but half-seriously too.

She laughed. "No, not at all. If those men were actually real, I think women would run the other way. No, there's something sexy in vulnerability, admitting weakness, and even showing flaws."

"Well, those pirates definitely have that. I mean, it is a flaw to be *that* sexy. A curse, really." And she started laughing at my sarcasm. But I heard something that made me hopeful. *Even flaws . . .*

I walked with her to the car, and I noticed she had very low energy after this treatment. It seemed to really drain everything out of her. Within no time at all, she fell asleep in the Jeep on the way home. I suggested she take a nap in her room, but it seemed like she didn't want to be alone. Instead, she went to the couch near Tutu's wicker armchair and started watching black-and-white TV reruns with her. Sebastian quickly came to her side, sniffing her relentlessly. I guess she smelled different now. I'd never even thought about that. I went to sit with them, happy to take the rest of the day off from the surf shack and play hooky.

Originally, I thought I would take Guin and Tutu to see some more sights around the island, but it didn't seem like Guin was going to be up for that anytime soon. She kept trying to carve out a spot to get comfortable so she could take a nap. I thought I could provide her some comfort, so I patted my left leg, inviting her to rest her head there if she wanted.

Tutu tsked. "She's not a dog, Locke." She eyed me as she said it. Well, Penny was the only successful female relationship that I had, so really, that should be a compliment.

Guin's enchanting, melodic voice filled the air as she politely declined, but I could see her practically squirming again. She looked so tired that she was uncomfortable. And she really was eyeing my leg. I watched her squirm with amusement.

"Comfy?" I asked and her eyes narrowed.

I patted my shoulder to give her another option and laughed as Tutu said, "Now you're just doing it on purpose, Locke."

But Guin relented, and to my surprise, she laid her head on my shoulder. My body tensed as enchanting sea pheromones swarmed around me. And the tension didn't ease, even when she fell asleep right away.

"Not a word," I said to Tutu.

She mimicked a quiet sound, and then immediately broke that promise. "How did her treatment go? Were you ok with taking her? Going inside?" Her rapid-fire questions flew quietly over to me.

This was her way of making sure I went inside. But I just said, "It went well, I think. We go back on Thursday. But don't think I've forgotten that you've got your end of the bargain to hold up."

"Well, if Louis comes around, I most certainly will," she replied slyly. We both knew that man was not coming around after being left on stage as she ran away. Tutu was going to need to reach out to him.

"Uh huh, we'll be talking about it." But my eyelids were falling heavily. You would have thought I'd had a treatment too. I had done nothing today other than accompany Guin to the center. Why was *I* so exhausted? But my eyelids continued to droop downward. And Clark Gable dancing with Joan Crawford was becoming all too fuzzy.

The next thing I knew, the phone was ringing beside me, and my upper body was laid out on the sofa with the Mermaid on top of me. *This had to stop happening.* I was *not* her sea anemone. But obviously she was my clown fish. Because I had my arms wrapped around her body, clinging to her like my life depended on it.

I released my hold immediately, hoping she hadn't noticed, trying to figure out a way to get to the phone without disturbing her. I couldn't believe my movements hadn't awoken her. She was in a deep slumber, and it was worrying me. I hadn't really believed her when she said she could sleep like the dead because of her conditions. Slowly, I picked the phone off the ringer with my one free hand so it would stop ringing. Then I said "one minute" quietly into the receiver, buying myself some time until I could get my sea anemone tentacles from around her.

I was sure it was Dean calling with a question from the shop and he would be kind enough to hold until I could properly make my exit. Surprisingly, it was very easy not to disturb Guin even with my clumsy movements. Feeling proud, I took the phone out onto the lanai. Few people called our landline phone, but Tutu still refused to get herself a cell phone. She said she'd survived almost eighty years without one, so what was a few more years? There was something to be said for that. Sometimes I felt like chucking mine into the sea, but I had a business to run.

"Hey, this is Locke. Sorry about that," I answered, expecting Dean.

I got a man's voice, but it wasn't Dean's jovial tone. No, it was a smooth, deep whiskey tone . . . *no, it couldn't be.* I seriously wanted to be this man when I was older. Or heck, how about now?

"Hey, Locke. This is, well . . . this is Louis from the other night. I was trying to reach Cass . . . uh Lani–Kelani . . . I mean your grandmother," he finally finished. *Yeah, you were.* Oh man, this guy had it bad. "Luna gave me this number, but–"

"No, it's alright. But–"

"But you don't think it's a good idea, huh?" Wow, he was blunt. I liked this guy.

"I didn't say that. . ."

"But it's not looking good, is it?" He laughed slightly. "Can you tell me my chances? How bad did I ruin things? I know you don't know me, but Luna told me a little about you and, well, you sound like a standup guy. I figured you'd shoot straight with me." There was a long pause. "Nevermind, I'm sorry I called. And uh, sorry about kissing your grandmother in front of you like that too." The deep timbre in his voice trembled for the first time, exposing a vulnerability under his smooth exterior. Apparently a lot when it came to my grandmother.

"No, wait. I heard the story."

There was a heavy exhale. "The real one?" he asked.

"Well, is there a decoy?"

He laughed, and it sounded like a Harlem jazz club announcer had just made a joke. "Yeah, I'm sure there is. So do I take this as a decent sign if you're still talking to me?"

"Yes, I'm pulling for you at least. My grandmother deserves to be treated well, *finally*. And she's obviously still very much in love with you, but you *didn't* hear it from me."

"Well, Luna was right about you." He chuckled. Then he sobered, pain lacing his tone. "Still? I wasn't ever sure there was a first place . . . Either way, I should have done more to fight for her. I should have stayed. Even if she wasn't ultimately going to choose me. It never was just about that . . ." His voice broke off. "How *much* do you know?"

"I'm pretty sure I know most of it, Louis. We had a long talk last night. I know she played the ukulele with you after her concerts and taught you what she knew about the instrument. And then she fell in love with you. And she wishes she would have gone with you to California. I wish she had too."

There was a long pause. "Part of me always thought she'd have a better life without me . . . with all the things I couldn't give her. When I heard your grandfather passed, I never had the courage to contact her . . . and then I saw her last night. And finally getting to sing together like we had always wanted–in the way we always wanted–did something to me. My stage name was even the Big Dipper–given to me by your grandmother no less–and I always hoped she might come join me as the little one." He laughed slightly as he said it. "I've always saved her a spot, always been waiting for her to complete that missing piece, and I just . . . I just got carried away last night. End of story, I'm sorry."

And I could tell he wasn't just talking about a missing piece in the band. "No, *you* were her great love. You better believe that, especially if you're going to go after her because I can tell you it won't be easy. But not because she wishes you had done things differently. That wasn't part of her story at all. She seems to blame herself somehow. She's the one that didn't go with you. And she still feels bad about it . . ." A debate came over me as I tried to decide what I should tell him next. "I don't know that I should tell you this, and you're not to 'know' unless she tells you herself . . ."

"Ok. . ." He braced himself. "You have my word." And I really felt like his "word" meant something. I looked through the glass doors, Tutu had found herself a quilt to work on so she could keep Guin company while she slept. A silent war raged in me. This felt like such a betrayal of trust.

"Louis, what my grandmother endured with my grandfather wasn't easy, but what she has ahead of her to endure is going to be even harder. I'm afraid life's not been fair, and that's always hardest to watch when it happens to the best person you know. But you seem to be the rainbow amongst it all for her. That's why I'm going to tell you this."

I could hear him swallow hard. "Locke, I'm sure I don't deserve to be called that. I let her down once already. I think it's much more likely that you're the rainbow in her life from what I can see. But I want the chance to be there for her now."

"How about tonight?" I asked.

"Just tell me the time and place," he responded without pause.

"You don't care what it is, do you?" I said with shock. What I had told Tutu had been correct. He was her Cary Grant.

"I care what it is for her, but not for me, if that's what you're asking."

"Yeah, that's what I figured. I knew you were a good guy. But, well, she's convinced it's unfair to you. That choosing you now would be the worst thing she could do to you . . . it's Alzheimer's, Louis." I had never said that word out loud. It was too painful. And we certainly didn't tell people who weren't family. My mom knew, and that was about it. Tutu's friends had basically guessed her condition, but we never spoke the word Alzheimer's. We left so many things unsaid.

"Locke, I will never stop loving your grandmother. She's it for me. Always has been. The only other woman that's ever been in my life is music. I just want my chance to be with her, even if I don't deserve it."

"That's exactly what I told her. But I don't think there's anyone that deserves it more, Louis. I'm going to make sure you get that chance tonight."

"You think you can get her to see me?" he asked hesitantly.

"Oh, I know it, Louis. You see, I have a deal with her. How do you feel about double dates?" I asked hopefully.

Locke

CHAPTER 25

I WAS FEELING REALLY proud of myself, but also like I'd just made a bit of a deal with the devil when I stepped back inside the living room. The devil being the fact that now I had to go on this double date myself. There was no other way to get Tutu there otherwise. Even if I tricked her into going somewhere, there was no way she would stay. I saw how quickly she'd fled that stage. But if she thought I was taking Mermaid out, then she *might* just stay. I wondered how I was going to convince Guin to do that for me. But she might do it if I let her in on the plan. She'd do it for Tutu. But it meant having to tell her my plan.

I wasn't exactly sure how I felt about finally getting to go on a date with someone who seemed so similar to me—someone who actually seemed to relate with me . . . only for it to be a *fake* date. I wasn't sure how well my battered dating self-esteem was going to take it, but for Tutu I would do anything. And maybe it would be good practice. Maybe I'd actually learn something. As long as I didn't blur the lines. Because truthfully, one thing I'd wanted most since the accident was for someone to actually see *me*.

Tutu looked up as soon as she heard me quietly close the door behind me, eyeing the phone in my hand. I saw her mind go on full alert. But I needed to talk to Guin first before I figured out how to approach her. I was just about to head over to the slumbering sea siren when Tutu got up. I was definitely fixed in her crosshairs now. *Uh-oh.* I set the phone down gently, wincing as if she could read my face and what I'd just done. That was the thing about me: I was ridiculously easy to read. *Aîa.* That arched eyebrow told me Tutu saw right through me. Before I could even sit down next to Guin, Tutu was shaking her head and pointing to the lanai. *Great.* This would not go well for me. I was not a matchmaker. I couldn't even herd these two together. And they were practically magnetized. It should be a done deal.

A disgruntled sigh left me. Looks like I was going back outside.

"Locke," she said, practically cornering me when we'd reached the balcony. "What have you been doing out here?"

"Nothing," I tried to say coolly.

"Nothing. Really? For all that time? You just dragged the landline out here to do a telethon. You're not exactly talkative enough to fill that much airtime. Let's try this again, shall we?"

"Fine, I wanted it to be a surprise, but I was trying to work out a nice evening for Guin."

She smiled cheekily. "What kind of evening?"

"Hopefully . . . a romantic one." I barely got the words out.

"What's the catch?" she asked right away.

I looked down at my hands, avoiding all eye contact, so she couldn't read me that way.

"Locke–"

"The evening would be for you too," I said as quickly as possible.

"I knew there was a catch. I hardly think I need to chaperone your date, *Keiki*. Sure, it could get awkward with her staying here if it doesn't go well, but I'm sure she'll be happy to remain friends. She's a good person, I can tell. And it's not like I can really help you in this area. Plus, you're more likely to get her unguarded reaction to things without a buffer."

I knew exactly what she meant. Now she was making me nervous, and this wasn't even an actual date. "I appreciate it, but that's not exactly it. This is more of a double-date scenario. I'm invoking the deal."

"*Oh no*. No, no, no." She turned to leave, but I grabbed her arm gently. Then she asked, "*Keiki*, what have you done?"

"I didn't really have to do anything." But she looked at me sternly. "You're in high demand, and a double date would help me feel better. It would help me feel more comfortable. So, when one of your suitors called, I extended an invitation."

She scoffed, "Because I have so many of those." She rolled her eyes. "Did he really call? Please tell me *you* did not call *him.*" I nodded to confirm. She looked perturbed but said, "This is really the only way you'll take Guin out?"

I nodded again. I couldn't believe this was working, but I knew she not only wanted to help me, she also secretly wanted to meet Louis. She would absolutely kill me if she knew I was faking it. Although, this double date did not seem like a bad idea considering what I had been through on the battlefield they called dating. However, I don't think anything screamed "I have issues" quite like taking your grandmother on your double date.

Tutu breathed heavily.

"Ok. Anything for you, you know that. *Tonight, really?*"

I nodded. It seemed to be all I could do. I guess I just didn't want to screw things up. The less I said, the better. I did not want to give her time to overthink it or back out.

She gently chided me, "Fine, but you need to work on your timing. More of a heads up would have been nice."

"I guess I get my time management skills from you. That VRBO check-in window was *awfully* small. But don't worry, you'll have a little more time than that one."

She just laughed at me. "I guess I should go get ready then. And Locke, wear a color tonight. I know you own something *other* than black."

I shook my head at her, but then I noticed Mermaid poking her head over the sofa to look at us. I guess it was weird for us to be having a secret huddle on the lanai. But it was going to be her turn next. *Great, round three for me.* And by far the toughest. I hoped I didn't get knocked out this time. I'd come so far.

"I'm proud of you, Locke. I think Guin could be a really great fit for you. At least she could show you there are caring women out there. That it is possible to still share a connection with someone and have some wonderful dates. Glad you finally admitted your feelings for her." Smiling, Tutu left me.

Feelings? Finally? What? No, this was for *her*. But she was right: this could be good for me. Even a good fake date would count as a victory. I ran a hand through my hair, sighing a little heavily. *Here we go.* I was going to look like a gigantic idiot if she said no. I had made some big promises.

I kept looking at Guin, hoping she would come out. And as if she read my mind, here she came. She slid the door open slightly and poked her head out. "Is it ok if I come out?" she asked almost bashfully. Since when was she timid with me? "Sorry I slept so long. Those treatments just really take it out of me."

"Yes, please come out. How are you feeling?" I asked.

"Better now after resting, thanks. And thanks again for coming with me today."

"Of course. I'm glad that I did. Thanks for asking me. But uh, there's something I wanted to ask you." I could already feel the lump forming in my throat. *Not real, Locke. It's not real.* I kept reminding myself. How was I even going to approach this? "Uh," I tried, raking my hands through my hair *again*.

"You ok?" she asked with concern.

"Yeah, it's just . . . I don't really know how to ask you this."

She moved a little closer. It was almost like I could feel her body pressed against mine. My mind had obviously memorized her outline from earlier on the sofa, creating an imprint just for her.

"Well, you just sat with me for hours today at a medical facility, and heard all my medical history as the nurses went over it with me. So whatever it is, I think you can ask."

"Would you go out on a date with me?" I blurted out, my body turning toward her. I raked a hand down my face. "I mean, it's not what you think." Quickly, I held my hands out in front of me. "Would you go on a *fake* double date with me tonight? I mean, if you feel up to it."

"Ok, I'm totally lost now." Her eyes were bigger than Ariel's.

My nerves had completely taken over as I rubbed my chin, trying to figure out a way to put this so as not to freak her out even more. I tried to slow down. "Would you be my double date so that Tutu can go out with Louis? I don't think I can get her to go out with him any other way. He called earlier, and this was the brilliant plan I came up with to give him an opening. Now I'm thinking maybe I should have just left him to fend for himself."

"No," she said, quickly.

"Right. Probably best. *Good call,*" I said so quickly the words ran together. I turned toward the door, but she reached for my arm, sending a shockwave through me. That got my attention. *All of it.* And I turned to peer deeply into those clear blue seas.

"No, Locke. I didn't mean that. I meant you shouldn't have just let him fend for himself. I love what you did. Of course, I'll be your double date. Did Tutu actually agree? She seemed really freaked out after that kiss. I mean, it was incredibly steamy, so I think I would have fled too."

Good to note. Stop it now, Locke. You are not taking any Mermaid notes. Take your little clam shell pad and chuck it way out of your reach.

"Well," I began, "That's the thing . . . We have to make this look real."

"What?" She seemed to pale. The word barely croaked out of her.

"Tutu seems to have a little fantasy about you and me

getting together. Probably because I'm sure she'd love for you to be her granddaughter. Nothing to worry about." But her mind seemed anything but worry free. Especially since her eyes stayed frozen on me. Almost like I'd delivered the worst news possible.

"So she thinks you really asked me out?" she questioned tightly.

"Yup."

"And why would Tutu believe you need this? Why would *you* need a double date?" she asked.

"Not really important, *Mermaid*," I said with strain.

"No, I think it's pretty important," she rebutted.

"Can we just focus? It's just one night, and then we'll tell her there weren't any sparks between us or however you'd like to phrase it. Hopefully, one night will be enough to set things off for her and Louis," I explained.

"Oh, no doubt. They already had the whole Fourth of July firework parade going." I laughed at her joke. "Kind of funny that we're going to get obliterated. That we can't even manage a few sparks. Now I kind of at least want a sparkler." I couldn't help but laugh again at her humor.

"Yeah, well, I wouldn't be so sure. Tutu is really nervous. She said she wouldn't see him again because of her condition. I had to really pull out all the stops for this one. And I never want to put any pressure on her. That's the last thing I would want to do. But I didn't want her to miss an opportunity because of self-doubt. My grandfather instilled enough of that in her. The double date takes some of the pressure off."

"So what's the plan then? Where are we going and what are we doing?" Her curiosity was rising.

"Well, I had thought about whale watching, but you're kind of stuck on a boat for that. Nowhere to run, so she might feel trapped. So I thought of dinner at Whalers Village followed by an outdoor movie shown by Tommy Bahama. Something low-key so the night can end at any time." I looked at Guin skeptically. "So, did I do ok?"

"Yes, you did perfectly. As stress-free of a date as you can get." Disbelief was written all over her face.

"Well, when you have enough stressful ones, you kind of learn. So casual and comfy for tonight works great. I don't want to make this weird for you. Although, I will miss that red dress." Her blush bloomed right along with mine. *Great, I hadn't meant to say that.* I had just made it weird. I really was clueless.

"Anything for Tutu. I'm happy to help. I want to see how things go for them. But, um, *how much* am I helping?" Her voice got small.

Right, we had to *act* interested. I put my hand up to my chin, rubbing it awkwardly. "Well, Tutu obviously thinks there's interest, so I think we should just leave it there. Good enough."

Wow, that probably made it worse.

"Going on a date is a little different, Locke. I know you don't actually want to go on one with me, but . . . well, that's why I kind of need to know–"

"I never said that," I cut her off, never wanting her to think that. "I just said I thought it was a *bad idea.*"

Guin looked down at the floor like it was the most interesting thing in the world. Why was this feisty woman going shy on me again?

My voice came out soft, something it kept doing on its own with her. "Hey, uh, how about we just treat tonight as a first date? We'll just do everything we would on a real first date, such as holding hands, etcetera," I said helpfully.

"You hold hands on a first date?" she said in sweet surprise, her eyes snapping up to mine. *Ensnared.* I gulped.

"Well, I would if my dates lasted long enough," I half-joked. "If I was on an actual first date with you, I definitely would."

Full blush ahead. The air had turned heady, and my hand already wanted to find its way to hers.

That seemed to scare her away sufficiently since she quickly said, "I'll go get ready so you don't have to wait on me. I'm super slow," she said, in a half-apology. She started toward the door, turning back briefly as if remembering something, and said, "No one should run away from you, Locke." Then she headed inside, taking her pink cheeks right along with her.

I sensed this was going to be a very long night. I had *already* started blurring the lines. And my wayward brain couldn't wait to blur them some more. Why did I want to be captured so badly by a mermaid? Why was I hoping she had any interest in me? And why was I willing to believe she'd be different from the others?

Perhaps this was as much for me as it was for Tutu. And that thought definitely scared me.

I SAT ON THE SOFA, waiting for Guin and Tutu to get ready. Honestly, I wasn't sure who I was prepared to see first. I wasn't even sure how I was going to get through this evening. Pretending wasn't in my nature. I was blunt and straightforward to a fault. So much so that it could scare people away and make me appear rough and intimidating. If you didn't know me and couldn't read me, then I didn't appear to be the warmest person. Once you knew me, though, I was hopefully more of a gentle giant than I seemed. Even King Kong had a softer side. Especially for one blonde in particular.

Tutu was the first one to make an appearance, coming out in a beautiful light blue dress. One I had never seen before. It certainly wasn't one of her Hawaiian floral dresses. It had a silky texture and looked like something from a bygone era. A loose, flowing dress with a 1940s style and fabric covered buttons all the way down the front. It seemed she might have been saving this one.

Her eyes flooded with doubt. "Uh, this dress is just something I used to wear when I played my ukulele concerts in the park. I used to go thrift store shopping to find old styles that matched my jazz music. You know me, such a romantic. *Silly me.*" She backed up and quickly found the door to her room.

"Tutu, stop. You look absolutely beautiful. Please don't change. I'm sure you look just as beautiful now as you did then."

She scoffed. "You're sweet. *Always* so sweet, Locke. But hardly. Luckily, I found one of the more generously cut dresses . . . I have to admit it is nice to wear again. I always felt so happy in it. And it was one of the best times of my life."

I knew she didn't need a generously cut one. Eating had become more difficult for her recently. She didn't have the same appetite anymore. I was constantly trying to get her to eat something. Food just didn't seem to have the same appeal. "Well, I can see why. You look gorgeous, Grandma."

She smiled. "Well, I added a belt. That covers a multitude of sins."

"I'm not even going to pretend to know what that means. Louis is *very* lucky." Her coloring paled at this, as if remembering whom she was going to meet. Obviously the dress was very much chosen for him. It sounded like she hadn't worn it since she had last been with him. And she probably had never worn it for anyone *but* him. The dress existed in a time capsule, just like their love.

I stood up from the sofa, and she came over to stand beside me. Her salt-and-pepper hair was pulled back with a white flower clip and twisted upward in the back. I'd never seen her like this. She truly looked like a different person. There was an infectious glow about her, and I could see nervous energy buzzing through her.

Tutu's eyes roamed over me with a twinkle, taking in the light aqua blue shirt I was wearing. I was *attempting* to show my softer side. And . . . the color made me think of Mermaid's eyes. So I thought it might be a color she liked. Not that I should think in that way. *Just remember . . . It's all fake, Locke.* But I needed to get in the mindset, I justified to myself.

I could tell Tutu was just about to say something to me when we both heard a creaking floorboard. Tutu's eyebrows lifted upward, both of us knowing exactly who that would be. *Here we go.* I felt an urge of sudden primal flight. I needed to remember this was for Tutu. *I could do this.* We both turned slowly, expecting to see Guin . . . "My date."

But my eyes were not prepared to see Guin in a devastating black dress. Her eyes had immediately found mine, assessing how I would react to her wearing that dress, which I think was put on this Earth to drive me mad. Definitely not something I thought she would choose to wear. The thinnest straps were holding the satin dress up, and a lightly embossed floral pattern shone on the fabric if the light hit it just right. I stared blankly, my throat going dry. *So much for comfy and casual.*

And here Tutu had told *me* to wear anything but black. It

was almost as if Guin had worn it for me, but she couldn't, possibly. This was fake. I couldn't even allow myself to think that way. It wasn't just dangerous; it was guaranteed destruction. Plus, it wasn't like she'd gone out and bought it specifically for our date. After all, she had packed it for this trip, intending to wear it. But that thought was doing nothing to assuage my worries. Because all I could see were her curves as she made her way down the hallway. Every step she took closer to me made me feel less and less prepared for this bewitching force. There was an undeniable quality about her. She was the first woman I'd been attracted to in a *very* long time. And she was the first one who seemed to understand what it was like to be looked at differently.

My wayward eyes scanned every inch of her, slowly making their way up her body to meet her eyes. I felt a surge of electricity between us. *Could she feel it too?* Suddenly, she halted. *Oh no, she had changed her mind.* Well, this was going to be embarrassing. *Geez, I couldn't even get a fake date.* But then she said, "Sorry, I forgot a jacket. I'll be back in one second."

I breathed out a sigh of relief at her words, but only momentarily. Because when she turned to go down the hallway, the back of her was even more devastating than the front. Those tiny straps continued in the back, making one large crisscross across her back that was on *full* display. The fabric starting just below the small of her back. *Nope, no way. I can't do this. Louis can do this by himself or I could call Reef. Maybe he's at Whalers tonight. Maybe he can handle a sea siren. But not me. Nope.* I raked a hand down my face. *Oh God, help me.*

Apparently the last words had not been so silent because Tutu laughed. "Still feeling good about this deal, Locke?" she joked with me. "You should be. Guess I should have let you wear black." But I was too speechless to respond. Tutu continued, "I think I might only impede your extremely hot date. How about I just stay home tonight? I think I'll change into some PJs. My Snuggie is around here somewhere."

But it was my turn to grab her arm.

She eyed me and then said, "You should feel good about this, *Keiki*. She obviously really likes you. Women don't put on dresses like that for men they don't like, Locke."

Unless it's pretend. And she was putting on quite the show. Perhaps that's why she went *so* above and beyond. She was going to need a lot of help to pull off this date. Maybe she thought the dress would do most of the work for her. I was certainly sold. It felt real to me.

But as I looked down at Tutu, her beautiful dress seemed to echo and validate her words. Seemed like she was speaking from experience–maybe even from the one of getting ready for tonight. "But . . . I told Guin she could wear something casual–comfortable." I felt bad. I sure hope she didn't feel she had to dress up for this.

"Exactly, *Keiki*." I groaned at her impish tone. "Can you just try to enjoy it? Finally, there's a very nice and beautiful woman who is interested in you . . . and who you like too."

"I don't–" But I stopped myself, remembering.

"Oh, but you do. You asked her out, didn't you?" Her eyes pierced me.

Oh no, she was already seeing through this, wasn't she?

Guin's sweet voice returned. "Sorry, I run so hot and cold. I sometimes get bone-aching chills. My body seems to think it's Halloween most of the time. I can't ever seem to get warm enough when they happen. I know it seems crazy to need a heavy sweater in Hawaii."

"Not at all, dear, but I'm pretty sure Locke can keep you

warm." Tutu's eyes drifted up to me mischievously. "Right, *Keiki*?"

"Oh, uh . . ." Guin seemed as flustered as I felt.

Great, Tutu was calling malarkey. I looked at the most beautiful women I'd ever seen and swallowed down my reservations before I lost my nerve. I would worry about the damage I did to myself later. "Yes, most definitely. I'd be lucky for a woman this beautiful to let me keep her warm . . . You look gorgeous," I said looking at Guin.

Guin's face rose in flames. She looked so taken aback that she literally stumbled backwards a little. Her black slides with the white soles thankfully caught her. I couldn't help but smile at her little slip-on sneakers. Not what I thought she would have worn with a dress like this, and I really couldn't have loved it more. I don't think I could have been attracted to her anymore.

I bridged the gap between us, her eyes looking at me with the utmost shock. I put an arm around her waist and steadied her. Finding her eyes, I looked into those beautiful blue pools and tried to stabilize her. And I suddenly found my face right beside hers. *What was I planning to do here?* Not really knowing what was first-fake-date appropriate, I lightly kissed her cheek. My instincts just kind of took over me. Her breath caught beside me and I had to stop myself from laughing. I kind of loved surprising her.

Her breath tickled my ear. "What happened to hand-holding?" she breathed.

"What happened to *just casual*?" I pulled away slightly to look down at her, our faces only inches apart, gazes locked. "All my plans went out the window when you wore that dress. There's no way a man won't respond to that. You just raised the ante. But don't worry, I will *still* hold your hand." Humor rose in me.

She looked at me, floored.

"Can I take that for you?" I said loud enough for Tutu to hear and nodded to her jacket. I think Guin's mouth was going to stay permanently open. I reached out my hand for her sweater, but she just shook her head. So I asked, "Are you ready?" I backed away to give Guin her space and to include Tutu in the conversation.

I looked over at the doggie bed where Penny and Sebastian were snuggled away for the evening. They were really becoming inseparable. I guess they had decided the excitement was over and they could get cozy for the evening. They had sat up on full alert every time Guin came out of her room this evening. Almost like they sensed the anticipation. I think I even heard one of them sigh when she'd gone back in her room the last time and they'd laid back down to wait on her. It was really cute to see.

Referring to the dogs, I said, "I fed them already. They should be fine until we get back if you're ok leaving them. But we can take Sebastian with us if you'd like. Restaurants aren't too lax about Penny, though. Neither are the patrons."

I knew all too well how people felt about emotional support dogs and the rights they should or *shouldn't* have.

Guin looked over at them, an expression of contemplation forming in her eyes. She'd said Sebastian was her emotional support as well. And when did you need emotional support more than on a date? Especially a stressful, fake one. I knew I relied on Penny to help with anxiety, *especially* social anxiety.

"Uh, no. That's ok. Thank you. I trust you to take care of me."

That had to be the sexiest thing anyone had ever said to me.

Adrenaline shot straight through my core and now pulsed through me. It wasn't enough for her to look like that. No, now she had to say things like this too. I was really doomed.

"Of course I will." There was no question about that. I would do everything I could to take care of her. And with those words, my hand slowly reached out to find hers. My fingers carefully brushed down her hand and intertwined with hers in a way I wasn't ever going to forget. This part *wasn't* fake. This part I meant. Actually, I realized my part would not be fake, at all, anymore. Perhaps none of it had been. But once I let this wall down, it was impossible to hide my feelings or lie to myself anymore. I was *completely* taken by this mermaid.

Guinevere

CHAPTER 26

WITH LOCKE'S fingers wound tightly around mine, I tried to look for anything to distract me. What did he think he was doing making that type of comment about my dress? I was completely confused. He'd wanted nothing to do with me, and now, suddenly, he was acting like I'd undone him with this simple piece of fabric. No, he must be just that good of an actor.

His words from the other night kept ringing in my ears: *"Not a good idea, Mermaid."*

Why had I even worn this? It was foolish. *So* very foolish of me. First the red dress and now this. It really wasn't like me. It felt like I was trying to get another reaction out of him, especially after his response to my dress last night. Like I was trying to go for round two. And the black dress that I had packed in case of emergency–that I never really intended to wear–had called to me from the very bottom of my suitcase.

The more I thought about how he had looked at me last night, the further I had dug into the depths of my luggage. I didn't know what emergency I was expecting when I had packed this dressy thing. I never wore anything like this. My wardrobe matched what you would expect from a children's book illustrator. I wore retro clothing that was fun in a nostalgic and wholesome way. I certainly didn't put my *whole* back on display. And being a children's book illustrator didn't help one bit. Locke's Disney princess references only confirmed that for me. So maybe I wanted to buck that stereotype a little. *Ok, maybe a lot.* I was just too intimidated to do it. But the more I thought about him sitting and reading to me today, and asking me if he could come back with me to my next appointment, the more courage I gained. And just like that, the black dress was on me. No looking back.

My eyes looked over to Tutu, trying to distract myself from the man standing so close to me. His massively tall frame was so near to me that I could feel his intoxicating body warmth. I didn't need to look at him to remember how he looked tonight; it was seared in my memory. I hadn't seen him wear anything but black before. All the wetsuits he wore were black; even the tee and jeans he wore today were both black. But now he was wearing a soft baby blue color. It was funny that Tutu was wearing blue too, but hers was a cornflower hue, and I'm sure they hadn't planned it. Because I was pretty sure Locke rarely wore much color.

The sleeves of his Columbia button-up shirt were rolled up, stretched tight against his forearm muscles, and his dark jeans hugged him in all the right places. I actually felt bad for checking him out like this. He wanted me to fake it, not actually do it. Not burn his sexy image into my retinas. He'd been clear with me several times. *So again, what was I doing in this dress?* Taunting myself. Because the one person—the one man—who wanted to sit beside me while I literally bled didn't *actually* want me.

I forced myself to move on to happier thoughts. Looking at the gorgeous dress Tutu was wearing I said, "Tutu you look stunning. Wow, Louis is so lucky. Are you excited to see him again tonight?"

"*You* look gorgeous, Guin. My grandson is the lucky one," Tutu said with a big grin, the biggest one I'd seen on her yet. She was loving this situation, and that fact made me feel a little guilty. I really hoped tonight worked out for her and Louis.

I felt Locke squeeze my hand as if he was agreeing with her, and it sent a jolt of electricity through me. I couldn't help but look over at him. Squeezes like that were just for me. *Why is he doing that?* Tutu couldn't hear or see his whispers or hand squeezes. He was only unnerving me further.

Tutu said, "I was just debating if I was ready for tonight." She chuckled, but it came out so nervously.

"We can wait. Take your time," I replied sincerely. I could only imagine. I didn't know the full story, but I knew it was going to take a lot of courage to show up tonight.

"No, he's probably been waiting for me to come to my

senses for decades. I don't want to keep him waiting any longer."

Locke quickly replied, "It's a little more complicated than that. You were in a difficult situation, Grandma. If anything, I'm sure he wishes he could have made things easier for you. Actually, I know that." His voice was firm but quiet when he spoke.

Tutu just looked at Locke. There seemed to be some sort of unspoken message passing between the two that I wasn't privy to. "Well, I'm as ready as I'm ever going to be. Although, my Snuggie sounds pretty good." She laughed. "But this is something I never thought I'd get to do . . . go on a double date with my grandson. I certainly don't want to miss that," she teased Locke, shifting the mood. "Let's see if my grandson has any Casanova moves in him."

"Oh yes, let's see," I said joyfully.

"Be careful what you ask for, Mermaid," he said, challenging me. Oh man, if I hadn't just upped the ante before, I now set the table on fire.

We made our way down to the Jeep, where Locke opened the doors for both Tutu and me, but not before he placed his hand on the small of my back against my skin. "Oh, the ante's going way up," he whispered against my ear as he opened the door for me.

"Is it too late to get *my* Snuggie?" I turned my face slightly toward him.

"Oh, *way* too late."

I could barely get my wobbly legs into the car. And the car ride wasn't much better. I certainly didn't need to worry about Tutu thinking this was fake. Our stubbornness had come out in full force, and neither one of us was going to be yelling "mercy" anytime soon in this dating game of chicken. I'm not sure how this escalated so quickly. Maybe that's what happens when you try bottling up your feelings. I guess I should have said no to this fake date after all. I was already having a lot of trouble with the "fake" part of this date, and the night was still young.

Faint streams of the remaining sunlight were weaving their way into the car as the sun became weaker, just like me. Locke's effect was gaining a bigger hold over me. I tried to talk with Tutu, who had insisted on sitting in the back, even though I had practically fought her for it. Although now I wish I had fought harder because I was left defenseless to Locke's "next level" of fake dating, and I wasn't fairing well. His hand was just above my knee, thumb moving in tantalizing circular patterns. And my breathing was becoming more edgy and ragged with each stroke.

He looked over at me. "You okay, Mermaid? Sounds like you're breathing a little hard. Do you need me to turn on the AC or something?"

He moved his hand up a little higher. "No." My voice squeaked higher with his movement. "I'm fine. I'm just worried about your driving ability. Don't you need *two* hands on the wheel?"

"Nope. I drive much better like this, actually. Thanks for your concern though."

I heaved out a sigh, my chest rising. And I looked up at the sky. He'd left the canvas off the Jeep since we weren't expecting rain. I counted to ten because feelings for him—ones I should *not* be having—were flooding me.

"Meditating?" he interrupted.

"No, but I think I should be," I replied sternly.

He started drawing larger circles, and my hand shot out and grasped onto his, effectively stopping his bone-melting movements. Although now his hand just felt ridiculously good in mine—all warm and rough. Like sea glass on a sunny day. Surfing and repair work had made his skin rough enough to rub against mine in all the best possible ways.

Now it was his turn to inhale raggedly. Tutu leaned forward slightly in between our seats. "So, this is a fun car ride . . . But um, Locke, mind telling me what you have planned?" I guess she thought it was a good idea to ease the mounting tension.

"It's a surprise. But I think you'll enjoy it. I promise, I've got your back. And if you want to leave, just use our sandcastle club sign." Tutu laughed at his words.

"Oh, I need to know the sign now. Tutu, please tell me," I requested swiftly.

"*No.*" Embarrassment flooded him. "And why would she? You'd probably be using it to bail on me," he joked.

"Yes, I can't give it to you. I have high hopes for this evening." Tutu grinned at me.

But Locke glanced over at my disappointed face. I saw this torn look on his features, like he didn't want me to be left out. It was actually pretty sweet of him. "Ok, but no laughing . . . especially if I'm letting you into the masked mouse sand club."

"The sand—"

"Watch it." I bit back a laugh at his stern tone.

Tutu cut in. "Oh yes, Locke was obsessed with both Mickey Mouse and Zorro. Well, Mickey's Steamboat Willie character. Those old reruns would come on late at night, and they always aired back-to-back. They were both in black and white, and he liked those best. Well, since he was so young, he started blurring the characters together. And he imagined this masked mouse. He'd get so excited after the TV shows that the only way to expel his energy, and save my furnishings, was to take him down to the beach. We would go hunt for hermit crabs in the moonlight. They came out of their holes on the shore at night and ventured further away from their homes. He would jump in the waves and dig in the sand to find the crabs when they burrowed back in their holes. He's always been a handful, but I wouldn't have him any other way. Those were our favorite nights together. Just the two of us. And when he had spent all his energy, we would lie on a blanket, and I would try teaching him the constellations."

Locke's grip on my hand tightened while Tutu told the story. I got the feeling few people got to hear this one. Maybe he was subconsciously asking me to take it easy on him. My eyes looked over at him, and I smiled. I hope he took that as my agreement. "So how does the sign come in?" I asked.

"Oh, he had a sign for when he spotted a crab. It also became the secret code for entry into our club or to signify when he wanted to go to the beach for our special time." I raised my eyebrows at her, waiting. "Let's just say he pretended to be a masked mouse with a cape. It was pretty adorable. I can't do it like he can. I couldn't even back then. It's a *full-body* gesture."

I couldn't stop laughing trying to envision all the different ways he might do that. "You should probably just tell me. My imagination is *very active*, Locke. And what I'm coming up with involves costumes, and I don't see you being able to work any of what I'm envisioning into tonight's activities as a signal." I could barely get the words out through my giggles.

Locke replied, "I don't see how this is anywhere in the realm of 'watching it,' Mermaid . . . *But* . . . I figured Tutu would just do a mask or cape gesture and I would get the picture."

"Yeah, because it's *so easy* to work those into normal

conversational hand gestures." I accidentally snorted in laughter. "Well, maybe for you it is though."

"You're going to be a permanent member of the club when you're sleeping on the beach." He threatened.

"Aww, so you want me to be part of the club? Like the three amigos. I'm honored, Locke. But just so I'm properly inducted, you should probably show me the signal," I teased relentlessly.

Tutu burst out laughing in the back. "I actually would love to see him do the full gesture again," she chimed. "It's like a modified version of the yoga dancer's pose, except he's supposed to be flying with a cape. And then his hand goes over his eyes like a mask–only he looks more like an explorer." She giggled.

"Tutu! That's our private family signal."

"I guess you'll just need to make Guin part of the family then," Tutu said plainly, like it was an obvious solution.

The Jeep seemed to veer a little and then it got a little bumpy as he had steered over to the rough shoulder of the road. I guess Tutu shouldn't have said anything that bold while Locke was driving.

Locke cleared his throat and let go of my hand, putting both hands tightly back on the wheel now. At least I'd won that brief victory.

"Let's just work on making sure she can do the signal first," he managed.

And with that, we drove the brief rest of the way in silence. Locke pulled the Jeep into the parking lot. It seemed like no time had passed at all. Things seemed to move way too fast. I was not ready for this night to begin officially. I wasn't even doing well with the warmup. *I think I've put in my time.* I was ready to Lyft back home.

But as I glanced at Tutu in the rearview mirror, I knew I would do no such thing. She looked truly exquisite but also extremely nervous, and I wanted to help her as much as I could. So I swallowed my pride and got out of the car. Locke was already at my door, holding it open for me since I had taken so long debating.

However, the bigger problem was that Tutu wasn't moving. Locke went to open her door too, but I stopped him, putting a hand on his chest. My gesture halted him immediately, and he looked down at me. His eyes searched mine for understanding.

"Just let her have some time, Locke. It's hard enough to be a woman going on a date, but I can't imagine what she must be facing.

He seemed to consider my words deeply as another thought struck him. "Guin, I really meant it when I said you looked gorgeous tonight. None of that was for show. I hope you know—"

"Why don't you show me that signal," I cut him off. The black sleeve covering my fistula seemed to dig deeper into my arm, like it was unbearably tight.

He just nodded with a half smile. "Ok, let me help you get inducted into the club. Do you know the yoga dancer's pose Tutu was talking about? I don't, but I'm assuming it should get us close enough. Then you're going to make a mask gesture." He started making these ridiculous movements over his face.

I burst out laughing. "Fine, I'll do that, but I'm not doing the yoga pose," I remarked looking down at my dress. His face grew slightly red as he laughed at his absentmindedness. Maybe at my attempted hand motions too. He was miming me, and we were having a weird war of over-exaggerated hand gestures when we heard the car door open.

"I'm going to put you out of your misery, Guin." Tutu chuckled. "Okay, let's go. I'm ready to see what my grandson could have planned." Locke went over to her and gave her a hug of encouragement. Then he came over and extended a hand to me, his palm up. It wasn't presumptuous. It was a sweet invitation, checking to see if I was still in for tonight. And after staring at his hand for probably a little too long, I took it. And there was something in me that breathed a sigh of relief as I did.

Guinevere

WE WALKED TOGETHER like we were going down the yellow brick road. I was pretty sure that was a fair depiction because Louis was Tutu's "somewhere *under* the rainbow." Their rendition still played through my mind, and my nerves kicked into overdrive for Tutu just remembering the other night.

When we arrived at the Hula Grill, Locke went to the

hostess stand to check us in, but we had already spotted who we were meeting. Louis would stick out anywhere with his "old school" jazz style of dress. His sapphire blue fedora was a splash of contrasting color against the straw of the tiki hut umbrellas. The ones that festively shaded the outdoor tables on the patio area overlooking the distant ocean. And Louis seemed to admire the view. Perhaps distracting himself to avoid thinking about the chance that Tutu might not show. I guess he was trying not to get his hopes up. His white button-up shirt, matching blue suspenders, and handkerchief made him look distinguished in the best possible way. He had his hand poised under his chin as if he was Rodin's *The Thinker*. And his leg was crossed over his knee in the cool way it seemed only musicians could pull off and not look like they were trying too hard.

But as soon as Louis felt Tutu's gaze, he knew she was here. His body went still, and slowly he turned, his eyes latching onto Tutu as he straightened. And his whole body took on a different posture and tone. He was completely alert, acutely aware of her presence. And his expression wrecked me . . . there was something so devastating about the way he looked at her. Like he'd been waiting his whole life to see something this beautiful again. Like he'd been lost without her. And without a second to spare he was on his feet, walking over to meet her.

And it wasn't Locke she grabbed this time. It was *me*. Locke's eyes drifted over to me in confusion. But now was not the time to second guess Tutu's choices. I would gladly help her however she needed. This was her moment, and I wanted her to have it. So I took a shot in the dark, hoping I wasn't overstepping.

"Tutu, I think we may share some of the same fears. And I know it can sometimes feel like we don't have enough to offer–

maybe not anything much to offer on some days–but to the right person, you have everything to give. To the right person, what you can give on your worst days is enough. Because it's *you* giving it." She nodded shakily at me. "I've never seen anyone look at someone the way he looks at you. Be brave enough for those of us who can't believe anyone could look at us that way. Help us believe."

Tutu nodded again, never breaking eye contact with Louis, and then she went to him. Making her way through the sea of tables to the love of her life. Being braver than I could ever be. Showing me that love knows no bounds, especially not the ones set by your conditions, and you just have to be brave enough to believe it.

I stared ahead, transfixed. Locke grabbed my forearm, trying to get my attention. "Guin," he began, but I just shook my head. Locke didn't speak anymore, but he didn't let go of my arm either. He stayed a step behind me as well, allowing me space. Something was feeling real here. And as I watched Louis and Tutu, dreams seemed like they could become possibilities.

I needed to leave. This had suddenly gotten into tender territory. As happy as I was for Tutu, it was time for me to go home. Because I knew this couldn't happen for me. I think my work here was done, anyway. She had successfully made her way to Louis and the two of them were standing together. It felt so intimate, like we shouldn't be here to witness it. Now was time to give them their space.

"I need to go. Locke, I'm sorry. I'll meet you all back home." I didn't look back at him.

"Guin, please don't leave, not like this. You're going to have *that*. Well, hopefully not the decades of *waiting thing*," he tried to joke. "You're too beautiful on the inside and out. Everything you said to Tutu applies to you too. Don't think it doesn't."

He slid his hand down my arm ever so tenderly and interlaced his fingers with mine. "'*O 'oe no*, *aloha*," he breathed. The words seemed to leave him mindlessly.

I turned my face to look back at him even though my eyes were glassy. "What does?–"

"It doesn't translate well. It's just like, 'Don't worry, beautiful.'" I smiled at his words, and he brought his other hand to my waist as he stood right behind me. "So what do you say, will you stay?"

"Well, we probably will need our own table." I glanced back over at the pair who were still taking each other in.

"Probably," he agreed, pulling me closer to him.

My heart was thrumming inside with our connection. And we both just stood there assessing, making sure Tutu didn't need us. Maybe trying to figure out what to do next. And as if the universe knew we needed some guidance, it sent us a rescue signal. Tutu glanced over her shoulder as if questioning why we weren't coming over. Louis seemed to look at us as well. I guess they wanted us to join them. It didn't seem like they were just being polite, either. I think they were both a little lost. They'd just been standing there, completely overwhelmed. Maybe they needed a little normalcy to ease the nerves and tension. Although they were probably barking up the wrong tree here.

"Truce?" Locke whispered behind me. "You don't have to pretend anymore. It's fine for my grandma to know–"

"No, it's ok. I think your grandma is enjoying it way too much. Plus . . . I was too."

He squeezed my hand. "Ok, but only if you're sure. I mean, you were winning anyway." He eyed my dress in such a way that made my knees buckle. I nodded meekly with a little "um hmm" that would have to suffice as a "yes." And he just crooked that smile at me and then guided me to the table with his hand never leaving my waist.

"Hey, sorry," Locke said, extending his arm to Louis. "I'm a little slow tonight. I keep getting mesmerized by my date."

I laughed slightly and shook my head, but Louis just took my hand to introduce himself properly and agreed with Locke. Then he said, "Yes, I was just saying the same thing about Lani." Although, I was pretty sure he had said nothing, but maybe that was the point. He was too speechless.

Locke smiled. "Yes, we're both really lucky."

Then he and Louis pulled out chairs for us. This was certainly a novel experience for me. And I could tell Tutu felt the same way by the look on her face. There was something so simple about the gesture. And I used to not really like things like this. They made me uncomfortable, but I guess I'd never truly had it done out of respect and appreciation. It suddenly took on a whole other feeling.

Seated under the tiki hut umbrella, my senses started soaking in the Hawaiian atmosphere. Under one of the other umbrellas was a ukulele band and a couple of hula dancers. The tiki torches blazed brightly and outlined the patio area with its beautiful view of the ocean. Another gorgeous spot in this paradise. There honestly didn't seem to be an unpleasant view here, especially when this man was beside me. And I wasn't even filtering these thoughts now because it had to be so obvious how I felt.

"Really, Lani," Louis spoke. "You look just as gorgeous as ever. And that dress . . . It's the one you used to wear when we–"

"Yes, when we played together. I saved some of my dresses from our time together. Actually, I haven't worn them since you left. I always thought I would if I ever saw you again. I just never thought it would be . . ."

"So long," he finished desperately.

I smiled and looked at Locke. They were absolutely adorable. There was no simmer; it was all steam. Their connection burned so hot I felt it in my seat. Really, I think they should have let us get our own table. Locke and I just sat there silently, not wanting to interrupt the moment, especially since they were finally talking. Their lost looks had given way to a flood of emotions through their words.

"Lani." There was such an ache in his voice, I didn't think I should be privy to it at this moment.

Locke's leg brushed up against mine under the table with a spine-tingling friction. His eyes locked with mine as he brushed up against me. Not taking it back. It was not a mistake. And I moved a little uncontrollably in my chair, shifting from the electricity reverberating throughout my body.

Isn't there a private tiki umbrella where he can kiss me senselessly? My thoughts roamed freely, *dangerously*. I stared at his lips as I bit mine. And it only encouraged him more. A little sigh escaped me, and his mouth quirked upward immediately.

"Guin, are you alright, dear?" Tutu asked. Apparently my renegade hormones were enough to break her trance. I felt bad for doing so.

"Mmm hmm," I managed, still staring at Locke.

"Are you sure? You're moving around a lot. Is your treatment making you uncomfortable?"

Locke chuckled and put his hand up to his mouth, rubbing it, physically trying to wipe off his grin.

"Oh yes, I'm ok. Something must be coursing through my bloodstream," I said breathily. A sexy, shocked expression registered on Locke's face. He went to reach for my hand across the table in response, but that did not help. I felt a flood of emotions wash over me from his stare, a faraway lost feeling taking over both of us, it seemed.

"Lani, I kind of feel bad for crashing your grandson's date now." Louis chuckled. And that was enough to snap me out of it. I blushed madly.

Locke said, "That's ok, Louis. I'm enjoying my grand fireworks display just as much. No sparklers here." And I just laughed at him. Louis looked absolutely confused. But Locke was letting me know we were absolutely holding our own, and I couldn't have agreed more. He was setting off a whole Fourth of July fireworks' finale inside of me.

Locke cleared his throat, coming back to the present moment. "I mean, how many times am I going to get to go on a double date with my grandmother? You have to tell me what she was like back in the day."

Louis smiled as if remembering. "Beautiful in every way. Just like now," he said without thinking. And there was no way it was a line. I'd never seen someone believe it more. "I still remember the first time I saw her. She probably doesn't even know this part. I had been having such a terrible week. My home life wasn't great. And I had stumbled upon her free concerts. I remember getting to that little grotto on the black sand shores and hearing her voice. It touched me in every part of my being, and then I saw her . . . And the woman who possessed that voice was even more stunning."

"Louis," Tutu began. "I had no idea. I thought you just became fond of me over time."

"No, Lani. Not exactly. I just wasn't ever bold enough to tell you." And she blushed even more at his words. "And I found a spot at the very back of the audience, as far away as possible. You made me so incredibly nervous and you didn't even know I existed. And I watched you interact with everyone. I saw the love you spread through your music. I saw the gift you were giving people. The gift you had given me. Music transported me away from all that pain. And I knew at that moment I wanted to do that for other people too. I would find a way, even though I had no money. And the more I listened and watched you, the more I could see your heart. There was no falling in love. There was just meant to be."

Tutu's eyes shone, and her shocked mouth tried to form words, but she couldn't. So he just continued, "I started coming to your concerts until I finally found the nerve to approach you and got enough money to buy a ukulele. I never expected you to be so generous with your time though. I really hoped I'd be able to show you my feelings one day, even though I knew I'd never deserve you. But once I saw the type of guy that was courting you, I knew I had no chance. But I was more than happy just to have a musical connection with you. And truly that's all it was ever supposed to be. I didn't mean–"

"Louis." Tutu's voice broke. "How could you think . . . I just saw no reason you would be interested in me."

"Lani. I've always been in love with you. Always have been, always will be." I swallowed hard at his words and Locke squeezed my hand in response. Louis continued, "You gave me so much. More than you could ever realize. And when I saw what was happening with the man pursuing you, it was only then that I gained the courage to show you my true feelings. I was pretty good at recognizing signs of different . . ." He trailed off, rubbing his ribs reflexively. "I think nothing could have hurt my heart more than the thought of you not being treated well. I loved you too much."

Louis paused. "Sorry, this is not what you asked, Locke.

Please forgive me. Your grandmother is just very special to me," he finished.

"No, please. Don't stop on my account and certainly don't hold back for my sake. I think everyone realized too late who my grandfather really was. My grandmother certainly deserves to be treated better," he said steadfastly. Locke's hand tightened on mine, and I knew how hard this must be for him. I also knew at that moment that he would be a different sort of man than his grandfather.

Louis nodded at Locke and hesitated. I could tell he still wanted to be careful about what he said especially since Locke knew the suitor was his grandfather. "Well, I started getting bolder. I mean, your grandmother was this gorgeous free spirit. Her infectious smile and kindness were so apparent. And I couldn't stay away. I would stay with her after the concerts so we could have our musical time together. It was the best part of any day for me. Just the two of us on those beautiful shores with our ukuleles. And she always made sure it was just the two of us, letting everyone else know that we had a scheduled practice time to keep. It gave me encouragement–hope. And then–"

Tutu explained to Locke, "Yes, I always made sure we had time to practice. Your grandfather used to get so mad at me. He hated those concerts I threw, and he especially hated that I stayed afterward to help a man for free with his music. But I wouldn't budge on it. I loved teaching Louis too much–it was too important. And that time with him was my favorite. Still is." She looked at Louis wistfully.

"I'm glad you said that because I always felt bad for–" Louis started.

"For just going for it like you did last night?" Tutu laughed, and then Louis joined her.

251

"Yes, I didn't know how else to show you. And you were just so beautiful playing your ukulele. I had to do it before I lost my nerve. Actually, I don't think I had a choice. I didn't even realize I had kissed you because I was so nervous. It was like an out-of-body experience. It really was a 'kiss to build a dream on.'"

"Well, I think you came back to your body when I started reciprocating. You just took me by surprise. All I wanted back then was for you to kiss me . . . But I caved to family pressures. I've always cherished what we created in that time though. Some of my best music came from the time I spent with you. We created 'Under the Rainbow' together, and music became our love language. Because we knew we couldn't have any other type of love."

A sad look crossed Louis' face, and Tutu spoke more quietly. "I didn't really know what I was getting into. It's no excuse, but . . . Well, it was a different time, and it was already hard enough just for Louis and I to perform together at different events. I saw the looks we would receive. People frowned on the age difference enough, but as far as everything else, it just wasn't done. I could only imagine how hard life would be for him, and I didn't want that for him. Especially when he got his offer–his big break. It would have made his career even more difficult with all the prejudice that existed in the States. Prejudice had a powerful hold, still does. We're lucky by how sheltered we are from it here. And I was never naïve enough to think that your grandfather wouldn't have done everything in his family's power to stop him from having a music career. The California offer would have evaporated as fast as it had appeared."

Louis seemed overwhelmed as he gazed deeply at Tutu. "I never knew . . . I never–" But he stopped. "Life was never easier without you, Lani. Life's never easier without true love. And there's been no one for me *but you*."

She looked at him so helplessly, as if seeing everything that could have been. And then her eyes shifted, and I couldn't help but think of those moments that Locke had told me about. The ones she had told him to take. Perhaps she was going to take hers now. "I agree. There's only ever been one true love under my rainbow," she replied softly.

Locke

CHAPTER 28

LOUIS SHIFTED TO LIGHTER TOPICS, telling me stories about my grandmother's ukulele playing and how iconic she had been in their community. I could tell he felt weird telling me intimate details about my grandmother but he also had wanted her to know that he still had feelings for her right from the start. As if he wanted to set the record straight finally and get it right this time. He wouldn't hide his emotions any longer. And I was seriously in awe of this man. I could learn a few things from him.

I was having trouble admitting my own feelings to myself, let alone showing them. But I guess decades spent apart would put things in perspective pretty quickly. I glanced across the table at Guin, who sent my heart racing every time I looked at her. And the words she had spoken to Tutu still rang throughout my mind. Something had changed inside me when she'd spoken those words. I couldn't deny what I felt for her any longer.

I was hoping some of Louis' courage would wear off on me and I'd be able to show Guin that these feelings I had for her weren't fake for me. That they never had been. That I'd fallen for her. And the scariest part was that I didn't know if she could accept all of me. But as I sat there witnessing the unconditional love that had lasted a lifetime between my grandmother and Louis, it felt possible. And as I dared to look at Guin, it certainly felt like anything was possible with this mermaid.

I have to admit this was by far the best date I'd ever been on, even if it was a double date with my grandmother. I was thoroughly enjoying the humorous stories Louis told of the old days, and Guin seemed equally amused. And I'd never seen my grandmother so happy, her face turning a romantic pink hue every time he called her Lani. That nickname was something I'd never heard anyone call her before. That nickname must have been reserved for Louis because she blushed every time he used it.

I had tried to plan as stress-free a date for my grandmother as possible, but it ended up being that way for me as well. I hoped Guin felt that way too, especially after what she had shared about her experiences of dating with health conditions. But she seemed completely relaxed, which was so at odds with her devastatingly gorgeous dress. Although, her little slip-on sneakers fit the relaxed vibe perfectly. They seemed to be a brilliant mix of her personality along with functionality to help ease her pain. Her adorable sneaker was still tucked right beside mine under the table. Guin's touch sent sparks coursing through me every time.

The ukulele music in the background with the hula dancers helped to keep the evening relaxed as well. I think we were all grateful for the music and the atmosphere. Especially when the band played a rendition of *The Rainbow Connection*. The pointed stares shared between my grandmother and Louis made it obvious this was another one of their secret songs. I hoped more than anything to have that kind of connection with someone. And by the look in Guin's eyes, it seemed she felt the same way too. And that unnerved me even more.

After dinner, I thought it might be best to let Tutu and Louis have some time alone together. Things seemed to go really well between them, and I didn't want to intrude on their date any further.

Hoping to give them some alone time, I said to Louis, "It's a really gorgeous evening. Maybe you should take my grandmother for a walk on the beach? She's always trying to teach me the constellations . . . She loves stargazing. I can take Guin to see the outdoor movie in the courtyard."

I suggested a walk on the beach for them since the movies were chosen for families and children. I knew a walk on the beach would be much more romantic for these two. An outdoor family movie would be a much better romance speed for the mermaid and me.

"Oh, I know," Louis said, looking fondly at Tutu. "That's why her nickname was Cassiopeia and all her band members had constellation stage names. I tried to lure her to my band with matching nicknames picked out for us." He laughed.

"You didn't need to lure me anywhere. Whatever constellation you were, I was always going to be the matching one," she said with a far-off look in her eyes. "I wish I had joined your band when you asked me. I wish I had done so many things differently."

A silence hung in the air, and then Louis spoke again. "Whatever you originally had planned for us is perfect, Locke. I never got a chance to take your grandmother to the movies."

After his words, there was this entire conversation happening between them that I couldn't understand. I was surprised that Louis had passed on my offer. I had just created the perfect opportunity for them to be alone. But if I had to guess he wanted my grandmother to feel comfortable and have a relaxed evening. He couldn't be more different from my grandfather.

A smile lit up my grandmother's lips as she hesitantly reached for Louis's hand. She obviously wasn't used to being able to do this freely. And it was beautiful to see. She had finally come out of her chrysalis. And for the first time, I believed she was with someone who wanted her to shine—who wanted her to be free to fly. A man who wasn't afraid for her to be anything she wanted to be in life.

So at his request, we made our way to the courtyard in Whalers Village, the twinkling lights creating a special atmosphere. A Disney movie was already playing when we arrived, so we found a spot off to the side with a nice grouping of extra-large bean bag chairs. I quickly realized that *Soul* was playing and the jazz musician movie could not have been more perfect for this pair of musical lovebirds.

Louis and Tutu found their way to some beanbag chairs, and Guin was just about to sit down as well when I caught her arm. Her eyes looked up at me with a questioning look. I pulled gently on her arm, letting her know my meaning. It was my way of asking her to sit with me. She just shook her head slightly with a little musical giggle. It reminded me how she had prompted me to ask her verbally to spend time with me. However, she was already drifting over toward me, so maybe I was more persuasive this time.

"What is it, Locke?" she asked. I raised an eyebrow at her in a "really, I have to ask you?" way. "Words, Thor," she said teasingly.

Well, I was being compared to Hemsworth again, so I took that as a good sign. "*E noho pu anei oe me au,*" I asked as I sat down on the beanbag. Trying to be clever as I asked her to sit down with me in Hawaiian.

"That I can understand, Locke," she teased.

"I think it's pretty clear, Mermaid," I bantered back. "I'm sorry my request for *The Little Mermaid* didn't go through in time," I said, nodding to the screen, "But let me make it up to you another way." Teasing her gently, I pulled on her arm a little more.

She laughed harder and moved closer until she was right in front of me. "*Please,*" I asked.

And with that, she sat right in front of me, her incredibly sexy back on display. Then she leaned back against me, and I leaned us back into the beanbag chair, my arms wrapped tightly around her. I was so ridiculously happy. I'm sure she could feel my heart pounding as hard as Thor's hammer and I didn't care one bit.

Oh, she felt so good resting against me.

That's why I barely heard Louis when he said, "Your grandson has some moves, Lani. Wish I had thought of them."

They both laughed together. "Yes, I'm glad he's got his mojo back. I was worried."

My face flamed, and I was glad Guin couldn't see it, but then she turned and looked at me with a smile on her face. *Well, so much for that.*

Tutu teased, "And Louis, it's a good thing you didn't try that one. With our arthritis, we'll be lucky to get up out of our own individual bean bag chairs. Let's leave the gymnastic moves to the young people."

But I could see the determination in Louis' eyes now. He reached his arm out to find hers and tugged on her ever so gently. "Please," he said, echoing my words. And who could say no to that man?

Tutu's face lit up with helpless amusement as she got up slowly and moved to him. He offered her his hand and helped ease her down to him as she made herself comfortable in his arms. A look of complete contentment covered both of their faces.

I couldn't believe one of the coolest men I'd ever met was copying my move. But I especially loved seeing my grandmother this way. It had been worth the risk of rejection to see this happen tonight. And I was so glad I took a chance on Guin because she was incredible.

Faintly, I heard Louis whisper to my grandmother. "I should have stayed. Lani, I should have fought for you. I'm so sorry." She turned to him and shook her head. He continued, "Yes, I'm so sorry for what you've had to go through. I thought maybe I'd read it wrong, that I'd projected. I thought you'd have a better life without me. And I thought that was what you wanted." He rubbed his side again. I could tell that self-conscious reflex had never gone away. Then he looked back up into her eyes. "But I promise, Lani, I'm not going anywhere. If you let me, I'll never leave you again. *Ho'i hou ke aloha.*"

And I knew exactly what that saying meant. It was perfect

for them, and my heart melted at his words: 'Let us fall in love all over again.' I looked from behind Guin over to them, trying not to be too obvious, but also a little transfixed. Guin was much more polite, or at least much more subtle, as she stared at the movie screen ahead. I, however, wanted to know so badly what my grandmother would do.

But it didn't take long as Tutu's eyes roamed over Louis, letting the words sink in. And ever so gently, she reached her hands up to his face, like she was reaching out for so many things she'd wanted in her life and never let herself have. I could see her hands tremble as she did so. And with so much love in her eyes, she said, "I've always wanted it to be you, Louis. From that first day you spoke to me. I thought to myself, he's going to make someone the luckiest person in the world one day. I just never imagined that person would be me. It has always been and will *always* be you."

And then she brought her lips to his in a kiss that had been meant for him from the very start. One that had always been waiting for him.

Locke

CHAPTER 29

GUIN AND TUTU came home from the convention the next day with renewed energy; but as happy as they were together, I knew my Grandmother would still make an excuse to stay home this afternoon. I'd invited her to come snorkeling with Guin and I, but she'd started making excuses about needing to stay home with the dogs. Even though the dogs would love going on the boat too. And sure enough, Tutu stuck to her plan, explaining she was exhausted from all the excitement of the convention. But as "exhausted" as she was,

Tutu had this glow about her that I had never seen before—except for last night. She thanked Guin repeatedly, and I could tell today had meant a lot to her.

Guin beamed at Tutu and said, "You'll have to go back with me to the convention on another day. There will be plenty of sessions and everyone loves having you there . . . *Especially* our guest speakers." There was this wink with some kind of secret message that I had missed. I had a feeling we'd been on a double date with one of those "special guests." I could tell by the looks on their faces that the two of them had grown even closer today. They had this unspoken musical bond now. I also saw a new aura around Guin too. One that was daring me to be brave where she was concerned.

"I'd really like to do that, *Ku'uipo*. But now I'm going to sit on the lanai and rest for a little while," Tutu said, smiling at me.

"Are you sure you don't want to join us?" Guin asked. "It sounds like it's going to be a beautiful afternoon. I don't want you to have to sit here by yourself."

"Oh, I have a feeling, I'll have some company soon enough." A little wink escaped with her voice. I knew there was no way Louis wouldn't be over here the first chance he got. He wouldn't let another day go by. They were going to be inseparable, making up for lost time.

"Ok, if you're sure. And I have a feeling you're right about not being here alone this afternoon," Guin said mischievously. But she seemed hesitant as she turned to me. "I'll just go change and get my things." A nervousness in her voice.

"Sounds good. I'll be here." I said in a slightly awkward tone. And with that, she left.

I'll be here? Where else would I be? I was really nervous. She brought every sense alive in me, stronger than a bloodhound. I needed to calm down. *Breathe, Locke. Everything Is fine. Things don't have to be weird after last night. It's just another excursion.*

But I practically jumped when she returned, because I was so on edge. She looked at me curiously. I would have done the same thing. Thankfully, little clues were telling me she was nervous too, and that oddly helped calm me down a little.

I drove the Jeep to Ma'alaea Harbor where I kept the boat my grandfather had left to Tutu and she'd passed on to me. I used it for both private and commercial excursions. As we neared the harbor, I pointed out the Maui Wildlife Center, which housed the highly acclaimed marine aquarium.

Her face lit up in excitement. "Can we go to the aquarium sometime? I would love to see the living reefs exhibit." Enthusiasm taking over her musical tone.

"I promise to take you on a rainy day. Our aquarium is pretty incredible. It's rated as one of the top aquariums in the United States. The underwater tunnels are really well done. But today, I'm taking you to the *real* outdoor aquarium and you get to swim in it."

She laughed at my incredibly corny joke, and it made my heart happy.

When we reached the harbor, the sun's bright rays were setting the aquamarine sea aglow with glittering reflections. The boats were swaying in their nautical beds in hypnotic welcome. The sea of white hulls provided a soothing sight as they rocked in their familiar rhythms.

After we parked, I led Guin down the dock to my boat, but she seemed to falter behind me. Sputtering like a car that just realized it was out of gasoline. I could tell from the look in her eyes that Guin had never been on a boat big enough to go out on the ocean. She hesitated and eyed some of the jet skis, apparently thinking they looked less daunting.

Reading her mermaid mind, I said, "I promise you don't want to ride one of those jet skis. All the waves out there would pummel you. When you hit one, it sends you flying in the air. And you get knocked back down even harder. I don't think that would be so good for your . . . Uh, I don't think it would be so enjoyable," I quickly corrected myself. I had almost said 'for your kidneys and conditions,' but thankfully caught myself. I never wanted her to feel bad about not being able to do something because of her health. But the last thing she needed was to have her kidneys pounded by the sea. I would much rather do things she could actually enjoy—that I hoped would be good for her. And I was praying for a gentle day on the water. I noticed she had smiled when I caught myself, so I guess she appreciated my blunt honesty.

I boarded the boat with our supplies and looked at her still standing hesitantly on the dock, even though I had taken some time to secure everything. "What is it, Mermaid? Afraid of seafaring vessels? Do you prefer *to swim* out to the island?" She laughed at me but kept looking at the boat. I asked her, "Didn't you say you lived near a lake?"

"Yes, but you can swim to shore," she quickly responded.

"*Ahh*, I see. Well, I'm not planning on sinking this thing and I have *lots* of safety precautions. I couldn't take tourists on ocean excursions without them. And what do you mean . . . getting lost at sea with me doesn't sound like a dream to you?" I teased. She continued to eye me. "Come on, *trust me*." I extended my hand to her. And just like last night, she looked at it for an unnerving amount of time before taking it. And that same rush of excitement came when she did. I sighed, never quite knowing what she was going to do. And oddly, loving it. She was a wild card, just like me.

I continued to try putting her mind at ease. "Some of the best and most iconic snorkeling and diving spots are around Molokini. It looks like a crescent-shaped island because it's an extinct volcanic crater. And if we snorkel inside the crescent, it should be calmer for you than the open sea. More protected. What do you think? I can take you anywhere, though, if you have somewhere else in mind."

"No, I trust you. Sounds perfect," she replied. And again, sexier words had *never* been spoken to me. I had to reorient myself as to what direction to navigate–to a place I'd gone countless times.

Guin stood by me at the helm, and I could tell she was actually a little nervous as I pulled out of the harbor. "Do you want to learn to drive?" I asked once I was safely out on the open sea with an expanse of endless horizon before us. I wanted her to sit and relax on the ride over to the island, but I had a feeling she was going to remain standing next to me in case we had a sinking ship.

"Ok," she said hesitantly.

"I promise I won't let you crash amongst all the dangerous obstacles," I said, motioning around to the wide-open expanse. Suddenly, I saw her shoulders relax.

I think learning how to command the boat actually made Guin feel more comfortable. I'd often found that knowledge provided people with a type of comfort. And in no time at all, we arrived at Molokini. I reached around Guin, helping her with the controls so she could learn how to anchor the boat. And in such proximity, her enchanting sea maiden scent and beauty captivated me once again. Guin had to call my name a few times to bring me back to the present so she could learn what to do after anchoring. I had most certainly left her hanging, as my hand lingered over hers on the controls while my eyes studied her face. I obviously couldn't teach mermaids.

And as embarrassing as it was, I just accepted it at this point. There wasn't much I could do about it. Believe me, I had tried. I busied myself by getting our gear together from below deck while Guin put her wetsuit on over her bikini. I needed to go down below before I had a repeat of our earlier shopping experience at my store. She already looked too beautiful with her blonde hair blowing in the sea breeze.

"Locke? Do you need some help?" She called down to me. I was obviously taking way too long to collect myself.

Yeah, apparently I do.

"No, just grabbing a few things." I surfaced quickly so she wouldn't worry about me, and then I was hit with the vision of her in that wetsuit again. I pinched the bridge of my nose as if I thought that was going to do anything.

"You ok?" she questioned.

"Yup, never better. The motion must be getting to me today." *The motion of her body in that wetsuit.* "So let's get you some flippers and put your snorkel mask on." That ought to help things. I should have found a more ridiculous pair for her to wear. Who was I kidding, the mermaid was going to look adorable.

I was helping her put on her fins and giving her some instructions about the snorkel mask when I saw her looking skeptically out toward the crater.

"What are you thinking, Mermaid?" I questioned.

"Uh, there aren't any sharks out there, right?" she asked a little nervously. I was definitely used to this question from tourists.

"Well, you might see some reef sharks. They won't bother

you, though. Just don't go chasing them. And that's why it's nice to stay inside the crater, it's more protected," I answered. "Why? Are you some shark movie junkie? Don't worry, they get everything wrong in those films."

"Well, that's good to know."

"Yeah, but still don't provoke them, hoping for some real-life *Jaws* action. I really don't want to wrestle a shark on your behalf."

"Well, I'll see what I can do," she said jokingly.

"That goes for eels and barracudas too. Now you have me worried that you're a *danger magnet*. Maybe I need to take the flare gun."

"Ha ha. Hilarious," she replied dryly.

But I seriously was thinking about grabbing it. Something told me she was as unlucky as I was. But I didn't want to make her even more nervous. I already took a diver's knife with me on excursions because you just never knew. But I sure wouldn't tell her that.

"The only flares you need to be worried about are my Lupus ones." And I laughed at her joke.

"Ok, let's go. I've got you. There's a whole reef to explore." I smiled at her reassuringly.

And with no further ado, we slipped into the silky, salty abyss. The water was so crystal clear we could see the bottom with no problem. I had anchored us at the Takos flats so it would be quick and easy to get to the shallow reef areas.

I helped position Guin's snorkel and then reached for her hand under the blissful blue waves, guiding her as she got used to her flippers. Within seconds of swimming, corals were bursting with color in front of us. Slowly at first, just some dull patches, and then a riot of color burst forth all at once. And the ocean life came alive too. There were sea turtles, blue and yellow tangs, clownfish, and seahorses, just to name a few of the beautiful sea life passing by us. I kept trying to point out different things to her and talk through my mask, but she just kept giggling. I'm sure I was pretty incoherent. But I was also sure I wasn't going to get enough of how she looked under the shimmering waves today. The sea had never looked so beautiful.

Guinevere

CHAPTER 30

I WAS ENJOYING my underwater exploration with Locke, who looked just as attractive under the sea as he did on dry land. I felt weird wearing flippers and a snorkel, though. And I wasn't exactly getting the hang of it. My snorkel kept filling with water as waves splashed over the top of it, and I didn't have the lung capacity to blow it out as simply as Locke had instructed me to do. I saw you needed to be pretty physically fit to be comfortable in the sea. Like Locke. He was the real mer-man. He fit here seamlessly.

I now knew why his surf shack did such good business. I had *not so* covertly looked up the online reviews on his business. And there were so many posts about how wonderful his excursions were. Although he wasn't offering many of those right now. But the photos posted with the reviews were simply adorable. And they all talked about the kind, goofy captain. And that had to be Locke. I was certainly seeing that side of him today.

Locke definitely came alive out on the sea and he had a natural ease around the water. And my favorite part was hearing him try to speak underwater to me. That was a new language I would treasure. He seemed to know every species of fish. Turtles, stingrays, angelfish, starfish, and sea urchins were just a few of the many types of sea life he pointed out to me. Each more beautiful than the last. I was obsessed with this new world my eyes were hungrily discovering. The sea had a uniquely beautiful color palette to explore and a language all of its own. The quiet whirl of the sea spoke to me and I wanted to stay there forever and listen to it.

The only problem was the flippers. In my struggle to make better use of them, I had hit something really hard. I was seriously struggling as I floundered about. Locke had warned me about fire coral, and I really hoped I hadn't hit any of it. Although, it didn't seem like it was sharp, just really hard. I checked my wet suit for cuts, and Locke looked over at me. At that moment, I realized what I had hit. I felt bad about it since he obviously didn't want me to know, or at the very least he didn't want to talk about it. But not talking about it felt like leaving a white elephant in the room, or in this case, a humpback whale in the sea. But I knew all too well what it felt like when people were too nosy which made you want to talk about it even less. However, I was too preoccupied to over-analyze it any further because motion sickness was overtaking me. I had tried to block out my nausea from the motion, wanting nothing to impede this beautiful afternoon, but now it was ambushing me.

Locke surfaced, taking out his snorkel. "What's wrong?" he asked, his face full of concern.

"Um, my motion sickness is getting a lot worse."

"Worse? Guin you should have said something earlier. I meant to give you something before we went out. I'm *really* sorry, I guess I got distracted." And his checks rose in color as he said it. "Snorkeling can be rough for people who have motion sickness. There's so much bobbing up and down in the water. I was hoping today would be calm, but even under the best of circumstances there's always a certain amount of up and down motion. Diving is much easier since you go under the water and can avoid the motion of the water on the surface, but you've got to be certified to dive."

There was no 'sneaking up on me' now: the motion sickness was upon me. I guess Locke could see it written on my ashen complexion, so he began speaking quickly, "Ok, I've got some things that can help. Let's just get you out of the water and back on the boat." He looked seriously at my face. "*Now.*"

Locke guided me back to the boat and ushered me on board. I was shivering pretty badly. I guess the seasickness was really getting to me. How embarrassing. I wasn't designed for ocean life *at all*. I'm just glad I hadn't thrown up while snorkeling. I don't want to know what type of sea life that might have attracted.

Locke got me to a shaded seat on the boat under the

awning. And I put my head in between my knees as instructed. Praying for some relief to take effect soon.

As he stroked my back, he said again, "I'm really sorry. I should have given you some MotionEaze before we got in the water. It's all essential oils, and it works really well. I bet it's something you can use. I'll get it for you now. I should have thought about it. Especially today since the water's rougher than usual here. A storm must be brewing. I promise it's usually much calmer here. You're just having a rough go of it. And with your conditions, I should have known your body would be more susceptible to the motion."

He started rubbing some liquid behind my ears from the bag he had grabbed out of the captain's helm. Then he suggested, "I have some pineapple rock candy too. You can try letting it melt in your mouth and see if the sugar helps. It usually works pretty quickly."

Everything felt like it was moving uncontrollably, and I reflexively grabbed at his calf to steady myself. As soon as I did, I realized I had grabbed the leg he hadn't wanted to talk about with me. His calf was rock hard, and I now knew my suspicions were correct. I tugged on him with even more urgency, but he didn't respond. I was trying to get his attention because I was pretty sure I was going to be sick and I needed that bag he'd brought over... *now*.

"Locke," I uttered. But he was just looking at me, frozen before me. His eyes seemed to fracture. There was no avoiding that conversation now. But I had no time left to stay; the motion sickness was winning. I got up and ran to the other side of the boat. Quickly, I leaned over the railing slightly, getting ready for the motion sickness to fully overtake me. I felt its grip closing around me. But miraculously the ocean calmed, and the freshness of the sea breeze combined with the other aids he'd given me took effect. I loosened my hold on the railing.

And then I noticed Locke standing beside me. "Is it letting up?" he asked in a strained voice. I wouldn't have recognized his voice except that it was just the two of us on the boat. That's how much he didn't sound like himself.

My drooped head turned slightly, and I smiled a little. "Yes, it's passing some. Thanks. I'm glad you know what you're doing." He nodded in response and then helped me to the bench seat in front of the helm. Then, he grabbed a towel and wrapped it around me after helping me out of my wetsuit. He was always mindful of my skin. I never would have thought he'd be so sensitive about things—so thoughtful.

I leaned against him, grateful for him as this solid and consistent anchoring place.

"Guin—" he said, as we looked out at the crescent island. But he stopped short. He looked down at me, lost. Those dark eyes were shifting, taking on a smoky haze.

So I created an opening for him. "There's a reason you wear wetsuits all the time, isn't there?" I asked, and he nodded slowly, looking slightly ashamed. I continued, "And it's why you wear long pants at the beach?" He nodded again. "And it's also the reason you don't particularly like romance? Or dating, I guess." He grimaced and nodded. I was trying to figure out what to say next. His right calf had felt so solid. It had to be a prosthesis, just as I thought it might be.

"Guin," he said painfully. I stared straight ahead at the wide open ocean. I was ready to get lost in it. I didn't want to go there if he didn't—especially if he wasn't ready. I had thought he'd open up on his own time, but that didn't seem like it was going to be the case based on his reaction now. He'd watched my vulnerabilities get uncovered one by one yesterday as he sat with me at the dialysis center, and it stung that he still didn't trust me with his. My vulnerabilities had been on full display, and yet he still wanted to keep his covered. Ironic that I was the one with an "invisible" medical condition, while he had a "visible" one, and yet he'd seen mine from the very beginning.

He looked at me, but I just gazed further out to sea. I got it. I really did. Having to show yourself like this was painful. It was like tearing off a scab before it recovered. Because having to share something like this before you were ready made it almost impossible to heal. So the wound just got messier, deeper, and more exposed. *More raw.*

I was just about to retreat when he did something that got my attention. He came over to sit beside me and started removing his surf shoe. I'd never seen his feet or legs uncovered. And then, he started removing his wetsuit. His pained face gazed at me as he did so. I knew at that moment I'd never seen true vulnerability before. I actually wanted to stop him from uncovering any more of his leg after seeing his wounded expression.

"Locke–" But my words ran dry. He just continued lowering his wetsuit. Past the bottom of his swim trunks, every-thing changed. Even his expression. But he kept right on. Below his right knee, the calf curved and transformed into a black prosthetic leg.

Under the bright Hawaiian sunlight, Locke stood there with the darkest expression. It was as if a dark cloud had come out, covering all brightness in its path. He unzipped the wetsuit at the ankle so that he could get it over the prosthetic foot with the surf shoe attached. Then he laid the wetsuit down, letting his right leg stretch out slightly beside mine. My eyes roamed over his face and he let out a painful sigh as he allowed his eyes to do the same.

"Ok, Mermaid. Now you see." His features raised and then fell so quickly. His statement was so nonchalant, as if he had just asked what takeout I would prefer. But it was one of the most important things he would ever show me, and I knew it. I understood it was the furthest thing from a careless gesture. This must be the point where people–women–ran. This must be his critical point. And I guess he didn't think I would pass. Surely, if he did, he would have shown me by now.

"Locke . . ." I looked at him tenderly. "I've known for a while now. But I didn't want to say anything or ask you about your leg if you weren't ready to talk about it. I know how invasive questions like that can be. And I figured you'd tell me when you were ready." I finished gently.

He seemed a little surprised. I guess since I hadn't said anything about it, he thought I hadn't noticed. "Oh . . . well, seeing it uncovered is different," Locke said, as he looked away from me.

"What?" Did he think I hadn't said anything because I wanted to ignore this part of him? That couldn't be further from the truth. I had waited for this and now I didn't feel like I was going to pass this crucial juncture, he was going to shut me out. And that stung, because he had seen me at my most vulnerable. Why could he not see I would accept him at his most vulnerable, too? Maybe since I hadn't asked about it, he was assuming I wanted to pretend that part of him didn't exist.

"This is the time when everyone runs." He swallowed hard, looking at his leg. "So just how unattractive is it?" he asked somewhat rhetorically, without an ounce of hope.

But he wasn't giving me any time to reply. It was as if he'd already decided what my response would be–had to be–based on everyone else's previous replies. He also knew I couldn't go anywhere–I couldn't run away. We were in the middle of the ocean. I was stranded on a boat, so he was going to respond for me.

When he started to get up, I knew he was the one running, not me. But as the gentle waves rocked us, my hand reached out, guiding its way reflexively to his right knee near his prosthesis. He jerked in reaction. Then he left his leg where it had been resting beside me. The conflicted look on his face sent shock waves through me. There was a quick spark in his eyes, but it extinguished quickly. As if too scared to hope.

And then he stood up, seeming to shake off that spark of hope, looking lost as he stood in front of me. I continued to watch him, really looking at him. Because this was the first time he'd truly let me see him. I got up with the towel wrapped around me as it fluttered in the breeze and slowly made my way to him. His expression filled with trepidation and an edge of weariness as he looked at me, like he didn't believe I knew what I was doing. Or maybe he thought the shock of seeing his prosthesis hadn't worn off. But I think he just couldn't believe someone was choosing him–the *real* him.

I stood before him, my eyes daring to move up to meet his. And there seemed to be an ache that lived in both of our eyes when they met. An understanding that we wouldn't inflict the pain we'd known from others on one another. That we would be different. I reached for his neck again, just as I had done that first night on the beach. My towel fell away, and the wind carried it toward the helm. And this time, his dark eyes shifted, turning the amber color of the waning sun. Calming me with their warmer color. Showing me how he felt about this moment, too. His desire was obvious, but there also seemed to be a deep longing for something else.

I moved closer toward him, knowing exactly what I wanted this time. I was done denying it. This stubborn man infuriated me, but in all the best possible ways . . . He made me feel so alive that I'd gotten back my energy to fight for the important things in life. Because he also had the best, most giving heart. And I realized he was the one who could understand my own. I was sure of that. All I'd needed was for him to be vulnerable with me–to open up to me–so I could know for sure. And once he did that, something had broken away inside of me.

Our banter and teasing connection had been the most fun I'd ever had with anyone. He had awakened my failing body. He was giving me a new appreciation for life and now I knew I wanted more. *So much more.*

I looked at his soft lips and moved toward them, wanting to linger amongst them. I was feeling the same gravitational pull as the moon toward the sun.

"Guin," he mumbled as I neared him. So quietly, the sound almost got lost in the expansive sea surrounding us. We were all alone out here, just the two of us and it felt symbolic. His word was almost a warning, but this time I didn't stop. Last time I shouldn't have either. He hadn't meant what he said. I was sure of that now. It wasn't a "bad idea;" he just didn't think I'd accept him. And there was this deep primal sound that escaped him as I got closer. Like he'd been waiting for someone to want him, all of him, for so long. And I took that as everything I needed to continue.

And within an instant, my fingers were kneading through his shaggy jet-black hair, gazing at him with intensity. Letting him know *exactly* what my intentions were with him. And his eyes scanned over my face in disbelief as I closed the distance between us, a longing burning inside me. I breathed in that salty, masculine scent that was purely his and waited. Not taking any of it back this time. And with this brief nod of his head, I bridged any gap left. A desire overtook me when our lips met, showing him how much I had wanted this and *him*. How attracted I was to him and had always been.

I needed him to know I didn't see him any differently, that this only helped me reach this level of intimacy with him. And when my lips moved over his, Locke responded. The softness of his lips molded into mine as he ignited sparks inside of me. And it unlocked something deep within me. A feeling that he was the only one who could do this for me. Maybe I'd somehow known all along, and that's why I'd been fighting against it with such determination. I'd been too scared. So afraid of everything this could be, of how much there could be to lose.

I pulled back and looked up at him with my beautifully swollen lips, feeling full of life. His eyes gazed purposefully over me as if memorizing every part of me. Then as if breaking a haze, he questioned me with the same intensity, "so this? . . ." And he let his leg stick out a little before me. I shook my head at what he was implying.

"So this? . . ." I answered in reply and allowed my left arm to float into the same space as his leg. He shook his head just as emphatically.

Then, without another moment's hesitation, he caressed my neck with both his hands. This time taking the lead and wasting no time. He brought my face to his, allowing his eyes to capture mine, getting lost in a way it seemed he must have wanted to do for quite some time now. Maybe he'd been just as afraid as me. And then he took my lips again, as effortlessly as the sea caressing your body.

Locke

CHAPTER 31

I HELD Guin tightly against me at the bow of the boat, her head resting softly against my chest. No woman had ever been this close to me since my accident. I'd never wanted one to be. Guin was the first woman who didn't seem to view me any differently because of my disability. My leg was a part of my story, a part of my life, but it was just a *single* part. It wasn't the full story. And I could tell by Guin's physical response that my prosthesis was just a single piece of me to her, and I loved it . . . I'd completely fallen for her. I think I had from the moment I'd sat with her at the dialysis center–and then again when she helped Tutu on our "fake date." But knowing that made me even more scared to show her *this* part of me. I had thought I'd rather she be oblivious to my circumstances. But I would never have known what I was missing. Not until now. Because what Tutu had been telling me was true, the right person will love all of you. Now her words were crystal clear.

I felt really terrible that I'd lied to her . . . that I'd swapped identities in the stories. The attack hadn't happened to my friend. *I* was the friend in the story. But I'd only fabricated the story to protect myself until I got to know her better. I'd always known it was only a matter of time until she found out about my prosthesis. People noticed at different lengths of time. I had stopped volunteering that information a while ago. Unfortunately, my approach was never going to work with her. I'd seen she was different from the others and yet I still couldn't bring myself to share anything about this part of myself. Telling her about my prosthesis only became more awkward the longer I waited. And the more I got to know her, the more I didn't want to be wrong about her reaction.

"I swapped the stories on you," I whispered as the bow of the boat creaked from the waves. The bright aqua color of the sea was soothing my nerves. Its crystal color was home to me.

"I figured." She laughed slightly, easing the tension. Then she asked quietly, "Did you *just* swap the stories or is there more?"

"Guin, it's not a story you want to hear. I promise." I didn't want to share this with her. Not the details. Seeing my prosthesis was enough. I'd already told her that the ocean was something you needed to respect, and that tourists and tour companies could be negligent. It was true. More than anything, that's what had prompted me to start my company. I think she could get a good enough idea of what had happened from my comments.

"But it's you . . . So, I'd like to know–if you want to tell me. I just–" She let it hang there. I understood her feelings because I felt the same way about her. I wanted to know everything I could about her. Every little thing she stopped short of telling me felt personal, like it was a part of herself she didn't trust me to have. She wasn't asking so she could feel the adrenaline rush of hearing a firsthand account of some grisly story. She was asking so she could learn more about me; to understand this piece of myself that I kept hidden. And I needed to decide if I was going to share it with her. I knew she could easily find my story in the newspaper's archives, but she seemed to be one of the few people who wouldn't do that. So I really could choose if she got to know about my accident or not.

My face twitched upward in indecision. I reflexively pulled Guin a little tighter to me. I didn't know if I was ready for my pain to be on display. Without even realizing it, I abruptly began, "I never share this story, but since it was all over the news, most people already know it, anyway. But people usually still try to get the story directly from me. I guess it's just natural human curiosity to want to hear it from the 'survivor.' But, I simply don't talk about it. Tutu and my mom are the only people who have actually heard me tell my story. Well, Reef, but he lived through it with me. And I didn't even want to tell Tutu or my mom because I knew it would be hard for them to hear . . . So why don't I just give you the broad strokes, ok?"

She pulled away from me slightly and looked up at me with those doe eyes. "Tell me as much as you want. I'm fine knowing as much as you want to share with me." She smiled weakly and then laid her head back on my chest. I guess she knew it would be easier for me this way. And it was. Although I knew she was going to hear my erratic heartbeats, which intimidated me.

"Uh . . ." I didn't even know where to begin. I wasn't used to telling my story. "So . . . I was with my friend, Reef. I told you the truth about that part . . . it was just all reversed. We went out on the same boat we're on now, but back then it belonged to my grandfather. Reef and I were spending the day together, diving. We hadn't gotten to do that in a long time." I looked at her, assessing. But she just nodded at me.

"Well, you know how I said tour companies aren't always careful? How they don't always put the tourists' best interest first or supervise them carefully, and that's why I wanted to start a company?"

"Yes," she replied solemnly.

My eyes closed as I felt the rush of water close all around me. I was transported back to that time, feeling myself being pulled down into the ocean's depths at lightning speed. My heart rate quickened. I didn't want her to see me as another victim. Or worse, think that my greatest accomplishment in life was being a "survivor." I hadn't done anything by just surviving. Surely that couldn't be my greatest accomplishment in this life. Hopefully, I was much more than that. But maybe she of all people would realize that. Maybe she would understand it was the aftermath that mattered. What I did as a survivor that counted.

"Ok, I'm more than happy to stop when you've heard enough. Just let me know." But she looked at me like that wouldn't happen, especially now that I'd said that. But before I could go further, I noticed the sun's rays streaming onto Guin's bare shoulders, so I suggested, "Let's get you into the shade. We can go back to the bench seat in front of the captain's helm."

Guin replied, "Locke, I was literally bleeding in front of you yesterday. You can trust me with this."

"Yeah, well, I'm about to lose a lot more blood in your imagination," I replied. She looked at me sternly. Man, she was stubborn. Just like me. She would not let me delay any longer. *Was this what it was like dealing with me?*

"Ok," I began as she held my gaze, holding me to my word. She was waiting and hoping I'd trust her. *Those eyes.* Those hauntingly beautiful *Mermaid eyes.* I was sunk. She could have *all* the pieces of me . . . So I told my story, "Reef and I had finally decided to take one of our bucket list dives at the Lanai Cathedrals. Even though we'd lived here our whole lives, we'd never been to the lower caves. It was just one of those things you take for granted and say you'll do in the future. The cathedrals are a really insane place to dive off the coast of Lanai. And they're special because there are a variety of dive spots with different ability levels that makes them accessible to divers of all ability levels. The Cathedrals were formed by lava tubes from volcanic activity that created these incredibly beautiful underwater rooms. The First Cathedral is a gigantic two-story tall cavern that has an impressive hole in the top where the roof collapsed. You enter through the hole into an enormous cavern illuminated by skylights. That's where you can find a vividly lit central piece of lava rock known as The Altar. There are also confessionals–small side chambers, that have many types of sea life in them. There's even a black coral chandelier. But there's not much light down there. And what light is there gets dispersed through holes in the rocks creating a beautiful 'stained glass effect.' Everywhere we flashed our lights uncovered a fascinating hidden world. And I guess the sensory deprivation just added to the effect.

"Anyway, we were seeing amazing ocean life: pufferfish, manta rays, stingrays, many types of reef fish, parrotfish, angelfish–my favorite–moray eels, octopuses, and sea turtles. It was incredible. Then suddenly, schools of fish came swarming into the caverns, and this wasn't a 'Little Mermaid' moment. No, when you get this many swarms of fish and this type of disturbance, you know something is going on. The fish just flooded into our cavern. It was kind of eerie. So we went back up to check it out."

I paused, needing a break. I tried to collect myself and decide what to say next. "We did our decompression 'safety stop' and then came up to the surface. Nothing looked unusual on the way up, and we surfaced near our boat. Everything looked fine. And there had been no one around when we arrived that day. We'd gotten lucky and gone on an off day and time. But when we came up, we noticed a boat not too far away from us. We figured they must have spooked the fish somehow. Then we heard them yelling. Noise travels really easily over water. They sounded like a group of drunk guys. Probably just doing something stupid that scared the fish. I remember looking at Reef and rolling my eyes. He just laughed and asked if I wanted to go back down. I glanced back at the boat, then turned to him and nodded yes because it was one of the best diving experiences of my life."

I closed my eyes and tried to stop the images that would come next. I didn't want to see them so vividly while I was telling her this. I didn't want *her* to see me like this.

"Hey," she breathed. "It's ok. I'm sorry I asked. You can stop now. It's ok. It's enough that you would share part of your story with me."

But it wasn't enough, and I realized that now. I willed my fists to unclench and took a deep breath, finding the strength to continue. "We were putting our masks back on and trying to talk to one another, but the screaming had gotten louder. They were really going crazy over something. It was difficult to make out what they were saying. And then I remember seeing this dead fish's head floating near us. I stared at Reef. And things started clicking into place. But it was too late. I didn't have time to say anything to him. I wanted to tell Reef we needed to head to the boat. That was the last thing I remember thinking before I felt this intense pressure on my leg. Like a massive clamp was pressing down on it, and then suddenly the water was swallowing me up and folding in on me. I was dragged down into the ocean's depths."

Guin's left hand immediately went to my right knee, a little above the rounded edge. I had extra sensitivity there because all the nerve endings had been mangled in the area. I didn't especially like being touched there. But our special connection, as well as her touch, felt good to me. And it wasn't lost on me that it was her left arm touching my right side. There was some sixth sense going on between us that I couldn't explain. It was like she could feel my emotions–my pain–almost as if they were her own. And that was how I had felt yesterday sitting with her at the dialysis center. The longer I sat with her, the more deeply I'd felt it . . . A special connection that was growing stronger between us until I wanted nothing more than to carry her pain for her. And as I looked at her, I knew she was going to want to do the same thing for me.

She pulled her hand back quickly as if she had forgotten herself. And normally someone touching me on my leg would upset me. But this was Guin. She was different. And I wanted her touch and its physical connection more than anything. She was showing me how much she cared for me. For me, it was even more intimate than a kiss.

I reached for her hand as soon as she said, "I'm sorry. I didn't mean to." Then I brought her hand back to my leg and placed mine on top of hers. My heart raced harder than it ever had with anyone before. Her eyes peeked timidly up at me from underneath thick, long lashes. Shy in a way I'd only seen her be with me.

Guin continued looking at me. She seemed to be a little intimidated at the connection between us. I could tell by her expression she was just as shocked as I was. And that made me hopeful.

"What did you do?" she half whispered.

"Well, when I finally registered what was happening. I realized whatever had me was only going to drag me down deeper and deeper. And my chances of surfacing were getting slimmer. Whatever had me in its grip was trying to drown me. So I started feeling around and the surface of this thing was so rough. Like sharp sandpaper. That confirmed what had me. So I just kept feeling around for a soft point until I finally found something. It felt a bit like jelly, and I dug my fist into it. I just kept going for it with everything I had. And finally, the pressure started lessening, but I was still too shocked to feel any pain, I guess. And I couldn't see anything around me, except that the water was red.

"As soon as the pressure lessened a little, my adrenaline kicked into a higher gear, and I pressed even harder. By this time, my oxygen was really giving out. But finally what I'd done was enough. The shark released me, and I somehow made it to the surface. Thank goodness it was salt water. If I'd been in a lake or something, I wouldn't have had any idea in which direction to go and there wouldn't have been any buoyancy to help direct me. As soon as I surfaced, Reef rushed over and got me to the boat. Thank God, I have such an amazing friend. He'd been trying to find me in the water. Most people would have immediately left me to get back on the boat to safety.

"After Reef got me on the boat, the adrenaline and shock wore off, and the pain kicked in. Reef radioed for med alert, and they airlifted me out of there. I remember the gurney dropping from the helicopter and someone strapping me into it, before flying to the hospital. Reef tried to come with me, but they told him he couldn't. So he had to meet us at the hospital. Luckily, I'm AB+, the universal receiver, so the blood transfusions were easier. And Reef even tried to donate blood for me, but it wouldn't have been fast enough. I'll always be grateful to everyone on the island who is a blood donor. It saved my life. They were able to keep me alive long enough to do surgery, and while I don't have all of my right leg, I am alive, thankfully. I have an incredible friend and community. So I know a little about needing a donor, just not in the same way."

She looked at me, stunned. "But you still go in the ocean. You take people out snorkeling and diving. And you even wear a shark's tooth necklace."

"Well, never to Lanai. That's for sure. Good thing it got marked off the bucket list that day." I laughed. "And the tooth is actually from the shark. They saved it for me from my surgery. They think it was a Tiger shark. Crazy, huh? That's one wicked reminder to always respect nature and all of Earth's creatures."

Guin looked at me so seriously that I replied, "Yeah, well, it wasn't the shark's fault."

"There's no way I could look at it like that." Her tone filled with disbelief.

"It really wasn't the shark's fault. Remember that other boat? And the dead fish I saw?" She nodded. "Well, those guys were out chumming for sharks. That's why they were yelling and got so excited, apparently. I realized what was happening as soon as I saw the fish head that floated over to us. I knew they must be seeing something cool, and usually tourists don't get that excited just over turtles. It had to be dolphins, whales, or sharks. And there's one reason people go out chumming: to see sharks. And guessing by the way they were acting; it had to be sharks. Plus, the way the fish were acting in the caves was a bit of an indicator. But I didn't even have time to say anything to Reef before . . ." Her eyes widened. "We would have gotten out of the water if we had known, and things would have been fine. But we had no idea. Chumming puts sharks into a feeding state. And we were in the feeding frenzy area. It's extremely dangerous to be chumming near well-known diving areas. *And so wrong.* It's risking everyone's life who's in the water near the chumming area."

Locke continued, "That's why I wanted to start my company. To make sure tourists are not only safe but also to make sure they respect the ocean. Those guys chumming near a popular dive sight never stopped to think they could cost someone their life. It could have been Reef's life too. And chumming is illegal in the state of Hawaii. We're really lucky that in Maui they're more vigilant because it isn't illegal in so many other places. But here, it's illegal in state water up to three miles offshore. The guys figured since they were eighteen miles from Maui, no one would care. They didn't think about Lanai being state waters or their boat drifting so close to an official dive spot. The local authorities gave them a misde-meanor charge once they found them since they had fled from the scene as soon as I was attacked."

"The guys on the fishing boat did nothing to help you?" she asked in shock.

"No, would you expect them to? It was a bunch of rich

guys who were bored and looking for a little excitement. Those guys were searching for an adrenaline rush. They've lived their lives in a world of privilege without consequences. They think the rules don't apply to them. But all our actions have consequences for others. We have to learn to live in harmony and respect for one another. I hope my surf company teaches that. I want to have *ho'ohana*–to work with purpose and intent."

She looked at me a little speechless. "I don't understand how you can get in the water after the shark attack. I'd be terrified."

"Reef is mostly to thank for that. He got me back in the water as soon as possible and even back to diving. The longer I waited, the harder it would have gotten. And I'll always think about it when I'm in the water. It will always be a part of me. But then I remember my love of the water. It's home for me. And I'll never be able to thank Reef enough for reminding me. It wasn't easy, but therapy helped. And Tutu was there for me, too. She moved in with me to help take care of me. When I noticed the signs that she needed help, I asked her to stay–to help me. But really, it's the other way around now. And we both know it, but we never say it. She really wants it to be the other way around. She's had to give up so much. So we just sort of pretend. And I am always going to need her. Tutu's love helped me survive. I just want to do the same for her."

"I know you do. I can see it," Guin spoke up. "You're not at all what I expected, Locke."

"I'm going to take that as a good thing." I looked at her deeply. "You aren't either, Mermaid. You're so much more than I expected."

Locke

CHAPTER 32

I'D FINALLY CONVINCED Guin to go back to the shaded area of the boat. Her motion sickness had calmed down, and I'd asked if she wanted to get back in the water before it got too late. But she said she'd enjoyed enough snorkeling for today. So we'd continued talking and the time slowly drifted by, until we were watching the sun drop lower and lower on the horizon.

This was turning into one of my favorite things to do with Guin. I had my arm wrapped around her shoulders, holding her like a treasure I'd found at sea. Because, in reality, that is very much what had happened. And I might not know what lay ahead, but I knew at this moment, I didn't want to let go of her. And as she leaned against my vulnerable side, with her arm resting on my right leg, it didn't bother me at all. I didn't even think about it. Not with her. It was like I'd forgotten to be insecure. I just felt complete with her. So much that it made me look at her hesitantly. Wondering how this could be real. Just waiting for this "too good to be true" moment to end. But it didn't. Our time together just kept getting more beautiful, just like the latest sunset.

She turned her face to me, glancing at me with a quirked eyebrow. "What?" she asked. "Does seeing the tubing bother you? I'm sure my sleeve has dried by now. I can put it back on."

Wow, that question really gutted me. Did she really think I'd be capable of thinking such a thing? I knew I wasn't particularly warm and fuzzy, and I had a guarded exterior with women–particularly beautiful mermaids–but I couldn't believe she'd think the sight of her tubing would 'bother' me.

"Guin, no. *Never.*" My solar plexus took a direct hit at the thought.

"Are you sure?" she asked shakily. "I know it's super unsexy."

"Yeah, because half a leg screams sex appeal." She laughed tersely at my joke, knowing all too well how I felt. Then I looked at her as I spoke seriously. "Guin, being attracted to you has never been the problem. There's not one part of you that I don't find sexy."

She dipped her head down and tucked a strand of hair behind her ear. For someone so bold, she sure got shy when it came to something like this. "Well then, what's the problem?" she asked teasingly.

"Well, it's definitely not you. There's never been a problem with *you*, Mermaid. It's me. I mean, you did–and you still do–really infuriate me, but now it just turns me on." I teased. She pushed her back against me playfully. I continued trying to explain it to her. "It's *my* sex appeal or rather . . . lack of it." I trailed off as I looked at the end of my leg.

Guin sputtered back in disbelief, "Locke, you're incredibly attractive. I'm usually only attracted to guys once I get to know them better, but with you, I was a goner from the moment you picked me up from my inglorious landing on the beach. You were like 'Hawaiian Baywatch' that day." I couldn't help but laugh. "The Rock version," she added. I laughed even more, and she said, "I think when you said that I 'wasn't your type,' and you started aggravating the heck out of me, then I was determined *not* to be attracted to you. Plus, I was so *over* dating and it seemed like you weren't particularly interested in dating, either. We were both obviously fighting our attraction to one another."

I looked at her seriously. "Maybe that's why we annoyed each other so much."

"I can almost guarantee it." She smiled.

I continued, "But you didn't see my leg that day. I always keep it covered–even around my family, with the exception of Tutu. Things probably would have worked out differently that first day had you seen my prosthesis."

"No, Locke, that's not true. I saw the indent in your wetsuit on our first day together. I realized what it was when you were trying to distract me from Tutu's care. I just was a little too disoriented to notice before that. So I have been and still am *very* attracted to you, Locke. Now, just as much as ever.

I'm not going anywhere. Your sharing has only made me *more* attracted to you."

I swallowed hard. This was not the reaction I had *ever* expected to get. It was jarring, and I was having trouble adjusting to it and to her kind heart. Most days, my prosthesis left me feeling pretty unattractive. And people's reactions to it could make me feel unloveable. Most women didn't even like to think about touching my leg, yet she'd treated it just like any other part of my body. And here she was saying she liked *all of me*. I couldn't be this lucky.

"Don't you have questions about it? Doesn't it bother you?" I asked gruffly.

"About what?" she asked, now really looking at me. The sun was dipping lower behind her, illuminating her in its soft, warm glow.

"Guin, what do you think I mean?" I returned with an ache.

"Should I have questions? Is this some test I'm not passing?" I closed my eyes at her sincere words.

"Well, usually there's a ton of questions if a woman doesn't run away like I'm the Hawaiian version of Frankenstein." She looked at me disapprovingly, but I continued. "You can pick a different monster if you like, but it's an accurate depiction."

"This would be a hilarious analogy except that you have it all wrong. *They're* the actual monsters, Locke. Anyone who treats you that way is the true 'Frankenstein.' They're missing one of the best pieces of humanity: compassion. And I feel truly sorry for them."

I had never looked at it that way, and her words went straight to my heart. An ache pulsated inside me from her understanding.

My voice barely came out. "Can you please just ask some

questions? Go ahead." There was such a hollow tone to my words. As much as her words had filled me with warmth, I was still bracing myself for the worst.

Guin looked at me like she was gathering her thoughts. She snuggled closer to me, the *opposite* reaction of what I was expecting.

She let her hand fall over my knee near my prosthesis. I couldn't believe how much I wanted to feel her touch there–how good it felt.

"Does it hurt?" she asked softly. "Is the attachment uncomfortable?" Those large blue eyes filled with so much compassion as she talked. *How can such a cool blue be so warm? Burn so hot?* But her eyes were the color of home to me.

"Huh?" Shock overcame me. No one had ever asked such questions. They usually wanted to know about the shark attack and how painful it had been. They wanted to know all about my 'limitations'–some of them *way* too personal. But they'd never asked about my comfort or my boring daily life.

"Do you still have a lot of pain in your leg since the surgery? Does the attachment hurt after wearing it for a while?" she asked, clarifying. "It seems like it would be really uncomfortable to put all your weight on it, unless you don't have any feeling there," she trailed off, blushing. "Sorry. You didn't really want that many questions, did you?"

"No, no, I did," I said with sincerity. And I pulled her even closer to me. For the first time since the accident, I wanted questions. And these were the sweetest ones I'd ever been asked. My heart felt like doing a happy dance inside my chest. "The end of my limb is actually super sensitive; all the nerves are bundled along the incision. If my weight comes down the wrong way, then it can be extremely painful. It gets really sore when I'm doing something new and especially when I'm 'breaking in' a new prosthesis. But more than anything, I get tired more easily. And there are times I've forgotten that I don't have all of my leg anymore. I know it sounds really weird, but sometimes I've gotten out of bed and fallen flat on my face. It sounds funny now, but it wasn't funny when it happened, that's for sure."

"No, that doesn't sound weird at all. I'm sure I'd *still* be forgetting about it, too. I'm lucky if I even remember to take all my medicine in the morning."

"Yeah, well, you catch on pretty fast after a few hard falls." I laughed dryly. "I used to really resent my prosthesis, but now I'm thankful for it. I'm able to do so many things with it that I wouldn't be able to do otherwise. But I'm still making peace with how people view it. That's not so easy. But as helpful as it is, the everyday logistics of wearing a prosthesis can be exhausting. Getting ready in the mornings takes so much longer and the daily care does too. Things like properly washing the prosthesis and getting the sand out of it in the showers after our surf lesson takes some extra time. It's just the little things that add up, especially compounded with the heat here. You can get hot spots from the silicone sleeve, so I have to be really careful. You learn to come up with creative things like using deodorant and silicone gel to help with hot spots from friction. There's a lot that goes into wearing it. So I look forward to when I can go to bed and finally be without it." I laughed. "Sleep is freeing. As you've noticed with my choice of pajamas."

"I can only imagine. I never really got used to my fistula at night, even after it healed. Did it take a really long time for your leg to heal?" Guin's eyes met mine and I loved that she was asking questions on her own now.

"Yeah, healing was a very lengthy process. It usually takes about six weeks and then you're supposed to have PT for around six months, but healing has such a mental component, too. No one really talks about that. And well, I had a lot of trouble with that aspect. I was really closed off and even averse to physical therapy. I didn't want to know how much I couldn't do. And I sure didn't want anyone to see how much it had affected my mental health. Men's mental health isn't exactly something we discuss in society. And I felt the last thing I could do was show that I was struggling in that area. But Tutu and Reef kept going with me. They kept supporting me and encouraging me to get through it. Who knows what state I'd be in now–both mentally and physically–without them. But I feel like I haven't gotten comfortable being in my own skin yet."

A sadness fell upon her features. "Locke, I always want you to be comfortable around me. You know, you can take your prosthesis off when I'm with you," she said softly.

"What?" Surprise filled me. *No one* ever wanted me to take it off. I must have heard her wrong. Well, except for a few people with some really strange fetishes that I did *not* indulge.

"You can take it off anytime it's bothering you. Like right now, we're just sitting down. I want you to do whatever's most comfortable for you. Unless it's not worth the trouble of putting it back on." I shook my head and she continued, "You could show me how to take it off and put it back on. I'm sure it gets tiresome. You might like someone to help and give you a break.

I just sat there motionless, overcome by her words. Finally, I nodded. But then I couldn't manage anything else and she seemed to realize that fact. So she continued speaking, "Will you show me what to do? I'd like to learn." She touched the sleeve on my thigh and asked, "Do you just roll this down first?" She looked at me questioningly, and then her face was covered in pink. She reached her hand back like she'd over-stepped, questioning whether she'd misread me. But it was too late. There were a few tears that had fallen down my face. *Tears*. And I couldn't stop them. Guin looked confused, "Locke, I'm really sorry. What did I do? I won't try to take it off again–"

I cleared my throat and forced myself to speak. "That's the first step. It just rolls down. But Guin my liner is going to be filled with ocean water. This isn't pretty, nor attractive or masculine. Let's just stop."

Her face was shocked, but after a slight hesitation, she returned her hand to my sleeve. "Locke, isn't that even more of a reason that it should come off? That can't be good for your skin. And this doesn't affect any of those things you just listed. Being *yourself* is what's most attractive." The look on her face tore away every hesitation that was left inside of me. I swallowed. She really didn't see me any differently.

I started going through the steps, sighing with relief when she removed the prosthesis. It was the most intimate undressing I'd ever experienced in my life–so raw and vulnerable. I watched as she gracefully laid the prosthesis beside me, within reach. It was a far more gentle treatment than the beat-up thing had ever received from me. Guin even offered to get the water hose so I could rinse off my leg, and then she returned to my arms. Like she hadn't just done the nicest thing possible for me. Her kind eyes roamed over me with uncertainty, making sure everything was okay, when in fact, she'd just cared for me in a way I hadn't known existed. Because that's what love does.

The only other person who had ever helped me with my leg was Tutu. My mom had tried, but after several awkward attempts, she left it in Tutu's capable hands, for which I was thankful. I liked fewer people having to do something like that for me. When Tutu cared for me, it was a gesture of love. Of taking care of someone because that's what family and communities do. It was a true depiction of *Ohana*. She'd instilled that in me. And when Guin did it, I felt yet another type of love. A love filled with deep connection and understanding. Because true love just knew. It wanted to care for you, and more than anything, it wanted to be there for you. And God, did I want to be there for her, too.

I held her as close as I could against the sunset as she said, "Better?"

"I think everything will be with you." And I *really* meant it. But I was having a very hard time not crying again, and it was actually humiliating.

I reached for her hand to watch the sunset again, but she turned to me instead. "I know I said I wanted a friend–and I could really use one–but I don't want you to be just a friend . . . I want you to be so much more, Locke."

I could hear the waves slapping against the side of the boat as I smiled at her and said, "I want more too. *So* much more." And I couldn't believe I was saying it.

Her smile faded as she looked solemnly at me. Her voice lowered. "Just as long as you know I can't stay on dialysis forever. It's got an expiration date." The last words stuck in her throat.

"I know, Guin. Just as long as you know I'm not spontaneously growing a limb." She laughed lightly at my attempt to lighten the mood again. "Seriously, I'm not going anywhere. I want to be here with you. *Anywhere* with you."

The way she looked at me told me what I'd just said hadn't been true from other people in her past. I lifted her chin and saw her eyes mist over. So I repeated, "I'm not going anywhere." She nodded at my words. "I mean, you've got my leg, so where am I going to go?" She pushed against me playfully. "You can keep it. Really, I don't want to be anywhere else."

"That is probably the strangest and yet most romantic gift I've ever been given." She laughed, but there were tears threatening to spill over in her eyes.

"I'd do anything to give you my kidney," I said seriously.

She nodded and swallowed hard. "Don't you know you're not allowed to give two such unconventional and romantic gifts in a row." She laughed. And I wiped her tears away.

"Sorry, I'll try to space them out better next time."

"Please do. A girl can only handle so much." She beamed.

"Guin, I think I'm falling for you," I whispered.

She turned to me. "Three, Locke. You can't do three." Her eyes scanned me, trying to find any hint of a lie. It seemed she was having a lot of trouble believing *any* of my three. "Locke, I'm like the lame horse they pull out of the race before it even begins. I'm not the type you want to begin the race with." It pained me to hear those words.

"Mermaid, I've fallen for you," I said steadfastly. Everything I had was laid out before her. Every insecurity. All the messiest parts. That was it. *All of me.*

She let out a little noise, and her chest rose and fell, quickly. Like my words were too much for her heart. She came toward me with those blue eyes pulling me into their riptides for the millionth time. Against the sunset, she let her lips crash over mine, and I hoped that was her reply. Because no one had ever kissed me like this. Never so sincerely and certainly never so passionately. Desire ignited in me. I knew she truly saw all of me, not just my disability. The "me" no one else took the time to see. Or maybe, the real me no one else *could* see.

Guinevere

CHAPTER 33

LOCKE DOCKED the boat in the Ma'alaea Harbor as the stars swirled above us in the balmy night sky. I realized that there weren't any other evenings quite like the ones under the Hawaiian skies. The heat of the day diminished and rewarded us with a cool, sultry evening that was a magical world all on its own. One that could never be experienced through photos. And I couldn't be happier that I'd come here. Even if my trip hadn't gone as I had imagined, the experience had turned out even better than I had expected. Way better than "perfect" because I had learned that *real* was what I wanted. Like the vulnerability I'd seen from Locke today. Because he was the best part of this new world.

And somehow, we fit so well together. Like our weathered edges were made for each other. A lot like sea glass. Our rough edges were being smoothed as the sea rocked us together. Maybe now we would be strong enough to weather the storms. Allowing something beautiful to be made of our lives.

As we tied the boat up to the dock, Locke spoke about getting something to eat for dinner. The more he talked, the more it sounded like a makeup date for our "fake" date. I just smiled foolishly because I couldn't wipe off the grin that was plastered across my face.

We started walking down the creaking pier, accompanied by the relaxing sounds of rocking boats. The lights on the dock poles guided our feet. Locke's hand was so close to mine, and I kept wanting to take it, but everything still seemed so uncertain to me–even if we had just kissed. He also glanced down at our hands, swinging his closer and then back out again like the ebbing tides of the sea. It was as if we both didn't dare go there. We didn't want to press our luck. There was something so vulnerable and intimate about holding hands. What we shared on the boat had been perfect, and maybe we needed to leave it there, at least for now. Physical intimacy was going to be hard for me. I realized it might be hard for him as well.

The large blue moon in the sky hung over us as Locke guided me across the street and down the path to the restaurant overlooking the harbor. I could feel the anxiety rising in me as we weaved through the tables on the patio. The dining area was perfectly lit by overhead twinkling lights and the blazing glow of the tiki torches that outlined the palm tree beds surrounding the patio area. I'd never been anywhere quite this picturesque with palm trees providing even more privacy–more intimacy to this fairy tale setting. "Romantic setting" would be an understatement for this place as the harbor lights twinkled in the background and glistened off the bay waters washing up on the sea wall.

My heart was racing as Locke pulled out my chair. *Why did he bring me here?* I would have thought a really vibrant, fun, loud place would be his thing. This was too much. And I was definitely dressed more for a food truck experience in my oversized, gold-button cover-up. As relaxed as Hawaii and even this place might be, I would have dressed more appropriately for a restaurant with this type of atmosphere. I might be in a type of dress, but it was not the right one. Even if there were other people who had come from their boat in similar attire, I felt sorely out of place. Anxiety was swelling inside of me–or maybe that was just my pounding adrenaline. Locke looked at me and seemed to realize the same thing.

While his Columbia button-down shirt and pants looked awfully nice on him, I had opted to *wear this* cover-up. But now I realized he had wanted to bring me somewhere special. And my heart rate was spiking even more as I sat with my salty, sea-blown hair pulled back into what was surely a disaster.

Do I get a re-do? Just a quick thirty-minute rewind, please?

"You look really beautiful," Locke said quietly, staring at me from across the candlelight.

Yeah right. And a little nervous laughter that I couldn't contain escaped me as he sat there bathed in the romantic outdoor lighting and looking ridiculously handsome. Was it the candlelight, the moonlight, the tikis, or the *twinkles* that were giving him this special "glow?" Seriously, I didn't have a prayer. It was unfair for a place to have *this* much mood lighting. Give a girl a fighting chance. And here I sat looking like candle wax–a real hot mess.

His face twisted. "What?"

"Locke, seriously, you could have told me we were coming to a place like this. I would have worn something else. It's hardly fair when you look like *this*."

His face slackened, relief and confusion taking over. "What are you talking about? You look perfect. Beautiful."

I was just about to respond with a teasing remark, but then I realized he was being sincere. Gentle Locke had struck again, and the cynic in me melted. And then I realized as I looked at him that he wasn't wearing pants as I had assumed. He had on swim shorts. I'd never seen his bare legs out in public before. And something kick-started in my heart. The squeezing in my chest sent butterflies flipping and soaring inside of me. Because I knew in my gut, this was something he didn't do. *Ever.*

Locke ran his fingers through his tousled hair. It was shaggy and beachy in a sexy way. And right now, I just needed him to stop looking so good because my hormones were going crazy.

A self-consciousness came over him as I stared at him way too obviously. "Uh, I didn't want to cover up my leg. I wanted our first date to be different–at least, that's what I was hoping this could be. And if so . . . I wanted it to be honest and . . . Uh–" But he stopped, too self-conscious to continue. I didn't realize when he asked me if I wanted to go to dinner that he was really asking me out on a date. Now, the determination he'd had in his voice made a little more sense.

A little sigh escaped me, like soft butterfly wings flapping. I don't think I'd ever been so attracted to someone before. *What is he doing to me?*

And before I knew it, my hand extended out, drifting across the tablecloth. Like an out-of-body experience. And it just lay there, open, palm up on the table. It probably looked more like a dorky move from *E.T.* than the vulnerable, romantic one I was feeling. I think my hand may have been shaking. I wouldn't take my hand.

But Locke definitely wasn't me. He took it right away and warmth spread through me like thick molten lava. My cheerful grin obliterated everything that had come before.

"Thank you," I breathed, because that's all the words the butterflies would let escape, other than my embarrassing sighs.

"No, I should thank you, Guin," he replied. His voice lowered, the husky tone filled me. "I, um, I haven't dated since my accident. Not really. Certainly never as my true self." He looked down briefly and then back up at me, his eyes deep with emotion. Their intensity created a dreamy home for me. What I had mistaken as icy darkness had become soothing warmth–a cocoon of understanding.

"Well, I can guarantee you weren't missing out on much." I laughed, trying to ease his pain. "I thought I'd found someone who didn't see my limitations, but unfortunately, he just called attention to them for control. He convinced me to keep my fistula covered because it was too unattractive. And sadly, I stayed in that relationship way longer than I should have. You were smart and probably just saw the warning flags earlier than I did. All that Baywatch training." I laughed, trying to lighten the mood. "It's certainly not easy dating with extra vulnerabilities."

Locke just squeezed my hand tighter. It was reassuring in a way I'd never known. I hadn't opened up about dating like this before, not even to my friends. A quiet contentment swelled in me. A calm peace came suddenly, feeling like I was with someone who would not harm me. Did he *feel the same?*

His voice brought me back, "No, Guin, that could never be true. You're beautiful and *so* much more. I hope you know that." A pained smile flickered across his lips. "You're much braver than I was. I gave up pretty quickly. So I'm a 'disability monk' . . . Never been kissed." He laughed. "Well, until now." And his smile melted me.

"I'm your first chronic illness kiss?" I replied in shock. This couldn't be further from what I'd expected from Locke. I realized then that I'd jumped to so many wrong assumptions about him.

"Yeah, Guin. Now I'm glad that I ran them all off." He laughed. "Because it had to be you."

My heart lurched at the thought of anyone 'running away' from him, but most of all I hated that any part of him believed they had a reason to.

I spoke gently. "Most people can't handle things that are 'different.' And you never know how much is too much until you hit that breaking point. That hurts the most," I said. Very much speaking from experience.

An understanding flashed in Locke's eyes, then a softness. "To the right person, Mermaid, there won't ever be too much. That person will always be there, wading through unfamiliar territory with you and helping you find your way, *together*." Little flecks danced in his eyes as the candles' flames reflected in them. I never knew such an answer could exist from someone.

I looked at him with so much appreciation. I never thought we'd have so much in common. I certainly never thought he'd be the one to understand me. I guess under all our bantering were two people trying to fight an undeniable attraction and connection. Because when you're chronically ill you get very good at assessing how quickly, and how far you can let your guard down with someone. It's an inherited sixth sense–a survival gift. But somewhere along the way, I had wanted nothing more than to be pulled along by the current because I knew it was going to lead to him. It was always supposed to lead to him. I believed that now with my whole being as I sat looking into his eyes.

Guinevere

THE REST of dinner went surprisingly more like a normal first date, except one that I actually enjoyed. So it wasn't really normal at all. Locke asked me questions about my life and we exchanged pieces of our stories. Little parts of ourselves floated about the romantic setting. And it had been perfect. And for one night, I'd felt truly accepted by someone. My life finally felt like it was the way it was supposed to be. I could feel the romance and the gorgeous night without worry. Such a wonderful, carefree feeling to be comfortable in your own skin.

And the brooding man with the weathered heart and gruff personality, the one who had first picked me up from the beach, turned out to be the sweetest, gentlest man I'd ever dated. And it was then that I thought maybe all those monsters and legends had something to them. Maybe they were meant to show us we shouldn't judge others based on first impressions. Maybe they're there to teach us to search for more. And while I was pretty sure Locke's mom had chosen his name because she loved water elements, I think his name had taken on more of a Loch Ness meaning for him. But that couldn't be further from the truth. The only similarity was that there was so much more to him, especially where first impressions were concerned.

Locke gently wrapped an arm around me, bringing me into him as we walked back to the boat. The night had cooled now, but his warmth had not. I was learning it never did. Then, with an ease that was obviously honed over years of experience, he untied us and set us free back into the harbor and out to sea. I'd never been on a boat at night and was actually expecting it to be a little creepy. I guess I had watched too many thriller movies. Usually this is where the dead body got thrown over . . . and *you* were that dead body. But with Locke, I always felt safe.

As he cast off the boat, he said to me. "How about some stargazing before we take the boat back to the dock? I made a promise to you." He grinned.

"You did, and I never thought you'd make good on it," I said cheekily.

"Well, considering this is my first *enjoyable* experience in dating with a disability, I want it to be special. So I'm going against my better judgment here." His grin spread even wider.

He found a spot outside the harbor to anchor and went below deck, leaving me to stare up at the glowing moon. Locke returned with two sleeping bags, pillows, and blankets.

I started laughing. "Do you camp out on the boat?"

"I just like to be prepared," he said playfully. "What if we got caught out in a terrible storm at sea? Then you'd be glad for all the supplies I have down there. Straws that turn saltwater into freshwater, etc. I'll show you sometime if you don't mock me."

I wasn't laughing now, thinking about what he had just said. He saw my face and said, "But that's never happened, Mermaid. I *promise* you'll be safe with me."

He unrolled the sleeping bags on the front of the boat's deck in one swift movement, spreading the blankets out for extra padding. "Your clamshell awaits, Ariel."

I had to bite my lip to keep from smiling too much. I also loved that this "disability monk" had brought out two sleeping bags instead of one. I'd assumed wrong again. Locke wasn't just gentle, he was respectful. And not just of my conditions but also my emotions.

My heart was thrumming again, whooshing like the ocean sound inside a conch shell. And I just stood there quietly.

"What, are you not going to try out your new clamshell, Mermaid?" Then, he seemed to have another thought. "Will the boat deck be too hard on your joints? I didn't think about that. Actually, I've never tried using sleeping bags on the deck before. I think I have some pads down below and some cushions—" He offered as he comically tested them out. He looked like he was being paid to test the sleeping bag for comfort and durability. Locke didn't seem to mind being a guinea pig for my comfort and care.

And as the waves inside me rushed harder, the blood pumped faster. This musical rhythm of desire overtook every part of me. I was pulled to this magnetic man; everything about him called to me. A full moon to my ocean heart. I began lowering myself beside him and he stopped his movements. His eyes caught on mine. I slowly reached for the sleeping bag top and pulled it back a little, assessing. Locke's eyes widened. And then slowly, I unzipped it so I could lie beside him. He was too stunned to make any room for me, his lower jaw dropping open.

He cleared his throat. "Uh, I've got it," he said, sending a shock wave through me. He brought me to his chest so he could reach his arm around me to pull the zipper up. I was tucked so close to him that every electric impulse started flaring inside of me. "Mermaid, I don't think these sleeping bags are meant for two people, but I'm happy to share." He chuckled. "Sorry your shell wasn't satisfactory."

"It really wasn't," I said in feigned disappointment.

"I should have known you would ensnare me in one of these." But there was nothing but a wink in his tone.

I pinched my lips together to keep from smiling foolishly. And then, without a thought, I brought my face closer to his, letting my feelings guide me—overpower me. I brought my nose to his, rubbing it lightly in affection. It felt so good to be this close to him.

"That's the wrong way to be looking at the stars, Mermaid," he said with a raw huskiness I'd never heard from him.

"Depends on what stars you're looking for," I replied softly, the butterflies letting a little sigh escape along the way.

"Oh God, Guin. I don't think you could make my heart race any faster. Take it easy on a guy."

"Yeah, well, I haven't even kissed you yet."

"Yeah, well, I think I'm going to need a minute. Pick a constellation."

"Ursula," I said cheekily.

"*Very funny*, Mermaid. I think you mean Ursa Major or Minor," he said clinically.

"No, I definitely mean Ursula," I said pointedly, referring to what I'd called him that first day on the beach.

"Fine, kiss me. Pull me all the way under. I'm done fighting the mermaid trap," he said, sighing in mock defeat. And I did just that, letting my lips capture his under that endless night sky. The look of falling for someone so apparent in his eyes. And I allowed every sense of him to wash over me; his salty smell, warm lips, and sweet taste. Until I was fully satisfied that he didn't feel like a monster in any way.

Locke

CHAPTER 35

AFTER A BEAUTIFUL EVENING under the night sky's constellations, we headed back to moor the boat. As much as I would love to fall asleep with Guin under the stars as she debated them with me, I knew it would not be comfortable for her. Plus, I knew we needed to get back to the dogs.

The stars guided us back home as we listened to jazz music, and she rested her head on my shoulder. And I realized then that the stars had been guiding us the whole evening. Meeting this woman must have been written in them. Just to know that someone like Guin existed changed something inside of me. And she probably had no idea what she'd done to me.

And maybe this hadn't been the most conventional date in the world, but I wouldn't want to have it any other way. I loved being seen by her. And for the first time, I wouldn't want to change anything about myself either. I felt more attractive than I ever had.

But something was tugging at my heart in warning. Her lack of a response wasn't lost on me when I'd mentioned my feelings for her. But tonight, I wouldn't worry about that. No, tonight was perfect, and I wouldn't let anything take that away from me. Not even those loud warning voices telling me it was time to protect myself and stop falling for her.

As soon as we entered the bungalow, it surprised me that Tutu and the dogs were nowhere to be seen. It certainly was earlier in the evening than the night when Guin and I had fallen asleep together on the beach.

I quickly went to say goodnight so I didn't make this awkward. "I had a great time, thank you. Best *real* first date. Although the 'fake' one wasn't bad either."

Guin smiled. "Me too, thank you. Seriously. I had given up on the existence of an enjoyable date." Her laugh came out a little strained. "I'm going to take my medicine now and check on the dogs."

I nodded as she went off in search of them and then I went to get ready for sleep.

I was sitting on the sofa in my Golden Retriever pajama bottoms when Guin came out with the dogs–they must have taken over her bed. Quickly, I stood up as she came closer. "I'm going to let the dogs out again just in case," she said.

"No, I'll do it. You go to bed," I said as I looked at her tired face. Then I took the dogs out the door before she could insist.

But when I returned, she was snuggled up on the sofa instead. She had on the most adorable and attractive, satin short and tank set I'd ever seen.

Why does she keep doing this to me?

And when I got closer, I noticed the *paw prints* on them. My pulse quickened .

"Uh, I don't really like my clamshell anymore," she said somewhat shyly, seriously making my blood pump harder.

"Oh," was all I could manage.

Great. That was really inviting.

"Yeah, it's a problem." She laughed melodically.

"Oh, is it? Well, you *already* took my clamshell." I nodded toward my room, and she laughed. "You want this one too?" And she burst out laughing.

"Locke." She looked down bashfully and then back up at me with this new confidence. "Can I stay with you?"

I looked at her questioningly. Then, as if she felt she needed to explain, she continued, "Locke, I never ask to stay in anyone's clamshell, but I'd like to fall asleep with you tonight if that's alright. I'd like to upgrade my Eric 2.0." She laughed, but my mouth went completely dry, I couldn't even swallow. I couldn't sleep with my prosthetic leg–I would get hot spots for sure. I'd been cowardly hiding it under the sofa. I didn't know if she understood what she was asking. I was *no* Eric 2.0 substitute. Thankfully, the other day when she'd caught me in my pajamas, I'd been able to lower the blanket *just* low enough for her to see my PJs, but not so low that she could see my residual limb.

"Mermaid, you better keep Eric 2.0. I'd be a lousy substitute." But she was already walking over to me with such desire in her eyes that it was melting my fears. Or at least making me forget they were even there. She stared into me, bringing that heat with her as she reached up on her tiptoes. And then I could think of nothing but those addicting, soft lips. She pulled her face back a few inches, not bothering to remove her hand that was threaded through my hair. "What are you scared of?"

"Guin, I can't wear my prosthesis at night," I said more quietly than I'd expected.

"I didn't expect you to. Hold me as you please." Those were the sweetest whispers. *This woman . . .*

"Ok," I finally breathed out. "Whose clamshell?" But apparently it didn't matter as she kept kissing me. She pulled back, and I looked at her with a deep appreciation. It was all I needed to initiate the next kiss.

Finally, we made our way toward the sofa, collapsing together with her head in the curve of my neck that would forever be hers. And before I knew it, she was sitting up on the edge of the sofa and reaching for the sleeve of my prosthesis. She was going to make sure this wasn't awkward. It was just a given that she wanted me to be myself and to be comfortable. And I was really thankful because I was too shocked to do much of anything.

She hesitated at the sleeve and looked at me, asking permission with her deep gaze. But I still couldn't respond. So she just sat patiently, never breaking eye contact with me.

Do I trust her? This would be the most intimate thing I'd ever done, definitely the most vulnerable. And without another thought, I nodded.

This time, she took the mobility aid off with no help, and again she laid it within reach. Something I never would have expected her to think about. But she just kept doing these things instinctively with me. It was so attractive. And then those beautiful ocean-colored eyes stared back at me, with more vulnerability than mine. As if she was the one exposed.

"Which side would you prefer me on?" She tucked her hair as she asked, not knowing what to do. That gesture of self-doubt that gave her away. So I sat up and took her in my arms, finally unfreezing. I brought her into my chest and back down to the sofa. I helped her curl into me as I spooned her against me. And she fit so perfectly. Like she always was meant to and always would.

"Perfect," I whispered in her ear.

She nodded. "I think Eric 2.0 better get worried. "

"Yes, very worried, I'm destroying all the pillows." And she laughed at my joke. "I don't think you know–" I began.

But she turned her head to me with tears in her eyes. "I know, Locke. *I know.*" And there was such a deep understanding. I had underestimated what tonight had done for her as well. And I pulled her into me, promising myself this was one mermaid I would never let go. Even if that was only in my memories.

Locke

CHAPTER 36

I AWOKE with the biggest crick in my neck, but happier than I remember being in a very long time. My sofa situation had been vastly upgraded last night. And it certainly looked a lot more beautiful.

I gazed at Guin, now sleeping on my chest. I don't think we had moved much from how we had fallen asleep last night, but how could we? The sofa wasn't exactly meant for sleeping two people. Looking at how soundly she was sleeping, my chest couldn't help but bloom with happiness. And I was going to take full advantage of this moment while I had it.

It was then that I decided I wanted to do something special for her. I would quietly slip out and go make breakfast. Hopefully, I could bring her breakfast in bed—well, sofa—before she woke up.

I had just successfully disentangled myself without disturbing her and was taking one last look at her before heading toward the kitchen. As I got up, my thoughts focused on being quiet so I could surprise her. But it didn't take long for me to realize that the leg I extended for my first step was a phantom one, and I hit the deck. *Hard*. And *loud* too.

This was utterly embarrassing. I hadn't done this in such a long time. And I don't even want to remember how many times I'd done this in the beginning. I had gotten *a lot* of bruises. But now, it was much harder to forget . . . unless you had "mermaid brain" . . . 24/7.

Within seconds, Penny had rushed over to me. She knew the drill. She would bring my prosthesis to me or help me up by lending me her back so I could stabilize myself. Usually, she tried to do both. Really, she could be a service dog. But most days I just needed her emotional support.

"Oh my—Locke, are you ok?" I heard Guin's voice slice through the air as I lay there, face-planted. But I wasn't ready to look at her yet. I was rooted to the ground. Within no time at all, both Penny and Guin were beside me. And I didn't know who was going to bring my leg faster, but I knew Penny was pretty territorial.

Guin's hand was on my back, rubbing smoothly back and forth. "Locke, say something. *Please*." I finally turned my head to face her, opening one eye with reluctance. I spotted Penny holding my prosthetic leg and Guin's concerned face. She reached over to Penny's mouth and Penny actually released the prosthesis to her. I was shocked. She really trusted Guin. That softened me completely.

"Uh, can you just pretend to go back to sleep for like fifteen minutes? Actually, make it twenty." I chuckled.

"Locke, no, I can't. What happened? Seriously, tell me what's going on. And let me help you."

"At this rate, you're going to be late for your appointment, and you'll never get to hear what happens to those sexy pirates. What if neither survives? What if there's a third Fabio?" I tried to joke, but I knew she did actually have an appointment today.

"Locke, I couldn't care less. The only 'Fabio' I care about is face down on the floor in front of me."

"Well, that's not a good look. I promise that won't sell any books."

"Locke!" I could hear her growing impatience.

I turned over, and Guin offered me a hand so I could sit up too. Penny actually let her. I sighed as I explained, "I wanted to make you breakfast, Mermaid. That's all. I wanted this to be special. This is what I get for attempting to be romantic."

"And you were going to cook it on the floor?" She teased.

"No." I sighed and looked away. "I guess I forgot I didn't have a leg attached today. That hasn't happened to me in a very long time. *Must be "mermaid" on the brain*," I mumbled softly to myself, hoping she wouldn't hear.

"I'm sorry. You have what?"

I turned to face her. "I have 'mermaid brain.' *All the time.* I've fallen into your snare, grabbed the shiny lure, went out to the siren call . . . However you want to put it, I'm a goner,

Mermaid. So gone, I thought I could walk without my aid, apparently. Ironic, since the mermaid is the one who's supposed to have trouble walking on dry land. I guess I just felt so good with you, that I thought I could defy gravity."

Her expression melted into something I'd never seen before. *Whoa, was that for me?* It was a look of overpowering emotion.

"Locke, everything with you is special. I don't need any of the extras. I would have been happy making breakfast with you or keeping you company so I didn't burn anything." She laughed at herself. "You don't need to do grand, romantic gestures. Believe me, you're more of a romantic gesture than you'll ever know. The way you make me feel–the way you care about me–those are the wonderful romantic gestures. And it's really special when you share things about yourself with me. That's what I really want." She handed me the prosthesis as she said it.

"Well, since it's *so* special, is now a good time to tell you that my phantom pain is acting up?" I grimaced, having trouble hiding it anyway. This one was definitely more severe. I wouldn't be able to hide it from her, anyway. It felt like a knife slicing through my nonexistent foot. Little electrodes were shocking me along the way. I cringed, grabbing my residual limb.

She scooted closer and nodded with concern. "Of course, what can I do?"

Now, it was my turn to smile, even through the pain. It felt like when I'd told her I didn't know what Lupus was. The playing field now felt more level between us. Just two equals really trying to understand and care for one another.

"Well, my brain thinks that I still have all of my leg," I said, trying to distract myself. "So I have to train and trick my brain.

Thankfully, there are ways to do that because your mind can really play games with you. Like wanting nothing more than to stretch out my nonexistent leg or extend it, but I can't. Or having an itch I'm dying to scratch, but there's no way to relieve it. It's like having chicken pox and putting on mittens." I laughed, but right now nothing was funny. Maybe if I did my exercises, then it would help to keep the pain at bay. But I wasn't so sure I wanted her to see me doing them. I'd been told that it looked a little weird.

She must have sensed my unease because she placed her hand on my neck, asking me to look at her. "How do you trick your brain? Can I help you . . . or even try to do it with you?"

Well, this is new. I exhaled sharply. This took the fun house mirrors to a whole new level. *Just wait until she sees.*

"Yeah, I just need this to pass first so I can get some things from my room. Usually the pain only lasts a few minutes," I said hesitantly. She tried to move her head so I was making eye contact with her but I couldn't look at her. I didn't want to see what I could lose. Even when the pain passed, I continued to look away, not sure if I was ready to let her into this part of my world.

But she brought her nose to mine anyway and started that adorable Eskimo kiss of hers. And my glacier heart started pumping blood so quickly that it had no choice but to thaw. Maybe that's one reason the Inuits do it. It certainly warmed me up. And I laughed silently.

"Let's see if we can help with that pain," she said. "I'll go with you, or I can get the things you need."

I nodded, the tension easing with her words. After what felt like a last wave of pain, I went with Guin to my room. She insisted on pulling out the mirror and pillows from my closet while I sat on the floor.

"So this is why you had all those pillows? Here I thought you were like the princess and the pea," she teased.

"Well, sort of. Sometimes I have to prop my leg in different positions at night, and using pillows can help with the phantom pain as well."

"What else have you been hiding from me?" she jokingly questioned. Then, as if it just hit her, she said, "I really hope last night didn't set this off."

"Well, there can be triggers, but a lot of times it just seems to happen for no reason at all. But even if last night caused the phantom pain, it was definitely worth it," I said, looking unconvincing as my smile turned into a grimace when another round struck me. I grabbed my residual limb. "And I guess there's a lot about my prosthetic leg I haven't told you. *Sorry.* But it's *only* about my prosthetic leg. I promise I will now. Or should I say *legs?* You can look in the hope chest. I keep my extra prosthetic leg and the foot attachments in there because I think it's unlikely anyone will look inside the chest. Sort of ironic since it's named 'hope." My sarcastic autopilot was taking over.

"Locke." Disbelief covered her face. But then she began walking over to the hope chest, a small smile forming on her face, seemingly happy I was finally letting her in. But I grabbed her arm to stop her.

"Wait, I actually want to show you. I can't believe I'm saying this. It was hard enough to show you my surfboards." I laughed. "But that was one of the best experiences I've had. So . . ." I trailed off. I couldn't believe I was going to show her *this* "collection." It certainly wasn't like my surfboards or wetsuits. But that feeling of pure happiness and intimacy overtook me again, the same one I'd had when she touched the surfboards.

And I was ready. I actually wanted this. "I'd really like to show you," I finished vulnerably.

Guin nodded slowly, a sweet and understated expression on her face. Yet it was everything to me at this moment. And somehow, it seemed to mean just as much to her. And I was amazed that I could be *this* lucky.

Guinevere

CHAPTER 37

I SAT beside Locke as he walked me through some of the mirror exercises. Locke really took his time explaining to me how they worked. I was surprised. I thought he would try to move quickly through everything and not share too much yet. But I could see that a weight was slowly being lifted off of him.

I listened carefully, not wanting to miss anything since I was finally being allowed into this extremely private area of his life.

He explained, "So I hold the mirror between my legs and have the mirror face toward my full leg. That way, when I look in the mirror, it appears like I still have all of my other leg. Then I run through different exercises, moving my leg and residual limb at the same time while looking in the mirror. I pretend my residual limb is doing the same thing as my full leg. It tricks my brain into thinking my leg is completely there and can help with the phantom limb syndrome," he explained nervously.

"That's really cool."

He seemed to relax at my words, saying, "Yeah, someone was pretty inventive to come up with this. I just need to do my exercises more often than I do. At first, I did a lot of physical therapy and was great at keeping up with it, but then I got lax about it."

"Oh, I know all about that," I replied. "There's only so many things you can do to improve your health. If I tried to keep up with everything, I'd do nothing else with my day. Sometimes it works out that way." I laughed.

He looked at me with gratitude to have someone who understood and I felt the same way. He continued to explain, "Massage helps too, and sometimes I play music to help relax my brain. The power of music . . . well, you definitely know." He smiled at me, referring to what brought me here. "And if I have a phantom itch, then I can try scratching my left leg and sometimes that will trick my mind, or I can try scratching my prosthesis. There's really nothing like having a scratch you can't itch, literally."

I was glad he was sharing so much of his world with me. "I had no idea. I'm glad you've found so many tricks to help, though. That makes all the difference in the world. Do you have people you can talk with online?" I wondered if he was like me in that regard. Even though I never went to support groups in person, I connected with other people who had Lupus on social media. We traded hacks and helped each other find our triggers. Anything we could do to support one another and make life easier. I was so grateful for my "spoonie" community. I hoped he had a group like that in his life, too.

He averted my eyes. I hated he might be embarrassed. He shouldn't be. About any of this. I put my hand on his shoulder, and it brought him back to me.

Locke spoke solemnly, "I haven't been able to open up to anyone about it. I don't go to support groups or do anything online. I just look at blog articles. Besides Tutu, my mom, and Reef, I don't really talk about it with anyone else. It was hard enough even talking to my physical therapist and prosthetist. People coming into the shop looking for custom equipment sometimes try to discuss it with me, but I just try to keep the focus on them."

"Locke, that sounds so lonely . . . but I understand." I really did. It was hard to open up about things like this. I always tried to talk about subjects other than myself, even when my grandparents and friends were nice enough to ask about me.

He moved the mirror and propped it beside the dresser. "So, are you sure you want to see more?" His eyes glanced over at the hope chest.

"Please, I want to see anything you're comfortable sharing," I replied earnestly.

"Ok." He swallowed but didn't move.

"Can I try the mirror first?" I asked. I was hoping to feel some of what he felt. To experience *something* that he experienced. At least in some way. He looked completely taken aback. *Great, I just keep overstepping.* And I would keep doing it with him because I cared so much and I wanted so badly to be part of his world.

I was just about to change the subject when he pulled the mirror back over and extended his hand to me. Then he gently walked me through some exercises. But it seemed hard for him. The gentle giant appeared overcome with emotions.

I didn't know if he was going to be okay to show me what was in the hope chest, but he still wanted to. Beneath a thin layer of blankets was an entire collection of prosthetic parts. I couldn't believe even in his room he covered them up. It really hurt to see.

Locke explained to me about the different prosthetic attachments. He had so many different types to help with his many different work activities and excursions. He even showed me all the different foot attachments and how to attach them.

Locke was showing me the differences between his two prosthetic legs when I asked, "Were you ever going to talk about your leg with me? Or were you just hoping I wouldn't notice?"

"Well, some people don't notice. Most people are looking at my face. And when I'm wearing pants and shoes it would be difficult to notice my prosthesis. But of course with the wetsuit, it's different. I was kind of hoping the black color and my cosmetic covering would disguise it. I've been fortunate to have an extra prosthesis that I can use solely at the beach. That way I can keep the cosmetic covering on to give it a more natural shape. I even have a 'surf foot' with a surf shoe glued on to it. And maybe I thought you'd be really interested in my charming face and not look anywhere else." He joked. "I don't know. I've grown mindful of blending in as much as possible. I do things like always resting my foot on the ground since the feet attachments don't bend or keeping people on my left side so they don't accidentally feel my prosthesis. These types of things have become second nature to me.

I gave a tiny laugh, but my face twisted.

"Guin, it's not you. It's never been you. I've gotten so used to hiding–believing that's what I needed to do to be loved or accepted in the outside world. When I help other people with disabilities at the shop to embrace themselves, they're beautiful and I see them as strong and capable. But I can't see it for myself. Believe me, I wanted to tell you. I just couldn't handle the idea of you not loving this part of me. So I didn't take a risk. And if you hadn't seen my prosthesis, I would have always regretted it. So thank you. And thanks for understanding my situation so well that you didn't say anything. I don't think I would have been ready to share with you. I'm sorry about that.

"Locke, never apologize for that." I moved to him. "You see my fistula covering. I understand. *All too well*." I took his hand, and he smiled slightly as he tried to search me to see if it was really okay. I decided to change the topic slightly. "So why isn't Penny a service dog? I've always wanted to ask about her."

"Well, a lot of amputees don't need a service dog; they actually just need an emotional support dog. It's only on rare occasions like this morning when Penny turns into more of a service dog."

"So how did you get Penny? You never told me–" But he seemed to cut me off as he looked away. *Right*. He was still going to be closed off. If I stumbled upon something, he would tell me, but he wasn't going to openly share. But then he surprised me.

He looked back and said, "It's not you, Guin. I'm just having a little trouble sharing all this with someone. But I *want* to. Because it's you." He smiled at me and I waited. "I was driving in the rain one day, and I was still having trouble adjusting to driving with my left foot since you know . . ." He looked down at his right leg. "And I have trouble driving that way. Or maybe I just had it in my mind that I couldn't do it. Either way, I was feeling really sorry for myself and listening to jazz on the radio. Really leaning into my sadness. And jazz welcomes you in any emotional state. It can heighten whatever emotion you're feeling. It's like the mood ring of music. And I wanted to be allowed to feel my loss–to commiserate. I needed it."

I looked at him. Still stunned that he listened to jazz. He seemed to figure as much.

"Yes, I listen to jazz. I didn't just turn it on in the car last night to set the mood." He laughed at my expression and continued. "Well, the rain came down even harder, and I probably should have pulled over. But I didn't. I wanted to prove I was just as capable of doing everything the way I could before the accident. Because I'm such an ableist."

"Locke–" I didn't want to push him anymore. For someone who wanted to stay hidden, this was a lot. A lot. I didn't want him to go too fast or have him regret anything with me.

He put a hand up gently. "I'm ok. I'm just a sap when it comes to Penny . . . I started swerving some and the curvy roads didn't help any. But then I saw something in the middle of the road, it made me pull over. Thank God, because the storm was only getting worse. And I remember hearing Billie Holiday sing *Pennies from Heaven* on the radio as I exited the Jeep to remove what was in the road. Really, it was just an excuse to pull over."

He exhaled, and I offered, "You don't have to finish. It's ok."

"No, I want to. For the first time, I really want to." He stared at me and continued, "I went to remove the cardboard box from the road and realized there was something in it. I figured it was an animal hiding out. I guess I was right in a way. It was a little Labrador golden retriever mixed mutt. *So skinny.* And the eyes really got me. The saddest eyes I'd ever seen. I forgot about getting out of the road until a car honked as it was passing by. I scooped up the box and took it back to my Jeep.

"I remember setting the box down on the passenger seat. Too afraid to get her out of the box. I wanted her out of it so badly, but I didn't know if she was too scared to be touched. She was obviously malnourished and neglected. I didn't know what else might have happened to her. And she kept staring up at me with those sad little eyes, and I'd be darned if that Billie Holiday song wasn't still playing. We just stared at each other. And I knew I was going to do everything I could to keep her. That this was a gift not to be taken lightly. She'd probably saved me from driving off the curvy roads that day. And she's continued saving me every day since. Not the other way around.

"I waited out the storm with her and slowly attempted to get her out of the box, which she was eventually happy to do. And while I wrapped some blankets around her from the back of my Jeep, I realized I needed to change my mindset. I needed to be grateful for the things I had and what my body could still do. And the things I could still give. It's probably wrong, but I didn't take her to a shelter. I just kept her as my own. I got her checked out by a vet, but I never turned her in. I believed she claimed me that day. So yeah, she's like a lucky penny. And so much more."

I knew the feeling so well, and I was too choked up to say anything. Instead, he looked at me and said, "So that's Penny. I guess I'm good at finding things. Like mermaids washing up on the beach at my feet." I laughed then, grateful for his humor. He added, "For someone who loves playing jazz on the ukulele, I'm kind of disappointed you never guessed that one. Plus, she has some red coloring like a 'penny from heaven.' I thought you'd get there, eventually."

I nudged him playfully, saying, "Yes, I guess that is pretty sad."

"So, how'd you . . . how'd you get Sebastian?" He hesitated, wondering if he should ask.

"Um, I passed out in my bathroom and when I woke up, no one was there." A shameful expression took shape on my face. It was humiliating to admit. "I moved in with my grandparents when I got sicker, but they'd gone out that morning. It's terrifying not knowing what is going to happen to you and also wondering if anyone will find you if something goes wrong. So my grandparents suggested I get a service dog."

"Is that why Sebastian goes with you to the bathroom?" he questioned. "I didn't want to ask about that before."

"Oh, you knocking on the door and asking if everything is alright is 'not asking,' huh? Bringing my dress was a nice cover, though," I teased, and he laughed.

"Yeah, well, I also wanted to get my shower chair out of the way. Not everything in this house is for Tutu, even if it appears to be that way." A slight heat crept up his face.

Realization dawned on me when he said that. I hadn't made the connection. I teased, "Oh, well, now that I know it's yours, I'll make good use of it myself." He smiled, and that heat went right away. "Yes, Sebe goes everywhere with me unless I have someone I trust with me. And I do have a fear of passing out alone after the bathroom incident." I looked downward, but Locke squeezed my hand. I continued, "So many people think I'm just faking it because I don't look sick, but I don't know what I would do without Sebe."

"Yeah, me too. People can be pretty quick to make judgements about emotional support dogs. But Penny has made such a difference in my life."

I nodded in understanding. "I still remember the day I went to get Sebe. I was so excited yet filled with nerves because I didn't want to choose wrong. But I didn't realize how it would really work. *I* wouldn't be the one choosing. I went inside, and he immediately looked up at me with those warm, chocolate eyes. I held him, and I still remember him chewing on my hair the whole time. He wouldn't let go of me, not even long enough for me to set him back down. And I just knew. It was like he'd chosen me, and it felt *so* good to be chosen. And I'd like to think after everything that's happened, he would still choose me again. I know I would certainly always choose him."

My eyes connected with Locke's in a way they never had before with anyone else. It all felt meant to be. As much as our dogs had been destined for us—as much as they were supposed to find each other—and now it seemed, it was kismet that we were supposed to meet.

AFTER LOCKE HAD FINISHED SHOWING me his hope chest, we headed over to the dialysis treatment center. When we arrived this time, there was such a difference. The atmosphere felt completely changed. There was no hesitancy on Locke's part this time. He just smiled at me, and we interlaced our hands. As if that would make everything alright because we were together. And his smile provided a warmth that could overpower even the deepest Lupus chill.

"I've got to hear how this story ends," he said with a playful grin. "You ready?" And the way he asked me was such a stark contrast to the last time. I couldn't help but be excited to go in with him as weird as that sounded. He was making everything better. I was actually eager to hear him read again. And more than anything I loved he wanted to be here for me, that he wanted to show up.

"Yes, I have to know which pirate gets the mermaid. I'm hoping a surfer comes in and steals her away."

And the grin that overtook his face left a wake of tingles all the way through me as we went inside.

As soon as we reached the check-in desk, the kind nurse from my last treatment spotted us and came over. Her wavy blonde hair swayed as she made her way to us. "I'm so excited to see you both. Please tell me you're going to read out loud again." She turned to the front desk receptionist. "Will you give them my section?" And the receptionist nodded.

I shook my head and chuckled at Locke. He leaned over to me, quietly saying, "See, the pirates are in high demand," as we made our way back to my chair. It only made me shake my head harder. And when I sat in the chair, Locke was already holding my hand, already there as a lifeline. And this time, it didn't feel like all my vulnerabilities were on display for him to see. It just felt like he was there to support me. Like this was just a thing we did together. As routine as getting a cup of coffee. As long as we did it together, that was what mattered most. When he was here, somehow, everything felt like it would be okay.

As the nurse started connecting me to the dialysis machine, I could tell she was eager to talk to us again. But I wasn't able to process much, except for the sparks in my stomach that were ignited from the look in Locke's eyes. The nurse seemed to understand and proceeded silently, only saying she'd be back to check on me shortly before she walked away.

As the blood started running, all I could do was look at him with appreciation and hold his hand tighter, so thankful I'd let him into my life. And this time, I knew he truly understood what a big deal that was.

Locke gently said, "*'O 'oe no¯, aloha,*" as he stared deeply at me. But I wasn't worried. And I definitely wasn't moving around uncomfortably like last time.

"Locke, I'm not worried. Thank you, though. I'm happy you're here."

There was a shift in his eyes as he smiled gently, and then he said, "Me too. So, would you like me to continue reading?"

I nodded eagerly, not caring if he knew how much I enjoyed this.

The nurse called out from the other station, "Yes, we do. We want to hear the end. Character voices again, *please.*"

Locke looked at me, a little embarrassed. "I didn't realize they were *that* noticeable."

"Oh Locke, let's just say you could put on a delightful children's puppet show. I think you may have missed your calling. It's not too late to turn the surf shack into a puppet theater."

He began laughing and then opened his phone to find where we had left off in the story, but his eyes drifted upward and caught mine. "I'm really glad I'm here with you, Guin. Thanks for letting me."

"Thanks for wanting to be here," I replied. He looked at me, nodding as he saw the mist in my eyes. "And thanks for being my personal Audible," I joked.

"Anytime," he replied.

Locke

CHAPTER 38

I WAS NEARING the end of the story, and I was enjoying reading it even more this time. To my surprise, I wasn't comparing myself to these fictional men anymore. I wasn't sitting here wondering if this was what women wanted–what *Guin* wanted. Because the way she looked at me, the way she treated me, told me that the type of man she was looking for wasn't on these pages. What she wanted, somehow, seemed to be me.

I held her gaze as I neared the last pages, halting. "Do you still wish that the surfer would come and win the mermaid's heart?"

Guin held my gaze steadfastly and said, "More than anything. Maybe we need to email the author to ask for an alternate ending to be included." I laughed, and she looked at me with assessing eyes. "You'd blow all those pirates out of the water, and I think you would look fantastic in swashbuckling pirate attire too," she said, raising her eyebrows in a humorously seductive manner.

I couldn't help but laugh. "Yeah, but I'm pretty sure that I would end up with a peg leg in that scenario." I cringed just thinking about that.

Guin responded, "An aid is what you make of it. Only *you* can let others make you feel less for using one. Only you can give others that power. So don't. Please *never* let them have that power. But I think you'd look attractive with whatever you used."

"Only you, Mermaid," I said somewhat quietly, trying to joke but completely unable to.

"As Eleanor Roosevelt said, 'No one can make you feel inferior without your consent.' It's one of my favorite quotes. So much easier said than done, but it's true. And you have absolutely nothing to feel inferior about. You have the biggest, most giving heart I know. I think you must get your big heart from Tutu. You should be proud of it and everything else that works together with your heart to make you so special," she said with so much feeling it struck me in the heart.

I was completely taken with this woman. She was the one for me. It was the only thought going through my head and it scared me. I had fallen so fast it felt like I wasn't even holding on to anything. I had become so cautious since my accident, but then she had come along and demolished every cautionary roadblock I had so carefully set in place. She was a force, and I guess it was time I realized I needed to just let go and fall. I was going to be brave and finally tell her she was the one–ʻo ʻoe no̅, aloha–in a language that she could understand. Tell her just how much I'd fallen for her and see if, by some miracle, she felt the same way.

But all I seemed to do was stare at her. Nothing was coming out. So I just held her gaze appreciatively and then went to finish the end of the novel.

"I guess I should finish. Sorry, I stopped at the worst time." I chuckled.

"Yes!" someone called out from a chair near Guin's and we both laughed.

"I guess you can finish," Guin replied to me, "but now I have my own ending."

And I was dying to hear hers. The alternative one. It was hard to finish reading as I thought about what her ending might be. But I could tell we were going to have a mutiny on our hands if I didn't finish reading the book.

"So," I said as I finished and everyone seemed satisfied with the pirate who had ultimately won the day, "what's on the schedule for the convention today?"

"Oh, let me see." She pulled out her phone, showing me the agenda. Then she gave it to me to scroll through. There was a ukulele folder on her phone, and she nodded her head, giving me permission to look through it. I loved being allowed into this part of her world and how freely she shared it with me.

"What's this?" I said when I got to what looked like a letter.

"Oh, that's the letter that told me I'd won a raffle ticket for the ukulele convention. It's actually really cool–" She continued talking, but I heard little of what she said after that.

I zoomed in on the letterhead that said "The Big Dipper Music Foundation." The icon had two ukuleles in a jazzy style with a lei and fedora beside them.

"When did you say you received your invitation?" I asked.

"Oh, it was a couple of weeks ago. Luna said she was going to give away three 'all-inclusive' tickets. And people could enter by submitting a video of their musical journey and explaining what music means to them."

"Really," I said in a fog. "Wow, I'd really love to see your video," I said earnestly. I also needed something to distract my brain from this crazy train of thinking.

"It's pretty embarrassing, Locke."

"There's no way. Plus, I think we're way past embarrassing, Mermaid. I'm thankful for that because I'm *so* good at embarrassing myself." She laughed at me. "I just want to know more about you, Guin. Please never feel embarrassed with me."

And then without another thought, she handed the phone over to me with a little sea siren smile.

AS SOON AS I brought Guin back to the bungalow, she went to collect her things for the convention. She was going to skip her nap, but considering she could barely keep her eyes open in the car I doubted that was going to happen. The way she trudged down the hallway, with her fingertips lingering on the wallpaper, told me she was headed for a collision with her pillow. And I have to say, I was relieved because I needed a moment with Tutu before I headed back out to the surf shop.

I located the mischievous Hawaiian "make a wish fairy"

herself out on our favorite balcony. I was having a Pavlovian aversion to it now, though, since it was becoming a place for secrets to surface.

Tutu grinned at me with a little impish twist of her lips, her hands seamlessly gliding along as she worked on her quilt pattern in the shade of her favorite tiki umbrella.

I smiled back, then I looked at her more pointedly and she seemed to sense the shift of my mood, moving a little uncomfortably under my suspicious gaze. "So Guin showed me something interesting while we were at her treatments."

"Oh, that's nice," Tutu replied.

I stared at her in disbelief. This woman thought she could get away with anything. "Yeah, a very nice letter with a certificate on her phone that showed where she won her ukulele ticket. It was from the Big Dipper Ukulele Foundation. Something like a musical 'make a wish' organization . . . almost."

"Oh, I didn't know they had–"

"Tutu, cut the nonsense. I know you named Louis the *Big Dipper,* and that he always wanted you to join his band and become the *Little Dipper.* It's extremely romantic. And I know its importance. There's no way that's a coincidence."

"Louis talks too much," Tutu responded, her eyes going wide. "He should not be telling my grandson these things."

"Yeah, well, I think it's good that he did. I appreciate having him as a good male role model. I very much like Louis and would be happy to grow up to be like him. But can we *focus* on something else now? Like, what did you do?"

This little infectious smile came over her that she wasn't able to hide, even though she knew she was in trouble. "It's no big deal, Locke, I just gave out some travel tickets."

"You did what now?" I asked in disbelief.

She sighed in a way that made it seem like I wasn't catching on fast enough. "I may have asked Luna if she could add some extra spots to the convention . . . for some very wonderful young women. I'd gotten to know some of them through the ukulele platform, and their stories were just so incredible. Locke, I didn't want them to miss this opportunity. I knew they wouldn't be able to come on their own. It was obvious through their interactions with the community and our messages."

"So you what? You sent them *fake* winning tickets? Are you *Mrs. Willy Wonka* now?" My voice and disbelief were rising.

"Well, not exactly. They won . . . *in a way*. I just helped things along. And I sent them packets with hotel accommodations and local bed-and-breakfast hosts as well . . . which consisted of me and my friends. It wasn't like I offered your house up to just anyone."

"Oh no, because that would have been crazy." I lifted my eyes toward the heavens. "Did you pay for all this? You did just offer them the convention ticket, right? And how many tickets are we talking about?"

"Well . . ."

"Tutu!" I said with exasperation.

"It was just for three ladies, Locke. And I didn't know if I could play the ukulele anymore. Or if I even *wanted* to play anymore. I didn't know if I had it in me . . . not until I saw Louis, anyway. I just attended those online sessions for the chats. And to connect with the ukulele community and the music. But these young ladies have a whole life of playing ahead of them and I wanted to do this for them. Music means so much to all of us. And you know I just sold my house, so I wanted to do something good with that money. While I still can. I don't have many ways left to help people. And I'm running out of time."

The tears were forming in her eyes, and that was something I couldn't handle. It pained me way too much. Her words were hard enough. "Tutu, there are still plenty of ways you help people. You don't need to do something like this. It's too much."

"It's not. It was a small price to pay compared to what the young ladies got . . . what I got. I only paid for one hotel. Two of the winners opted to stay with hosts. And, of course, Luna took care of all the convention expenses. She loved the idea. And so that just left the plane tickets."

"You paid for the plane tickets too?" Shock took over my voice. "Tutu–"

"I only wish I could have done more. And I plan to continue to do *more* in the future. There were so many other people that needed the healing power of music." I just looked at her. Not knowing what to do with her and her big heart. "And you've met Guin. You see what I mean."

"Yeah, I met Guin alright, but you could have told me."

"I didn't know how you would take it. Especially after what happened. I didn't think you'd drag one of them off the beach. I never expected you to show up with one of them in your arms. What were the chances?"

"I guess they were pretty decent since she was waiting for her room and she seems to get herself in trouble," I said sarcastically.

"Locke," Tutu said as she rolled her eyes in exasperation. "Well, that may be, but it's not my fault that you fell for one of the 'raffle ticket winners.' That's not what this was about. You weren't supposed to fall head over heels . . . Especially not for our very own houseguest."

"Oh, so the woman I picked up from the beach and carried here caveman style would have been fine, but *not* our houseguest."

"Show some decorum, *Keiki*. You're supposed to keep things platonic on VRBO. No one wants a perverted Bed and Breakfast' host."

"Thanks for that lovely image," I said sardonically.

"You're welcome." She nodded her thanks at my words. "I had changed my mind about hosting anyone because I didn't want to have to tell you . . . I knew you'd ask too many questions, but when Guin reached out to me and said she had a service dog, too, I didn't want to turn her away. It was like fate, *Keiki*. And then the more I started chatting with her, the more I knew I had to let her stay here."

"So this wasn't some sort of bachelor setup?" I asked, somewhat suspiciously now.

"No, Locke. I just got lucky on that one," she teased. "I couldn't have done any better if I had tried. But I'd be happy to provide you with a rose to give her if you feel cheated ."

"*Right.* I'm not really sure what to do about telling Guin." I looked toward Tutu. "I guess it's probably better to leave it this way. It would be nicer for her to think she won the ticket through Luna, but I don't want to hide anything from her."

Tutu nodded at me. And then I looked back through the glass door, hoping I was doing the right thing.

Guinevere

CHAPTER 39

TUTU and I returned from the convention later that afternoon with Sebastian by our side. We'd left early so that I could go out on the boat for Dean's training. Apparently, I was to be part of Dean's "practice" tour. To me, it just sounded like an excuse to have Dean's family out for a fun evening–a perk of the job. An especially good one for a family who had gone through a lot in the past couple of years. It sounded like a very 'Locke' thing to do.

Locke had told me a little about Dean's wife and what the family had been through. And I was honored to be included in this outing. Hopefully, I wouldn't make this too much of a "practice tour" for Dean. My motion sickness didn't make it easy on the captain and crew of *any* boat. So I crossed my fingers as I changed into a bikini and cover-up, packing a bag as well. Then I fed the dogs and took them out to play while I waited anxiously for Locke to pick me up.

As if on cue, he pulled up in his Jeep and got out to greet me and the dogs. Locke gave me a warm smile. The one that was becoming iconic to me. "I'm going to go change, and then I'll be back. Want me to take the dogs inside? Or do you think Sebastian would want to come with us? Penny loves the boat."

"I love that idea," I replied. "Um, I just need my bag that's by the door."

But when I moved to go inside, he offered to get my bag for me. So I waited in the open air of the Jeep. Not really sure why he needed to change since he already had his wetsuit and surf shoes on. I sat there still dumbfounded that he had kept that part of his identity secret for so long. But I was shocked when I saw him come out to join me. He was wearing a swimsuit, and the dogs were trailing behind him. The dedicated 'beach leg' he'd shown me just this morning was on full display. Blue ocean wave shorts giving it away. No secret there. And through my shock, the biggest smile became plastered across my face.

Locke set our bags in the back of the Jeep and buckled the dogs into their backseat "doggie" hammock. Then he came to sit beside me at the wheel. And he just stared at me. A change had come over him, and I couldn't help but be absorbed by it.

He looked down at my sleeve that covered my fistula still. Old habits die hard. And with no preamble, he gently went to take it off as he looked at me for permission. I nodded, even though I was still in shock, and he placed it in my bag.

He turned back to me and said, "I'm tired of hiding, aren't you? You're way too beautiful for that." And with those words he pulled my face toward his in the open air, letting all the sweet sounds and sea breezes engulf us. *Allowing me to truly feel the heartbeats of the island.* His hands gently caressed my neck. And yes, I was so tired. *So very exhausted from not being accepted, of not being "normal," of not being enough.* And most of all, I was tired of putting all these restrictions on myself–of allowing myself to feel this way. But not with him. Not with these people. Not any longer.

And my sigh of agreement made him smile as he gazed at me and asked, "Are you ready?"

"Yes, although I would like to know what we're doing," I replied, still a little breathless.

"Oh, I'm not ruining the surprise. You'll see soon enough." Then he glanced back at me. "If you need your sleeve for protection from the water, I'll understand. I'm now second guessing my symbolic gesture," he said, somewhat flustered.

I laughed. "I'll put it back on if we get in the water. Otherwise, I won't need it. And by the way, I loved your symbolic gesture," I said as I reached for his hand. He smiled and started driving us to meet the others at the dock.

AS WE WALKED down the pier, I saw Dean and his family were already at the boat. Locke's hand was intertwined with mine and the dogs were trailing close behind us. Dean's wife and two little girls were further down the pier exploring the other boats, but Dean was standing guard at Locke's boat, waiting for us. His face lit up as soon as he saw us, his eyes zeroing in on Locke's choice of swim attire. A big grin crept across his features.

I looked over to Locke, who was shaking his head. "Hey, Dean," he said with a tone that showed he knew some good-natured ribbing was in store for him.

"There's my favorite Lobster," Dean called. And Locke's head only shook more now, but there was this big smile that told me he was enjoying Dean's good-natured teasing. When we reached him, Dean said, "I don't think I've ever seen you look so good. It must be Guin." But Dean was obviously happy to see Locke being comfortable in his own skin. And he seemed pretty happy about me too, since he kept smiling at our intertwined hands.

"Thanks, man. It's definitely Guin. She can make anything beautiful. So, are you ready for more training? Or the better question might be, is your tour group ready for *their* 'excursion?'" He chuckled.

"I don't think they're ever really ready, Locke. But they are excited. I appreciate this. Again, thanks. *Really.*"

Locke made a "don't mention it" motion. I could tell he didn't enjoy getting thanks or credit. Then Locke asked me to wait on the dock with the dogs while he and Dean got the boat ready, just as they would do if it was a real excursion. Locke went over everything with Dean, quizzing him on their preparations, which I could tell he enjoyed as they joked around quite a bit, too.

Dean's wife and two little girls came bounding up the dock, very excited about this trip. His girls had to be the two most adorable kids I'd ever seen. No older than five and seven. And their eyes lit up when they saw not one but two doggies. Dean's wife, Ella, made the people introductions, and I made the doggie ones. As soon as we boarded the boat, the girls found Locke. Apparently, he was a favorite.

Locke had two small, pink life vests for them in his hands, ready to help the girls put them on for the voyage. Tracey, the oldest girl, stopped short, already spotting the difference in him, but it was Etta, the youngest, who reached out to Locke first. My eyes widened when I saw what she was about to do.

"Locke, I didn't know you were a superhero," she said as she reached for his leg, the *right* one. My breath caught in my lungs when her tiny hand connected with the hard metallic post. Locke hadn't even put on his cosmetic covering.

"Oh my–Locke, I'm really sorry." Dean raced over. "Etta, honey, you can't just touch people like that–*even* Uncle Locke. Ok?"

"Dean, she's fine," Locke said as he waved him away. "I can help her put on a pink vest. Don't you have a boat you need to be getting ready?" he teased, trying to reassure him. I was shocked that Locke was being so relaxed about this. Wasn't this the same guy that had gone to such great lengths to cover up his leg in front of me? Locke turned back to Etta who still had her tiny hand on the lower part of his prosthetic leg. He said to her, "I really don't think I qualify as a superhero, but this thing is pretty cool, huh?"

"Yeah. You definitely qualify, Uncle Locke. You could take bullets, or whatever, and it wouldn't even bother you. Would it?" Now Tracy started pondering his leg, too. She asked, "Can I touch it, too?"

"Sure, you can, Tracey. Well, a bullet wouldn't hurt me in this leg, but it would certainly slow me down since I need it to walk." They both laughed at him.

"It's *so* cool," Etta said as she started knocking on it to test the sound of it. And I couldn't help but giggle at that.

Locke shot me a look. "Like you haven't wanted to try that, too," he teased, as I came over to them.

"Guilty, there's a lot of things I want to try." His eyebrows shot up at my words.

"Uncle Locke, does it change shape and color, and stuff?" Etta asked. Becoming even more curious now. I couldn't help but giggle. She was too cute.

"Let's get your life vests on, and then I'll show you how it works," Locke said with a genuine smile, and they cheered like they knew they were getting something special. And really they were, they had no idea. Locke was letting them into his real world. It was the most precious thing, almost as adorable as Locke putting on their Barbie-pink vests. He was great with them. I don't know why I was so shocked, but I was. The gentle giant would probably wear one and have imaginary tea with them if that would make them happy. Maybe I should suggest it. I'd love to see that.

Locke sat down on the bench seat in front of the captain's helm of the boat. Each little girl bounded up on the seat to sit on each side of him. He looked like "The Rock" in a Disney movie. My heart went to jelly. Then Locke looked at me and cocked his head, nodding to an open spot on the bench. I gladly accepted the invitation, not wanting to miss the demonstration. And he showed the girls how his prosthesis worked, giving me déjà vu from earlier this morning. He'd been so open and patient with me as I asked questions. Nothing but gentle and kind as I fumbled my way around them. And he was the same with these beautiful, big-hearted girls. And that's when I realized what the difference was. Both times were special because our questions were asked out of love. Sure, not all our questions were politically correct or phrased properly, but they didn't have to be. It didn't matter. Our questions came from a place of wanting to understand his situation and were asked with care and respect. Nothing but love, and Locke gave it all back. Graciously. And it was beautiful to see, especially with such small human beings. If they could be this way, why couldn't everybody else? Why couldn't people have pure hearts when faced with such painful vulnerability?

Locke looked over to me, and it was then that I realized tears had spilled from my eyes. I wanted this so badly for him. There were very few moments in life that reached deep down inside of me and pulled hard at my being. There were few things more precious to a person with a disability. Feeling that care and connection was certainly near the top. At least it was for me, and by the look in his eyes and the overwhelming joy on his face, I'd say it was for him too.

Dean walked over and stood in front of us and asked. "Are you girls behaving?" He eyed them as they experimented with the prosthesis that was now unattached. They'd begged Locke to take it off. I saw the fear and debate in his eyes, not knowing if it might freak out the children. But they were having the best time with his leg. Dean cautioned his girls, "You need to be careful. Don't break Uncle Locke's leg."

Locke responded, "Don't worry, that thing is indestructible." And then he elbowed me. "Probably even mermaid proof."

"Ok, well maybe so, but I think it's time to give Uncle Locke his leg back," Dean said, a little worried.

I couldn't help but laugh at his worry, seeing that there was no way they could break his prosthetic leg. And Locke just grinned at me. "You're the one he needs to be worried about." And it felt so good to joke and laugh about such things. To know you had people that cared for you enough, so you could do so safely. Maybe our wounds were finally healing.

Finally, we gave Locke a break from his "superhero" leg demonstrations and started taking the boat out to the open sea. We put two cute doggie life vests on the dogs to keep them safe. Good thing Sebe was around the same size as Penny. I didn't know what he would think about the sea once we were really under way, but so far he was loving it. Both dogs roamed freely about the boat as Penny showed Sebe the ropes. Although I didn't think it would be long before they were both snuggling below deck. I'd heard that's where the water bowl was kept. I'd also heard there was a bed that Locke couldn't keep Penny from claiming as her own. Sounded like she got them all.

Best of all, I don't think I'd ever seen Locke so happy. He guided me in front of him, wrapping his arms around me. We stood close to Dean at the helm as he steered the boat, just in case he needed help, but it seemed he was becoming quite comfortable navigating. Locke rested his head beside mine as I leaned back into his sturdy chest.

"Thanks, Mermaid," he whispered in my ear.

"For what?" I asked, turning my head slightly.

"You know . . ." He brushed his right leg up against mine. His love tap shot a warmth through my core. I sighed out a little "um hmm" and he chuckled. Then he kissed my neck, not being at all shy about it.

"Hey lobsters," Dean jokingly called beside us. "What are you going to do when you see the whales? That's the romantic part of the cruise. Save something, will ya?"

Locke shot his arm out and shoved Dean playfully in his

captain's chair. "You're supposed to be watching sonar, not us, you creeper."

"Kind of hard when you guys are so much more attention-grabbing."

Locke refuted, "Well, I don't think anything can compete with the whales, so no worries there."

"No, I'm pretty sure you'll still be winning." Dean laughed, and Locke shoved him harder.

"Well, I take that as a challenge," I said jokingly.

Locke pulled me in playfully, and Dean's laugh burst out. "Oh man, Locke, you caught the right Lobster for sure."

"Wait, whales?" I said with glee, turning around in Locke's arms to look at him.

"Yeah, Mermaid. We're going whale watching. But *not* sunset dancing," he said playfully, remembering my earlier requests.

Dean called back, "Oh, I'm the captain tonight, Locke. And my itinerary says there will definitely be dancing. Lots and lots of dancing."

"Just keep your eyes peeled, *Captain*," Locke said, pointing out some promising whale-watching locations. "This is probably an excellent area to be at twilight if you want to stop and grab a bite to eat while we wait."

So Dean moored the boat and then we all sat around the table Locke had set up for our meal. Ella had packed the cutest little lunch boxes for the girls and then surprised me by handing one to me too.

"Sorry, I just wanted to keep your food separate. I didn't want it to get confused. It's gluten-free and low sodium," she said. And I was seriously touched as I held the adorable container in my hands.

"*The Little Mermaid*," Locke said as he leaned over to me

and looked down at the lunch box. "She couldn't have accepted any less." He laughed.

"It's so thoughtful. Thank you," I said to Ella, feeling tears form in my eyes. This was seriously the sweetest family. And then we enjoyed a wholesome meal as we talked together, like a family gathered around the dinner table, while the sea gently rocked us. Something you just didn't see near enough these days. It all seemed too serene as the dogs waited patiently by our feet. And the girls' sweet giggles enveloped us, which really got to me. Locke's hand on my knee told me I wasn't the only one.

When we packed up, twilight was creeping in, and I was told that this was the perfect time to see these magnificent creatures. We thought we might have spotted some off in the distance as we were eating, but honestly, we had been too distracted to know for sure.

So we started moving the boat toward the potential whale sighting area, with the sky dimming and the early night breeze gently floating by. And in the distance we saw movement. We gathered at the boat's railing and huddled side by side. The adorable girls stood on their seats, clutching the rails, with their mom by their side, and Locke's arm wrapped tightly around mine.

Then we saw the most wonderful sight–two whales breaching at the same time. Their bodies gliding up together through the air in perfect time and their massive fins hitting the water with an epic splash.

"*Whoa,*" the girls cried out in unison, and I was just as blown away too. The biggest smile planted firmly on my face.

Dean slowed the boat down just in case there were more whales in the area before putting the engine into neutral. And then we waited until we saw another breach, just as spectacular as the first. I leaned into Locke, my heart swelling with so many emotions. If my life was going to be short, then this was the way I wanted to live it, with someone like him by my side. This realization not only unnerved me but scared me too.

And then as if God wanted me to keep believing in beauty, miracles, and possibilities; two whales came right up to our boat. It had to be the most magical thing I'd ever seen. And all I could do was thank God for this gift. And it was then that I realized I'd been bitter for far too long. Feeling rejected and undeserving. But now God was sending me all these beautiful things as a gift. Sending me these wonderful people–their acceptance and love–along with this special evening on the ocean. Like God wanted me to see that I could choose beauty. That I could choose to surround myself with people that loved me and wanted me. That I was *still* deserving.

And something happened at that moment. I decided Locke was right: this was my moment, and I was going to take it. I was going to live it, no matter how short it might be. I was being given this beautiful moment–this Esther timing–and I would not waste it any longer. I was going to be thankful for it. And I had no time to waste on being bitter any longer.

And as those whales moved closer to the boat, they looked so much like storybook creatures. And all I could do was to be struck by awe at their beauty.

Locke looked at me. "You ok, Mermaid?" he asked gently.

"The moment for which we were created," I somehow managed. And his eyes seemed to pool so deeply, somehow looking endless. He nodded with a glassy, dazed expression.

"Yeah, Mermaid." And he took my hand, the warmth comforting me. His whole being provided a much-needed shelter from this storm I'd been trying to survive on my own for way too long.

Locke

THERE WAS something breathtaking about her at that moment. Something had changed, and I searched her face trying to figure out what had happened. But I loved whatever had transpired. There was this true inner peace and beauty that had washed over her.

And I can't say that the whales didn't gravely affect me as well, but there was something mesmerizing about seeing her reaction to them. It was strange. I'd been whale watching plenty of times before. I'd taken tourists out on several excursions. And I'd seen the sense of wonder and awe on their faces when they saw the whales breaching. And the whales *never* failed to be magnificent. Yet I had to admit, they'd never come up to the boat this close before. Probably it had something to do with a certain sea siren call. Guin was magnetic, even to the creatures of the sea. I'd never been affected like this. She made all the difference.

As the whales made their way back into the deep sea and the night sky gave way to starry darkness, I was feeling completely at ease. That was until Dean's mischievous smile lit up the night sky and his music cut through the twinkling starlight. His girls started jumping up and down, apparently super-pleased at this turn of events.

Dean said, "Sorry, Locke. I'm with Guin on this one. I want to see you shake your little lobster booty." And the girls cheered, very much in agreement. I rolled my eyes at him as Elvis's smooth voice sailed out of the speakers singing *Suspicious Minds*.

Dean teased, "Looks like you are in a bit of a lobster trap. Might as well make the most of it." Dean went over to dance with Ella and his girls, literally bumping me on his way, knocking me a little closer to Guin.

She blushed. "It's ok, Locke. We can just sit and enjoy the night sky. I love doing that with you."

"Well, Mermaid, that may be preferable. I haven't ever tried dancing with my prosthesis. Not that I was a super talented dancer to begin with." But I looked at her sweet face as she moved to sit down and I nervously fumbled for her hand. She glanced back at me in question. "No, Guin. I want to dance with you. Under the stars. *Properly.*"

Those soft pink lips that I couldn't get enough of turned upward. But I didn't think she was going to feel that way much longer once we started dancing. However, if I was going to embarrass myself with someone, I wanted it to be her. But when she found her way into my arms and buried her head in my chest, I knew I was certainly mistaken. This was one of the best gifts a woman could give me. This deep feeling of being wanted–of feeling like home for someone.

I asked, "Is this ok?" as we swayed, not really sure how many moves I wanted to try. I was physically active with surfing and snorkeling, so dancing shouldn't be a problem, but mentally, I wasn't so sure. The nerves were making this difficult. But Guin felt so good in my arms and the more she enjoyed it, the more I eased. Until we were really dancing and enjoying ourselves. And surprisingly, as awkward as it could be–since I was in my head so much–it was the best dance of my life.

Guin smiled contagiously at me. "Locke, you're an incredible dancer," she said, and of course, I stumbled as soon as she said it.

"Ok, Mermaid. If Mr. Toad's wild ride had a dancing component, then maybe I'd qualify. You're the one saving this dance." And I spun her out, needing a moment. Then she landed right back in my arms just as quickly. The moonlight bathed her beautiful face, and her scent was even more intoxicating in this proximity.

"Locke, I'm serious," she said, and her expressive eyes washed over me. "You're a really, *excellent* dancer." Her voice took on a husky, seductive tone. I can't believe my dancing could turn anyone on, but I would certainly take it.

"No, Guin you're the one who's really the great–" But she cut me off, tugging lightly at my shirt with both hands and drawing me into her. Her scent engulfed me even more, and I was completely lost in it. And if I thought her eyes had crashed over me, they had nothing on her lips. I guess she thought she would put us out of our misery and just cut to the chase.

Dean's voice cut across the muffled waves slapping the bow and the energetic, upbeat music. "I told you that you'd like dancing, Locke!" Then there was a brief chorus of laughter and tiny "kissy" noises from the little girls making fun of Uncle Locke. Guin laid her head on my shoulder and moved in closer to me, smiling as renditions of "Uncle Locke sitting in a tree k-i-s-s-i-n-g" broke through our perfect little bubble.

WE SAID goodbye to Dean and his family when we got back to the harbor. Dean had docked the boat with very little help. He was getting great at navigating it. He soon wouldn't need many more "practice tours." But they were helping him to feel more comfortable with the boat, and honestly, I enjoyed them as much as he did. And his family especially loved them. Hopefully, we would continue boating together even when he started going on excursions by himself. Maybe we could have a standing night to all go out together as family and friends. They certainly felt like family to me.

I sat back down with Guin to rest for a moment before packing up the boat for the evening. The dogs lay curled on the bow, resting together harmoniously, thoroughly worn out from the evening. The harbor was so peaceful at this time of night with the dock lit by soft lights and the waves lapping ever so gently. And, of course, one of my favorite parts of the evening was the Maui moon shining brightly over the bay. I couldn't get enough of this place. Sometimes I would just come here to think. I'd sit on the bow of the boat and just escape everything. It was the first place that I sat with my leg on full display. No one passing by could really see it, but I knew. I just wanted to see what it felt like. It was the bravest I had gotten around other people, besides in the bungalow with Tutu, until Guin came along.

I wrapped my arm around her as I soaked in the moonlight rippling on the waves. I really didn't know how it was possible for her to look even more beautiful. And I felt even more connected to her too. I was being pulled out by that current of emotion again. Feeling substantially lost and not caring. It was bliss to be surrounded by her.

So much so that I almost didn't hear her when she said, "Locke, there's something I need to tell you." She breathed out heavily, an exhale that didn't seem to end. Then she said, "Wow, those whales really got to me. That should be a therapy excursion. You really should package that."

And I laughed lightly, but I was actually concerned. Something had come over her. I had seen it. And there had been such a change in her the second she said the words about our Esther timing.

She seemed to have trouble speaking, so I said to her, "Do you want to go somewhere more comfortable? I can bring out the clamshells." I was joking with her, but I thought she might really need them. Or at least she might need some help to relax. "Or we can go down below. It's sort of a mess, but there's a galley. I can make tea and there's a small sitting area."

"I don't know how well my motion sickness will do in an enclosed cabin, but it sounds nice . . . really cozy. And tea would be perfect."

"Yeah? Ok," I said eagerly. "I'll get you some more Motion-Eaze and put pineapple rock candy in your tea. That should help some. I *won't* forget this time. We can always come up if the motion of the boat bothers you."

I was actually excited for her to come below deck. I never allowed people down there. Tourists were often too curious for their own good, and I liked to keep that part of the boat separate. Maybe I was just too much of a private person. I had hoped to make some overnight excursions on the boat in the future. I dreamed of sailing around the other Hawaiian islands for practice and then the ones off the coast of California. So I'd really been working on making the kitchen nicer. I'd put rope lighting around the base of the cabin and twinkle lights around the top. I guess the romantic in me–who I knew was not so secret–had hoped one day someone would travel with me. Maybe I'd even take this thing on a honeymoon excursion if I was lucky enough. Travel to another island. Dean's words had really hit a nerve with that one. I had given up on that dream, but now it seemed like it might be a possibility for me one day. That maybe someone would still want me.

I opened the portholes to let the sea breeze come inside the cabin to help her with the motion sickness. I realized Guin might not be the best candidate for those excursions, but my heart sure liked the idea. I was really hoping to see how she did down here, and I realized that thought was literally insane.

I turned on the accent lighting, trying to make it cozy, but then thought maybe it looked like I was trying to 'set the mood.' As if this was a one-button bachelor pad. I seemed to overthink *everything* with this woman. I immediately went to the light panel to turn on the overhead lights, not wanting to look like *that guy*, but then she stopped me.

"The lighting is perfect, Locke. Really cozy. Unless you need to see better." Now I could tell she was overthinking it, too. Glad I wasn't the only one.

"No, believe me, I know where everything is in the dark."

Oh great, that really sounded forward, but she just laughed. I moved to get her the MotionEaze and make her some tea. I set the kettle on the little electric stove as she began looking around.

"Wow, this is really nice, Locke. You've done an amazing job with the cabin. I love all the nautical accents and decor." I saw her hand brush over the anchor pillows and then stop in front of a mounted ship in a bottle. Her eyes scanned over boating and Hawaiian wall hangings. Then she found her way over to the ancient stereo with a stack of CDs of local Hawaiian music laying beside it.

"Would you like to hear some music?" I asked, pointing to the stereo.

"No, I think I prefer the sound of the ocean waves, if that's ok. Dean filled my music quota for the night." And I laughed. I loved hearing the night music of Maui, but right now I was hearing more of the music of my heart as it thrummed madly. My heart felt like it was ready to jump ship.

"Please, make yourself at home," I said as I finished making the tea. I watched her find a place on the sofa and curl up around a pillow. I could see her beginning to relax. "There are some blankets in the closet by the bed. I'm sure Penny already showed Sebastian the bed. No doubt that's where we'll find them."

"Thank you," she replied, but after a few moments I heard awkward laughter. "Locke, is this a trick?"

"What do you mean?" Now I was worried.

"I mean these knobs. Is this a trick? Really not cool for someone with Lupus hands." She was laughing playfully now.

"Oh, sorry. Yeah, things work a little differently on a boat. You push in the button, and then it pops out to become a knob." I showed her how it worked and she blushed with embarrassment. I reassured her, "Mermaid, there's so many weird things on a boat. You can't possibly know about all this stuff. It's ok. Just ask me."

And I loved the look that spread over her face. Warm, buttery softness was overtaking her, and I was happy she was letting me see more of it. I brushed by her, grazing the side of her body in the tight corridors, and then I opened the tiny closet to select a blanket for her. "This is my favorite. It's the softest. Trust me."

"Thank you." And she kissed my cheek like I'd just done the nicest thing for her. I wanted to say "uh huh," or something else equally lame, as she walked back to curl up in her spot on the sofa, but apparently I'd gone to jelly with just that brief contact.

Get it together, Locke.

I brought the tea over and found a spot by her side on the sofa. It didn't help that she was looking at me with dreamy eyes. I guess the Hawaiian night streaming in through the portholes, along with the harbor sounds and the lighting, was getting to her. Surely it couldn't be me. I looked down at my leg self-conscious, now beginning to wish I'd worn pants. But that look on her face was unphased, unchanging.

I waited for her to take a few sips of her tea. "So, what did you want to tell me?" I managed, not wanting this dream to end.

She breathed shakily. "Oh, nothing now. Can we forget about it? Everything's too perfect down here. Somehow you've created the perfect retreat and I want to soak up every moment."

"Well, that's why this is the best place to talk. Nothing bad can happen in Grandmother's haven 2.0," I joked.

I stretched out my leg. The end of my thigh was really aching. I guess "dancing" had gotten to me after all, especially since it was something I wasn't used to.

Her voice challenged me, "You can take it off."

"My shirt?" I asked teasingly. "How forward of you, Mermaid."

She scoffed. "Your prosthesis."

"Somehow that's not near as sexy. No, my self-esteem prefers for it to stay on right now. Thanks though. Something about you in this mood lighting has me a little in my head."

"There's nothing sexy about staying in pain or not being yourself with me." But as I continued to look down, she lightened her tone and bantered with me instead. "So this was supposed to be your secret romantic getaway, after all?" She raised her eyebrows comically.

"There's no winning with you. All I said was the way you look in this lighting was having too much of an effect on me. That's it."

"Not buying it," she replied quickly.

"*Fine*, I'll tell you *if* you go first."

"But mine is a buzzkill," she heaved.

"Ok, so we'll end with mine. I have a feeling if I go first, then you won't tell me about yours."

"Ok, but please consider taking the prosthesis off if it's hurting you." She crossed her arms. I had a feeling she wouldn't talk if I didn't make myself comfortable.

"Why are you so darn stubborn?" *And why does it turn me on so much?* "Fine, but only because I want to hear what you've going to tell me," I said pointedly, and she smiled at her victory.

I took off my prosthesis, rubbing the end of my residual limb and wincing a little. It did smart. Somehow, my leg being exposed seemed to loosen her up. Like she could breathe easier. A reminder that she wasn't alone in this battle with her body. That she wasn't the only one *choosing* to be vulnerable here. And for once, it felt like we both got to choose.

She sighed. "I wasn't *completely* honest with you, Locke." My eyes snapped up to her from where I was rubbing my limb.

Oh no, what bad news is she going to give me? There was always a catch. *Please, not with her.* My leg somehow felt even more exposed.

I went to reach for my prosthesis, but she stopped me. "It has nothing to do with you, Locke. It's about me." Disbelief raced through me.

Her lips twisted painfully. "Locke, I had a kidney match." The words just hung there in the cabin's intimacy. I stilled, already feeling an ache. "One of my friends matched. And it was an actual surprise, because there's such a slim chance that someone outside of your family will be a match. And it was incredibly kind of her to get tested. I mean, my boyfriend at the time never did. He kept saying, 'I'm going to go do that.' Like it was something on a to-do list." She wrung her hands. "We'd talked about this scenario ever since we had seen a celebrity receive a kidney donation from her best friend. We saw their photos in the hospital beds together, and their unconditional love for each other looked so beautiful to us. But I guess it's easy to look at a photo and . . . just talk about it. We had discussed all these what-ifs when I was first diagnosed. . . . But we never really thought that would be me. And I couldn't help the hope that surged through me when she was a match. But in the end, she couldn't do it. I reassured her I understood. Because I really did. Giving an organ is one of the biggest, most selfless acts one human can do for another. And it was okay with me that she felt like she couldn't donate, but I still wanted and *needed* my friend. It turns out she couldn't do that either. And *that's* what I didn't understand. "

"Guin, I didn't know–"

"So you know how we were talking the other night about how messy is *too* messy? Where's the line when you become unlovable? When do you become too much? I've actually found that line, Locke. And I think it has made me more scared to open my heart. It's definitely left me feeling undeserving."

I leaned over and reached for her hand, wanting more than anything to make this better for her. To take this pain away from her because I knew about it, too. "I wish I could say I don't understand, Guin. But I know all too well about that unlovable line. I guess finding where that line is with people usually happens early on for me at least."

She nodded painfully, looking down into her tea like she could escape into it as she said, "It was one thing to be diagnosed with my health disorders, but I wasn't prepared for the ripple effect it created in my life. And certainly not for all the things it took away from me."

"Yeah, I wasn't either," I said to her softly. "We have a proverb here *Ku'ia kahele aka na'au ha'aha'a* and it means that 'a humble person walks carefully so as not to hurt others.' Imagine if we all walked in that way what the world would be like. Just one footstep has the potential to shift the entire framework. It's amazing what an effect one change can make. Our entire world is a chain reaction."

"A butterfly wing's flap," Guin said softly. "For the first time in a long time, I'm seeing what love and acceptance looks like again. There was something about seeing those whales today. Like they were sent to me to show me that I'm worthy of beauty and miracles. That I shouldn't give up. Ever since I lost my mom at a young age, I've always been more closed off. My mother absolutely loved the beach and music. She was a music teacher, and I guess that's where I got my love of music. That's what I remember most about her–all the love she shared with everyone, especially through her music. Before I lost her and went to live with my grandparents, she'd been planning to take me on a trip to the beach. And so I wanted to take this trip for her, for us. And somehow it feels like she's guiding me here too . . . I don't even know how to explain it."

I swallowed as I answered, "No, I think you're doing a great job and I'm sure she's guiding you too. I wish I could have met her." Guin's eyes looked downward, like she couldn't handle my words. "The miracles of Maui–the people and the love here–can definitely restore your faith. Please don't let other people take love away from you or make you feel unworthy. Just know those are the people who need love the most. And all we can do is try to show them kindness in hopes they will receive it and pass it onto others."

"Locke." She held my hand tighter, urging me to trust in her. "I promise–"

But I cut her off. I didn't want her to validate herself to me. "I know you're different. I've known that from the start." And she smiled at my words. "After my unpleasant dating experiences, I tried to find love in other areas of my life. I was determined to surf again. And making customized boards for those with physical disabilities has given me purpose in life. It saved me. I'm so glad you've been able to fulfill some of your dreams through your book illustrations and coming here to attend the ukulele convention. And I hope you'll keep fulfilling your dreams–that you always go stargazing."

The biggest smile crossed her face. "Yes, I hope so too. Especially now that I've decided to really live my moments. I think I'm going to start by writing a children's book that features a character like me . . . and maybe someone like you." She looked at me nervously, afraid of my reaction. She brought the tea to her lips, shielding her eyes slightly.

I moved over closer to her and wrapped an arm around her shoulders. "I think that sounds like a wonderful idea. And I'd love to help you."

"Really?" She glowed. I nodded, happy to answer any questions she might have. "It's just that I've been illustrating so many books, and no one in them looks like me or you . . . And there are so many children with disabilities. There's such beauty and validation in being seen–in no longer feeling invisible."

I looked deeply into her eyes, taken with her heart and what this could mean for so many children. "You're really incredible, Mermaid. I think I just fell even harder for you." Those big underwater blues stared back at me. I don't think even Pixar could have captured them.

And in the silence, I pulled her close as she fidgeted with her double dolphin necklace–the one she never took off. If I had to guess, I'd say it was from her mother. She rubbed the charm before asking me, "So, are you going to tell me about your dreams for this boat?" She pulled out a cheeky smile now, lightening the mood. But I was feeling a little vulnerable, considering what I had just told her. And it wasn't like she'd said that she had fallen for me too.

So I responded, "Oh, it's nothing. Just trying to fix the boat up. It was kind of a mess down here when my grandfather left it to me."

She narrowed her eyes, looking at me playfully. "No, you said you would share your plans for this boat after I shared with you. Now I want to hear about this romantic getaway."

Locke

CHAPTER 41

"Uﬀ, let's just leave it at that." I felt extra vulnerable with my bare limb resting next to her. It actually felt weird to sit on this side of her. I'd worked so hard to be mindful of always keeping her on my left side.

As if sensing that, she placed her hand tenderly on me. "No, I really want to hear about your dreams. Will you please share? I was only kidding about the romantic getaway thing."

Her words eased something inside of me, but I still wasn't sure if going "further out to sea" was a good idea for me. I would get lost or shipwrecked. "Uh, well you're not that far off–"

"Locke." She backed up a little in mock surprise. "Are you really a Casanova as Tutu suggested?"

I pulled her in tighter, relaxing with her banter. "Ok, I'll tell you, but *no* laughing."

"My lips are . . . *locked*." She chuckled. Why did I need to share my unrealistic dream with someone as incredible as Guin? The dream that was never coming true. It was too embarrassing.

"Ok." I looked at her, testing out her promise of "silence." And she didn't move. "I guess I started working on this boat hoping one day I would find someone who would want to sail with me. If I ever found someone who accepted and loved me as I was, then I wanted us to go on adventures together–to make memories together. If that ever happened, then I wanted this boat to be as nice as it could be for her. I don't know, I even had the crazy idea that maybe it could be a . . ."

But I stopped myself because I was sounding crazy, I slowly looked down at her. Allowing my eyes to travel downward to meet her oceans of blue. Then she asked quickly, "It could be?"

"Guin, it's silly." She squeezed me on a double tap, begging me to continue, and I laughed lightly. "I don't know, I guess I just started channeling my energy into this project in hopes of 'one day.' If I just waited, maybe by some miracle, it would happen for me. And I just thought if she was someone who enjoyed traveling and exploring, then it might even be a good honeymoon option. Sailing the blue seas and going to some island together sounded pretty perfect to me. Maybe it was the fantasy I needed to get through everything else that happened to me. I still have some more work to do on it, but it's coming along. The boat, not the fantasy." I laughed nervously.

Guin looked at me with intense longing and desire. There was a burning in those crystals that not even I could deny. Her voice barely came out. "Is that why you wanted to see if I could stay down here without getting motion sick? You want someone who can . . . travel with you?"

"Oh, I know you get motion sickness so I . . . Well, I just wanted you to feel ok . . . I didn't mean–" But her lips were very much on mine. I guess my expression and awkward voice had given me away. My mind couldn't help but wonder if Guin might be that special person who would want to travel with me one day.

She pulled back softly, saying, "I feel ok. Actually, more than ok. I feel perfect here." Guin gazed at me. "Anyone would be lucky to be your special person, Locke. I'd travel the world in a heartbeat with you." She breathed out those last words as my heart pounded out a rhythm just for her, and then she looked over at our dogs snuggled on the bed. Their puppy love couldn't be more apparent, and they seemed to enjoy each new place together more than the last. I understood that sentiment all too well myself.

"Nothing would make me happier than to travel with you one day, Guin." My heart spring boarded over itself.

She eyed the dogs again and then turned back to me. "How about a trial run?" I looked at her quizzically. She continued, "Are we able to see how I do here overnight? What do you say to snuggling with some puppies?"

I'd say every fantasy and then some were coming true. "Really, are you sure? I don't exactly have everything up to–"

"Locke, it's incredibly nice down here. I don't know how you plan to make it *any* nicer, honestly."

I laughed at her, "Well, adding *you* is a start." And she smiled with a bloom of pink on her cheeks.

"I like that plan," she whispered.

"Me too, so let me show you how everything works," I began rambling.

"Locke, I really want to snuggle with you, like now."

"Ok, Mermaid. That I can do. Let me just put on my prosthesis–"

"You don't have to do that on my account."

"I appreciate it, but I'm planning on carrying you over to the dogs. I have this pretty vivid fantasy, and I'd like to fulfill it, and that means my prosthesis needs to be on."

She beamed, and after I reattached my prosthesis, I took her tea and set it on the table in front of us. Then I came to pick her up in one swift movement, quite happy that I had pulled it off. I carried her over to the bed and set her down by our dogs. Her face looked up at me with appreciation and filled with so many emotions I wish I could decipher.

I went around and carved out a spot on the other side of the dogs. And without thinking about it, I took off my prosthesis. Like it was a natural decision with her. Then I sat up and opened the porthole window above us, allowing the starry night with its cool, crisp breeze to enter the boat's cabin. Guin rolled onto her side to look at me and then back up at the stars. The dogs even sat up from their cozy position to take notice.

"Locke, it's gorgeous," she whispered.

"Well, I want you to have the full trial run," I teased. "Really trying to pass that motion sickness test here. I figured the fresh air would help."

"Locke, it's perfect . . . but if you really want me to pass the test, you should hold me," she teased back.

"Yeah, well, our dogs are currently creating quite the barricade between us," I said as I rolled onto my side to face her. "Which is kind of funny since they've been trying to push us together."

She smiled mischievously and slowly moved around them. Then she wedged herself into the small space between the dogs and me. She tucked herself into me and carved out the place that was already hers. And would always continue to be.

"I don't need much room," she said cheekily.

"I see that," I barely managed. I pulled her closer to me, inhaling her scent. "Uh, what about your medications? There's a stocked bathroom with hopefully everything else, but–"

"I brought them to take after dinner. I'm fine, Locke. Thanks for asking though."

But my mind was racing. "Are you doing ok so far?–"

"Locke," She said in such a way that it completely silenced my mind. "I feel perfect with you." She sighed happily as the dogs moved closer to her as if in agreement, diminishing our space even further. And I agreed, it couldn't have been more perfect.

Locke

CHAPTER 42

THERE WAS something special about waking up on the sea, even if it was in the harbor. It still felt like we were in the wide, open ocean in my imagination. And waking up in the warmth of this woman and these two adorable doggies made a wave of emotions slam into me. This was something I never thought I'd be able to have in my life.

Guin snuggled in closer to my side as if wanting as much of my warmth and protection as possible. Letting herself soak it all up. I could feel the morning rays coming in through the glass of the hatch to greet us. I had closed the glass over the screen to keep any generator fumes from entering. I always wanted to keep her as safe as possible. She seemed to find this really attractive, especially as I taught her about the safety features of the boat. I guess safety could be sexy.

I groggily started opening my eyes as I pulled her closer, embracing her in my arms. I already wore a gigantic smile on my face, especially for it being so early in the morning.

Little happy sighs escaped me. "Did you sleep ok?" I was eager to hear her response, but she snuggled into me even closer, and I guess that was her answer. "That bad, huh?" I asked.

"Absolutely terrible. The most adorable dogs and man under the stars with breathtaking mood lighting . . . yuck," she teased back.

"Well, you'll just have to give me a chance in the future to make it better." I smiled at her, and her face lit up in reply.

"I'm going to hold you to it, although maybe one of these times we'll fall asleep together in a more *normal* place." She laughed.

"Normal is way overrated. You taught me that." And I looked at her with appreciation.

"I couldn't agree more." She beamed. "So, can we do something together today?"

"Oh, *you* want to do something together? How the tables have turned." I teased, remembering how I had nervously asked her that very question on the beach not so long ago. She nodded yes with a laugh. "Well, if we have the whole day, then–"

"Oh no, I'm scared now. Maybe I'll take it back."

I squeezed her. "If we have the whole day," I began again, louder, "then we could go to Paia. It's a free-spirited town with lots of fun shops and local artists' works. And we could take the Road to Hana. Maybe even see some waterfalls. You could just leave it up to me, the *local*, you know?"

"Never," she joked. "That would make too much sense."

"That's what I thought."

"No, I love that idea. Ok, lead the way," she stated in a relaxed and trusting way.

"Really?"

"Well, don't sound *so* surprised." And I stopped myself before she changed her mind. I knew she was kidding, but I also knew how guarded Guin's heart was. And now that I knew it was for good reasons, I didn't want to do anything that might cause her to put those shields back up.

WE TOOK the dogs back to the bungalow and grabbed a bite to eat before heading out. I went to find Tutu to tell her the plans for the day and to see if, by chance, she wanted to join us. To my surprise, I found both she and Louis sitting on the lanai having breakfast together. They looked so casual and relaxed, as if this was how they were always meant to be. As if this was a routine they'd shared every day for countless years. I almost didn't recognize Louis without his fedora and with his sophisticated suspenders now casually hanging down. He'd rolled up his sleeves in a relaxed, cool way as he sat close to Tutu.

I hated to break this moment, their shared laughter making me smile, but I always let Tutu know where I would be in case she needed me. I cleared my throat slightly so they would know I was there as I stepped onto the porch.

"Hey, Locke. Sorry for the early morning intrusion," Louis said, sitting up straighter as Tutu smiled up at me.

"Hey Louis, it's good to see you. And it's fantastic to see my grandmother smiling so much. You're welcome here every morning if you're going to make her this happy."

"*Keiki*," Tutu said in a teasing tone.

"*Yesss?*" I said back to her in a singsong voice. "Guin and I are going to Paia today and then the Road to Hana. You're welcome to join us if you like. I know it holds some pretty wonderful memories for you."

Tutu was about to say something, but Louis looked at her with a lost, nostalgic look. "Lani, what do you say? Would you like to go?" That baritone vocal smoothly sang out of him. I definitely would have said yes to the man.

"Oh, uh," my grandmother said, looking flustered. His look certainly could do that to a person. Then she looked at me. "Are you sure, Locke? Don't you want some time alone with just Guin?"

"I'd love for you to come, and I know she would too. I can call Reef to come check on the dogs. The parks don't allow dogs because the hikes aren't always safe for them," I reassured her.

Louis looked at her again, and her cheeks bloomed with color. "Ok, if you're sure. I'll go get changed."

She went to grab the plates, but Louis reached for her hand, stopping her and letting her know he had them. She blushed even harder. My grandfather never would have done anything he thought of as "women's duties." He certainly never would have offered to help. I could tell it went against all her instincts to leave the dishes with him. But when she looked at his face, she relaxed and smiled, heading to change for the day, an added excitement in her step.

I sat down with Louis for a moment before I made something for Guin and me to eat. "You really make Tutu happy, you know?" I said to him and he looked down slightly. It was the first time I'd seen him go shy.

Louis spoke softly, "Locke, I know I just came back into her life and I'm going to have to earn a lot of trust–and that I also just came into your life. And I certainly don't want to mess up anything you have here because it's so special, but if things keep going how they are, and you feel you can trust me . . . And most importantly, if Lani feels she can trust me, do you think–" He looked off into the distance and then back to me, suddenly making direct eye contact. I could see how much his self-confidence wavered. I could tell he had little to begin with in this area–especially where my grandmother was concerned– and that astonished me. "Well, Locke, I'd really like to spend what time we have left *together*, and I think she would too. I don't want to rush anything, but I wanted you to know my intentions for when you think the time might be right. If you think it might be possible."

I spoke, a little shocked, but he spoke before I could.

"I'm not saying any of this correctly," Louis said, looking flustered again. "I want to do it right this time. I want to do it how I dreamed of it being the first time. A beautiful church wedding that I never could have afforded when I was younger. Maybe at the little white chapel in Wailea. The one with the glass floor that sits on the koi pond by the ocean and has so many stained-glass windows. It's my dream for us. I guess I'm going to be asking for your blessing one day. But I figured you would know when the time might be right. If it would ever be ok for her to live with me in new surroundings. I haven't . . . I haven't seen any of the memory problems you were talking about. I don't know how she will respond to me or if I will help her as well as you can. So I thought—"

"Louis, I will help you however I can. And you have my blessing." My heart felt so full after hearing his words. I just hoped when one of her episodes happened he would still feel the same way. As I knew all too well, it was so easy for people to talk, but Louis didn't seem like one of those people to me. I sure hoped I wasn't wrong.

AFTER EVERYONE WAS ready to go, we said goodbye to the dogs and loaded up the Jeep. As I started driving, I looked over at Guin, her blonde hair blowing wildly across her face. She gazed back over to me and smiled. I could still see the outline of those pink wings across her cheeks that she'd gotten the first day we'd met. I could tell she kept trying to cover them up with makeup, but today it seemed she hadn't bothered. And it was freeing to see. She was beautiful just the way she was—naturally beautiful. And honestly, there was something special about those pink wings because they belonged to her. She looked like a butterfly had kissed her. It was a reminder of her gentle and kind nature. She was very much like the butterfly wing's flap she talked about.

It gave me an idea as I reached for her hand. "How about visiting the butterfly farm today? It's on the way to Paia."

She tucked strands of her blonde hair behind her ear as she tried to tame them. "A butterfly farm? Really?"

"Yeah, there are screened in areas for the endangered butterfly species and you can walk through the enclosed areas." I saw her bite her lip, and I laughed, knowing her answer. I started to call out over my shoulder, but Louis was too fast.

"We would love to go," he answered before I had time to ask. "Butterflies, rainbows, and constellations are kind of our thing, Locke." He laughed.

Right. I should have known from the songs they used to write and sing together. And the idea of metamorphosis seemed perfect for everyone in this car. We may all have been in different stages of our transformation, but we were all experiencing it through the power of love and acceptance. Through the power of kindness and compassion, and from finally being seen. And it was beautiful. Just like a butterfly emerging from its cocoon.

I nodded. "Ok, to the butterfly farm it is then. I'm pretty sure it's mostly for kids, but that's alright."

"We're all young at heart here," Louis said, and I saw him take my grandmother's hand. And I couldn't have agreed more. Because as we started walking through the screened tents, it really felt like we were kids again. Wonder lit up our faces as butterflies of all different sizes, shapes, and colors landed on us. You could say they were from "all different flights of life" as they originated from different places in the world. Just like us. And they all blended together seamlessly–harmoniously.

I looked over at Guin just as a butterfly landed on her nose, right in the middle of her butterfly rash. Its little iridescent wings flitting to the pace of my heartbeats. "Uh, you've got a little something," I began, and then I got lost in her childlike expression and her crystal blue waves of wonder. "Never mind, it's too perfect."

She giggled slightly, and the butterfly flitted off. She said, "It would have to land there."

"Definitely, it found the best spot," I said. She shook her head no, so I continued, "I think so. I love your beautiful face with your butterfly wings and everything in between. I especially love that spot for something else you've taught me to do." Then, I demonstrated her adorable Eskimo kiss. "But even better . . ." I began as I looked at her with this heat pulsating between us–one I knew wasn't just from the humidity that was rising for the day. "Even better is the special place for butterfly kisses. I'm glad it didn't land there. I'm definitely claiming that spot."

Her lips parted, and a brief flutter of sound escaped. "Well, you better do it fast then," she instructed. And I certainly complied as the butterflies continued to dance around us. Symbolizing so many things that my mind could not process. Because all I could do was get wrapped in those gentle lips that seemed to understand and care for me so well.

I faintly heard Louis' voice saying something to my grandmother, and it broke through my bubbled fantasy. "Lani, you really underestimated how many moves your grandson has. I definitely should learn from him. And you thought he was going to need some help. Like he has anything to learn from me." He laughed.

"Well, I'm sure he does. But in the meantime, I'll take some butterfly kisses too. I think it's only fair. The butterflies are dancing their hearts out for us."

I looked over to Tutu and Louis as I held Guin in my arms, and what I saw were two teenage kids so completely in love. And I couldn't have been happier for my grandma. We took our time walking through the rest of the farm. Really soaking up the kaleidoscope of colors and the beauty of the day. Then with some reluctance, we decided we better leave for our next destination.

It was a bit of a drive from the butterfly farm to Paia, but the car was easily filled with conversation, especially since Louis had joined us. He was like the friend you picked up with and he didn't miss a beat. I loved that. He was a good guy and so down to earth. Exactly what my grandmother needed.

I parked the Jeep close to some of the local shops and as we made our way over to them, I could see both Guin's and Tutu's eyes light up with anticipation. But I wasn't sure I was up for another shopping excursion with them. They had already given me quite the shopping initiation last time. Although I had enjoyed it.

However, their mischievous eyes were making me reconsider. "Just a few shops, and then we have to get going if we actually want to see anything on the Road to Hana," I said, knowing their capacity for shopping. I looked at their slightly disappointed faces. "Or we can stay here if you prefer."

Guin spoke up, "No, I definitely want to see the waterfalls, but it means we'll just have to make the *most* of our time here." She sported an impish grin.

And oh boy, did they make every second count. They made it through quite an array of local shops while Louis and I trailed behind, letting them have their space. It was really nice to have another guy around. But by around the fifth or sixth shop, Louis had gravitated over to Tutu. They were completely absorbed in each other as they enjoyed the local artists' booths. I figured now was a good time to ask what they would like to do. But I was pretty sure my grandmother would definitely prefer to continue shopping, and I liked the idea of having some time with Guin at the falls.

So with as much attention as I could muster from them, I tried to ask my grandmother their preference, and she easily said they would like to continue shopping. So I told the love birds goodbye and offered the smiling Mermaid my hand, so we could make our way back to the Jeep together. I had a feeling this sea siren was going to be right at home among the waterfalls.

Locke

CHAPTER 43

WHEN WE LEFT Tutu and Louis to continue their shopping in Paia, it felt really strange leaving Tutu with someone else, but I knew she was in excellent hands. I already trusted Louis just from the way he treated Tutu and the way she looked at him. Maybe it was crazy to trust someone that quickly, but I did. Just like I had with Guin. Maybe she was changing something in me.

I wanted to surprise Guin by taking her to the Wai'āna-panapa State Park before we visited the waterfalls on the road to Hana. The park was famous for its sandy black beaches and for its lava tube cave that looked like a little grotto. And I knew Guin would be interested in the place where Tutu used to hold her concerts. Especially since it was also where Tutu and Louis had played their music together. The place where they had fallen in love. And for that reason alone, I knew Guin was going to love it.

So I headed the Jeep in that direction and it was definitely worth seeing the look on her face when we arrived. Exploring those black lava, sandy shores with her and the little grotto cave was magical. To be somewhere marked by my grandmother's beautiful memories, and to be there with the woman I had opened my heart up to so completely, was pretty surreal. And Guin seemed to be just as affected by our surroundings as I was.

We explored the edges of the lava cave and then stepped out into its radiant sunlit opening. I went to Guin and wrapped my arms around her waist as I stood behind her. With my head nestled beside hers, I gazed out to the ocean, feeling warmly cocooned inside this perfect moment and our lava formed time capsule. We continued to stand together without words, feeling fortunate to have found each other just as Tutu and Louis had. Music had brought us all together.

Eventually, we moved from our perfect spot and made our way back to the car, intertwined around one another. When we reached the car, I finally broke the silence, asking what else she would like to see and do with the rest of our day.

We decided to see Twin Falls next since there were some smaller waterfalls close to the parking lot. If Guin didn't feel up to walking, then she would at least be able to see some of the smaller falls. If she felt up to walking, then the impressive upper falls were only about a mile away. This way, we could "play it by ear," depending on what Guin felt like doing. I could tell she was already nervous about "hiking," and I didn't want her to be. I didn't want her to feel any anxiety with me. So when we pulled into the parking lot, I suggested visiting the fruit stand that was part of the farm first. This seemed to ease some of her tension immediately. Plus, the stand was pretty adorable with its painted red surfboard sign hanging over the retro van. It seemed very Guin.

After we finished our delicious coconut drinks, we headed to the nearby falls. I could tell Guin was completely relaxed. She even slipped her hand in mine as we started walking. The falls nearest the road were beautiful, but they were barely a few feet deep. The pools were still a good size, but I was really hoping she'd be able to see some of the larger ones with the bigger drops. But I wanted her to make that call.

As we stood before one of the smaller falls, she looked over at me. I guess she could tell that I was debating what to do next. I was trying to figure out if walking any further was a good idea or not.

"So," she started, "are these all the falls? They're not very big."

"Uh, well, there are some larger waterfalls, but they're about a mile away." I left it there and continued looking at the falls.

Guin responded, "Oh, that doesn't sound too far. I was thinking the hike would be several miles each way."

I looked over at her. She seemed to feel good today and have a pretty decent amount of energy. Maybe it would be okay to take the hike if we took our time along the way. But it was pretty warm today. "The hike is worth it if you're feeling ok.

The falls are really breathtaking. But I can also find more falls later today on our drive that are closer to the road."

"No," she said with an edge of excitement to her voice. "I'd like to see these falls. But I might need to take some breaks and walk at a slower pace."

"Well, I'm still sore from dancing and I'm walking slower anyway, so it should work out just fine for both of us." And she smiled at me.

We'd both worn waterproof hiking boots because of having to cross several streams. That was one thing she had from growing up around the Smoky Mountains. And luckily, so far, Guin seemed like she was doing really well with the hike and enjoying it too. I offered her my arm when things got rocky or we crossed a stream, and Guin seemed happy for the help. It was like we were a team now. And I was so glad to see that she viewed my offer of help differently now.

I could hear the sounds of the waterfalls faintly in the distance when I felt Guin slow down substantially. Then she stopped completely. "Locke," she said to me, breathlessly. I could tell the heat and humidity were getting to her. Her face was flushed pink all over. And her nose and cheeks were colored with bright red marks in the shape of a butterfly. I knew she didn't do well in the heat, but since most of our outdoor activities had taken place in the water, she'd been doing well on our other excursions. The water really helped to keep her cool. I had been worried about hiking to these water-falls, but my concern had been more about her energy levels and fatigue. I obviously hadn't given enough thought to the heat and humidity.

Her eyes had a glassy expression, and I could see a look of disorientation forming in them. *Oh no, this isn't good.* I'd had people pass out before on excursions, and it seemed she had reached that point. Her conditions were definitely coming out in full force. I knew Sebastian had been trained to warn her of impending episodes, but I definitely wasn't as good as Sebe at that job. I felt like I'd dropped the ball on this one. She looked way past going. I should have noticed sooner.

All I could think was that maybe if I could get her somewhere cool to rest, hopefully that would help the situation. "Guin, tell me what's going on. I'm going to need some help here." I looked deeper into her blues, trying to find some answers, but she seemed to slip further away from me.

"Locke, I just–" she paused and put a hand up to her head. I reached my hands out to her waist and held onto her tightly, as did my heart. She had already come to mean so much to me. I couldn't let anything happen to her. I swallowed, waiting. She continued, "I think I'm overheating, and it's flaring both my Lupus and my migraines. I just need . . . My body is going to shut itself down soon. It's too late to reverse it, so is there somewhere we can find . . ."

"We've got to get you somewhere cool, fast. Hopefully, that will help. I'll find you a place where you can lie down too." I looked around, assessing my options. Trying to think of anything that would help her and then I saw Guin close her eyes and start swaying. "Whoa. I need to get you to a better place than this. Just try to hold on for a few more minutes." But I knew immediately that was an idiotic thing to say. I saw that wouldn't happen. There was no holding on. "Ok, I'm picking you up, Guin. We're close to the water. I can hear it. I'll get you into one of the pools at the base of the waterfalls. The water should help to cool you down some."

She was easy to pick up. She had gone limp like a rag doll– no fighting me on it. Not that she had the first time we'd met either. Her arms wrapped weakly around my neck, and her head fell onto my shoulder. She said almost incoherently, "You really are my very own Creature from the Black Lagoon. So sexy."

"Ok, well just wait until I carry you into the pool of water." I laughed. I'd had such a hang-up about creatures and monsters, but when Guin used the comparison, it didn't bother me. I knew she would never see me the way other women had. She was just comparing the way the creature carried the film star around in the movie, and for the first time, I felt like a weight had been lifted off of my shoulders. Even if I identified with the creature because I often felt just as judged or misunderstood, that didn't make me one. And Guin wasn't the creature's damsel in distress either. She was strong and fearless. She just needed a little help sometimes, just like me. I now saw what a privilege it was to be given the opportunity to take care of Guin when she was in a vulnerable position. And she was showing me it was ok to ask for help. That being one of those people she asked was a privilege in itself too.

Guin smiled up at me. "You have no idea how many fantasies you are fulfilling today." Her words came out a little more coherently now. I guess being able to rest in my arms had helped her some. She continued, "I've even been to Crystal River in Florida, where they filmed the *Black Lagoon* movie. I went when I was really young. We stopped there on our way to Disney World when I was on a trip with my mom. But now I'm really enjoying this private interactive take on the Black Lagoon tour."

"Well, you'll have to take me there sometime. But in the meantime, I'm happy to fulfill as many fantasies as possible today," I said, and I couldn't help but raise my eyebrows to get a laugh from her.

"You better be careful what you say, Locke. You might regret it."

"Doubtful. Very doubtful, Mermaid," I said, as we made our way further on the trail with the sound of water getting louder. I knew that this wasn't the smoothest mode of transportation with the extra weight on my prosthesis and the uneven terrain. I had been acutely aware of these same things the first time I had carried her on the beach, but today I didn't worry or feel embarrassed that this was a somewhat "bumpier" experience. Because Guin had shown me that being different wasn't bad. Being true to myself was definitely preferred.

Up ahead, a gorgeous emerald-green pool came into view with lots of lush foliage surrounding it. I could see a spectacular waterfall with white water cascading down, creating an ethereal rainbow. There was a rocky overhang from which the water fell, tangled with vines, roots, and assorted plants. I wished Guin felt better so she could enjoy it too. This was truly spectacular.

Guin looked up at me with a little more energy and a beautiful smile. I scanned her face, still seeing splotchy pink throughout and the red mask under her eyes. "Ok, I'm taking you in," I said, only stopping long enough to set the pack down. Then I headed straight for the pool.

"Locke, let me at least take off my clothes." She laughed.

"Ok, if you insist," I joked.

"Yes, I think my swimsuit would be much better. I really don't want to walk back in soaking wet clothing."

"I'm pretty sure I'll be *carrying* you the rest of the way, Mermaid." She shook her head, and I set her down so she could undress, not wanting to argue with her. Then she started walking toward the water. I reached for her arm and she looked back at me questioningly. But I just moved over and picked her back up. "I'm not letting you miss your Black Lagoon fantasy."

I waded into the water with her, taking extra care to get my footing. I felt the cool water's immediate relief from the heat as its silky tendrils wrapped around me. I could only imagine what she must be feeling.

I heard Guin let out a deep exhale, and I took that as a sign that the water was helping her feel better. After I had waded all the way in, I continued to hold her in my arms as she floated buoyantly. Stress seemed to leave her as she held onto me. Finally, a relaxed expression moved over her wearied features.

"Better?" I asked, and she nodded her head in agreement. I knew there wouldn't be too many times when I could actually provide her relief. I loved that this time I actually could do something. It made you feel powerless when you couldn't help someone you cared so much about.

I started drifting nearer the waterfall. The steady sound of droplets lulled us into a serene sense of security. Guin seemed to realize what I was about to do, and I grinned at the look on her face. Quickly, I ducked under the stream from the falls, getting us both wet.

"You could have gone around the waterfall to get us to the backside," she said with a playful smile.

"Could have. But I figured we both needed a little more cooling off." Plus, I loved to see her hair all tousled and wet. I was really hoping the shade from the overhang would help her feel even cooler, as well as the dampness from the enclosed cove blanketed by the curtain of white water.

"Your coloring looks better. Are you–" But I didn't finish my question as I noticed the look of wonder on her face as she took in her surroundings. "Um, are you feeling–" Well, I'd managed one more word as she wrapped her arms tighter around me and then her legs. I pinched my eyes, trying to focus. "Feeling better?" I finally finished, opening my eyes. This had to be the most romantic place I'd ever been with a woman. It was like our own personal hideaway. And Guin was making it impossible to even think past caveman level vocabulary, apparently.

"Uh, huh," she said as she looked at me, nodding. But those weren't enough words to satisfy me. She really had looked like she was going to pass out on me earlier. I realized at that moment there wasn't anything I wouldn't do to keep her safe. How much I wanted to protect her. Memories of going down to the dialysis center while Dean covered for me at the surf shack sailed through my mind. I'd asked the center how to find out if you were a match to be a kidney donor for someone, and I had already started the process. I knew with my blood type I wouldn't be a match for Guin, but I had to hear that "no" for myself.

"Guin, are you sure you're ok? Back there–" I asked again, looking into her eyes with concern. But the shimmering waves of blue wanted something different from me.

"Locke, I'm fine now. You did *exactly* the right thing for me. It's like you know me so well. Sometimes I get a longer warning before I pass out. That allows me to try to prevent it from happening or at least get to a safe place. Sebe usually alerts me, but you could do that for me today. Thank you so much."

"I think you can thank the overheated tourists and the unfortunate heat stroke that I see–" I started technically.

"Locke." Her arms tightened more around me and her tone took on a huskiness to it, like she was trying to get my attention. That wasn't the problem.

"Mermaid, I don't think–"

"You are seriously the only guy that wouldn't be taking

advantage of this situation right now. I'm literally wrapped around you, begging you to kiss me in the most romantic place I've ever been."

Well, she thought so too, huh?

"Is that what you're doing?" I asked playfully.

"Yeah, it is."

"Well, your health will always come first." There was no question in my voice. *She* would always come first. And by the look in her eyes, I knew she would do the same for me. She was the type to put the oxygen mask on me before herself. It didn't matter what instructions she was given. And I knew at that moment it was the same for me as well.

A little noise hitched in her chest. "I don't even know–" She looked so lost. So completely overwhelmed. "I'm not used to–" She looked off. "I'm used to just being valuable as a 'pretty face,' fulfilling stereotypical roles. You know, wherever you can insert the word *babe* . . . babe, come meet my boss; babe, I'm hungry; babe, wear the red one."

"It definitely doesn't work like that with me, Mermaid. And I will officially never call you *babe*, I promise." And she laughed lightly. But I knew it wasn't the nickname that was the problem, although someone had surely abused it.

She looked at me with so much desire and said, "When did this notion start that good guys finish last? That they never win?"

And the way she was staring at me made me know she thought I was one of them. And it meant so much to me. "Probably because they usually do." I laughed.

"Well, we need to change that," she replied as her lips reached mine.

Locke

CHAPTER 44

WE CONTINUED to sit in the cool, little oasis cave under the waterfall after our swim. It was relaxing and refreshing, and I was pretty sure that was just what Guin needed today. At least she'd been able to see some of the Road to Hana on the drive. But I'd rather be under this waterfall with her, anyway. Now I just had to figure out a way to get her back safely.

We still had to walk back to the Jeep, and then, hopefully if Guin still felt better, we could meet up with Tutu and Louis for dinner. I hoped they'd enjoyed the rest of their day shopping. It seemed like they were having a great time checking out all the local artisan booths when we left them earlier today. But I was pretty sure they would love whatever they did as long as they were together. That was the mark of a truly strong partnership. And I looked at Guin with that thought. So far, there wasn't anything that wouldn't be better with her.

She contemplated me in return as we sat under the cool overhang with the smooth, rejuvenating rocks underneath us. "Thank you for taking care of me today."

I started to speak, but she stopped me.

"No, really. I sometimes forget how much I rely on Sebe. He's given me so much more freedom. I used to be consumed with carefully planning my day. There were so many things I didn't do for fear of having an episode, especially socially. Sebe has brought me such comfort and given so much of my life back to me. I could even live by myself now that I have him. I never want to put that responsibility on anyone else, but I can't tell you how much your help has meant to me. Overheating is a big trigger and I should have said something sooner, but I didn't realize what was happening until it was too late. So thank you."

"Guin, I will always notice you. I'm just glad there was something I could do to help." My eyes tried to convey how much she meant to me.

"You're the real deal, aren't you?"

I looked at her, not sure how to respond. "I just really care about you, Guin . . . So how bad is your migraine? "

"It's bearable, but I think I'll need to take some medicine

for it. I didn't want to take any on the walk because it dehydrates me."

"Why do I feel that bearable for you isn't the same as it is for everyone else?" I skeptically asked her.

"I guess it's a sliding scale with chronic pain. You just expect it. If I woke up with none, then I would be shocked and probably worried too." She laughed lightly.

"Well, let's go get your medicine and then see if you're up to finding Tutu and Louis. Hopefully, they've had a good day. We can get you some electrolytes too. Hopefully that will help as well."

"Yes, that definitely helps especially in this heat." She looked at me, a little overcome. I was thankful I had learned how to care for people in this type of weather. "And I'm sure Tutu and Louis had a great day. They are completely adorable together." I laughed at her words, but I completely agreed. They were good together, and it had been way too long since my grandmother had been this happy.

I CALLED Louis when we were getting close to Paia, but he didn't pick up. I thought they were probably busy looking in a shop or might have even stopped for some shaved ice. But when we drove down by the shops to find some parking, we quickly found out that wasn't the case. Guin spotted them sitting on a bench outside one storefront, Louis' iconic fedora facing Tutu.

"Locke." Her voice had an edge to it that worried me. "I think something happened."

With her words propelling me, I parked as quickly as possible. I went to walk around the Jeep to Guin, but she was already in front of it. She was in just as big of a hurry to get to them as I was.

I saw Louis' face first when we approached them, since he was turned in our direction. There was concern etched in his features and he had a hand on Tutu's back, rubbing her gently as he spoke in soft tones to her. His face looked up quickly as we got closer, worry burrowed deep into his creases. I couldn't tell by his features how he wanted to proceed, but I certainly had a good idea what had happened.

I didn't know how to talk to Tutu with Louis around. He added a whole new dynamic. Usually, it was just Tutu and me. I tried to keep things as relaxed as possible. So I casually asked Tutu, "Hey, how was the shopping?" Then I added, "I'm sure Louis has a whole new collection of hats by now."

Louis nodded to me. I could tell he wanted to speak with me. I looked over at Guin. She wasn't in Tutu's long-term memory, so I didn't know if it was okay for her to be the one to stay with her. But Tutu seemed to do a little better now. And I didn't need to say anything to Guin: she already understood. She went over and sat beside Tutu. She began talking to her and Tutu smiled. Whether she recognized Guin in this state, she seemed happy to talk with her and felt comfortable with her. She seemed to have an innate sense of whom she could trust, maybe a subconscious understanding.

Louis slowly got up, seeing that Tutu was comfortable with Guin. Following his lead, I went over to a shop window with him, just out of earshot from Tutu.

"What happened? Is she alright?" I asked him slowly.

He looked at me. Then I knew for sure he'd seen one of her

episodes for the first time. This was going to be the deciding point. Was he "all talk" like my grandfather, or was he more? I waited, my heart too scared to hope.

"Uh, Locke, I think your grandmother had an episode. She seems fine now. She became disoriented and didn't know where we were or what we were doing. It scared her and . . ." I could see the pain on his face. Not fear, but *pain*. It hurt him to see her this way. Now my optimistic heart couldn't help but hope. Louis continued, "But she still recognized me. Eventually I could take her outside so we could talk. I was just about to take her down to the beach and see if that would help her when you arrived. I thought the ocean waves and the quiet surroundings might relieve her. I think it still might help her, if you don't mind."

I was shocked. I thought he'd want to pass her off to me. But no, he wanted to take care of her. He wasn't scared in the slightest; he was just hurting for her.

I swallowed back my tears. "Yeah, I think that's a great idea. Thank you." He nodded, and I could tell he just wanted to get back to her now. "Um, Guin and I can come with you, if that's alright. We can sit in a different area, and if Tutu feels better, we can still all go to dinner together. Her episodes usually pass pretty quickly but she stays rattled for a while. I really appreciate your care for her."

Louis really looked at me then. "Locke, I'm not going anywhere. *I promise.* I want you to know that. I know you don't let people into your grandmother's life lightly, and I know it's a privilege. One I appreciate that you've given to me. I will love her just as much at the end of this day as I did at the beginning."

He looked at me for understanding. But I wasn't capable of

speaking. At this moment, all I could do was embrace him. It was the only thing I had to offer as a thank you, and I hope he understood. But the way he reciprocated said that he did. And in that moment, something shifted between us. An understanding. He was quickly becoming the grandfather figure I never had and the man Tutu had always deserved.

I backed away from him, so incredibly thankful he had come into our lives. He spoke more quietly now in that smoky tone of his, "I'm going to see if your grandmother wants to go sit on the beach. I hope you and Guin will join us."

And I just nodded because that's all I could do. He looked at me with a soft smile and said, "Ok." Then he moved toward Tutu. Tenderly speaking to her and taking her arm in his as they made their way toward the sandy shores.

I went over to Guin and sat down beside her on the bench. She patiently let me sit in silence while I tried to collect the thoughts that came whirling through my mind, faster than the waves crashing on the shore. After I explained to Guin what had happened, we went to join Tutu and Louis on the beach.

Guin and I stopped at the beginning of the path that led down to Ho'okipa Beach. There on the shore, just above the break of the waves, Louis sat with his arm tenderly wrapped around Tutu. Her head rested on his shoulder, and she looked completely relaxed, completely at home. They looked like a couple in love for the first time, just like they had at the beginning of our day. I imagined this might have been very similar to what they looked like all those many years ago.

My hand tightened on Guin's, and she squeezed mine back in response. Then she looked up at me through the lingering rays of sunshine. "Locke, I think she's going to be alright. You couldn't ask for more than to have someone like you and Louis by her side. That's really all anyone wants. Someone to laugh and cry with you through it all–*every part*. If you have that, then you can get through anything."

I brought her into me and tried to tuck her away, wanting to keep her there and protect her from everything. But I had a feeling she wouldn't stay. And I wanted that more than anything.

Guinevere

CHAPTER 45

TIME HAD MOVED EVER SO QUICKLY. I couldn't believe my week here was ending. But we had already fallen into a copacetic rhythm. This morning, Locke headed out to the surf shack since I had convinced Tutu to go back to the ukulele convention with me today. And I couldn't have been more excited for her to join me and I was eager to learn whatever I could from her.

Tutu was collecting her things when the phone rang. I picked it up expecting to hear Locke's voice, but instead I heard Dean's. And he sounded way more serious than usual. I had become accustomed to his more playful tone.

"Guin?" he asked, and I confirmed his suspicions. "Hey, I had something I wanted to talk with you about."

I figured he wanted to speak with me about something related to Locke, but I couldn't have been further off. And when I hung up the phone, I sat on the sofa in a dazed state with Sebe beside me, my phone in my hands and my purse beside me as I waited on Tutu.

"Ok, I'm ready, *Ku'iupo*. I'm sorry you had to wait on me," Tutu's cheery tone sang out to me. And her voice was exactly what I needed to snap me out of my trance. I smiled as she came into the living room. "Everything alright?" she asked as she came over to me. Apparently I had not done as good a job as I had thought in hiding my emotions.

I quickly gathered up Sebe as I assured Tutu everything was fine and then I drove us to the convention in my rental car. It was a quick drive to The Westin Resort & Spa, where the convention was being hosted. The Westin Resort looked like something out of a fairy tale.

Even though there were signs pointing the way to the conference rooms used for the convention, I couldn't help but want to explore a little of the hotel grounds with Tutu before the sessions started. They were just too magical to miss.

The three of us walked through the lobby and then it transitioned to a koi pond and a man-made waterfall. The area was open to the outdoors with plenty of sunshine and fresh Hawaiian air. Our eyes traveled over the boardwalk that crossed over the koi pond and looped around the waterfall. In the middle of the pond was a large, floating area filled with convention guests excitedly talking about the convention.

I quickly recognized Luna sitting on the boardwalk with a few of the other ukulele players. They were easy to spot with their colorful array of wood tone ukes propped beside them. Luna quickly motioned us over, and we began walking across the boardwalk to meet them.

"Tutu, I'm so happy you came! And Guin, it's so good to see you again." A huge smile spread across her face when she said my name. Perhaps she remembered the "coconut smoochie" escapade. "Come sit with us," she said in a warm and welcoming tone.

As we took a seat on one of the carved wooden sofas, I couldn't help but think how good it felt to be a part of this community. To belong to a group where I felt so at home.

Luna began, "We were just discussing how we found our way to the ukulele and why some of us started using music as therapy." She gently turned toward one lady in the group. "Sharon lost her husband of thirty years and said she wouldn't listen to music. It reminded her too much of him. But this one particular record kept mysteriously playing on her husband's antique record player. So Sharon took it as a sign from her husband and became determined to learn how to play the song." Luna turned to another woman with a scarf over her head. "And Liz was diagnosed with stage three cancer and had always wanted to learn to play an instrument. She wanted something that would be soothing, so she gravitated toward the ukulele." She turned to a younger woman, "Amber went through an abusive relationship and felt like she wasn't able to express herself. So she started writing song lyrics as an outlet for her emotions. And then she began learning to play the ukulele to add music to her lyrics." Luna looked at us. "Would you like to share your musical journey with us?"

I was taken with their stories. I hadn't realized how many people in this community had needed the healing power of music. I had assumed most of them probably just wanted to learn how to play an instrument and the ukulele appealed to them since it was small and easy to carry. Light baggage, so to speak. *Easy breezy, right? That's what people think of when they think of the ukulele, isn't it?* But no, I had made assumptions like so many other people had about this instrument. It could do so much more than people realized. It was all in how you handled it and played it. All in what you made of it. Like so many things in life.

There was such deep meaning in their collective choice to be here, as well as why they had chosen this special instrument. The one that had brought me so much peace through its soothing strings. And then a feeling of completeness washed over me. I felt like I finally fit somewhere and that I was with people who would understand me.

I looked around at the faces of these beautiful women that had just shared such a big part of their hearts, and I actually couldn't wait to share my story with them. That hadn't ever happened to me before, except for when I'd met Tutu online. I looked over at her face, and I could tell she felt the same way. Only music could bond us together in this way.

I held Luna's gaze, and she nodded to me in a reassuring way. I didn't even realize I was holding my breath when I began. "I didn't realize I was depressed when I bought my first ukulele online. I was too embarrassed to even buy one in the store. Music represented another thing I probably couldn't do with my conditions. I'd started learning to play the guitar before I became really ill and I thought since I had more time, I would try it again. But I found out I wasn't able to press down the strings of my guitar anymore, so. . . ." I trailed off.

Luna just looked at me again, the patience and care she always showed in our sessions was so apparent on her face. So I continued. "I quickly became frustrated with the guitar, so I shoved it aside as one more thing I couldn't do. But there were all these emotions churning around inside of me, ones I didn't really feel I could explore and I needed to find a safe way to do that. And suddenly in the middle of the night, I woke up with all these song lyrics in my head and I wrote them down. It kept happening to me. And then I watched ukulele instruction videos on YouTube. But it wasn't until I found Luna's videos and watched them all that I got the courage to buy a ukulele and join the online community. And slowly, through playing and singing, the expression of music lifted some of the darkness that had crept across my soul without my knowledge. Suddenly those strings and this community provided a light I never knew I needed. And I allowed myself to indulge my emotions wherever they took me and to truly feel them. No part was off limits, it was all therapy."

Luna looked at me slightly overcome, just as when she spoke about the other women's stories. "I know that darkness, Guin. Sometimes music feels like the only place that has light. And lyrics are the only thing that makes sense." I nodded slowly at her. Then she asked, "Did it spread? The light?"

I nodded my head and finally spoke, "Yes, everywhere." My eyes wandered around and landed on Tutu. There's no way I would have been able to come here if it hadn't. I would have missed out on so many beautiful parts of life.

WE FOUND the room for the jazz chord workshop that was focused on learning to transpose chords down the fretboard of the ukulele. I was so excited about this workshop because this was an area where I was severely lacking. I had been particularly excited that Tutu had joined us because I knew she was an expert, ever since I'd heard her play and watched how seamlessly her hands moved up and down the frets. And I could definitely use the extra help. Sometimes the brain fog made concepts harder to grasp and today felt like it was going to be one of those days.

So I was already in a daze as we entered the room. The events of the morning were contributing to my brain fog. Tutu grabbed my arm. "Guin," she said, pulling me to the side. She looked at me and then guided me over to a bench so we could sit down. "What's wrong, Guin?"

"Oh, nothing's wrong." I tried to control my facial expressions.

But she continued to look at me, holding me accountable. "Guin, you can always talk to me. Whatever it is. I hope you know that."

"It's nothing, really. I think I was just nervous about today. That's all. I was just letting my anxiety get the better of me."

Her warm eyes looked at me, and now they seemed hesitant too. "I understand, Guin. I have been really nervous to come to the convention with you. It's been a while since I've played the ukulele, especially in front of other people. And I . . . Well, I just don't . . . Well, sometimes you just want to remain blissfully unaware. You don't want to know your limitations. You don't want to see what happens when your memory slips *or* how much it already has. Or how it will affect your playing ability."

"Tutu, you're amazing. You played so well with Louis the other night. And I look up to you so much. '*O 'oe no¯, aloha,* '" I said to Tutu.

She looked at me, confused. "I'm the one, what one?"

I turned my head to the side, not understanding. "What? Did I say it wrong? Or use the wrong saying?" I guess my attempt at saying *don't worry, beautiful* didn't come out nearly as well as when Locke said it to me.

"Well, no . . . I guess not, dear. I'm very flattered. I think of you like a grandchild now, and I'm happy to be your Hawaiian grandmother, so I'll be your 'one.'"

"Wait, I'm confused."

Tutu responded, "Yes, I think you are. I'm not sure the phrase means what you think it means."

"What does it mean?" I asked hesitantly.

"It means 'you are the one.' And 'aloha' has so many meanings for us here . . . hello, goodbye, a way of life, unconditional love, compassion, a life with purpose, a way to lift each other up . . . but in this case, it's a term of endearment and great respect." She looked at me hesitantly. "What did you think it meant?"

My world was spinning. Locke had said that phrase to me on our fake date. And he'd continued to say it to me even when I hadn't reciprocated his feelings–when he'd said "he'd fallen for me" and I said nothing back to him. Because I couldn't. I'd already let him get *too* close to me.

I must have gone a little pale because Tutu said, "Who has been saying–Oh . . ." And then it hit her. "Never mind. I think it must mean whatever you originally thought," she said, trying to do some damage control. My eyes went wide as I stared at her. Tutu continued, "Guin, can we just pretend . . . has Locke really never told you what it means?"

"No, he said he'd fallen for me, but I didn't know he'd been saying *this* ever since . . . I didn't–" But I stopped myself. I didn't want to tell her I couldn't voice my feelings to him.

"Well, that's Locke for you. He has always been shy. I suppose he just couldn't hold it inside any longer. Or maybe he was building up the courage to tell you by testing the words out safely first. I used to have him practice what he would say to the schoolyard bullies to help him build up his courage. I guess he's still using that method. I'm sure he was going to tell you. And maybe in his own way he has." I swallowed hard at her words.

And that's when I knew I had done the right thing after my phone call with Dean. But it wouldn't make things any easier. I looked at Tutu as I felt my eyes water. I fought back against the unwelcome tears.

"Guin, are you alright?" she asked.

I nodded slightly. "I just need to tell you something," was all I could say.

Locke

CHAPTER 46

THE PHONE RANG at the surf shack, and I picked it up mindlessly, still laughing about some remark Dean had just made. I was on a mermaid endorphin high these days. "Ohana, Surf Shack, Locke speaking." I tried to squelch the laughter and my overjoyous tone. But it was pretty impossible these days.

"*Keiki*, you need to come home. *Now.*" Tutu's urgency cut through the line, obliterating everything else like a tidal wave.

"What happened? Are you ok?" I turned my head away from the phone. "Dean!" I called, then I lowered my voice as I remembered he was right beside me. "Cover for me, ok?"

"*Keiki.*" There was a pleading tone in Tutu's voice. "It's not me, it's Guin."

"What?" The blood drained from my face. Many terrible possibilities wiping everything else from my mind. "What's happened?" I could barely croak out my question. Dean was hovering right beside me now, a concerned look on his face.

"Locke, it would be better if you came home–"

"*What happened,*" I stressed, willing Tutu to tell me.

"I don't want to tell you over the phone like this." There was an ache in her voice. She paused and sighed. "Okay, I'll start at the beginning because once I tell you what has happened, then you won't hear anything else . . . Locke, Guin knows."

"She knows what? I'm aware she knows about my leg, Penny, and my accident. What else could she know?"

"Locke, things kind of collapsed today. Like a sandcastle got knocked over by a rogue wave."

My face went slack. What the heck did that mean? Dean was looking at me and making an impatient hand gesture. I pulled the phone away from my face and mouthed, "I have no idea." He made an executive decision and put the phone on speaker while I still held it in my hand. Then he put the closed sign on the door and sat down on the stool next to me.

"Maybe I don't want you to hear this," I said, conflicted. He made a "too bad" motion, and I just rolled my eyes, putting the phone down on the counter.

Tutu asked, "What did you say, *Keiki*?"

"Nothing, Dean is just worried about Guin, that's all. What were you saying about me being a sandcastle collapsing in a hurricane?" Dean's eyes widened. I put my hands up. I really didn't understand.

"Uh, no, *Keiki*. I said that was what today had been like. Apparently there were some things Guin didn't know about and it would have been nice if you had shared that information with your grandmother." I swallowed hard, and Dean raised his eyebrows. I went to push a button so I could take the phone off speaker, but he slapped my hand away. Tutu continued, "First, I didn't realize that you hadn't told her about the ukulele scholarship and that it came from me . . . Also, she didn't know the 'Big Dipper' scholarship was named after Louis. I thought after I told you about those things, you decided to explain them to her."

I breathed in slowly. "Well, that's not so bad. I mean, you did an incredibly generous thing. She's loved her trip to Hawaii, or at least I think she has." Dean nodded in agreement, his solidarity helping to reassure me.

"Yes," Tutu said hesitantly. "It threw her off and wouldn't have been so bad if . . ."

"*If*?" I questioned urgently.

"If . . . *Keiki*, remember I love you. And I will always be your favorite Tutu–"

"Tutu!" I spoke sternly. "If you do not tell me what is going on–"

"Fine, fine. I'm trying. It's just difficult." She exhaled again. "Ok. Second, it may have slipped out that you were getting tested to see if you were a match to be a kidney donor for her and that there were other people who wanted to do the same."

"*Noooo*." I shook my head. "No, please tell me you didn't.

Tell me you didn't let *that* slip. You didn't–" I wasn't making any sense.

"Oh, man," Dean breathed out, and I looked at his horrified face. "Locke, you hadn't told her about any of these things?"

"Dean, you have to know Guin. She never would have let me get tested. And she never needed to know if no one matched. No harm, no foul. That is . . ."

Tutu's voice interrupted me. "Is Dean there?"

"Hello, Kelani," Dean said gently. "I'm here. I was trying to be supportive of Locke, but–"

"Yeah, he's dug a pretty big hole, Dean," she replied.

I let my head fall with a bang on the counter in front of me. Dean put a hand on my back. "Hey man, we can fix this. It's fine. You have an enormous heart. You were just using it."

"Yes," Tutu said meekly. "And that brings us to number three."

"What, number three?" The words came out muffled since I didn't bother moving my head from the counter.

"Locke, you really shouldn't be throwing around the phrase '*o 'oe no⁻, aloha.*' You can't just casually say that to *someone* who doesn't know the Hawaiian language. And it's a little awkward when that *someone* then uses it improperly with others and has to be corrected . . ."

I lifted my head enough so I could rake a hand down my face. "You didn't tell her what it means . . . did you?"

"Dang, Locke," Dean said emphatically, and I just looked at him. "You've been tellin' people 'they're the one' without them knowing what you're saying? That's cryptic, dude. What kinds of things have you been saying to me this whole time?"

I gave him a warning look. I was in no mood for his jokes, even as much as I usually loved them. Because I was *so* screwed.

I looked at him pointedly and said, "Yes, Dean. My sentiments exactly. That's why I told her it means 'don't worry, beautiful.' The phrase just kinda slipped out the first time. It was an accident. Then I was too scared to tell her what it really meant. I figured if I kept saying it, then eventually I would get the courage to tell her what it meant. I did finally tell her that I'd fallen for her, but when she didn't respond to that, how was I supposed to tell her she was "the one for me?"

"*Nooooo, dude, you didn't.*" Dean was in shock.

"Oh, but yes, he did," Tutu replied.

"Locke, you can't secretly tell people 'they're the one' and then tell them it means 'don't worry, beautiful,' just because it accidentally slipped out."

My head banged against the counter again. "Can we just work on damage control now and not rehash my failures? In my defense, it was too early in our relationship for me to say it . . . It was too early to even admit to myself. Again, it came out without me even realizing it. I was just swept up in her mermaid pheromones, her beauty in the moonlight, and whatever else. So just give me a break. And it's not like telling her I was 'falling for her' ever elicited a response. So I think I made the right call here. She wasn't ready to hear it yet. She's *still* not ready to hear it. Because what lunatic falls for someone so quickly? . . . *Wait. Don't answer that!*"

Tutu and Dean both went dead silent. Then Dean said quietly, "Is this the wrong time to say 'lobstered?'" And I started laughing hysterically because I couldn't be in a worse position. I would have to fall for a woman who didn't live here, didn't reciprocate my feelings, and had no intention of letting her heart get any closer. And I'd already handed mine over.

"*Keiki.*" Tutu's voice hesitantly came over the line. "But you do *aloha oe ia¯ ia,* right?"

"Yes, Tutu. I love her. But I don't think it matters. I'm pretty sure I've got my answer," I breathed out.

"Good, because I needed to know your answer before I told you this . . ."

Good? I didn't see how any of this was good. "What else could you possibly tell me?" I asked in utter defeat.

"*Keiki*, she's gone." There was no sugarcoating it, Tutu just laid it out there.

"What?" I could barely be heard through the hoarseness of my voice.

"She's leaving the island, *Keiki*. We left the convention early, and she came back here to 'lay down.' But she really came back to pack her things. I thought we'd talked through everything at the convention and she was alright, but she just didn't want me to tell you she was leaving. She's on her way to the airport now. Guin told me goodbye and thanked me for everything. She asked me to thank you for everything too. She said this had been the best week of her life and she owed that to us, to *you*." Tutu paused as if debating. "Locke, she said it was easier this way. But that she'd never forget you and that she hoped you would always go stargazing."

A long silence followed, and Dean looked at me with a heavy gaze. Tutu continued, "I'm sorry, *Keiki*. But if you love her, and you said that you do, then you should go after her. Because if you don't, then you'll never know. If you don't at least try, you'll always wonder *what if*. And I have a feeling she's never coming back. She doesn't want her life affecting yours. She doesn't want it to have any negative impact on you."

Dean looked at me eagerly, trying to determine what I was going to do. I shook my head, but he just nodded up and down. "Dude, get those little lobster claws in motion. She may not know it, but she's waiting on you. Sometimes we don't realize we're lovable until someone truly loves us. Or that we're not broken until someone makes us feel whole. Sometimes we have to be shown love to know that we can be loved. Go show her."

I stood up without a second's hesitation, knocking the phone off the counter. As I rushed out the door, I saw Dean pick it up, and heard Tutu ask pleadingly, "Dean, what's happening? Is he going after her?"

"Yeah, he's going to get his lobster," Dean replied seamlessly.

Locke

CHAPTER 47

I NEVER IMAGINED I'd be the type of guy to race to an airport terminal. But here I was doing just that, with Tutu's words still ringing in my mind. I couldn't believe Guin was going to leave this way. Maybe it was the only way she felt she could. And I always knew she had to go back home sometime. But I could never have been prepared for this feeling of desperation that came over me.

The sea breeze was pushing me toward her as I raced to the doors of the airport. I didn't know what my plan was here, but

I wanted to take whatever opening I could get. I could surely come up with something. Because there was no doubt in my mind that I was going to fight for her.

The burst of cold air as I entered the airport was a shock to my system. I hurriedly looked through the sea of people to see if, by some chance, I'd get lucky enough to spot her. But it looked like I was going to have to buy a ticket. That was the only way. I needed to catch her at her gate. I just hoped I wasn't too late. She'd made sure there wasn't much time. I doubt she thought Tutu could even tell me in time.

When it was *finally* my turn at the counter, the desk clerk was moving about as slow as molasses. Or maybe it was just my impatience.

"Sir, that flight is just about to leave. I don't think you'll make it," she slowly informed me after hitting an inordinate amount of keys.

"That's fine. I just need to get to the gate. Can you please hurry?"

"I'm not the one who should have planned their time better," she said in a clipped tone, obviously having had enough of this job for the day. Or maybe just enough of me.

"Please, the woman I love is getting on that flight."

"Oh, please. If I had a quarter for every time someone used *that* excuse." She seemed to move even slower now, just to spite me.

I threw back my head and sighed. Then I did something I *never* did. It went against everything inside of me, but I was desperate. I had tried asking for grace first even though it had cost me time, so now I put my prosthetic leg up on the scale. The sound of my clumsy movement woke her from this bad day she was having and her eyes widened as I started rolling up my pant leg. I emphatically continued, "You see, the woman I love came through here with a service dog a little earlier. You probably remember her now. I'm sure someone here does. She's not *only* the first person to truly understand me, but the first woman to treat me with respect. And that would be true whether or not she had a service dog." I looked down at my prosthetic leg. "I just thought this would make my point a lot clearer, in a much faster way to you."

"Very clear, sir," she said with wide eyes.

"Do you remember her now?"

"Yes, I do. And I will have someone assist you to the gate right away." I eyed her. That was not at all why I had done this. I just wanted her to understand, and I thought this would do it. The agent hastily added, "Not that I think you need help, but it will get you there sooner."

"Thank you," I said, breathing heavily. And then she handed me a piece of paper. Apparently it was a dummy ticket or something. Or maybe a real one. I wouldn't question it.

I reached for my credit card, but she waved it away. She knew I had no intention of getting on that flight. She simply said, "Have a pleasant flight, sir," to which I smiled and waved, making my way toward the gate. "But sir, what about your assistance?" She called after me. But there was no way I was waiting for assistance or showing up to meet Guin with a whole airport security team. My thoughts raced faster than my body as I rushed to her gate with the ticket in my hand. I felt like a penguin rolling his pebble on an arduous trek to meet his soulmate. Well, maybe more like a lobster with his piece of coral in this case.

As soon as I reached the boarding area, I saw the space was desolate. The chairs were empty, and no one was waiting. This was bad.

"Sir, passengers are lined up outside on the gateway. We'll

need to take your ticket now," one of the flight attendants at the desk called. *I really hope this dummy ticket works.* And miraculously, it did. Luck felt like it might be on my side today.

As soon as the warm, humid Hawaiian air hit me, I saw Sebastian waiting patiently near the end of the line. And it didn't take but a second for my eyes to land on Guin. The heat of the tarmac was nothing compared to the urgency inside me.

But I just stood there, completely frozen. Trying to figure out how I was going to win this Goliath fight. Her beautiful blue sundress swished as her head slowly turned to find the source of the heat gazing upon her. But she already knew. There was such a pained look in her eyes. And she was already shaking her head, telling me to stay away. But I had absolutely no intention of doing any such thing.

With each step I took, her head started shaking a little more, the line moving around her. A silent word kept escaping her as she stayed glued in place. And before I knew it, I stood in front of her, only feet away. The soft, warm breeze was the only thing separating us as Sebastian looked up at me with curiosity. I hoped Penny at least got to say goodbye because this was pure torture for me.

The palms around the airport fence provided some coverage from the intense warmth of this day, but there was nothing to shield me from her fierce, sad blue eyes. They were beckoning me to wade in deeper and get lost again. But there was such heartbreak in them that I felt they were already closed off to me. And I didn't even know where to begin.

"Guin–" And when the word left me, I realized she wasn't the only one wearing her pain. I swallowed. I had fought hard to get here, and now I was completely ruining it. "Guin–"

"What are you doing here, Locke? You're supposed to be at the surf shop," she said with a little ache in her voice.

"Yeah, and you're supposed to be at the convention. Guin, what are you doing? You're just going to leave without saying goodbye? After everything?" I tried to move closer to her, but she backed away from me.

"Locke, why didn't you tell me?" she asked quietly.

"About what?"

"Come on, don't act like you don't know. First, it was the water accident when I thought it was Reef who got hurt. Fine, I definitely understood that. But *this*. And *now* you're having people get tested to see if they're a kidney match for me?"

I closed my eyes. This was bad. But it wasn't like I had asked others to do it. When I started the testing process, then others wanted to do the same. So many people here already loved Guin. This was one of the biggest things you could do for a person, but no one had to say if they were a match until they decided if they wanted to donate their kidney.

"Tutu. Really, Locke?"

"What?"

"Oh, come on. She wants to start the process. Not that I would *ever* accept a kidney from her. But she sure is ready to give me one. She has the biggest heart, and she feels like she's running out of time to help people. And more than anything, Locke, she wants to see you happy while she still can. Do you know how terrible it felt to turn down her offer to get tested?."

I began, "No, I told her not to get tested." I couldn't believe Tutu. Of course she wanted to start the process. She loved Guin the most of anyone, other than me. She probably was already trying to start the process to become a donor for *someone*, whether she matched with Guin, after hearing Guin's story. *Had she tried to start the testing process? There's no way they would let her, right?*

"Oh, so who is allowed to get tested, huh? Because apparently the entire community did. I had a delightful conversation with Dean, who has an excellent shot at being a match based on his medical history and blood type. He called this morning to ask me about starting the tissue typing and crossmatching testing."

"Really? Oh, my God, Guin. Are you serious? You're going to take him up on it, aren't you?" I couldn't keep the happiness from my tone. He hadn't told me yet. I guess everything that had happened this afternoon distracted him. Or maybe he wanted to talk with Guin first.

"Does it look like I am, Locke?" she said with a wounded tone.

"Guin, I don't think you understand what *Ohana* means here. And you've become *Ohana*. That's what this island represents, what this community is all about. We're all family. We help each other out as if we were blood because we are. There is nothing stronger than the *Ohana* bond."

"Really, is that the *correct* translation, Locke? '*O 'oe no¯, aloha.*'" She stared pointedly at me. I pinched my eyes. *Oh, this all looks so bad.* "When did *you* start getting tested, Locke?"

"After your first infusion. I went back to the center and asked about being tested. And since they remembered I'd been with you at your treatment . . . well, they were more than happy to tell me how to go about getting tested to become a kidney donor. And then I told Tutu and Dean about it, just in case the center called with more information for me. After that happened, people started taking it upon themselves to get tested. I didn't mean for anyone else to do it."

She continued to look at me dumbfounded. "So ʻo ʻoe no ̄ʼ really does means ʻyou're the one?'"

"Yeah, Guin. It does and always will."

"But you said that phrase to me on our fake first date," she said with astonishment.

"Nothing has been fake with you. I've just been fighting it. And I remember the moment I fell for you. When you gave Tutu the courage to go on her date with Louis. I don't think I've ever seen anyone be more beautiful. That was the moment I knew I was done fighting my feelings for you. That was the moment I knew you were the one."

"Three, Locke, that's three," she breathed.

"But they were all done with good intentions, Guin. And I was going to tell you about each one. I just wanted it to be the right time. I wanted you to be ready to hear it. There was never any malicious intent."

"I'm *not* a charity case, Locke," Guin said firmly. "That's not why I came here. I came to escape all that. And you are the *last* person who was supposed to see me that way. The last person I wanted to see me that way."

I could hear the break in her voice. I tried to step closer to her, but she still wasn't ready to let me near her. I looked past my shoulder at the line that had now moved substantially forward.

"Guin, that's the last thing you could ever be to me. I wish more than anything I could be the person to give you a kidney, but not for that reason. I'm not even the right blood type. And I'm probably wrong for you in so many other ways too . . . But I love you–'Aloha wau ia ̄ ʻoe.'" My plea fell on soul-crushing silence as she just stood there.

I moved to her, and she numbly looked up at me as I placed my hands on her waist. My heart was already breaking, so I said it again. "I love you, Guin," I breathed. The baby blues raged war at my words.

"Miss, the plane is boarding. Can you move up with the line if you're planning to join us?" someone called from the front of the tarmac, obviously worried Guin was going to miss her flight.

"Oh yes, sorry," Guin called back as she looked that way, but she didn't move. "Locke, I have to go. My plane is boarding. I'm sorry. This week has been amazing with you, and I will always remember it, but I'm scheduled for destruction and I need to get you out of my wake. You have so much life ahead of you. And you have so much to give someone. Remember that, *please*. You deserve the best, Locke, and I'm sure you're going to find it. *Don't settle.*"

She turned to leave, and I shook my head and grabbed her waist again. "No, Guin. Don't do this. You have so much here. A potential donor. A new *Ohana*. And someone who loves you. *Stay*. That's three." She was shaking her head slightly at me, a shimmer of tears forming in her eyes. I pleaded, "What are you so scared of? Please stay a little longer. Just see what happens. That's all I'm asking. Can you please stay with me?"

"Miss, you're going to need to give us your boarding pass if you don't want to miss the flight," the same voice called more urgently now. Guin nodded.

"Guin, I might not know everything about you, but I see you. I've always seen you. I was just too scared to admit it. And isn't that what you want, someone who knows who you really are? Isn't that what we all want? And I'm so in love with you. It doesn't matter if I don't know everything about you yet because I know the important parts. I know your heart." And I truly meant it. *Because what good is knowing someone's favorite color if you don't know the colors of their heart.*

I looked at her and at the airplane soaring overhead as if it was foreshadowing what was to come. "Guin, don't get on that plane. Let me see you every day. Let me love you every day."

She looked at me blankly, so I continued. "Please, we'll figure the rest out. But let me have a chance. Whatever time you have left, please let me share it with you. Let me be a part of it."

She went to open her mouth, but I wouldn't let her because I knew what she was going to say. I could tell by her expression. "I *never* have the right words, Guin, and this time won't be any different. And this is probably going to all sound wrong, but it wouldn't make a difference to me if you had one month or one week. I would still be here fighting for you. I want whatever time you have. There are no guarantees for any of us. Isn't that what you said to Tutu? What would you say to her if she were in your position? *Let me see you*, Guin."

"Locke, I–" she started.

"I'm never going to have enough time with you, no matter the circumstances. But if you want to spend the time you have with me, then stay. *Please. Stay.* Let me love you. *All of you* . . . I'm asking you to take a chance on me, too."

And then her painfully detached voice cut through the air. "Goodbye, Locke. It's better this way, ok." She turned to go, and my hands fell from her. Sebastian sat there unbudging. If I wanted to play dirty, I would have brought Penny. Then Sebe wouldn't have moved, that's for sure. But I never expected this from him. I didn't know he liked me so much. "Sebe, come on." Guin said a little more forcefully, pulling weakly on his harness. A broken plea escaped her.

I just looked from Sebastian to Guin. I couldn't believe she was leaving with no intention of ever returning. Or ever talking to me again, it appeared. She was completely disappearing, leaving me in "calm, unchurned waters." A place where I wouldn't truly be living, just existing. I certainly didn't want to live life that way. I wanted to be where I had to fight against currents and streams. Because that's where life was lived, amongst all the chaos; in the surf, where ripples turned into waves. No one ever gained anything without taking a risk, and no one ever became a better version of themselves without wading through rough waters.

But unfortunately, there wasn't anything left to say. I had fought with everything I had, and I could tell nothing I said was going to change her mind. She was as stubborn as me and if I truly loved her, I would let her go. The tears on her face told me that's what I had to do. So I bent down to Sebastian and patted his head. "Take good care of her, ok Sebastian? You'll always have a home here." Then through my strangled throat, I said, "Go on, boy." And he did.

I watched the only woman I would ever love board that plane. Knowing what I offered wasn't enough. Knowing I would never know if she felt the same about me or if she was just protecting me. But one thing was for certain; I would never hear those words from her. There was something so final about her decision. Even as I remained hopelessly on that tarmac, waiting like a fool for her to step off that plane. For her to change her mind. But she never did. And finally, I couldn't watch any longer. Not when that door closed. It was done.

Locke

CHAPTER 48

I MADE my way home in a fog, opening the bungalow door to find Tutu pacing back and forth on the lanai. It was fitting, since that was our thinking place. I slowly made my way out to her, not ready to have this conversation. I just wanted to hide myself away–to wallow, but she deserved to know.

As soon as I opened the sliding door, her face fell. She knew. She stopped pacing immediately. Frozen.

"No," she barely whispered. "*Keiki,* no," she said with a heartbreak that shattered me even more.

I swallowed hard. "It's fine. We knew each other for such a short time. What did I expect?" The lump tightened in my throat. "You don't ask someone to stay with you after that short amount of time. You don't say '*o 'oe no* '–and especially not 'I love you'–so soon after meeting them. We had a wonderful experience together and I need to be thankful for that. She gave me the greatest gift. We both know I had given up on dating before she came along. But maybe I can just hang on to my love for her forever and never date again." I laughed awkwardly.

"You don't mean it." She shook her head.

"Tutu, I'm going to need to mean it," I said firmly, going into survival mode.

Now a little tear escaped and ran down her cheek as she came over to hug me. She landed with a tiny thud against my chest. *What is it about me today?* I was making all the women in my life cry.

"It's fine. I'm sure she will get a donor back home. *I know it. I have to believe it.* And maybe she'll come back when things in her life are better. When she's ready. And I will certainly be ready for her." Tutu just shook her head harder at my words.

"This is not how it's supposed to be."

"Well, I don't think you're supposed to say or do what I did after this short amount of time, so I'm sure–"

"Locke, stop that," she said, pulling away from me. "You know time doesn't mean anything. That it means nothing to a pure heart." She looked up at me with a newfound zeal. Like she was ready to wage a battle. "Did you tell her? Locke, did you *really* tell her? Did you fight for her?"

"Yes, Tutu. I fought *really* hard. And I lost," I said, finally allowing myself to lay it all out there. I thought about what Tutu had said about Louis. I didn't want to lose all that time.

And it was time we might not have, anyway. I had been ready to fight for us as soon as I went after her. As soon as Tutu had said she'd left.

"Locke, I'm so sorry. I had no idea when I offered your home as a place to stay that this would happen. I didn't know when I offered those raffle tickets that I was really offering a ticket to your heart. I was just trying to give back through the gift of music. I never expected . . . I hope you don't think that's what this was about. I certainly never expected you to pick her up off the beach." She laughed a little, trying to ease my heartache.

"Yeah, I never would have expected that either. And you did an amazing thing, Tutu. I'm so thankful for what you gave to Guin . . . and to me. I hope you'll keep giving back through music. Just *maybe* don't offer our place again." There was a pain in my words.I could see the guilt on Tutu's face, but there's no way she could have known. Especially since I hadn't shown any interest in anyone for so long now. I wouldn't even open myself up to the possibility. I didn't even date anymore. How was she supposed to know that I would fall for one of the raffle ticket winners?

She hugged me again. "Guin's going to realize, *Keiki. She will.* She's so in love with you. *I promise.*" I huffed at those words. Because I was pretty sure that wasn't true, especially since I hadn't ever heard those words from her, *not once.* Tutu continued, "*Keiki,* it is. Think about how much she shared with you. Think about all the love she *showed* you. She just doesn't want to see you get hurt. That's true love. True sacrifice. There's a reason she didn't tell you–that she didn't say the words. And there's a reason she left the way she did. She wants you to be able to move on." Tutu paused. "Did she kiss you goodbye?"

My eyebrows raised in shock. "Grandma, I don't think that's appropriate for you to ask."

"I didn't think so. She's trying to leave with as little impact as possible. No 'I love you' or any promise of communication. That says it all."

"Yeah, it says this meant nothing at all."

Tutu sighed and pushed against me. "She's protecting you, Locke. And she's afraid. Terrified. You should have seen her face after she received the call from Dean this morning. Just imagine what she's feeling. You didn't tell her people were getting tested, and you *certainly* didn't tell her you were getting tested. And Locke, even if she gets a match, there's a chance it won't work out or that her body won't accept the kidney. And she'll have to take all these immunosuppressant medications to give it the best shot. That will transform her life dramatically. She'll have to be careful even going to the grocery store because of the possibility of picking up illnesses. She's looking at going through a lot with the transplant, Locke. It's not just a magic fix. Nothing with chronic illness ever is."

I swallowed hard. "But she's strong enough to do it. And I want to be there when she does. Besides you, she's the strongest person I know."

"Exactly, Locke. She's strong enough to give you up. To know she doesn't want you to have to go through all those things with her."

"Isn't there some way–" I began, but I heard this clawing at the sliding door. Penny was scratching at it relentlessly. She must sense my distress. She was the best emotional support– she always seemed to know. I headed to the sliding door to let her out, wanting nothing more than her company, when a bark rang out through the air.

I froze as an electric shock pulsed through me. Every nerve

on high alert. I looked at Penny's closed mouth as if she was a mirage, but she simply clawed harder. And as the barks in the distance became more frequent, suddenly so did Penny's. I opened the door as she rushed to the edge of the lanai and I glanced over at Tutu hesitantly. And there on her face was the biggest smile. A proper *I-told-you-so* look.

She came over and patted my shoulder, glancing at me. A quick glance of sheer happiness. Something told me this was the moment she'd been desperately waiting to see happen for me. Then she slipped back inside without a word.

All I could do was stare at the sliding glass door. My heart was hammering in my chest at the possibilities. And when I turned, I saw Penny's tail wagging madly as she sat at the railing on the balcony. Her head turned to me as if asking what I was waiting for, little yips and whines escaping from her.

I breathed heavily as if that could help me make the trek to the edge. And when I peered down, there *she* was. A golden-haired mermaid, standing beneath the palm trees, bathed in the flickering sunlight. She looked so beautiful in the outdoor courtyard with her luggage and Sebastian flanking her, the adorable dog waiting not so patiently at her side. A look of longing and fear on her face.

Well, if this wasn't a reverse Romeo and Juliet. I just stood there dumbfounded, not knowing what to say in the slightest. I had seen that plane door close. I'd seen–I don't know what I'd seen anymore. Because all I could do was stare at the beautiful woman before me. The one I didn't think I'd ever see again. And my heart spasmed so hard with hope.

A pain seemed to swallow her as she called up to me. "They let me off the plane." I could barely hear her words. I could barely register them. "They . . ." She couldn't finish. "Sebastian started going crazy on the plane. Barking like mad when I–"

I held up my hand in a wait gesture, but I wasn't sure she would. She looked so scared and tiny down there. I hesitated, scared to leave this spot, scared she would disappear. But with one last look at her, I raced through the bungalow, past a laughing Tutu, and down the stairs, Penny right behind me. And it was only when I saw her staring fixedly at my empty spot on the lanai that I slowed. So thankful she was still there.

But that was not the case for Penny—she continued running for Sebastian. They met playfully in between us, as far as Sebastian's leash would reach. And the pull on Mermaid's arm was enough to get her attention. Her eyes traveled down the leash to the reunited dogs and then finally back up to me. Those deep blue seas were storming.

"So uh," she continued nervously. "They really had no choice. Apparently panic attacks make other flyers nervous." She laughed slightly. "So the panic attack and Sebe got me off the plane. And here I am." I started making my way to her, letting nothing stop me this time. An urgency and desire burned in equal measure. My hands found her shoulders, and then I tilted her face up to mine. And I knew what I should have done the first time. But now, I wouldn't waste any time. My thumbs gently explored the soft curves of her cheeks, not believing they were truly here. And then I brought my lips to hers as if I needed to show her instead of using words, separating our lips on her tender moan.

Her eyes looked up at mine, and I wondered if she had any clue what she had done to me. "I love you, Locke," she whispered. "'O 'oe no¯, aloha.'" That phrase caught me out of the blue. I didn't think I'd ever hear her say those words. I was worried if I'd heard her correctly. But her expression was unmistakable. It was the one she'd been giving me for quite some time. Tutu was right, yet again. She spoke softly, "I'm scared, but you can have me. You can have all of me. Whatever good parts are left."

"No, Guin, you're wrong. They're *all* good." And I looked at her deeply. "We may have broken parts–even literal ones–but they only help us realize how well we fit together. All your pieces fit with mine. They complete me."

And all I could do was bring her lips back to meet mine, tugging her in by the waist this time. Never wanting to let go of her again. Our hearts were finally beating together in perfect time; we had each found the one soul who could unlock that magical heartbeat.

Epilogue

EPILOGUE | GUINEVERE | 6 MONTHS LATER

"ARE YOU READY?" Locke asked, his hand seamlessly intertwined with mine.

He leaned over the side of the hospital bed as he sat beside me. I could see concern spreading in those inky eyes that always gave me such comfort, their warmth never failing me. The care this man carried for me was beyond anything I could have ever envisioned.

I hadn't wanted him to be here for this part of my journey because I had wanted to protect him. Maybe a small part of me had wanted to protect myself, too. I didn't know what lay ahead, but there wasn't a day that went by that I didn't thank God for this man. The man who wanted to be by my side for everything, the good *and* the bad. I was learning to accept that there were people in this life like him. *That love like this existed.*

And that's what the last six months had taught me. Because it wasn't only Locke here with me today. There was a whole waiting room full of people out there. Without hesitation, I'd been accepted into this beautiful Aloha community as one of their own. It didn't matter how wounded I was because I felt whole when I was with them.

I grabbed onto Locke's hand even tighter. I had hoped and prayed for this day but also feared it a little too. And honestly, it had never been my intention to stay here in Maui. I had made my decision to leave the island the day I boarded that plane. Shutting out everything, every thought and feeling, in order to leave; especially every wonderful feeling that Locke and this island had given to me.

But as I sat in my seat on the airplane, all I could feel was Locke's love spreading over me. And suddenly it wasn't a choice anymore. His words . . . *let me love you, all of you*, reverberated through every part of my being. The very words I had always hoped to one day hear. *Take a chance on me*, rang through my ears. And then it was like I didn't have control of my body anymore.

How did Louis describe it? An out-of-body experience? Yes, I was floating above myself, watching this panic attack play out as I realized I could lose the man I loved . . . yes, *loved*. And Sebastian went crazy, the timbre of his deep, booming barks setting off an alarm, much to the chagrin of all the other passengers. I think he was more than happy to get me off that plane. He might have tried an exit strategy anyway, even if I hadn't had the panic attack. And the crew was more than relieved to escort me off the plane.

And when I went to find Locke, I didn't have any plans. My whole life was back home. I didn't even know how much longer I could stay. And I definitely never intended to accept a gift like this one. The gift of his love, this new family, and this new home was more than I could have ever asked for. Because the longer I stayed, the more I realized I wasn't ever going to leave. That the safety of his love gave me a new strength–a new voice.

Because I realized I had the definition of unconditional love *all* wrong. I learned it was showing up for someone and letting them know you were there for them. Even if they weren't ready to accept what you had to offer yet. Even if that meant waiting until they were ready. It was just simply being there. Giving whatever you could out of care and compassion. And Locke always had. From the very start. Just like these last couple of months when I wasn't ready yet to accept this gift, he just waited. Giving me whatever support I needed. *Always* showing up. And I couldn't love him more for it. Because at the end of the day, that's what we really need . . . someone to be there for us.

And to help me work through my emotions, both Locke and Tutu encouraged me to write my own children's books. They saw how discouraged I had become at never seeing anyone like myself in fiction. Knowing that children with disabilities had to grow up without representation in the books they read, without being able to truly see themselves. I started by illustrating the stories and then the words came. *My* voice came. Stories about little boys who looked like Locke. Little girls who looked like me. And plenty of service dogs in between. I not only had a home, but my stories did too. My books sat in the little surf shop window by Tutu's quilts, honorably displayed by a man who couldn't be more proud of us both. Locke even set up special events where I could hold book signings and Tutu's artist friends could share their work and talk about their artistic processes. And the dogs who always felt quite at home at the surf shack were also quite the sales reps. This man's heart knew no bounds, and it was one of my favorite things about him.

I thought back to the day at the dialysis center when Locke had been the one to hold my hand so tightly. How the tables had turned as I gripped his hand so tightly now. He looked at me steadfastly and said, "I'm right here. I'll be here as long as they'll let me be, ok?"

I nodded, emotions welling in my eyes. "Locke, did I ever thank you for just being you?"

"Well not at first, but I'll certainly take it now." I laughed at his joke. "Guin?"

"Yes, Locke?" I answered seriously, sitting up a little straighter in my unflattering hospital gown.

"I'm so glad you finally said yes to this. But I'm really sorry it couldn't be me." Now concern spread over his face.

"Locke–" I began, but he wouldn't let me finish. I knew he wanted nothing more than to do this for me. And it had practically killed him that I had taken so long to accept this offer. But he hadn't pushed. It had about crushed him, but he just stood by supporting me.

"I'm wondering if you might say yes to something else . . ." he trailed off. There was a nervousness in him that was shaking me up a bit. I was used to him being my rock. The secure ground that would always be my safe place.

"Locke, I think this yes is all I can handle right now–" I didn't know what he was talking about. I was at full capacity. But then he was down on one knee before I could even finish. His hand anxiously raked through his shaggy black hair, and the other one clung to me. Of all the places this man could pick . . .

"Guin–"

I started shaking my head. He could not do this here. He started chuckling.

"Locke, this is *Hawaii*. Honeymoon capital of the world. There are romantic spots literally *everywhere* you turn, and a hospital room sounded like a good idea to you?"

He just laughed harder and said, "Anywhere sounds like a good idea as long as I'm with you." *Oh geez. He was killing me.* I looked down at my hospital gown. "Guin you're the most beautiful woman in the world to me, no matter where we are or what you're wearing." I looked down with more disbelief, knowing he could read my thoughts.

"Locke," I said as I put my hand up to my face, but he just gently took it down with his other hand.

"I have this elaborate plan and you're currently ruining it." I couldn't help but laugh at his joke. I was so nervous, but he was the one who didn't seem capable of speaking right now. "Guin no matter what happens, I want you to know what you mean to me. And I want you to always have a part of me. Well, not just a part, *all* of me. You know you already do, but I want you to have this promise. This forever reminder of my love for you." He pulled out an ice-blue velvet box with shaky hands.

And I could hardly look at him when he opened the box. The mist in my eyes was overwhelming me. Inside the box was a light blue aquamarine, rose gold ring. A single stone with two diamond bands twisting around it, becoming one. Just like our lives had come together the day he pulled me from those aquamarine shores. The rose gold reminded me of the sand where he had picked up so many pieces of me. And now our broken pieces fit together so seamlessly I couldn't tell where one of us began and the other ended, just like the ring.

"Locke." But the tears swallowed all my words. I had never wanted to be this person. The one that wept when their loved one got down on one knee. But here I was, weeping like a sad Disney princess in my hideous hospital gown without an ounce of makeup on. Well, at least it wouldn't smear.

"Don't cry, Mermaid. It's not that bad. I can exchange it. I knew I should have gone with a diamond." He laughed, but there was worry in his handsome features.

"No, it's perfect. You're so perfect. No, you're better than that. *You're you*." I loved all his "quirks," his "imperfections," every "Lockism" that had helped to make me whole. That made me truly believe again.

He looked so taken aback. Like he was having trouble processing it. "So–" he tried, words failing him. This long pause engulfed us.

"You're killing me," a voice shot out from the other side of the room from behind the curtain. "Please, just ask her! Dude, she can't say yes if you don't ask!" Dean's jovial tone boomed over to us.

We both laughed helplessly, somehow at this moment having forgotten Dean was in the room with us. The hospital staff had pulled the curtain closed earlier for our intake and I guess they hadn't moved it back afterwards, or maybe Dean already knew Locke's plans.

For whatever reason, it gave Locke the courage to continue.

I guess Dean could tell how nervous he truly was and wanted to help calm his nerves. Locke looked at me with so much love and asked, "I love you, Guin. Will you sail around the world with me?"

And I nodded like a fool, a smile so big it hurt. "Of course I will. Yes, I love you–'*Aloha wau ia¯ 'oe,*'" I said, thankfully with better pronunciation now. I'd had a lot of practice. It hadn't taken me long to get comfortable admitting my feelings for Locke or for him to teach me how to say it properly in the Hawaiian language.

"*Aloha wau ia¯ 'oe,*" Locke said as he slid the ring on my finger and came closer to kiss me. The curtain moved back, rattling the rings at the top of it, revealing a grinning Dean in his hospital bed. "Lobstered," he said with raised eyebrows. "Finally. Took you long enough." Then he called out, "She said yes!"

Applause and shouts of congratulations rang out. And my head shot around to look at Dean. *What in the world?* But it only took me a second before I saw Tutu's head peek in through a crack in the door, and then his–our–whole Aloha family came through the door. I was pretty sure you weren't allowed to have this many people in a hospital room. But maybe they'd made an exception. Or Tutu had worked her magic and pulled some strings. Even the dogs came through the door to check out the good news. Their tails wagging in a way that matched the excitement in the air. I'm sure they thought their humans had been incredibly slow to realize what they knew from the beginning.

And as I looked around the room at all the people who were here today to support me, the sense of family and community overwhelmed me. Tutu immediately grabbed my hand to find proof of the ring, Louis right beside her. I could see the look on Louis' face as Tutu approved the ring. If I had to guess, she'd already seen the ring and probably even helped select it. And Louis' face was saying he was going to be stealing Locke's move soon. The love in his eyes for Tutu burned so brightly, as did his special care of her. Louis seemed to excel at sensing what she needed, and just like Locke, he was waiting for her to make her peace with the idea. Giving her space and room to accept that his love was here to stay. And with each day and every episode they weathered together, I could see Tutu's reluctancy crumble just a little more. And there was something much more beautiful being built in its place.

In the excitement, Locke's mom tried to take a turn looking at the ring, but Tutu wasn't letting go of my hand. Reef and Luna were smiling and congratulating Locke. Dean's family had come in as well and were standing beside his bed. And my grandparents had made the trip here, and they didn't look surprised in the slightest, so I imagine Locke had already asked them for their blessing. I was pretty sure Locke had probably offered them the option to stay here with me. I didn't know what his plans might be, but his big heart really knew no limits.

It wasn't lost on me that the kindness he had shown Dean was now being passed on to me—in a much bigger way. That flap of a butterfly's wing had amplified into a hurricane. That was the power of kindness. You never knew what a little of it could do for someone. How much it could change a life. Because Locke's kindness had forever changed my world and now Dean's gift would save my life. And the entire community's compassion had restored my faith. That was the power of kindness—of grace.

A nurse entered the room with a big grin, and then she switched to a more serious face. "Ok guys, you know the drill.

You have to go to the waiting room now." But Locke held onto my hand tighter, making it clear he wasn't letting go. The nurse sighed, her resolve already breaking. "Ok, one person can stay with each patient. You can go as far as the OR doors. No further. *I mean it.*"

The rest of the group took their exit, promising to see us both soon. Tutu and Luna took Dean's children with them. And I looked over at him, I saw his wife gripping his hand just as tightly as Locke was gripping mine.

My eyes swelled. I couldn't believe what Dean was about to do for me. I would never take his compassion and gift for granted. I would find a way to pass it on. The chain would not be broken with me. And as the nurses started rolling us out of the room, with Locke right beside me and his hand tucked perfectly in mine, I looked over at Dean and he looked back at me.

He reached his hand out to me. *"Ohana,"* he said seamlessly.

I reached for Dean's hand as the tears fell from my eyes, Locke's hand still squeezing mine. Memories of so many other times that his hand had fit perfectly with mine flashed through my mind. And visions of so many future times I hoped to have with Locke because of Dean. Because of a flap of those beautiful, kind butterfly wings. Because of this Hawaiian family. I grabbed hold of Dean's hand with everything I had. *"Ohana,"* I said with a newfound meaning and life in my soul.

Inspiration for Guin and Sebe

"GUIN & SEBE"

Deleted & Extended Scenes

Deleted and extended scenes available at www.brookegilbertau-thor.com/bonuscontent. You can sign up to become a "site member" if you would like to access the growing bonus content library. By becoming a site member, you will receive monthly or bi-monthly newsletters as well :) If you're already a site member then you can access it now! Thank you!

Also by Brooke Gilbert

The Paris Soulmate: A Sweet Romance Novel

A woman with a "no dating policy." A mysterious, cocky British stranger. A dream trip to Paris. What could go wrong?

Reeling from the reality of turning thirty soon, Christine decides to take her bucket list trip. She has dreamed of going back to Paris, but since being diagnosed with several rare autoimmune disorders, she never imagined she would get the chance. Now, she finds herself on her way to the City of Love with an unexpected surprise . . . An extremely handsome British stranger seems to have mysteriously fallen onto her path. Is it just a coincidence that they are both traveling to the city of love? It all seems too good to be true.

"Own Voices" Crohn's, Lupus, Mast Cell Disorder, & Mental Health Representation.

The Irish Fall: A Sweet Romantic Comedy Novel

A woman goes to find her heart in Ireland, what she doesn't realize is she will leave it there.

Eyre decides on a desperate whim to take the first appealing flight out of town. This lands her right at the gorgeous cliffs of Moher where she meets the attractive, but infuriating tour guide Darby–not to be confused with Jane Austen's Mr. Darcy. Darby shows Eyre the heart of Ireland and in doing so, shows her how much heart she still has left to give. But Darby has demons of his own. Can Ireland's healing powers mend a wounded heart?

"Own Voices" Crohn's, ovarian cysts, suspected endometriosis, & mental health Representation. PTSD is also represented.

Author's Note

Thank you for taking this journey with me! I hope you enjoyed the characters' love stories! :) If you've made it to this part of the book and are taking time to read this, thank you!! The author's note is really important to me :) Ohana is one of the biggest themes of this book and I want to thank you for being a part of this book family! The people I've connected with on this journey has been the biggest blessing to me. There are so many incredible readers, authors, and spoonies who I would never have gotten the chance to know if not for my writing. And I will always be incredibly thankful for this opportunity. Our conversations are always the highlight of my day. And so many of you have been with me since the very beginning, ever since reading *The Paris Soulmate*, and I cannot thank you enough for your support! You continually encourage me and spread the word about my books, and words cannot express the gratitude I have for you. More than that, I feel that I have found a family and connections that will last a lifetime :) I couldn't be blessed with more beautiful readers!!!

I really struggled this year, not only with my health, but also with being an author. I fell prey to comparison. And the part in this book about comparisons was written from this experience. I started to re-evaluate my whole way of writing and I had to take a hard look at what success meant to me and the reasons *I* write. I had to define what this meant to me if I was going to continue to publish and I have so many of you to thank for helping me. Success to me is someone being able to pick up my book and see themself, to be able to connect and not feel alone. If I have done that then I have succeeded. I don't write for anything else. I write for therapy and for *you*, the reader, to be seen. I write so we can have a spot on the romance shelf and in fiction. I write so we can believe in ourselves, our worth, beauty, and dreams. And hopefully in the process, I am able to spread awareness and make hard topics like mental health easier to discuss in society. *That* is success to me. And it's why this book is being published. And I hope you close this book believing in yourself and loving yourself just the way you are. I had the privilege of working with a two time Pulitzer Prize finalist on a book trailer for his novel and to my great protest, he read *The Paris Soulmate*. Michael was the nicest man and he said something pretty powerful to me. He said sometimes you have to see something first to believe it or think it's possible. And I hope that's what I'm doing here. This conversation was the inspiration for Dean telling Locke sometimes you have to be shown love and acceptance before you can give it to yourself. In this world we live in, with so many labels and such ableist views, sometimes we need someone to look at us and see us not as "broken," but as the *person* we are. And I really loved that Guin and Locke could do that for each other. So I will keep living out my dream by writing and I will keep writing characters who live out their dreams as well. No matter how they have to adapt or what that looks like for them. Because there is such beauty in being yourself. And I hope my books inspire you to do the same.

So let's dive into some aspects of the book (oh, you know that pun was intended)! The idea for this book came to me while I was writing *The Paris Soulmate*, my first novel, back in February 2022. It felt very unrealistic that I would ever write a second book. I thought it was a one time thing. But I'm so glad I've found writing as therapy and so many wonderful people to share my work with. You truly are incredible :) Since my first novel, this musical storyline kept tugging at me. On nights when I couldn't sleep from pain or insomnia, I would play my ukulele into the wee hours of the morning. So I started dreaming about Guin who, like me, wanted to attend a ukulele convention and the rest is history. Guin's journey with the ukulele is all based on my own and I don't know what I would have done without music, this instrument, the online ukelele community, and music lessons. The ukulele provided so much light when my conditions were covering my life with so much darkness. Guin's Lupus was also written from my own experiences. I thought it would be an ironic juxtaposition to have a woman who loves the beach (but it just doesn't like her) to meet this surfer guy who lives to be out on the sea. I am a beach/water fanatic like Guin. It has always been my favorite place to go. But like Guin, it's no longer the same for me. I have to experience the beach very differently now, especially with my Lupus. Nothing angers it quite like the sun and those pernicious little UV rays. I really wanted to be able to put in the tips and tricks I've learned with my Lupus. And I hope if you have a chronic illness that you might pick up some useful ones! I have readers message me to ask about my conditions or the ones I write about to learn more about them for family members or friends. I love to see people caring for each other in this way. And it gave me the idea to include a tips and tricks section. For me, spreading awareness and meeting people that want to learn more about chronic illness is one of the best parts of this journey. And I love meeting beautiful people like this who want to learn more in order to understand or help a loved one. The human condition never ceases to be beautiful or amaze me.

I knew from the beginning that I wanted Guin to have a service dog because having a dog has helped me so much with my conditions. But the story evolved and Locke ended up having one as well. And of course the dogs had to fall in love first! Puppy love was just too hard to pass up. Lol. There are so many things that Sebastian does for Guin that are from my own experience. My mom's golden retriever Labrador mix has become an emotional support dog for me. There's a lot of stress, anxiety, and depression that can come with chronic illness, so on days when the pain or mental health is too overwhelming and the tears come, Bella is always there. She always knows. So Sebastian is extremely close to my heart and so is Penny. Because the emotional support that Locke needs very much comes from my own experience with anxiety, depression, suicidal thoughts, and even panic attacks. And if these are things you struggle with as well, I hope this book helps you feel less alone. These are things that are a part of so many people's life experiences who suffer from chronic health and it's important that we talk about it. I also think it's important for these conditions to be depicted in romance to show that they can exist in this medium.

Guin's transplant story arc developed because I was greatly affected by Selena Gomez's story. She actually had her transplant the same year I started taking medication for Lupus. I remember it very clearly. And I wanted to write a love story with this chronic health representation, organ donation awareness, and hopefully a story with hope. I also had a close connection with someone who was possibly going to need a kidney transplant, but who wouldn't have been eligible for the list because of their conditions. It motivated me even more to make sure this novel got published. The organ donation list is so long and competitive that many people who need an organ will never receive one. And kidneys are the most needed organ. The statistics are staggering–as they are for organ donation in general. I had no idea until I researched this book. So when you are looking at the donation check box on the back of your driver's license, please think about it very carefully because that box represents *a chance of living for so many people*. I will never look at that box the same and I hope after reading this novel you might not either. Because if more people check that box, we could save more lives. More people and their families could be given hope. So when we look at that box, I hope we will see the potential to give the greatest gift of a future.

The other chronic illness condition in this novel, Alzheimer's, was extremely important for me to include. I lost my grandfather to this disease and it was one the most painful battles to watch. Tutu is one of my favorite characters I have ever written, but her story was also the most difficult. The themes of emotional abuse which are also so incredibly important to me were some of the toughest I have written as well, but also some of the most rewarding. Our society tends to sweep this type of abuse under the rug or downplay it, and that's one of the reasons it was so important to me to include it. Emotional abuse is just as real and damaging as any other type. The scars of emotional abuse are deep and crippling. They will forever leave a scar on your psyche. And I really wanted to show that with this type of abuse, it can be very difficult to recognize an abuser. It can be extremely difficult to know this is happening to someone. These abusers are very good at hiding and making the victim out to be the bad guy. I felt it was crucial to highlight this gaslighting as well. It seems to be a hallmark of emotional abuse. And this won't be the last time it's explored in one of my novels.

Online Help Resource for emotional abuse: https://www.thehotline.org/resources/what-is-emotional-abuse/

In recognition of the conditions discussed in this novel, 5% of the net Amz profits from this book will be donated to Lupus and Alzheimer research. I believe that we must advocate for more time and money to be spent on autoimmune disorder research. The spoonie community tends to get overlooked. I was once told by a medical intern that I was going to need to advocate for myself and that I should never stop doing that. I believe that's what we need to do for ourselves and for each other. Together we are stronger.

To make a donation to the Lupus Foundation of America: https://www.lupus.org/give/ways-to-give

To make a donation to the Alzheimer's Association: https://www.alz.org/get-involved-now/donate

Online Help Resource for organ transplant patients: https://transplantliving.org/before-the-transplant/waiting-for-your-transplant/emotional-aspects-of-waiting/

Tutu is an extremely personal character for so many reasons, but one reason is that Locke and Tutu's relationship is based on my relationship with my mom. Tutu also has aspects of my grandma and one of my non-biological grandmas as well. My grandmother and mother were/are piano teachers and wonderful musicians. And my mom definitely inspired this aspect of the character and my love of music. She also has the biggest heart, just like Tutu. And of course all these beautiful ladies have a little bit of a mischievous matchmaker in them! But it is really my mom's neverending encouragement and the fight she has for me in all aspects of my life that made Tutu special. She's never let me give up on my dreams or my health, just like Tutu did with Locke.

I'd like to take a little time to talk about Locke and the reasons I wrote his story arc the way that I did. First, I bet you're wondering why the shark attack? . . . This was not the original plot. It was always supposed to be a boating accident because I wanted to highlight the scary practices that happen on the water in general. I grew up spending summers on the lake and accidents happened all the time, many that could have been easily avoided. As Locke says, the water should be respected. I felt it was extremely important to me to bring awareness to the practice of chumming. Maui is vigilant, but unfortunately, chumming is a dangerous practice that is still legal in many places. My dad's family lived in Florida when he was growing up and the summer that the movie *Jaws* was released, there were surfers who were attacked because of people chumming close to the piers looking for sharks. And this still happens in areas today. So I wanted to spread awareness of this practice. As far as Locke being airlifted, I did actually see this happen while hiking to the top of the Diamond Head mountain on Oahu. This was an experience I will never forget and I cannot get over the bravery these first responders show on a daily basis!

As for Locke's physical disability, I always envisioned the character this way. It was very important to me to see this type of representation in a romance novel and I hope I did this representation justice. I don't have personal experience with this type of physical disability so I am especially grateful to everyone who helped me along the way. I had the privilege of speaking with a local prosthetist and she helped me immensely with Locke's experience. The representation would not have been the same without her help :) There were so many things I wanted to put in the content caution, but beta readers did not think the physical disability aspect of this novel should be disclosed. It just gave too much of the book away. One of the big things I wanted to disclose up front was the fact that I knew it would be really hard not to notice Locke's prosthesis in a wetsuit and that you would have to suspend some disbelief for this aspect of the story. The prosthetist I spoke with helped me so much with the surfing aspect and Locke's disability. She came up with the idea to glue on Locke's surf shoe to his surf foot. And I decided that Locke's first prosthetic leg would be an extra one that he uses for the beach. Since it's an extra leg I decided he would keep on his cosmetic covering, which would make his prosthesis less noticeable to Guin. This is something that people are going to take off for the beach, but since he wants his leg not to be noticeable I had him keep it on. The surf shoe would also make it harder to see the outline as well. But of course, the wetsuit is tight. However, it was important for me to write the book this way so I hope you were able to suspend some disbelief for the purpose of the plot and themes. I do appreciate the grace you gave me in reading this novel, especially since this was not disclosed up front.

But while on the topic, I did want to take this time to discuss why I wrote about this type of disability. And I definitely want to be up front about a few aspects of this representation. Even though I have spent many hours researching this disability, I'm sure I have gotten some things wrong. Besides talking with people in the community, I also watched many hours of first hand accounts online and did much research, but there is no substitute for "Own Voices." And I want to be honest about this! But I always envisioned this character so clearly and I wanted to write this story a certain way. I believe everyone deserves an HEA and deserves to see themselves in fiction. And I hope you enjoyed Locke's character and maybe even felt seen or less alone. That is truly what this is all about :) I have tried my best to portray this disability as accurately as possible, especially with the help of readers and speaking with people in the community. Accurate and positive representation is extremely important to me and I hope you find it to be so. However, if you find areas that could be more accurate, please don't hesitate to reach out to me directly. I am always up for revising an edition in order to make sure the representation is as accurate and positive as possible for everyone who reads it!

Even though I don't have his physical disability, there are so many parts of me in Locke. I tried to cover and hide my disabilities for so long when I was first diagnosed. And that's why this part of his journey was so important to me. I wanted to see

Locke slowly accept and show his disability to the world, stating he had *nothing* to hide or to be "ashamed" or "embarrassed" about. His journey was extremely therapeutic for me. I want nothing more than for us to be able to love and accept ourselves just as we are. If nothing else, I hope you take that away from this story. Please don't ever hide! Allow yourself to shine, even if others aren't ready for it.

I also liked that Guin didn't notice Locke's disability at first. This was important to me because a lot of times it feels like people with disabilities are mainly viewed as limited or less capable. And these sentiments are definitely seen through Locke's character. So I really wanted Guin, and thus readers, not to notice his physical disability in the beginning of their story. I just wanted her to see *him*. And while she's shocked that she didn't notice his disability, she's not shocked about all the things he's able to do. Nor is she fascinated about all the things he's "overcome" or "survived." She just views it as learning more about him. It's just another piece of Locke. I wanted people to see a character have *that* type of reaction. I also love that Locke found a way to adapt to his situation so he could keep doing what he loves and help others do that as well. It shows we can find ways to work with our bodies if we can accept them and kick the ableist mindset. Something I'm still working on. I thought that was a really nice balance with Guin and her book illustrations. It was so therapeutic to write about a couple that could *help each other accept themselves—all* of themselves—and encourage each other on their journey to become the best version of themselves. I was listening to something recently that talked about the character "overcoming" their disability. And for some reason that made her extremely attractive to the other character. That's *not* what this is about. It's *not* about "overcoming" something. It's about becoming the best version of yourself, living with your disability because it is a part of you, and learning to love yourself as you are. Because you're incredible just the way you are. And it's about finding someone who will be there for you along the way. And I hope you have found that or believe that this is out there for you, too.

Of course this book would not be possible without the beautiful Hawaiian culture and island of Maui. I learned so much through the proverbs alone. And the themes of Ohana and the flap of a butterfly wing were inspired by the beauty of this culture. The Lupus butterfly rash turned into a symbol of grace and kindness with the butterfly wing flap analogy. I truly believe people come into our lives at the right time and that was part of the inspiration for the "Esther moments." And there is a whole story behind that as well, but one I won't get into here. Lol. Suffice it to say, we never truly know what's going on with someone and we never know how much impact we will have on them, just like the tiny flap of a butterfly's wing. A small act of kindness has the potential for a much bigger impact. That's why I knew "butterfly" had to be in the title as did "aloha." Because aloha can mean so many things. And these different meanings were important to the storyline as well. I hope we can start channeling more aloha into our daily lives because you never know the battle someone may be facing. I hope to start carrying the weight of this word with me every day.

Thus, 5% of net Amz sales of this book will be donated to the Maui Strong Fund to help with Maui relief.

To make a donation to the Maui Strong Fund: https://www. hawaiicommunityfoundation.org/maui-strong.

I believe chronic illness and disability voices need to be heard and that we deserve a spot on the romance shelf. I especially believe we need more "Own Voices" books. Something like disability doesn't just affect one part of your life, it seeps into every part. While I hope to provide a lot of escape in my novels, I also tackle a lot of heavier topics because chronic illness affects *every* part of your life. And that's why you'll see it affect every aspect of this book from start to finish–even a most unconventional proposal. But I hope you could tell it was an "Own Voices" book in this regard. When my pain is at its worst, I find solace in writing and thinking about ways these words and characters might reach someone in their pain as well. I've left it all out there. So if you connected and enjoyed it, please share. Please help this book find more readers who might need it and might be feeling alone with their conditions. And I hope if you haven't done so already, you'll friend me on social and join our little happy community. Because it's not so little any more–it's growing and it's *definitely* special. I'm truly honored to be a part of it and so lucky to have found these people. And while reviews are *so* incredibly appreciated, I haven't been able to go on review platforms to read/respond to them as much because of my mental health. It's not always easy to be a disability author and I've decided going forward I need to be more careful about the review platforms. But I will respond on social media because with your help I've been able to create a positive space and I LOVE our community. The connections I've made through my writing with readers and other authors, and the way this community has grown *is the success. You* reading this right now is more than I could have ever envisioned for myself and I can't thank you enough. If you had told me eight years ago when I was bed bound that this would be my life, I wouldn't have believed it. So if you are in that place right now, keep believing. *You have dreams that are waiting on you!*

The community is here if you ever need to talk; hopefully we continue to build one where we can talk about the struggles and successes in our life, and lift each other up. I believe literature has the power to do that–it has the power to connect us and help to heal us. And that's exactly why I wrote my author's note this way. Please know my door is always open :) I could never cover everything here so if you have a question, feel free to send me an e-mail or IG message! I'm always happy to join book discussions too!

Sending all the love & spoons,
Brooke

If you enjoyed this novel, I would greatly appreciate it if you would consider leaving a review on Goodreads, BookBub, The StoryGraph, LibraryThing, or recommend my book to any family members or friends who you think might enjoy it! Reviews are invaluable for authors and help us be able to continue to do what we love and, hopefully, what you enjoy us doing, too. I also love seeing readers post photos with the book on social media! Meeting readers is one of the best parts of this journey :)

Sign up for the newsletter at www.brookegilbertauthor.com and receive a free romance quiz to see what type of man is your perfect match! You'll also be matched with a leading man from one of my current or upcoming novels! There's also a giveaway in every newsletter!

I am constantly writing and hope to release more novels soon. I am currently working on publishing my next one. It's my *healthy* addiction. I'd love to connect with you whether to discuss writing, literature, pets, hobbies, travel dreams, spoon theory, or everyday life!

Connect with Me:

Official Website: brookegilbertauthor.com
Email: brookegilbertauthor@gmail.com
Instagram: @brookegilbertauthor
TikTok: https://www.tiktok.com/@brookegilbertauthor
Youtube: https://youtube.com/@brookegilbertauthor
Pinterest: www.pinterest.com/brookegilbertauthor

Follow Me On:
Author Central:
https://www.amazon.com/author/brookegilbert
Goodreads:https://www.goodreads.com/author/show/
23026582.Brooke_Gilbert
BookBub: https://www.bookbub.com/authors/brooke-gilbert
The StoryGraph: https://app.thestorygraph.com/authors/
5826ed0e-5120-433f-90b7-bceb6d8ed7f0

LibraryThing: https://www.librarything.com/author/gilbert-
brooke#https://allauthor.com/author/brookegilbertauthor/
Allauthor: https://allauthor.com/author/
brookegilbertauthor/
https://linktr.ee/brookegilbertauthor
Etsy: brookegilbertauthor.etsy.com
Audible: *The Irish Fall* is COMING SOON!!!

Fact or Fiction

There are so many parts of this book that are inspired by aspects of my life and are not totally fictional. I know it is not the "norm" to share so many personal details, but it's important to me to do so. My writing is extremely personal and hopefully that helps you be able to relate and connect to it. I hope by sharing with you in this way that you feel less alone, are able to feel seen, and are able to connect with my writing more. So I thought it would be fun to play a round of fact or fiction.

• Guin's ukulele journey is my own.
  ◦ FACT. I have five ukuleles and a healthy obsession. Lol. I found Cynthia Lin's channel online and never looked back.

• Did you start writing songs first?

◦ FACT. The first creative writing I did when I fell ill was actually song writing. I would wake up in the middle of the night just as Guin described and a song would pour out of me and then I'd go back to sleep. Song writing bloomed into a hunger to write more, thus, my first book was born.

• Do you have a service dog?

◦ FICTION. My mom's golden retriever/lab mix has turned into an emotional support dog for me. And yes, I have almost passed out several times in the bathroom. And yes, Bella insists on going in with me because she worries about me. And no, I'm not embarrassed to share this with you. I'm done with feeling that way and I hope you are too! I've also blacked out after physical therapy exercises and Bella's always there. Probably should get her trained!

• The beginning scene happened to you.

◦ FICTION. It happened to my mom. She actually got beached on the shore in Maui from the gigantic waves. And it made quite an impact on my memory! However, I don't think my very young self and my tiny friend were as good of a rescue crew as Locke. Lol. But I love a good, unconventional meet cute, so I hope you enjoyed it!

• Guin was bullied and turned to illustration because of an undiagnosed learning disability. Did this happen to you?

◦ FACT. That whole story is true. I was the last to learn to read in my class and I would often color the pictures in the book when I should have been reading. That's why I love to make covers for other authors.

• Is the storyline of the friend with Lupus who is losing her eyesight true?
  ◦ FACT. Yes.

• My grandmother had Alzheimer's.
  ◦ FICTION. My grandfather did and it was extremely important to me to highlight this disorder.

• My mom is a music teacher.
  ◦ FACT. She's an incredibly gifted musician like Tutu, which is where that inspiration came from and where my love of music is born. If you enjoy the music references in my novels, you can thank her! Lol.

• Are the characters named after jazz musicians?
  ◦ FACT. If the characters don't have a Hawaiian name, then most are named after jazz musicians such as Louis Armstrong, Ella Fitzgerald, Etta James, Tracey Chapman, and Dean Martin.

• Do you have a Creature from the Black Lagoon fantasy?
  ◦ Apparently. Lol. FACT. I have been to crystal springs with my mom like Guin. And yes, I was dreaming about the Creature instead of Ken.

• Is the pet adoption story for either dog real?
  ◦ FACT. Sebe's adoption story is true of my dog, Rio Blue, who is a border collie. She literally wouldn't let go of my hair so I couldn't put her down. She did choose me.

  ◦ Have you seen all the movies referenced?

° FACT. It's important to me to include movie and TV references. Throughout my disorders, classic film and TV, along with rom-coms and thrillers, saw me through so many sleepless and painful nights. They allowed me to travel and see the world and provided me escape on days when I was bed bound. They are such a part of my journey and I can't help but enjoy incorporating them. Hopefully, you'll find some to enjoy as well!

Movie List

In need of ideas for a movie night? Grab some popcorn and relax with the movies/TV shows mentioned in this novel. Haven't heard of some of these references? That's okay! I'm hoping you will find some new ones to enjoy along the way as you read this novel! Find the movie list on Letterboxd at
https://bit.ly/thealohabutterflykissmovies.

• *Jaws*

• *10 Things I Hate About You.*
• *The Little Mermaid*
• *Creature from the Black Lagoon*
• *Indiana Jones*
• *1o1 Dalmatians*
• *Hulk*
• *Pretty in Pink*
• *White Lotus*
• *Legally Blonde*
• *Beethoven*
• *The Three Stooges*
• *I Dream of Jeannie*
• *The Hunchback of Notre Dame*
• *The Phantom of the Opera*
• *Rocky*
• *The Big Bang Theory*
• *Sleeping Beauty*
• *House*
• *Mary Poppins (1964 & 2018)*
• *I Love Lucy*
• *Splash*
• *The Avengers*
• *Friends*
• *Catwoman*
• *Gremlins*
• *Cléo from 5 to 7*
• *Star Wars*
• *Beauty and the Beast*
• *Laverne and Shirley*
• *Charade*
• *Romeo and Juliet*
• *A Walk to Remember*

- *Dancing Lady*
- *King Kong*
- *The Wizard of Oz*
- *Soul*
- *Frankenstein*
- *Willy Wonka and the Chocolate Factory*

Lupus Tips & Tricks for Summer

- Rash guards and dive skins are a lifesaver. I buy everything with UV protection, especially wide brim sun hats. And of course UV, polarized sunglasses are wonderful to protect your eyes. And yes, I have a hope chest where I keep my rash guards and skins so I can enjoy time on the lake. Lol.
- UV umbrellas have become my biggest friend and if I sit outside, then I have one up.
- Stay inside during peak UV sun hours
- Take vitamin D. It boosts the immune system, and all these sun protecting and UV shielding devices will block your vitamin D absorption.
- To help with the butterfly rash, I buy foundation with high SPF and organic sunscreen with zinc oxide. The story about being compared to a cuttlefish was definitely true and while it was a weird doctor's appointment, I actually have experienced weirder ones.
- Coconut water is my go to for hydration. This helps with headaches too. I used to not like the taste, but now my body

craves it. I don't have to worry about artificial sweeteners or flavors like I do with electrolyte mixes.

• I have a personal neck fan that I always keep in my bag. It helps me not get overheated.

• Specialized Diet (low inflammatory). See my blog for the diet I follow.

• Pregnancy pillow for back & GI pain for sleeping

• Yin Yoga at night or Nidra is great to help with joint pain and swelling. I swell a lot in the morning during the summer.

• Heated blanket and heating pad to help with joint and GI pain in the morning. Morning baths with Epsom salts are also good!

• Connect online with other Lupus warriors through blogs and social media. It's helped me so much to share tips and tricks. And also to find common triggers. This is truly a beautiful community of women!

Tutu's Salve

The recipe below is for a quick liquid application, but you can make this recipe into an actual salve with a double boiler. The salve uses a larger quantity of ingredients. Use 2 cups coconut oil and ¼ cup beeswax pellets as the base and melt them in the double boiler. You can keep everything else the same and just increase the essential oils to around 30 drops. The recipe below is easier to make when you need it and you can apply it right away! Just combine and use :)

- 2 Tbsp liquid coconut oil
- 1 tsp vitamin e oil
- 1 tsp aloe vera
- A few drops honey
- 2 drops rosemary, eucalyptus, tea tree, frankincense, and myrrh
- 1 tsp crushed lavender and chamomile flowers
- OR

- 5 drops of lavender and 5 drops chamomile essential oil

Fish & Plantains Recipe

Fish and Plaintains

SERVINGS: 2   PREP TIME: 15 MIN   COOKING TIME: 12 MIN

Ingredients

- 1 lb Mahi Mahi
- 4 bananas
- coconut sugar
- lemon
- salt
- 1/2 cup coconut milk
- 1/2 tsp coconut oil
- 1/2 cup white cheddar
- 4 tbsp mango preserves

Directions

1. Heat oven to 400°F (can also use air fryer).
2. Spray the pan. Place mahi mahi in pan. Pour coconut milk and squeeze lemon juice over top. Salt and sprinkle coconut sugar (~1 Tbsp).
3. Cook for 10 minutes. Pull out of oven and spread preserves and sprinkle white cheddar. Place back in the oven for 2 minutes. Make sure to check that the fish is done and flaky!
4. Melt 1/2 Tbsp coconut oil in a pan on the stove. Slice bananas or plantains in half. Saute on each side until golden brown (~2 minutes per side). Sprinkle coconut sugar after you flip the fish so it doesn't burn!
5. NOTE: This is wonderful over jasmine rice!

Brookegilbertauthor.com | @brookegilbertauthor

Discussion Questions

A few questions to start the discussion at your next book club meeting. If you are choosing *The Aloha Butterfly Kiss* for your Book Club meeting, I would love to join your discussion! Send me a message at brookegilbertauthor.com, @brookegilbertauthor on IG, or email me at brookegilbertauthor@gmail.com.

Question 1
• How do you feel about the disability representation in the novel? Can you relate? Did it make you feel more connected to the main characters?

Question 2
• What is your favorite quality about Locke?

• Did you think he was a good fit for Guin?
• Did you know why he needed an emotional support dog? Did you guess why he did before Guin found out?

Question 3

• One of the things the author often hears is how relatable Guin is with her health concerns. Can you relate to Guin?
• What is your favorite quality about Guin?
• Guin doesn't want to date because she feels it isn't fair. Even at the end she wants to protect Locke. How did you feel about that? Can you relate?

Question 4

• A major theme of this book is learning to accept and love yourself, including your disability. • Do you feel the characters were able to do that?
• Dean talks about having to be shown love or having someone accept us before we can do this for ourselves. Do you agree?

Question 5

• What's your favorite quality about Louis?
• Do you think Louis is a good fit for Tutu?
• Alzheimer's is a major part of Tutu's reluctance to start a relationship. Do you think she was right to open her heart up to Louis?
• Tutu and Louis had to overcome a lot to be together. How did you feel about the struggles they faced?

Question 6

• Like Locke, so many of us with disabilities, especially at the beginning of our journey, have trouble accepting ourselves and the way people view us. Could you relate?

• How did you feel about the lengths Locke undertook to cover his prosthesis?

• If you were Guin, how would you have felt about Locke not talking about his prosthesis with you?

Question 7

• How do you feel about the mental health representation in the novel? Which character do you feel grew the most through their struggle in the novel?

• Was the mental health representation portrayed differently than in other novels you've read? If so, how?

• Emotional abuse and gaslighting are themes in this novel. Do you think discussing them in literature will help them become more easily discussed in our society?

Question 8

• What do you think about how Guin and Locke met? Did you enjoy their service dogs and their puppy love? Did you learn a lot about service dogs or enjoy the representation?

• What was your favorite Penny and Sebe scene?

• Guin and Locke's love of their dogs and the role they play in their lives really connects them. It's the reason Guin keeps her VRBO plan. But soon they start opening up more to one another and find out they have so much in common. How do you think Guin changes throughout the book? What growth did you see in her?

• What about Locke?

Question 9

• One of the main themes is Ohana and *found* family. What did you think about this theme? Is it one you enjoy?

• Did you enjoy learning about Hawaiian culture and

language? Is there a spot in the book or an activity you would like to do the most?

• One of the other major themes is the "butterfly wing's flap." Do you agree with this analogy and the metaphor of kindness and grace? What did this theme mean to you? Did you have a favorite quote?

Question 10

• What do you envision for the characters' futures? Tutu and Louis? Guin and Locke?

Question 11

• What is your favorite scene in the novel?

• If you had to pick just one place to visit that was mentioned in their story, where would it be?

• If you were going to travel with one character from the novel, who would it be?

Acknowledgments

It certainly takes a village to write a novel and I don't think that statement has ever been more true than for this one. There are so many people behind the scenes that helped to make this book possible and made sure it reached publication day! Which I had to admit, because of health reasons, was very questionable this time around. Lol. But I have been blessed with a truly incredible support system, and the best book and spoonie community!

Like in so many families, the real unsung hero of this novel is my mother. She has worked tirelessly to make sure this novel came to fruition. Through every developmental change and crazy new idea I had, she stood by my side and cheered me on. She's edited every version and then some, and this book would not be here today without her. She's helped me to believe I have something to say and that I should keep pursuing my dream. What Locke says about Tutu is so true. We all need someone in our corner fighting for us, believing in us, and my mother is that person for me. It's not only been a fight to keep publishing this year but also a fight with my health. It's been eight years of fighting these disorders and being a medical mystery, and this year only got harder. I think it's so easy to give up and say 'this is the best my quality of life is going to be' or to give up on finding answers. And that's where I would have been this year if not for her. She's never let me give up. Not on my health and not on this dream. Without her, none of this would be possible. She is the Tutu in my life. Mom, thank you for all the late nights we stayed up talking through scenes, all the care you took in making sure I said what I needed to say, and for making sure this book was the best it could be. It means the world to me, and *you*, of course, mean the world to me. "Thank you" would never be enough. The bond built through this experience has only made us closer. And as always, thanks for making sure I never went "a bridge too far." I love you!

The other unsung hero of this book is my amazing rainy day partner-in-crime and honorary spoonie member, Tomi Tabb. I don't know what I would have done without her this year. She appeared when I needed a friend so badly. When I was so lost in this new world of publishing, I will forever be grateful to her. The kindness she has shown me and all the help and encouragement she has given me could never be repaid. God truly knows what he is doing. Thank you, Tomi.

And I truly believe that people are sent to you just when you need them. I searched for help with the physical disability aspect of this book for months. I kept hitting dead end after dead end. A few weeks before publication. I got the phone call I desperately needed. This book and the representation would not be the same without Jessica from Hanger Prosthetics of Knoxville. I was so nervous to ask my questions, but she was so incredibly kind. Jessica spent so much time with me even though she'd experienced food poisoning the day before our talk. That is an incredible person for you! Our community is truly wonderful. If you enjoyed the physical disability representation and found it to be accurate, then I assure you it was thanks to her, the rest is on me. Lol.

I've truly been blessed with so many "honorary spoonies"

and such a beautiful spoonie community in my life. Writing has given me so much, but I am especially thankful that it has given me you. Thank you for all the kind words and encouragement you give me daily. You've made all the difference in my life. And I am so incredibly grateful for the many friends and family who have supported me through the years as well. They have stood by my side through my chronic conditions, through the good *and* the bad and reminded me of my self-worth. I cannot express my gratitude enough. You have been such a blessing in my life. A special thank you to Caroline Wolfe Grimm and my beautiful Aunt Teena who continually encourage my writing and are always there to check on me. It's been such a gift to have you in my life.

One of the biggest parts of this 'village' that made this book possible were the incredibly caring medical professionals in my life. The reason I have been able to write is the fact that they have worked tirelessly to get me to this point in my health journey. It is no coincidence that I could write my first novel after starting a new medication, naltrexone, off-label. There are so many medical professionals that have helped me with the disorders discussed in this novel! Thank you to Dr. Annapureddy, Dr. Bell, Dr. Braden, Dr. Harris, Megan Micaletti, and Sonyia Ballew for all the care you gave me during this journey. Your belief in me and all the care you've given me has made all the difference in the world. You truly put the 'care' in Healthcare.

Thank you so much to Caitlin Miller, who is an incredible editor! This is my third time working with Caitlin, and I was so excited to be fortunate enough to work with her again! She was so patient and kind throughout the entire process. Her sweet and compassionate nature made the editing process fun and less nerve-racking. I am so lucky to have her meticulous proofreading, which helped make this book the best it could be! I feel so blessed to call her a friend and editor! I'm so grateful that God brought us together to work on these projects, and I can't wait to see what the future has in store!

Thank you to all the Beta readers, sensitivity readers, ARC readers, and Bookstagrammers who have encouraged me daily. Becoming a part of this community has been one of the best experiences of my life. I have never met such a welcoming community. I will never forget your compassion, kind words, sweet postings, beautiful reviews, and fun book discussions. And I also want to thank the spoonie community, who makes up part of the book community as well. I have found such a wonderful support group with you, and I no longer feel alone with my conditions. Your beauty and strength encourage me every day. And I hope you know my door is always open if you need to talk.

I'd be very remiss if I didn't include the authors and voice-over artists I have had the pleasure of meeting along the way. I am always amazed at the encouragement you give one another, and I am so thankful you have accepted me as one of your own. From the first moment, you made me feel like I belonged. Coming from the competitive world of medical sciences, I can say it was an extremely pleasant shock to my system! I have loved learning from you and hope to pay it forward one day!

And of course, I would like to say a big thank you to every person who takes the time to read this novel. I know there are so many options, and that you read my book truly means the world to me. You make this experience so rewarding and mean-ingful. I am humbled and honored that you have taken this journey with me. And if, by chance, it resonates with you or provides you with some escape, then you will have made this whole writing journey worthwhile.

To my parents, who have supported every creative dream I

have ever imagined, I want to say thank you from the bottom of my heart. I know having a creative daughter who marches to the beat of her own drum has been a handful, but I appreciate all the love you've always shown me. I'm sure you never envisioned having "Mrs. Maisel" as a daughter, but just as her parents did, you have always supported me and fought for me. Thank you to my mother, who always wanted me to be a writer and encouraged me. I never imagined I'd ever become one. It's still surreal to have written a novel. Your love has been a light and a guide, especially in times of trouble. Thank you to my father for shaping my sense of humor and always providing laughter in my life. It is laughter that has made the difficult times bearable. You have helped mold me into the person I am today, and I will be forever grateful. Your continued support has meant the world to me. I love you both very much.

Most of all, thank you to God for showing me that "all things work together for good for those who believe in the Lord" (Romans 8:28). And for proving that faith can overcome all odds. I am humbled and unbelievably grateful for this Job moment.

About the Author

Brooke Gilbert is a Tennessee native, a microbiology graduate of the University of Tennessee, and a border collie mom. She is, as you may have already guessed, a hopeless romantic and a lover of Jane Austen. When she isn't writing, she works as a jewelry designer, an audiobook narrator, and a graphic designer. Her writing features characters with autoimmune disorders, something she deals with herself. She believes it is important for these types of characters to be seen in modern literature and started writing so she could see someone like herself in literature. She is considered a medical mystery and has several rare autoimmune disorders. These disorders caused her to withdraw from Physician Assistant School, but she is happy to be pursuing her dreams of designing, creating, and writing. She thanks God for leading her heart on this new path and recites "perhaps this is the moment for which you were created" in times of doubt (Esther 4:14).

She loves watching classic films (thrillers and romantic comedies, too), reading, playing the ukulele, painting, dancing, Pilates, and spending time with her dog, family, and friends. One of her favorite quotes is from Flashdance: "When you give up on your dreams, you die." She believes that if you're waiting to pursue your dreams, stop waiting and start doing. Your time is now. And may you never stop being a hopeless romantic. Contrary to popular belief, it's a very good quality. She's still looking for her Mr. Darcy. Visit brookegilbertauthor.com to connect and stay updated on her latest projects.